Promise You'll Wait

BOOKS BY ELAINE JOHNS

A Cornish Wartime Story
Be Brave for Me

Elaine Johns

Promise You'll Wait

bookouture

Published by Bookouture in 2022

An imprint of Storyfire Ltd.
Carmelite House
50 Victoria Embankment
London EC4Y 0DZ

www.bookouture.com

Copyright © Elaine Johns, 2022

Elaine Johns has asserted her right to be identified as the author of this work.

All rights reserved. No part of this publication may be reproduced, stored in any retrieval system, or transmitted, in any form or by any means, electronic, mechanical, photocopying, recording or otherwise, without the prior written permission of the publishers.

ISBN: 978-1-80314-709-3
eBook ISBN: 978-1-80314-708-6

This book is a work of fiction. Names, characters, businesses, organizations, places and events other than those clearly in the public domain, are either the product of the author's imagination or are used fictitiously. Any resemblance to actual persons, living or dead, events or locales is entirely coincidental.

To Mar and Frank, and Delboy with love and thanks for all your support over time.

PART ONE

1

CORNWALL

27 JULY 1942

The killing was far away now. Left behind in a different world. Rosemary Ellis stood on the cliff-top and stared at the ocean, mesmerised by its fury, the chilling beauty of the wild Cornish seascape. The waves pounded the shoreline, and in their retreat left behind small flecks of pure white foam.

They were at the top of East Cliff and her eyes shifted to the collection of clapboard bungalows huddled below, tiny from right up there, clinging to the cliff edge with a determination that seemed to defy gravity. One day they might disappear, taken greedily by the ocean and the winds that battered the rock face.

Over on the other side of the bay was West Cliff, thrusting its way into the sky like a jagged monolith. That's where their boarding house was. Halfway up, along a narrow path. A bit of a climb, but then they were young and fit. Nothing to it. *Two rooms*, not one. She'd insisted on that. Anything else would have been improper.

And down there in the valley, nestling between both cliffs,

was their special place. A restaurant with tables outside. Rosemary had never been to a restaurant with tables outside before, somewhere you could sit and watch the evening sun slide into the ocean, and eat crab. It seemed exotic, with all the allure of foreign places that she'd only read about and dreamed of seeing one day. A world apart from the drabness of wartime London and the Blitz.

Rosemary was an attractive, uncomplicated girl, whose charm lay in her honesty and sincerity. It was those qualities that gave her a quiet dignity and had first drawn her companion Danny Welland to her. He'd told her she was 'wholesome'. *Was that a compliment? It sounded more like an advertisement for some sort of food.* But no, he'd assured her that to be wholesome was good. It meant she was straightforward, and natural, didn't put on airs like some of those sophisticated and cynical society women his mother threw at him.

Two people from different backgrounds, both Londoners: Rosemary was an East End girl, proud of her Cockney roots, and Danny came from the rarefied air of Dulwich. But love ignores borders, vaults over class barriers in a single bound.

They'd met on his last leave. She'd rescued him, he said, from the greatest disaster in history. Some woman called Marjory with a face like a horse and a voice to go with it. His mother had been ready with the confetti. He'd fled to the Lyons Corner House on Coventry Street. Rosemary recalled his face when he'd spotted the spare seat at her table – it had crinkled up and she'd thought he was in pain or having some kind of seizure, but apparently it was *ecstasy* at the sight of her. *Men, eh! They could lay it on thick when they wanted to.*

But she'd let him sit at her table anyway. Had moved her gas mask off the seat to make room for him. He'd looked harmless enough, and handsome in his RAF uniform, and Rosemary was having one of her let's-be-adventurous days.

She had guessed he was only there to look at the charming

'Nippy' waitresses in their new uniforms. Joseph Lyons had smartened up all the waitresses in his Corner Houses and teashops with attractive and modern black and white outfits. Figure-hugging with two rows of tiny pearl buttons down the front. She reckoned that most of the blokes eating their lunch were only there for the added attraction of the Nippies.

And now? Well, now he called her *his Rosie* and her 'deep green eyes had found their way to his soul'. *A poet as well as a pilot.*

She tried to picture his mother and the women he'd rejected. Their hair – was it coiffured in the latest short style, or did they sport the 'peekaboo' long locks of Veronica Lake: a cascade of blonde hair falling over their shoulders, coyly covering one eye with a soft wave? *They were bound to look like film stars, weren't they?*

Her own hair fell in long glossy tresses – not easy to keep shiny now, what with the shortage of good shampoo – but she tried. The shade of Rosemary's hair changed when the light of the sun shone through it. Sometimes it was red with traces of copper, and then when she turned in her quick, impatient way, it could be a shimmering brown.

She imagined again the society women his mother had flung at him. Their fancy floral evening dresses. It was wartime but some women, those with wealth, still managed to deck themselves out in lavish finery. Rosemary's dresses weren't exactly elegant, but she did her best with 'make do and mend', like the pamphlet said. Coaxing new life out of old clothes, doing her bit for the war effort. Not like some people.

There were some who acted as if the world was the same as before. It wasn't. Everything had changed. How people lived. How they loved, like tomorrow might never come. How they worked. Now women were *allowed* to work, and in men's jobs too. But Rosemary wasn't naive, she knew that might change. Change back when women weren't needed anymore. When the men came home from war. Not that she didn't want them home. It's what she prayed for every night: that it would all be over soon and laughter could return and mothers, sisters, wives could grieve properly for their men. Men like her dad.

Harry Ellis had been one of the poor sods left behind at Dunkirk, doing his bit as part of the rear-guard, so that other blokes could escape back home across the Channel. He was a prisoner of war now, they'd heard. Somewhere in Poland. *Well, he'd always wanted to travel* – that had been her mother's reaction when she'd heard the bad news from the War Office. Gallows humour. There was a lot of that going around.

She squeezed Danny's hand and his eyes sought hers in reply, a question in them.

'Remember how you teased me when we met?' she said.

'Me? No!'

'You were a *monster*,' she said, and poked him in the ribs with a finger. 'Called me Rosie the Riveter.'

'It was a joke. You told me your name was Rosie and you worked in a factory, helped with the war effort. I was impressed.'

'You were?'

'But I was nervous. What was I supposed to say?'

Him, nervous? She couldn't imagine it. He always seemed so confident, so self-assured. A fighter pilot.

'Yes, but Rosie the Riveter. Really?' The cartoon poster of 'Rosie the Riveter' came from America. Rosie, with her red and white polka-dot turban, navy blue overalls with the sleeves rolled up, her hand clenched in a fist pump, flexing serious arm muscles. Challenging the world with her 'We can do it!' attitude. But Rosemary didn't need any old poster to tell her she was capable of doing anything, including a man's job. She knew she could. And she didn't need to turn into a man to do it. She was beautiful – Danny had told her so.

'Tell me again,' she said now. 'You know' – she smiled shyly

– 'that you think I'm pretty.' She didn't *need* to hear it, but even so, it gave her a thrill and tiny goose bumps when it came from his lips.

'What? That your eyes are deep liquid pools of green, just like the ocean?'

'Really?'

'Well, not exactly like the ocean, obviously. A close second, though.' He grinned.

'Fool! On a scale of one to ten, then.'

'An eight. Definitely an eight.'

'Swine.' She poked him in the ribs again. He was getting thin and bony, his uniform loose in places. Not eating enough, smoking too much and too much stress. He worried her. Rosemary's forehead creased into a frown.

'What's wrong?' he said.

'Nothing.' *A lie.*

'An eight's not bad, you know,' he said, and took a strand of her hair, curled it around his finger.

It was a game they played, pretending that they weren't perfect for each other. It was wartime. It didn't do to build your hopes too high. One day his kite might go down, he might not come back. She might not survive. It was 1942 after all: bombs were still decimating London; one of them could easily have her name on it.

Cornwall had been a great idea, as they both loved it there. They stared out at the ocean and fell into a comfortable silence, broken only by the sound of their breathing. Together. *Even our breathing is together*, thought Rosemary. They were like one body.

One body with two minds, though, for Rose Ellis would never let anyone tell her what to think. She had strong opinions, was not afraid to voice them. And ideas about how women should be equal with men. Ideas that weren't always welcome, even in her own family, for her dad had called it *idiotic* – the notion that a woman could ever do the job of a man. But Danny understood, encouraged her to be herself and never give up on her dreams.

She heard a sigh and Rosemary shifted her gaze back to the man beside her. He was tall. Much taller than she was, for people described her as slight. Her mother said she was 'dainty', which always struck Rosemary as another word for 'weak'. She wasn't weak, the opposite. Danny called her 'petite', and that sounded much better – colourful and glamorous. *French*.

Maybe she'd visit France one day. Maybe he'd take her there, this man who had an old-fashioned elegance. It came from his bearing rather than his wardrobe, and that breezy confidence of his; some might think it had something to do with his upbringing, but Rosemary believed it came from deep within him. A core of self-belief. Danny had a strength that made her feel secure.

Yet, oddly, there was also vulnerability in his eyes, like a puppy that had given his trust and been hurt in the process.

She wanted to protect him from any more pain.

His face was strangely at odds with the RAF uniform he wore. So young, she thought, for the weighty responsibility of a squadron leader. But then they were all young, just boys, flying out day after day to face the terror that hid in the skies. In that summer of 1942 they had no other choice. The blokes in the squadron called him the 'old man', and compared to some of the other fliers, twenty-two *was* old. And sometimes, when he let his guard down, she could see it in the mirrors of his eyes. The things he'd seen. Been forced to do for his country, for the uniform.

She shivered slightly, her mood broken, as knowledge of the future impinged on the happiness of the present. Soon Danny would leave, and these three precious days would retreat farther back into his mind, to be locked away in the drawer where he kept his memories.

'Did I tell you the squadron has been passed as qualified for night ops?' He said it with quiet pride.

Rosemary tensed, as the spectre of horrific mid-air collisions punctuating an inky-blackness scraped agonisingly across the fertile bed of her imagination. She swallowed her fear and smiled. 'That's good. You must be pleased. I'm sure it takes a lot of skill to fly at night.'

Danny Welland nodded eagerly, pleased with her understanding, her interest. 'Well, I think we've stared at this bit of coastline long enough,' he said. 'We'll be wearing it out. Shall we walk back along the cliff path?'

He took her hand and once again she felt the happiness tingling through her finger-tips.

And so they spent their last day together before they had to go their separate ways: he to Hampshire and his Hurricanes, she back to London. To sew her parachutes and hope that one of hers would someday save a life like Danny's.

She hated the thought of going home to London, with its daily fight for survival and almost hysterical spirit of cheerfulness that pervaded the place. It was so different here. Their own magical Brigadoon – the village of Havenporth, where they had spent so much of their time together, also seemed timeless, mystical; untouched by the grating, raw reality of war.

'Let's make this our own special place, shall we? Promise we'll always return here – every summer.'

She studied him, unsure of what he was trying to say.

'We should! That'd be great,' he continued, excited as a kid at Christmas. 'What's the date?' he asked.

'The twenty-seventh of July. But I don't understand.'

'We'll make it an anniversary. Visit here every year on the same date. A sort of pilgrimage. Don't you think that's romantic?'

'You mean meet here every year?'

He laughed. 'No, you silly goose. I don't mean *meet* here. I mean come back here together.'

Rosemary's face flushed. She felt awkward, embarrassed. Surely he knew by now she wasn't *that* kind of girl.

'In my clumsy, cloddish way, Rosie Ellis – I'm asking you to marry me. Should I get down on one knee? I suppose I could run to something athletic like that, if you think it's necessary.' Danny Welland beamed.

Rosemary's joy knew no bounds. It was an infinite emotion, not constricted by time or space. This was what she'd been created for. Put on this earth for. She was sure of that. She'd found her soul mate. It was so simple, yet profound.

They decided to get married during Danny's next leave, on her twentieth birthday, in October. A double celebration.

Rosemary returned to London breathlessly, ecstatically happy. The war seemed a remote thing now, one that only involved other people. She closed her mind to the dangers he faced, for they were young, alive, vital, and most importantly – in love. They were indestructible.

2

LONDON

OCTOBER 1942

Danny Welland was part of a fighter escort on a huge bombing raid when it happened.

In one cruel, bone-jarring instant, the vibrant life force was tugged from Rosemary's body, and the colours around her turned to grey.

Officially he was listed as missing, thought to have been shot down somewhere over the Dutch coast. At first, she clung to the word *missing*, like it was a magic talisman that would keep him safe. Missing was better than dead. Rosemary refused to believe that life could be so cruel to them both; that fate could pull them apart, before they'd even had a chance to marry. To consummate their love.

But weeks turned agonisingly slowly into months, and nothing was heard of him.

Gradually it dawned on her that he must be gone. If he were a POW, the Red Cross would have turned up something by now, to say nothing of the Air Ministry, whom she pestered daily for any scrap of news.

Eventually, Rosemary let go of the slender thread of hope and retreated into a world of silence and shadows. The glossy chestnut hair that had once been her pride became lacklustre; her full, oval face was haggard; her mouth pinched with the pain of loss.

She rarely spoke, and only then, when forced by her mother or sister Gracie, in short, brittle monosyllables. They hovered over her, tried to get her to eat the meagre rations that her mother miraculously turned into food. She got thinner. But then nobody got fatter: there was a war on.

It was a freezing-cold start to 1943. Rosemary didn't care – it matched her feelings, her body, her mind.

'I'm off to work,' she said, one frosty evening.

'But you just did a long shift!' complained her mother. Lil Ellis had the knack of turning her mouth into a thin, mean line when she was angry. She hated being left alone in the house at night, especially if there was a raid and she'd have to find her way to the underground shelter in the blackout.

'There's a war on,' said Rosemary, wearily.

'Hold the front page. Roll the presses!' *Her sister Gracie could be a right tit at times.*

'And my job's important,' Rosemary shot back.

But she didn't really believe that anymore. She didn't have the energy or the faith to believe anything now. But at least going to the parachute factory was an escape of a kind. She threw herself manically into the work, a mind-numbing exercise. The factory was a bolt hole far from the stifling confines of the house and their nagging. And whining. Her sister and Ma fought all the time now, rubbing each other's nerves to shreds. Her mother called Grace 'a good-time girl' and 'flighty', flinging herself at any bloke who winked at her. 'A disgrace – that's our Gracie,' she'd say.

Good for her! Take joy where you find it, for it soon gets ripped from your grasp. Bitter? Well, yes. But then she had reason to be.

Rosemary closed the door of the small terraced house behind her. Their home in Royston Street, Bethnal Green, was tiny, but it had been a miracle to find it after being bombed out of their last house a few months before. Lucky to have a roof over your head at all in these dangerous and troubled times. They'd been stuck in a temporary church shelter until Rosemary had found this place.

She stepped carefully over her mother's spotless front step. Lil Ellis was proud of her clean doorstep, scoured to within an inch of its life. It sent the world a message – a proud, hard-working housewife lived here, understood her responsibilities. War or no war, standards had to be kept up, the house neat and tidy, rugs beaten, copper on and weekly wash done on Monday. And every morning – rain, sleet, or lightning bolt – that front step had to be stained white with the donkey-stone.

Rosemary made her way along Royston Street, heading for the factory. A twenty-minute walk through narrow streets with terraced houses crammed together on either side. Acres of wet washing in backyards, flailing like flags in the wind. Once, this strange herding together of people had felt comforting, the sense of community a gift to be cherished. But not now. Now everything had changed in her life, and the closeness felt claustrophobic, as if it might smother her.

Her body was stiff and rigid as Rosemary moved through the East End streets pockmarked with bomb craters. Constant reminders of the new normality. *Nothing was normal, would ever be normal again.*

She pulled her head farther down into the collar of her coat. The wind seemed more bitter than usual, but then it was January so you'd hardly expect anything different. A new year already. And what would 1943 have in store for them all? More of the same probably. She used to be such an optimist, but it was hard to get in touch with the light when all around was darkness.

Head down, eyes fixed on the road, always looking down. Safer that way, especially with the blackout. No eye contact with other people, for they'd only see the pain in her and she'd recognise the weariness in them. That good old East End spirit that Bethnal Green was famous for had taken a battering. Some of them had been bombed out of their houses two or three times since the beginning of the Blitz. The East End had been pounded when Hitler sent his *Luftwaffe* over day and night, its closeness to the docks making it one of the hardest hit in the relentless German bombing. Bethnal Green alone had taken 80 tons of bombs.

That was over now, the Blitz proper. But they all still needed the shelters, for there were lots of tit-for-tat raids that demolished houses, killed civilians. When Berlin was bombed you couldn't expect to get off scot-free. *One for you, one for us. Like kids playing a game.*

Except it wasn't a game of course. Loads of good men had been killed – on *all* sides. And women and men on the home front, and kids. Innocent kids who'd never done anything to deserve it.

A month after Danny had gone missing, fate had played another of its ugly tricks and Rosemary and her family had been bombed out of their old house in Wilmot Street.

She still remembered her mother and her coming out of the shelter at Bethnal Green tube, heading to their house and finding the kitchen sink blown out into the middle of the street. Sitting there, it was – large as life and twice as daft. Her ma had sunk to her knees in the rubble, had laughed hysterically and then she'd cried.

Why us? her ma had asked her.

Rosemary had no answer. Besides, they weren't alone, for many others had lost their homes that night, their belongings, their lives. The whole street had been taken out, leaving just the school standing by itself, its roof shattered but the rest of the old building clinging on tenaciously.

And the smell. Who could ever forget the smell? The acrid, choking smell of burned-out buildings, the nausea of a broken gas main, and the strange musty odour of damp plasterboard hanging from the remains of houses. Places that used to be homes.

Their old house may not have been a mansion, but it was the place where she'd been born. Somewhere she'd built memories.

Rosemary tried to recall the family times they'd had in that house; the things they'd all done; the Christmases they'd enjoyed before the war when her father had been there with them. And Danny! The last time she'd seen him had been in the front parlour there. They'd made plans for the future and drunk tea and her ma had produced some strange oatmeal cake that she'd been proud of. Then they'd taken a walk up to the schoolhouse and Danny had told her about getting the marriage licence, about the car he'd borrowed to take them on a two-day honeymoon. He hadn't told her where they were going. But he had winked. So, she'd guessed it was Cornwall, their favourite place.

But there had been no wedding. No honeymoon.

She shuddered, thinking about the pain. There'd been so much of it. Her da, missing. Their old home, missing. But the worst pain of all? That had been an agony of pain that wouldn't go away. The loss of her precious Danny. No pain could ever surpass the suffering that came from that.

She tried to shrug off the blackness that had enveloped her and quickened her pace, for the light was already being sucked from the late afternoon sky. Dangerous out walking in the dark of the blackout. You could easily turn an ankle in the rubble.

'That you, Rosie Ellis?'

She didn't reply. The man knew who she was, and now he'd be using her appearance as an excuse to get chatty. He'd tried to get chummy with her before, at the factory, in the canteen. They came from the same area, so maybe he figured that gave him some sort of property rights over her. Some men were like that. Still didn't see women as their equals.

She'd had several offers – blokes willing to *take her on*, they'd said. Take her on? Bloody insulting. Why would she need a bloke to look after her when she could look after herself? A skivvy, that's all most of them wanted. Somebody to cook their dinners, keep their house clean, take their orders.

'Walk you to work?' he said. 'Dangerous place with the dark coming in.'

She said nothing. *What did it take to discourage the man? Did he not get the hint that she wasn't interested in him?*

In him or any bloke.

'Not much of a talker, are you, Rosie?' He slipped his arm through hers.

'Don't you *dare* call me that!' She ripped her arm away. The violence took him by surprise. But she wouldn't let any man call her Rosie now. That's what *he*'d called her. Danny. His memory had to be held intact, a memorial, nothing about their history to be lessened, especially by somebody like Albert Green. A man who hadn't even served his country, was in a reserved occupation, but then that was just an excuse with some of them. Blokes who knew somebody special who could pull a few strings to get them off the fighting. Cowards! Not like her Dan.

'Touchy little thing, ain't you?' said Albert. 'I was only going to see you safe to work. Not offering to marry you. Not that ou'd be much of a catch. Stuck-up, skinny little bitch like you. We're not good enough for you, eh? Now that you've got this bloke of yours with his pilot's wings and his fancy house in the suburbs.'

Her breath stung her throat. The hurt dug into her again, reminding her of the loss. Not that this idiot knew anything about Danny, or what had happened to him. It wasn't like she'd broadcast the news of his death all over Bethnal Green. Some things were private.

She ran the rest of the way to work. Tears threatened to overtake her, but she battled them ruthlessly, couldn't let them all see how weak she was. She waited in line with the others to clock in, get her overall and hairnet. Just being part of the swirling mass of bodies made her feel better. A random mix of people, they all had things in common but were also very different. In a weird way she felt more at home there than she did with her family in their tiny house in Royston Street. Here, she could be one of the many. *Invisible*. And that's what Rosemary liked.

'Alright, love? You bring your bed here?' The enquiry came from Maisy Clark, the woman next to Rosemary in the queue. 'Might as well sleep here. You spend more time here, Rose, than in that house of yours.'

Rosemary nodded. Didn't speak. Still had a picture of Albert in her head and how he'd insulted her. 'Skinny' she didn't mind. But 'stuck-up'? Is that what they thought of her? Sad. Pessimistic. Weary. She would own up to all of those. But stuck-up – never. She was an East Ender same as the rest of them in there, didn't take on airs and graces, never needed to. All she wanted was to be left alone to get on with her job, no jokes, no banter and definitely no war-talk. She could bury herself in the work, and stifle painful thoughts, murder them fiercely at birth. To be left alone – it wasn't much to ask, was it?

'Well?'

Maisy was persistent. You had to give her that. And she was also the closest to a friend Rosemary had in the place – anywhere really, when you thought about it. Since Danny had died, she didn't encourage friendship, had built a prickly shell around herself that took care of that.

'Sorry.'

'Wow! Words,' said Maisy.

If she ever smiled now – and it was rare – it was Maisy who managed to drag one from her. This one arrived on her face before she even knew it was there.

'Okay, I deserved that,' she said. 'But I'm really trying, you know. To be *normal*.'

'Normal? Who wants to be normal?' said Maisy. 'Where's the fun in that? Anyway, you hear the latest?'

'Huh?'

'We're having a visitor. Somebody special. Coming to give us the old morale boost.'

'Who?' she asked. Not that it mattered. It was always the same. They came for an hour and left. Foreman rushed them through on a whistle-stop tour, and then when the excitement died down, it was back to the normal slog again.

'Reckon it's one of them *really* special people this time. Seems like they're going to town, smartening everything up – even the canteen's got bunting up. Could be one of the royals... what d'you reckon?'

Rosemary stepped up and took her card from its slot, put it in the machine, clocked in. She wasn't fussed who was coming, if anybody was. Rumours were always rife in a place like this. Five hundred people working there, you got five hundred rumours. Didn't pay to listen, and Rosemary didn't usually, but then her friend Maisy was getting really worked up about it. Like Christmas had come early.

'We'll find out when they're ready to tell us.' She looked up at the supervisor's cabin high above their heads. He lived in the glass bubble up there where he could see them all, and only scuttled down to the shop floor when something piqued his interest. And it was usually something bad. She'd never heard of Mr Hardcastle coming down to offer praise. You did a good job, that was normal, something he took for granted. An everyday expectation. And Mr Hardcastle was a man with high expectations. You were *doing it for the war effort*: it was a mantra so often on his thin, bloodless lips that it had become a kind of shorthand for the man, and something said behind his back by mimics fed up with the continual slog, looking for some comic relief.

A strangled voice came over the tannoy. It was Mr Hardcastle doing his impression of somebody posh. He was still getting to grips with the new speaker system and seemed to think that his own working-class voice wasn't good enough.

Rosemary didn't get it. You were what you were, and she saw no earthly reason to apologise for it. She was a Bethnal Green girl and proud of it.

'Ladies and gentlemen, can I have your attention, please?'

Maisy laughed. '*Ladies?* That's nice.' She gave Rosemary's shoulder a friendly squeeze. 'Chin up, girl. See you later?'

'Maybe.'

Rosemary watched her friend head towards the canteen. Maisy was off to work her cook's magic with the paltry lot of rations she had to juggle. Abra-ca-bleedin-dabra! Making meat pies with no meat in them. They should call them carrot pies. But what the heck, it was better than nothing. *Was that optimism?* Rosemary smiled to herself. Her second smile that evening.

She wound her way to her machine station, past massive tables with girls on either side packing up the finished parachutes. There were others stacking the rolled-up chutes onto row upon row of shelves that stretched the whole length of the ground floor. In her own job, on her industrial sewing machine,

Rosemary was always surrounded by great swathes of white parachute silk. *Make lovely knickers*, the girls used to say, and laugh. But nobody took any. That would be unpatriotic.

The tannoy made some more strange noises as Mr Hardcastle hit it with something, to check it was working. The grating sound made all heads on the factory floor turn up to his glass tower. Anything to break the boredom, the repetition of their work.

'Ladies and gentlemen...'

'Didn't he say that already?' moaned Norman. Norman was a grizzled old man on the sewing machine next to Rosemary's, and she'd never seen him smile. Not once. He usually had a puzzled frown on his face, as if life confused him. Norman would take first prize in any grumpy-old-geezers competition.

'...can I have your attention, please?'

'Get on with it,' shouted some wit at the back of the room. 'War'll be over before he gets round to it.'

Easy to be a critic when you don't have to do it, thought Rosemary.

'Can I please see Rosemary Ellis up here at her earliest convenience?' said the voice.

'Ah *ha*! What you been up to then, Rosie?' Norman waggled an accusing finger at her.

She was so flustered she didn't even remind the man her name was Rosemary. *What had she done?* She could think of nothing. Dear God, that awful man Albert Green hadn't made a complaint about her, had he? But she hadn't done anything. It wasn't fair. *He* was the one should be getting an earful, not her. He'd tried to get familiar when she hadn't asked him to.

But then life wasn't always fair, was it?

She straightened her overall and slowly made her way up to the glass tower. There were catcalls and whistles as she passed and it felt like every eye in the place was on her. She held her body stiff, like a piece of steel. She could be brave. She could do this. Whatever it was, it could hardly be worse than what she'd already experienced.

———

'Where you off to dressed like that? Thought you'd work today,' said Lil.

Though she didn't make a whole song and dance about it, Lil Ellis was proud of her daughter Gracie. Of both her daughters and what they were doing for the war effort. But it didn't always do to say stuff like that. Didn't want them getting no ideas above their station. Gracie was already headstrong enough for a girl of seventeen, and she could be flighty around the blokes.

Even so, Lil's chest swelled with pride when she thought of her Gracie standing up there on the draughty platform of a big old London bus in her uniform, a clippie in charge of all them passengers and her just a slip of a thing. Ferrying people back and forth to their work.

And once, during a raid, Gracie had kept them all calm. Ordered the passengers to lie on the floor, arms over their heads, protecting themselves from flying debris. They were safe enough from glass shards for Gracie's bus had the usual blast-proof mesh over its windows; still, you didn't want a chunk of bus landing on your head.

The driver had run, abandoned them all at the first sound of the siren, but Gracie had stayed at her post, a sheepdog guarding her charges. No one got hurt, but they might have done. And Gracie had been famous for five minutes, with a line in the local paper for her cool head and bravery, and a pat on the back from her boss.

'You hear me, missy?'
'What, Ma?'
'Why you dressed all fancy? Where's your uniform?'

'Day off,' said Gracie. 'Me and Nora's going up west. Lunch in Piccadilly.'

'What!'

'Ma, it's only a corner house. Not the bloomin' Ritz.'

'You be careful. I hear there's lots of GIs go up west.'

'Yeah, sure.' Gracie shrugged her shoulders. 'A million and a half Yanks over here and I ain't managed to meet one of them yet.' She didn't look her ma in the eye. Instead, Gracie dropped her gaze to the floor. To an interesting stain on the linoleum. She hoped her ma would buy the lie.

'Just you keep it like that,' said Lil. 'It ain't all what it's cracked up to be.'

'How d'you mean, Ma?' asked Gracie, an innocent look on her face.

'Those Yankee fellas. They ain't all rich, like movie stars.'

'I ain't given it much thought,' said Gracie. 'Don't mean nothin' to me.'

But Gracie's secret ambition had been to find a gorgeous American serviceman who would whisk her off her feet, and take her to a new life in his magical country where there was no rationing, no bombs, everybody chewed gum, and you fell over movie stars on every street corner.

'And Nora's going with you?'

'Sure, Ma. And it's not like I could get up to anything exciting with her in tow, is it?'

But she'd lied about Nora. Nora wouldn't be going. She was a friend, sure – but she'd only slow her down. Nora – with her church-going ways, and strange ideas about saving yourself for sex till you were married. Just like her sister, Rosie.

'Okay. But you'll be careful, right? Don't want no GI Joe leaving you with a little war brat, do we? And don't think they wouldn't. They'd be off back home to their fancy New York before you could knit your first baby bonnet.'

'*Nothing*'s going to happen, Ma.' Gracie tried to think of the word that meant saying one thing and meaning the opposite. 'And where's our Rosie?' *Always good to pull the conversation round to Rosie. Took the heat off her for a bit.* Gracie grinned. Her ma was so easy to handle, not like their Rosie. Seemed like Rose could read your thoughts.

'Still in work. I'll swear the girl loves that place. Unless...'

'What?'

'Well, maybe she's got herself a fancy-man in there. She say anything like that to you, Gracie?'

'How could she have a fancy-man and still be as bleedin' miserable as she is? Not a smile for months,' said Grace. 'Not a civil word. No, I reckon our Rose only cared for one bloke and I can't see *nobody* filling his shoes.'

'Two weeks before their wedding, too.'

'What?'

'Him,' said Lil. 'Shot down before his wedding like that.'

'What – you think making Rose a widow would've been better?'

'Better a widow than a sour old maid,' said Lil.

'She's only twenty, Ma. She'll find somebody.'

'She better make it quick, before what's left gets took. And you're *right*, though I hate to say it, what shouldn't. That girl's been a proper misery. Grieving's one thing,' said Lil. 'But taking it out on your family? It ain't right.'

―――

Rosemary *was* smiling. Right then she had a proper grin on her face. That can happen when you think you've been called in for a bawling out, maybe even an official reprimand, and instead the supervisor offers you butterscotch. (*Sweeties! How on earth did he get those?*)

'So – should I wear a special dress or something, Mr Hardcastle?'

'It's a great honour, Rosemary, certainly. To be picked to do the presentation. But I think that when you hand over the bouquet to Her Majesty she'd expect you to be in your working clothes. Hairnet and all.' He smiled, and it wasn't often Mr Hardcastle smiled. 'After all, she's a very down-to-earth lady. And I'm sure she's interested in seeing our normal working conditions.'

Queen Elizabeth coming here. Rosemary liked the woman. Although she was the wife of King George, she wasn't stuck up or arrogant, like some of them other royals had been for years. And she was brave, faced the same dangers as everybody else in this war; hadn't rushed off to hide in the countryside. And her and her hubby didn't stay safely tucked away in some old palace, neither. They were right there in the thick of it, visiting people in the East End who'd been bombed out, and they knew all about the Blitz – had their own place at Buck House bombed as well.

'Right you are, Mr Hardcastle. Working clothes it is.'

But such a special occasion called for a bit more, as well. She'd give her hair a proper do, a holiday – even though it would all be trapped under a hairnet. She still had a bit of that good Amami shampoo left. There'd been no reason to use it lately and she couldn't bring herself to think about how she looked, not when there were men out there fighting for their lives. Men like her wonderful Danny.

This time when she thought about him, she didn't cry. A moment of panic made her head swirl and there was a weird buzzing sound in her ears. Did that mean she was forgetting him? She mustn't forget. *C'mon, breathe. Think!* She concentrated hard, closed her eyes, conjured up his face in her mind, and started breathing normally again. *Panic over.* His face was right there in front of her, with his shock of unruly black hair and that mischievous grin. Of course she hadn't forgotten him, and she made herself a promise – she never would.

3

ROTTERDAM

THREE MONTHS EARLIER

The air was heavy and thick with black smoke that clogged his lungs, made it hard to suck in the next desperate breath. And the chemical smell of burning tyres and oil filled his nostrils, gummed his eyes shut. He tried to prise them open. *They didn't work. He couldn't see.* What the hell was going on? Where was he? *Who* was he?

Danny Welland crawled his way on elbows and knees that were flayed raw. The skin was hanging off them, but he couldn't see any of that. He just kept crawling, even though he had no idea where he was crawling to. He felt the heat from the burning plane on his back and instinct told him to head away from it, keep going, get as far away from the fire and the smell as he could. Other than that there was no plan. How could there be?

'What the hell?'

All of a sudden he was being dragged by something. By some*one*. It was terrifying not to see, not to have control of your own body. He was being lifted now and could hear voices. Low, frantic whispers – in a language he didn't understand.

'Put me down. Leave me *alone*,' he screamed. Agony ripped through him. He just wanted it to stop.

'*Quiet*, British! You scream like that again and I have to gag you. You'll get us all killed.'

Hands pulled on him, thrust him into the back of what felt like a wooden cart, threw a heavy cover over him. That's when he passed out.

———

They took him to Adam Pietersen's house, to the basement. Adam didn't live there anymore, had escaped to London to join the Dutch navy in exile when the Netherlands were overrun. But his wife Sara and his daughter Anna still lived there, doing useful work for the Dutch Resistance.

'What the hell can we do with him?' said Edwin Jansen. 'He needs a doctor.'

'We'll do what we can,' said Anna. No one had heard her creep quietly down the cellar stairs. She smiled to reassure them. They were all frightened. So was she, but she was young, it was easier for her. 'The man's a hero. We can't abandon him. We have to help.'

'He'll die anyway,' said Jansen. 'Look at him.'

———

He didn't die, not *then*. Which everyone agreed was a small miracle. But a part of him died that night. The part that remembered Danny Welland. Who he was. What he did. And, most importantly of all – who he loved.

———

'Who's there?'

He was in a lot of pain – it was screeching through his nerve endings till he thought he would scream with it. But an instinct told him not to scream, that for some reason it would be dangerous. Other than that, he knew nothing, not even his name. And he couldn't see. *When did he go blind?* He couldn't remember. There was only blackness in front of his eyes, deep black with not even the faintest flicker of light. But he could hear. He'd heard the footsteps.

'It's only me again.'

'Who?'

'I told you before. You don't remember?'

'No.' A girl's voice, or a woman's, he thought. It sounded deep, though – and he pictured her as tall.

'Not to worry. You've been very ill. Had a high fever for days now, been delirious.'

'And my eyes?' asked Danny, as his hand touched a bandage around them. 'Will they be okay?'

'I'm not a doctor,' she said. 'I cannot say. But I washed them out and put the cloth around.'

'So, you've been looking after me?'

'Yes.'

'Thank you.' He licked his dry lips. 'You have some water?'

'Here.' She held the cup to his mouth. 'Drink slowly,' she ordered. 'And there's a little soup here, if you can manage it.'

Danny Welland couldn't see to eat by himself, so she fed him.

'What's your name?' he asked, after a bout of coughing had left him exhausted.

'Anna.'

'Pretty name.'

She was silent. He felt the warmth of her close to him. It was comforting when all he'd had to think about was the pain. *Enough of that* – it wasn't on, feeling sorry for yourself. He didn't know why he felt like that, because he didn't know anything about himself. Was he a good man, an ethical man? Was he a criminal? How had he ended up with her, with this girl?

'Anna what?'

'Pietersen. Anna Pietersen is my name.'

The way she said it, the syntax of her sentence, made her sound foreign. Different from him. And how did he know that? He didn't even know what *he* was. But he could hear from his own voice that his accent was not like hers.

'Pietersen – is that Norwegian?'

'Dutch. I'm Dutch. We all are. All the people who rescued you.'

'I've been rescued?'

Anna Pietersen laughed. It was a noisy, boisterous laugh, and he liked it.

Anna put her hand over her mouth to deaden the noise she was making. Noise was dangerous, even down there in the cellar. The Bosch had ears and eyes everywhere.

'Yes,' she said. 'Mr Mystery Man, you've been rescued.'

It wasn't strictly true, of course. Only half a mystery, because they knew he was a British pilot, had been wearing an RAF uniform, had been spotted crawling away from a burning Hurricane. But no one knew his name. And they'd all decided that, for the time being at least, that's how it should remain. Safer that way. The Dutch Resistance was still in its infancy and you never knew who you could trust – not all German collaborators were easy to spot. So it had been decided that no one would attempt to get a message through to England about this flier. At least not yet.

And anyway, no one was sure whether the man would live or die. Anna knew that some in the Resistance there, in Rotterdam, would prefer this pilot to die. Less complicated. *But not her.* She felt something special for the Englishman, a bond. And maybe he felt it too. He seemed at ease with her. He couldn't see her, of course – maybe that was it.

Anna was confident in her own skin even though others might see her as flawed. She saw how some of the young lads looked at her, but she didn't care – she was what she was and couldn't change it. She was not pretty like some girls she knew, had always been forced into the role of tomboy because of her size and masculine-looking features. So she'd gone along with it, cutting her thick black hair short. Not a bob, like some women, but close to the skull. Some of them sniggered behind her back, called her a dyke, queer. But she wasn't. And what business was it of theirs, anyway?

Although she'd soon be eighteen, she didn't have a boyfriend, had never had one. Lads her own age were frightened of her. She was taller than any of them, with large feet and hands. Hands that had pounded a few heads when she was growing up.

But this man, lying in her cellar, couldn't see the shape of her face or her massive feet. All he could hear was her voice. And when he'd heard it for the first time – he'd smiled in spite of his pain.

Anna Pietersen allowed herself to hope. Hope that this man would survive. That the Bosch wouldn't find him. *That he might even like her.* All of a sudden, she realised that the last small hope was the most important one of all.

———

He heard their voices and thought it was still part of his dream. Horrific nightmares had enveloped him in their madness: mid-air crashes where the sky lit up in a mosaic of orange and silver flashes; a demented screaming cacophony of sound and light, his own free firework display; and then him, falling through the freezing night with its thin, unbreathable air, hoping he wouldn't pass out from the lack of oxygen before he could pull the ripcord of his parachute.

Parachute. The word bounced around in his head. It meant something, something special, but he couldn't grab hold of its magic. He knew it was important, though. When he had thought about his parachute, a smile had tried to break through his terrifying nightmare. Then the voices woke him up.

'That you, Anna?'

He was pleased he'd remembered her name. Had picked it out from his scrambled brain.

'I'm here,' she said. 'And some others. They want to talk to you.'

There was a tightness in her voice that hadn't been there before; it worried him.

'My parachute. Have you got my parachute?'

'Parachute?' she said. 'Why would you want a parachute?'

'I don't know why. But I think it's important. It's a clue to who I am.' It was feeble, he knew, and he didn't know why he'd said that.

'There *was* no parachute,' said Anna. Her voice was weary. 'You didn't fall from the sky in a piece of silk. Your parachute was destroyed in the fire, I expect, along with everything else.'

'Well, then how—?'

'—did you survive? God's hand, maybe. He flung you from a crashed plane – a burning plane. A miracle.'

He heard a heavy sigh. A man's voice. He was beginning to pick up on their rhythms now, the small nuances of these people who had rescued him. Though what he was doing in a plane he couldn't imagine. Even the idea of being up in the air, being thrown around the sky, made him feel queasy.

'Okay, flyboy. We need to move you. Too dangerous for you to stay here.' *The man again.*

'What Mr Jansen means,' said Anna, 'is that the Bosch is having another one of their purges. Retribution.'

'Retribution? For what?' Danny asked.

'Amsterdam again,' Jansen told him. 'They tried mass industrial strikes before, protesting against the treatment of Jews – back in '40. Didn't work then. Won't work now.' Jansen sighed. 'Mr Hitler just turns up the flame. Pulls in some more Dutch. Lines them against a wall.'

A sharp intake of breath. It was the girl, Anna. He recognised the timbre of the sound, drew a picture in his mind of what she might look like.

She'd tried to explain stuff to him. There was a war on. The idiots had gone and done it again, when the last one was supposed to be the one that ended all wars. Not that many had believed that.

They helped him to his feet. Two of them, one on either side. Strong arms lifting him, practically dragging him up the cellar steps, for Danny couldn't find the strength to manage it by himself. He felt stupid, useless, like a small child having to rely on these good people who were putting themselves in danger for him. The least he could do was walk when they asked him to, but it seemed he couldn't remember how to do such simple things.

'There you go,' said Jansen, and there was humour in his voice this time. 'Not bad for a dead man.'

4

'Stop fussing, Ma.' But secretly Rosemary enjoyed the sensation, the luxury of having someone else wash your hair. Even though it was your mother. Some weird switch in her brain must have clicked on, because yesterday when Ma had fussed over her, tried to get her to eat, to rest, to sleep like other people, she'd stormed out in a temper.

'Fussing? *Fussing*, she says!' Lily Ellis nodded to the room, as if seeking agreement from some invisible audience. 'And why should I *not* be fussing? It's not every day a daughter of mine gets picked to meet the king and queen.'

'*Queen*. The king's busy doing other stuff, I expect.'

'Even so, what an honour.'

'Yes,' said Rosemary, 'it is.' And she felt a small reawakening of her old optimism. 'Oi, watch it. That hurt.'

'Well, you shouldn't have so many rats' tails. When was the last time you washed this?'

She couldn't remember. 'There's a war on, Ma.'

'Sure there is, but that doesn't mean we let things slip, does it now?'

Rosemary turned her head to face her mother, got shampoo

in her eyes, and water all over the kitchen floor. 'No, it doesn't, Ma. You're right.'

And that was it. The two women built a bridge between them, a bridge to the past, to how things had once been. They hadn't been perfect, but they'd been okay.

Rosemary sat in front of the fire and began drying her wet hair. 'Where's our Gracie?'

'Went up west with her friend, Nora. She's back now, but she didn't come home.'

'Oh?'

'I met Sid in the butcher's queue. Said Gracie was down the shelter, getting stuff ready for the concert party tonight.'

Bethnal Green tube station was like a whole underground city nowadays. One of the few deep-level stations in the East End, it had been a natural choice for a massive public air-raid shelter. The new station hadn't been completed when the war started, so the rails had been covered over with a huge wooden platform where concert parties and singalongs were sometimes organised. Once, they'd even had a wedding party down there. Worked miracles for morale.

The station platforms were used for sleeping. *One night at the height of the Blitz there'd been 7,000 people packed in down there. Not an inch of space to spare*, Rosemary recalled. Sardines had more room in their cans. But people hadn't complained, took it all in good grace with hardly a grumble.

The place had 5,000 bunks and the rest had huddled together against the cold. People picked up their rolled-up bedding from collection shops at street level after their day's work, and then trudged down the stairway for another night below ground. Folks tried to keep up their spirits, but sometimes it wasn't easy with so many bodies all crammed in, and the stench of living close together, and dodgy toilets. In the morning, the overpowering smell of TCP disinfectant would drift out onto the street after a night's grim bombing. Even so, Rosemary could think of a few love stories that had had their beginnings in those fear-filled nights underground. People who had found each other. Romance that had bloomed. Something good out of something bad.

Then there was Gracie. The locals loved Gracie. A born performer who cheered up folks with her singing and dancing, getting them to join in the singalongs. Rosemary admired her sister, but she wasn't looking forward to another night deep underground: the smells enough to turn your stomach, and shivering in the cold. Still, some things you just did. For family.

'She's got a lovely voice, our Grace,' said Rosemary.

'She's got the knack,' said Lil, proudly. 'Born with it.'

'So, the concert party...' said Rosemary. 'Maybe we should go later – if Gracie's doing her bit. Keep the family flag flying.'

'Didn't know we had a family flag,' her mother said. 'Tell you what, though...'

'What?'

'After tomorrow, when you've done your curtsey to the queen, we'll maybe have a fancy family crest we can stick on the sideboard.'

They both laughed. It was the first time Rosemary had laughed in months. It felt good.

The next day, things got even better.

Gracie's concert had been grand, a big success. There had been a party feeling about the place, as if the cold tiled walls of the underground chamber had magically morphed into a sunny, tropical beach or at the very least a charabanc ride to Southend.

Rosemary had practised her curtsey and made a fair enough job of it, and there was an air of excitement that even a grumpy soul like Norman seemed to catch.

The queen was charming and scattered smiles on everyone

she met, and they didn't seem false. She somehow managed to make everybody feel special, including Rosemary.

Rose handed over the bouquet when Mr Hardcastle gave her the nod and the queen took it graciously – considering it was a bit on the sparse, scrappy side. But then *there was a war on*, as people were at pains to remind you.

'Thank you, my dear. Rosemary, isn't it?'

'Yes, Your Majesty,' she said. They'd all warned her she might be tongue-tied, but she wasn't. And why should she be? She was a person, just like this woman. Well, okay – maybe not exactly like this woman. But Rosemary was proud of who she was, where she came from.

A flash went off as some bloke in a fancy suit took a photograph.

'And now I've got a little surprise for *you* as well.' Queen Elizabeth turned to the table behind and took something from it. 'We're all very proud of how hard you've worked for the war effort, Rosie. Do you mind if I call you Rosie?'

Now she really was tongue-tied. She just nodded as this woman in the cornflower-blue coat shook hands with her, and then handed Rosemary something that looked like a photo frame. But she remembered to curtsey again. She was getting the hang of it now.

Mr Hardcastle gave her a strange look and before it was too late she squeezed out a strangled, 'Thanks.' The bloke took another photograph and winked at her.

They offered her tea in the canteen, but she went for the orange squash instead, for it was a long time since Rosemary had tasted squash. She let it trickle slowly down her throat, savouring it, and once again looked at the certificate in its golden frame. Well, not gold, obviously (*there was a war on*) but impressive just the same. It would look great on the sideboard and she knew her ma would dust it incessantly.

It said that Rosemary Ellis had produced the most parachutes in the last year of anyone in the factory (it actually mentioned the whole of the British Isles, but that seemed a bit boastful and Rose wasn't one to boast). She'd been tireless in her work, taking extra shifts while others had slept.

The citation was effusive in its praise and Rosemary felt a little embarrassed, and guilty, because only *she* knew why she had been so 'tireless'. She had thrown herself into her work as an escape from the pain that froze all other emotions in her. So maybe she didn't really deserve this, maybe she was just one great big fraud.

No! That wasn't true. She'd accept the accolade graciously, it had been handed out in good faith, and anything else would just be impolite.

———

'All la-di-da now, eh? Now that you've been in the company of royals!'

'Huh?' She couldn't believe her sister was being like this. She'd never have said that if Ma was home.

'Miss Hoity-Toity. You'll be taking tea from china cups and crooking yer little finger next.'

'What? No! What's wrong with you, our Gracie?'

'Our Gracie? Stop that! Makes me feel like Gracie-sodding-bloody-Fields.'

'Nothing wrong with Gracie Fields.'

'Yeah, well, I'm not her, am I? Never will be now.' Her shoulders heaved with a massive sigh.

'C'mon, Grace. Out with it. What the hell's wrong?'

Rosemary watched her sister's face screw up into a tight ball of pain.

'Jesus, Grace. What *is* it? It can't be that bad! You were on top of the world last night, people screaming and yelling, telling you how you should be on stage an' all. When this lot's over, you got a great future ahead. Big West End star. We'll all be right proud of you.'

'Sure. Big West End *star*,' said Gracie. 'That's rich. More like little East End tart, you mean.'

Rosemary took her sister by the arm. Shook her. 'Don't say that. Don't you put yourself down, Gracie Ellis – there'll be enough people out there ready to do that without you helping them. We love you. Your family loves you, and you're special.'

'Yeah? Think Ma will figure I'm special when she finds out I'm cooking a little American bastard in here?' Gracie wrapped her arms protectively around her belly and rocked backwards and forwards.

'What? Never! Can't be.'

'See. Even *you're* shocked. What the hell chance I got with her? And the neighbours. My God, the neighbours! Ma's gonna love that.'

It was true. Of course Gracie was right – the tongues would wag and the knives would be sharpened and her sister Gracie would be the latest juicy bit of gossip behind every front door in Royston Street.

But so-bloody-what?

'You're sure? Maybe you're just late,' said Rosemary. 'None of us are eating enough, we're working flat out, and then there's the stress of the bombing. Maybe your period's just gone away for a bit.'

'Oh, yeah? Like taken itself off for a wee holiday in the sun,' said Gracie. 'That would be nice.'

'You've checked then?'

''Course I've bleedin' checked. Seen a doctor an' all.'

'That's it, then. If old Doc Parish knows, so does the whole of Bethnal Green,' said Rosemary.

'Don't be daft. I'd never go near that old alky. I went to some bloke in Cheapside. I may be pregnant, our Rosie, but I ain't stupid.'

'No? Stupid enough to get yourself knocked up.'

Rosemary wanted to put the hateful words back in her mouth, but it was too late. The damage was done and she grabbed her sister in a hug, pulled her in tight; tried to calm Gracie's sobs and the tremors that were rippling through her body in a river of pain.

'It's okay, Gracie. We'll fix it. Find the American, tell him he's a daddy. I'll go with you.'

'Oh, sure. Like I didn't already try that? The bastard's married. One small detail he forgot to mention before he had his jollies. Claims it's somebody else's brat. It's not, Rosie. Honest to God, it's not. I loved this bloke – ain't *never* been with no one else, not in *that* way.'

'Shush now.' Rosemary rocked her little sister in her arms, like she was a baby again. 'It'll work out, you'll see. Not the end of the world, and I'll stand by you when you tell Ma.'

'Think I'd tell Ma this? She's got enough in her head. On top of our da, and being bombed out, something like this could mess her up good and proper. And she don't deserve that, Rosie. Whatever we think sometimes, she don't deserve no more grief.'

'So?'

'I'll have the kid without her knowing *nothing*. 'Cause whatever else I am, Rosie, I ain't no murderer. The poor wee thing didn't ask to be born and I won't have no abortion.'

'Good for you. But how you figure on doing that?'

'What?'

'The bit about her not knowing,' said Rosemary.

'I'll take meself off some place.'

'Oh, that'll work! Ma's got spies everywhere. She'll find out.'

'Not there, she won't. I'm taking off to the country. Lots of nice clean air too.' Gracie produced a cynical snort. 'I've joined the bleedin' Women's Land Army. Just waiting for me papers. I'll be miles away from this lot here when little Harry or Harriet decides to gouge their way into this lunatic bloody world.'

So, the swine that got her up the duff was called Harry, was he? And the Women's Land Army? No way could she see Gracie with her sleeves rolled up 'digging for victory'.

'They won't take you at seventeen,' said Rose.

'Seventeen and a *half*,' said Gracie defiantly. '*And they already did!*'

Sadness bubbled up in Rosemary as she studied her sister's face. For what she saw there was not the image she was used to, of a young girl fizzing with excitement and expectation, ready for anything this crazy world threw at her. Now she saw the hardened face of a bitter crone who has lost all belief in the joy of life.

Tears trickled down Rosemary's face. Tears of sorrow for her sister, and this baby. But tears of regret for herself, as well, and for Danny. He would have made a fine father; they could have brought a baby into the world, taught it, supported it, loved it. A treasure for them both to share, but now it would never be.

Instead, the first baby to come into the Ellis family would have an absent father, a selfish man who cared nothing for Gracie, or his child. Rosemary didn't even want to know his name, this man who had cruelly cast her sister aside. But she was sure of one thing: he may have abandoned Gracie, but *she* never would. Whatever Gracie had done, they were family. And family looked out for each other.

5

ROTTERDAM

17 OCTOBER 1942

The Britisher had been trundled all over the city in the back of a milk cart. Its first bone-jarring moment had made him pass out. Which Edwin Jansen reckoned was a bonus. At least it would keep him quiet. Make the journey less hazardous. They were going to Jansen's house. He was the leader of this small underground cell, and at fifty, the oldest one there.

'We've been lucky,' said Jansen. 'Not a single German patrol.'

'Bosch got other fish to fry. I heard somebody blew up a rail track last night,' said De Groot.

'Seems so,' said Edwin.

'And kids been putting sugar in their petrol tanks again. Really pisses them off,' said De Groot. Although the man's name was William, few called him that. He was known by his nickname, De Groot, which meant *the large*. Jansen wondered how anyone could still be that big with all the food shortages, for the man had hands like ham hocks and feet the size of industrial shovels. Maybe he had a pig stashed somewhere that the Bosch hadn't found.

Edwin Jansen was relieved to get the airman settled into his apple cellar – although it had been a long time since any apples had been kept in there. Apples were a luxury now, like many other things. The Germans had stripped the countryside and towns alike, causing food shortages for civilians. The invading soldiers were like a plague of greedy locusts.

The Resistance had reason to be grateful to Edwin Jansen. He'd put himself in danger many times, and had also given refuge to three *onderduikers*, people in hiding, Dutchmen who also happened to be Jews. He'd hidden them in his cellar for three months before they'd finally been able to escape to Britain.

Jansen looked down at Danny, lying on a mattress on the cellar floor. 'Let's hope this *British* hasn't left his rabbit's foot at home,' he said. And he meant it.

He'd seen how Anna fussed over the flier, had taken him under her substantial wing, how her face flushed crimson when she spoke to the man.

Anna was a good girl, a brave girl who took on dangerous jobs for the Resistance, cycling around with messages right under the nose of the Bosch. But Anna was a young woman who found it hard to smile. And yet he'd noticed her smile more readily in these last weeks with this Englishman.

Jansen had promised his good friend Adam Pietersen to look out for his family, that Sara and Anna Pietersen would be safe. He'd tried to be a second father to his best friend's daughter now that Adam was in England. But it hadn't been easy. Anna had rarely been happy before, but she was happy now. And that was okay with Jansen.

It had taken him four months to drag his battered and weary body back to some kind of normality, to become a functioning human again. Well, almost functioning. He could only see out of one eye, but sometimes one eye was all you needed.

And gradually pieces of him, of his history, began to slot themselves into places that made sense. He was a pilot. Had crashed his Hurricane here in Holland and been rescued by the Dutch Underground.

He'd been in Edwin's cellar for three tedious months now and was going stir crazy. The damp walls were pressing in on him like a claustrophobic cocoon; the smell of mould permanently in his nostrils. Soon – very soon, they'd all promised him – he could go above ground, into daylight. Because now after his long confinement, he was finally doing something important.

He'd been surprised at how quickly and easily he'd learned Dutch. But then Anna was a good and patient teacher. And he'd taken readily to his new job of organising and printing the propaganda leaflets for the Resistance, and the one-page newspaper that they ran off copies for once a week on their duplicating machine. *He'd never expected to find himself in the publishing business, but fair enough.*

It was February 1943. A month when there was good and bad news for his paper. The Germans had finally surrendered at Stalingrad. When they'd heard that, they'd all celebrated with the last of the vile homebrew Jansen had produced for Christmas. But the bad news cancelled out the sudden euphoria. *More reprisals.* This time for the murder of Dutch collaborator General Seyffardt by a Resistance cell. Six hundred students had been arrested from campuses all over the Netherlands and taken to a concentration camp in Vught.

This last brutal reprisal made him even more determined to get back home and rejoin his squadron. Go to Berlin and bomb the hell out of the bastards.

And now that his memory was gradually coming back, he

understood one more thing. That he was loved. That somewhere in London was a wonderful woman who loved him. Who was waiting to marry him.

Her name was Rosemary.

―――

Talk about the Secret-bloody-Service. Rosemary would have made a decent recruit. She'd been sworn to secrecy by Gracie. *Mum's the word.* There were winks and nudges from her sister, reminders that blood was thicker than water. Oh, yeah? It wasn't like their mother was stupid, and once she'd cottoned on to the truth... well, both of them would be finding out exactly how thick that blood was.

Because Lil Ellis would be shedding some of it.

Rosemary lived on a knife edge, constantly watching for signs of her sister's expanding waistline, and the first hint that their ma had smelled a rat. But Lil was in a happy little bubble, while Rosemary knew that Ma was proud of both her and Gracie – though she didn't always say it – what with Gracie with her glorious voice and now herself with that fancy new certificate sitting there on the sideboard.

She watched her ma dust the frame yet again, though there wasn't a speck of dust on the thing.

'This chap you said came looking for me,' said Rose. 'What exactly did he say?'

'You and your sister, you're both the same,' said Lil. 'Never bleedin' listen. Told you. Said he was from the ministry of something or other. Looked like a spiv in his fancy suit.'

'Never mind his wardrobe, Ma. What did he want?'

'Bloke said he knew you. Took photos of you before. Said you was to meet him at the factory,' said Lil.

'But why?' asked Rosemary.

'Your Mr Hardcastle sent him round. Reckons it's part of the war effort,' said Lil.

'Don't see how,' said Rosemary.

'Bloke reckons he'll make you a poster girl. Wants to take photos of you. So you'd best put your new dress on, our Rose.'

She wasn't sure. Maybe she should just wear her overalls. But her ma went and ironed the dress anyway, so she put it on. It was her Sunday best. One that she'd used up all her clothing coupons on.

A poster girl, the man had said. *What? Like Rosie the Riveter?* The thought took her back to Danny and how he'd joked about it when they first met. And the sadness ganged up on her again.

6

LONDON

FEBRUARY 1943

'Propaganda,' said Robert Batley. 'That's the name of the game.'

Rosemary smiled at him. *You had to be civil.* Still, she wasn't sure she wanted to be 'propaganda'. Somehow it felt a bit fake. But her boss Mr Hardcastle had assured her it was all part of the war effort. Anything less would mean that Herr Hitler would be parking his tanks in The Mall, filling up the pantries of Buck House with German sausage and sauerkraut. She needed to do whatever Mr Batley from the Ministry of Information required of her.

It was the same photographer who had taken pictures of her and the queen. The man had winked at her. That much she remembered. And he wasn't bad-looking – young, around twenty-five, twenty-six maybe. Escaped the call-up from his country then, which meant relatives in high places or flat feet.

It was all the same to Rosemary. She had no time for them, not when there were men like Danny and her da who'd stood up whatever the cost.

'Charming,' he said, as he walked into the supervisor's

office. 'Utterly charming.' He kissed her hand. *Blimey. No one had ever done that before.* He seemed very sophisticated, and he acted and sounded like a toff, but that didn't make him any better than her. Just different.

First, he took her to the canteen for a cuppa and started asking all sorts of questions. Personal questions. Ones that made her start to wonder what he was going to put in this article of his.

'I don't really get it, Mr Batley. Could you not just put that other photo in with a line or two underneath?'

'If we're to do a real poster campaign, Rosie... Do you mind me calling you Rosie?'

'Yes, I do. Rosemary's my name.'

'Oh. But when you met Her Majesty, she called you that.'

'That was different.'

'I see.'

Rosemary finished her tea quickly. She didn't like the man. There was something *off* about him, and if Mr Hardcastle hadn't gone on about Hitler's tanks rolling up The Mall she'd have gone straight home without doing any of this nonsense. But she was a patriot. Loved her country. Didn't fancy eating German sausage.

'Okay, then, Mr Batley. Can we get on?'

'Robert. Call me Robert.' Robert Batley's face creased into a charming smile. He followed it up with a wink.

The charm offensive was wasted on Rosemary. The man struck her as false and insincere, and she certainly wouldn't call him by his first name. First names were for friends.

'So – what happens now, *Mr Batley?*' she asked.

'Ah... well, Rosemary, if it's alright with you, we'll need to go outside to get a few shots. Against the background of the factory wall. Make a good visual juxtaposition, I believe.'

'Oh?' Rosemary wasn't sure she wanted to be alone with

this bloke, especially outside with no one around. 'In what way?'

'In what way what?'

'This juxtaposition of yours…' She refused to ask him what the poncey word meant.

'Well…'

Rosemary watched him move restlessly from one foot to the other. He looked uncomfortable, as if her questions had unsettled him. Maybe he wasn't used to women having minds of their own. Needed them to be subservient, like most blokes did.

'The contrast – side by side like that,' Batley explained, 'between a stark brick wall and an attractive young woman… who is *also* tough and resolute.' He added the last words quickly. 'It makes for a powerful visual image.'

They went outside and Rosemary was sorry she didn't have her coat on, and that she'd listened to her mother and worn her summer dress. She could feel goose bumps coming up on her legs already. She'd didn't have nylon stockings on, had just drawn the line up the back of her leg where the seam would be. It was what you did when you didn't own nylons anymore. Not many could afford the ridiculous price the spivs charged for them on the black market.

She felt silly now. Why hadn't she worn her overalls? And that strange look on Mr Hardcastle's face when he'd seen what she was wearing. Did he think the same thing? That it wasn't quite right?

'Maybe I should go back in and put my working clothes on,' said Rosemary.

'Why on earth would you do that?'

'For a start, Mr Batley, it's blooming cold out here. And it's not like I do my work in something fancy like this.'

'You look perfect, Rosemary. The image – it works well.'

'Maybe I could get my coat?'

'You're *cold*?' he asked, surprise in his voice.

She studied his face. Up close like this it was fleshy, with the beginnings of a double chin. It had become red in places, as if some internal furnace was heating the man up. Rosemary couldn't think why she'd first thought him good-looking. And the strange way he was staring at her – as if she were a specimen trapped under a microscope.

'My coat...?' she said again, harshly. With an impatience that said *she* was the one in charge, not him.

'Okay. We'll get through as quickly as we can. Shouldn't take much longer. Can you just put one arm up over your head like this?' He raised his own arm above his head to demonstrate. 'Up against the wall like this. That's good. Yes, that's great! And the other arm – bring it round the front, like so.'

———

Batley went over to her. He licked his lips. They were dry, and his hand was shaking. The closeness of her, the colour of her skin, and the smell of her hair – it was the final straw, the one where the camel collapses. What was she doing to him, this girl, this slip of a thing? No, she wasn't a girl, but a woman. And that spark in her eyes, it was like electricity being shot through him. The jolt scorching its way to his nerve ends. He was becoming infatuated with her. If she didn't want him to feel like this, why did she look this good? Why had she worn that dress, fixed her hair that way? She was the one to blame. They were all the same. Teases.

He couldn't help himself, even though he knew it wasn't right. But what could anyone say – or do, for that matter? They were out there alone in this yard with its grimy brick, and her like a beautiful butterfly trapped there, pinned to the wall.

Robert Batley ran his hand up her leg and underneath her

flimsy dress until he touched something that felt like warm cotton. And that was the last thing he remembered.

Rosemary fled and made straight for Mr Hardcastle's office high up in the rafters, far above the industrious ants below. That's what she felt like now. Like one of the masses. Inferior. Like she didn't have a value. And dirty. Really dirty.

She sat on the only other chair in Mr Hardcastle's office and shook. She couldn't *stop* shaking. That's why the supervisor had gone to the canteen himself to get her a cup of tea. *When in doubt bring on the tea.* And it was meant to be good for shock.

She knew that Mr Hardcastle was shocked too. He'd said so when she told him. And he believed her, Rosemary could tell; believed that this sleazy bloke had done exactly what she'd accused him of.

The supervisor came back with the tea and Rosemary thanked him. She was grateful. The tea was strong. And sweet. *Very* sweet. She guessed he must have heaped at least three spoonfuls of sugar in there, as if there was no such thing as rationing. There was a biscuit, too.

'Now, Rose, we need to get this written down,' said Mr Hardcastle.

'Do we have to?' she asked. She just wanted to go home. Wanted it all to be over.

'Can't have any of that hanky-panky going on here. I should get the police, Rose. Make an official complaint.'

'No, don't do that. *Please*, Mr Hardcastle.' She thought about her mother and the bubble of joy she'd been in lately. All false, of course. But Rosie couldn't heap any more pain onto her poor ma's shoulders. There'd been enough of that. And anyway, it wouldn't help. She knew how it went – her word against his. And he was a toff. Stood to sense who'd come off best in that.

'But we can't let him get away with it, Rose.'

'He didn't get away with it.' And Rosemary smiled at last. 'I broke his nose.'

'I saw the blood,' said Mr Hardcastle, giving her a small smile.

'You went down there? What he say?' She felt her throat constrict when she remembered.

'He was gone. Just the remains of his fancy camera lying round. You do that too?'

'I jumped on it hard. Smashed the bloody thing to bits.' She put a hand to her mouth. 'Sorry, Mr Hardcastle,' she said, 'swearing an' all.'

'Never heard a thing, Rose.'

She finished her tea quickly and the lovely digestive biscuit that he'd brought with it.

'You trot on home now. Come in tomorrow. Come up and see me when you get here and just tell that lot down there that we're discussing new work shifts. Okay? Don't have to tell anybody about this if you don't want to. But I'll be putting an official complaint in to his boss.'

Rosemary was relieved. She didn't want them all to know in there. Not even her friend Maisy. No smoke without fire, that's what people loved to say. She didn't want to make a whole production number out of it. That would mean the bastard had won some sort of victory.

7

ROTTERDAM

2 MARCH 1943

Danny was thrilled. He'd escaped above ground for the first time, could breathe *real* air, during a trip across the city with Edwin Jansen, over to the hospital.

It was a shock, the devastation. He hadn't expected it, but most of the city centre had been wiped out when the Germans bombed Rotterdam in their *Blitzkrieg*. Fires had burned for days, Jansen told him. Now the city was a sad, fire-blackened, rubble-strewn shadow of its former self.

They were going to meet a friend of Jansen's, an eye specialist and a man who could be trusted. Danny had no idea of the man's name. But he understood. It was the way it had to be, to keep the Resistance cell secure. He already suspected that the sight couldn't be restored in his injured eye. But the strange thing was that Danny's good eye seemed to be compensating for both of them. The biggest difference between now and before the crash was in his peripheral vision: now he had to turn his head to look out of the corner of his eye.

He sensed that Edwin Jansen believed their hospital trip

futile. But Anna had insisted on it, and Danny had watched the man go along with it. He'd noticed it before, the way Edwin seemed to want to please the girl. In many ways he treated her more like a daughter than another colleague from the Resistance.

But whatever the outcome of the day's visit, right then Danny was happy. Excited to smell the fresh air. Air that wasn't tainted with mould like his cellar home. To walk with the wind on his face. And the best bit was that they trusted him.

It also meant his Dutch was okay, would pass muster if they were stopped, even though they all made fun of his accent. But he knew it was a game they played, especially Edwin. He was gaining their trust and their respect. They had always had his. To put your life on the line took real courage, for if this Resistance cell had been discovered hiding someone – especially a *Britischer* pilot – they would be hauled off to a concentration camp. Or worse, put up against a wall.

Immediate execution was one of the Bosch's best tools. A dramatic warning.

He wanted it to last forever, this outing. But it didn't, of course, and the news about his eyes had been what he expected. He could live with that – after all, it was what he'd been doing for the last five months. And it seemed that his one good eye was in great shape. The doctor had also pronounced him to be in excellent physical shape, a remarkable recovery considering all he'd been through.

Danny was sorry when the trip was over, but he could see that Anna was relieved, was glad to have them all back safely. She sat on one of the fruit crates in Edwin's cellar, her hands busy with something. He couldn't tell if it was needlework or some sort of craft thing. She was always busy with something.

'Edwin tells me you could be home soon.'

'What?'

'If they can coordinate the plan with London, you could be

there by the end of the week. Two of you. Another British. SOE headquarters are sending a plane to pick him up.'

'SOE?' asked Danny.

'*Special Operations Executive* in London. They're coming to pick up one of their agents and Edwin thinks they might give you a lift home.'

'*Home?*' said Danny. 'But... that's wonderful!' It was incredible news. But when he looked at Anna, he saw only sadness on her face, not the excitement of his own, and he felt crass. An insensitive lout. He knew the woman had feelings for him. She hadn't tried to hide them, but he couldn't find those same emotions in himself, and you can't manufacture that kind of thing.

His heart was somewhere else. Had been given a long time ago, and he hoped Rosie still felt the same way about him as she had that day on the cliff-top at Havenporth when she'd agreed to marry him.

'I'd like you to do something for me.' Anna looked at him shyly, and there was a flush of red starting on her neck, creeping up her face.

'Of course, Anna. Anything.'

'My father's in London. Try and find him. Tell him about us, Mama and me. Tell him we're fine; he mustn't worry. Give him our love and give him this. I've been making it especially for him – when I knew you'd be going back.'

She showed him the thing she'd been working on. It was a cross, and very unusual for something like that. It was large, and made out of leather: two pieces sewn roughly together, and a sort of hook stitched into one end; for a chain he guessed, or maybe it was meant as a bookmark.

'I'll find him, I promise.'

She smiled at him. 'Tell him I'm sorry about the chain. Remind him we're at war here!' She laughed and threaded a lump of string through the hook.

Danny took the cross from her hands. Even if you didn't believe in stuff like that, it was good to have something to hang on to. A lucky charm. 'I'll get it to him,' he said.

'Thank you.'

'No, thank *you*. No words can say what...'

'Don't say them then,' said Anna. 'I understand.'

And just like that, she was gone, rushing up the cellar steps. He didn't go after her. Knew she wouldn't want that, to be seen as vulnerable, for him to see the tears. But he'd seen them anyway.

———

'Right then, hurry on down the bus, please.' The pilot laughed and winked at them both. Danny smiled back, but his companion remained silent and unmoved. The man looked as if he'd been in his own private war: bruises all over his face, dark shadows under his eyes; eyes that held a deeply haunted look. His name was Alexander, no last name offered, and Danny hadn't asked. Sometimes, it was better not to know.

Whoever this Alexander was, he was important, though. A special plane had been sent from the SOE intelligence agency to pick him up – and Danny had been lucky enough to get a ride.

'Okay, let's get you war heroes home.' The pilot laughed again. That's what pilots did: they ribbed each other, all in good humour though. Danny had missed that. But if anyone was a hero, it was this chap – the pilot from the RAF *Special Duties Squadron*, flying behind enemy lines, working for the intelligence agency. This British pilot in his Lizzie – the affectionate name for the Lysander – had put his flimsy crate down on a feeble airstrip that he couldn't even be sure was there, and had waited long enough to pick up his strange cargo of burnt-out human beings and transport them somewhere safe.

Not that Danny felt burnt out, but the bloke standing beside him certainly looked it.

Danny swallowed hard; didn't even want to think about what that poor blighter might have been through.

Today was a date that would live in his mind forever – 5 March 1943. Whatever else came along in life, it would always be a day of celebration. He was on his way home. He had two dates to be kept alive now. Because there was also 27 July, an anniversary. A very special day on a cliff-top in Cornwall. Memories of Rosie, how she had looked that day, her eyes, her smile; they had all flooded back to him. He was grateful to have his memory back, to picture her face in his mind. And soon, with luck he would see her again. The thought drew a smile from him.

The Lizzie had a permanent ladder attached to the rear cockpit. Danny climbed up first and scrambled into a space that would comfortably have fitted one, but had now been adapted to fit up to three desperate people if needed.

Getting off the ground had been dramatic, but both the Lizzie and her pilot had struggled valiantly, miraculously clearing a hedge like magicians. Once airborne, the shudders and creaks of the small plane were a symphony to Danny's ears, even though his companion Alexander jumped nervously each time they hit a thermal.

It had been a tough goodbye, although they'd all tried not to show it. *Hard men. Flinty.* It was what they needed to be able to survive. But in the end even Edwin had succumbed to emotion, and after giving Danny a simple clap on the back had grasped him in a huge bear hug. They'd miss him, they said, *and* his pathetic Dutch accent. He'd been useful to the cause.

De Groot had patted Dan's tousled wavy hair, until embarrassment made him stop. Anna had stayed home with her mother.

No one had told him anything: who was collecting him,

where they were taking him. Maybe they didn't know. Safer that way. He'd been shoved into the back of a lorry and told to keep quiet. Not that anyone had to tell him that. He'd been in occupied Holland long enough by then to know what it took to stay safe, to stay alive. And he didn't want to bring down any kind of reprisals on these brave people who were helping exfiltrate him. The Bosch were good at reprisals.

'This is your captain speaking,' came the jovial announcement over their headsets. ''Fraid we don't have much in the way of in-flight catering, chaps. But if one of you would care to search around back there, you'll find we do a rather decent line in cocoa and some pathetic cheese sandwiches that have given up hope. Curled up at the edges, I'm afraid. Still, better than nothing, eh?'

Better than nothing? Surely he meant manna from heaven? Danny Welland's grin took over the whole of his face. He couldn't remember the last time he'd had a cheese sandwich, curled up or otherwise. He felt around at his feet for the flask of cocoa. *Still warm. Made in England.*

What a strange thought. Danny felt a tsunami of emotion rise up in him, threaten to overwhelm him. He hadn't let himself think about it – ever – what it might feel like to be going home, for it seemed such an impossible dream. But here he was. God, but it felt good.

'Got it,' he said. 'And thanks. I've died and gone to heaven.'

'Long as you don't take us with you, old boy.' The pilot's voice boomed in Danny's headphones. 'Look ahead of us.'

'The Channel?'

'Can't imagine how it feels, but thought you'd be glad to get your first look.'

And there it was laid out in front of him through the Lizzie's cockpit. The English Channel. Home was on the other side.

'Can never say for sure, but should be an easy ride in now –

at least we're safe from the flak. And we've practically been hugging the ground under their radar. Always get the odd hungry *Messerschmitt* trawling the Channel for easy pickings, but fingers crossed.'

Danny Welland took one more look at the water below them and something strange happened to him. He felt warm tears flood his cheeks. He tried to stop them, but they kept on flowing and his shoulders shook with emotion. Relief, sadness, what? He didn't know. But he felt weak and stupid for letting his emotions get the better of him. He was a fighter pilot. He couldn't afford to wallow in that sort of stuff.

He immediately wiped the tears with the coarse material of his jacket – a workman's jacket that Edwin had given him – and opened the flask of cocoa, then passed a mug to Alexander, along with one very worried-looking cheese sandwich.

8

'I tried my best, Rose.' Mr Hardcastle's face had a sour look, like he'd just sucked on a lemon. Not that you could get lemons anymore. 'Didn't make a difference. They won't fire the bloke. Said they'd give him a "reprimand". But I wouldn't go holding your breath. They'll be out with their brooms, shove it all under the rug.'

'Thanks, anyway,' said Rosemary.

'For what?'

'At least for trying.'

'Said I would. You're a good little worker, Rose. One of the best.'

So he'd said. And didn't she have the certificate on Ma's sideboard to prove it? But where did that get you?

'I'll be getting on back to work, then. Can't stop up here too long.' She looked through the window at the people working below. 'They'll think there's something up.'

Maisy caught up with her at lunchtime. Lentil rissoles, and some kind of grey mass that passed itself off as mashed spud.

Oh, joy! Pom again. How she longed for real potato – even spam fritters started to look good now, but the canteen had run out of spam and had to resort to the lentils again. *All good protein*, the sign on the front of the counter boasted. All the same, at least spam fritters had some sort of meat content in them. They'd tried flogging whale meat steaks a while back. But they hadn't been a success. Like chewing rubber, and some of the workers had either thrown up or spent the rest of the time on the lav.

'You okay?' asked Maisy.

'Sure, why?'

'Just that Betty was in earlier. Said you was on the carpet for something. Saw you going into old Hardcastle's office.'

'On the carpet? No, I'm not in trouble. Don't know where she got that from!'

'You know this place,' said Maisy. 'If they don't know it, they'll make it up. So...?'

'It was nothing. Mr Hardcastle just wanted me to work a double shift next week.'

'Hope you told him to shove it where the sun don't shine. You're far too accommodating sometimes. They'll take advantage. You need to watch that, Rose. And mark my words, this cosy world of theirs will all change once the war's over.'

'Yeah. Maybe.'

'No *maybe* about it. The downtrodden masses can only take so much. Take it from me, there's a revolution on the way,' said Maisy, sagely.

'You don't strike me as one of the downtrodden.'

'Think those toffs stick to only five inches of water in their bath? I don't *think* so!'

'We're at war. Everybody makes sacrifices,' said Rosemary.

'Only some more than others, eh? You can be naive at times, Rose.'

Was she? Her friend was becoming more political as the war dragged on. And maybe that was a good thing. Better wages and conditions for workers, better housing. Women earning the same as men. (That was a joke, right? The blokes in charge would never allow that.) Still, it was something to shoot for, but first they had to win the damn war. It was all exhausting. She couldn't think about stuff like that right now, not when there were things to worry about closer to home. Like her sister Gracie and this baby. And thoughts about Danny and how things might have been if he'd survived. They'd be married now.

Sometimes she wondered about how he had died. Did he die alone? Her imagination plagued her at times with harrowing thoughts and images, which she tried to ignore. Because something Rosemary knew, above all else, was that Danny would have wanted her to be happy. Not miserable or sad.

She took her lentil rissoles and went to find a table. She got stuck with Norman, with his continual miserable grumbling and pessimism about the world. It wasn't enough she had to have the man right next to her when she worked, now he sat down beside her and gave her a running commentary about the inside of a cow's stomach. She'd no idea how they'd got onto that, but she nodded in the right places, and let her mind travel back to Gracie.

Gracie was about to go off to be a Land Girl and still hadn't broken the news to their ma. Rose wouldn't be surprised if she snuck away without saying goodbye, with maybe just a note to explain her disappearance, leaving Rose to sort out the flak. Gracie didn't *do* confrontations. Who did? But sometimes you just had to face up to it.

Her sister was terrified. Rose already knew that. Frightened of having the baby, of being on her own, of being away from home for the first time. Gracie would be having lots of *firsts*. And in a way, Rosemary was proud of her, of how she was dealing with all this. It took courage. But facing up to the leviathan that was Lil Ellis was a step too far for her.

'You guys going to the dance tonight?' Maisy took a seat beside them, putting down her plate of powdered egg. The stuff looked almost as bad as the rissoles.

'Same old rubbish,' said Norm. 'I'm not bothering.'

'Not that you ever bother, do you, Norm?' Maisy giggled. And Norman left – grumbling something about pearls before swine.

'Yeah? But who's the pearls and who's the swine?' Maisy shouted at his back. She turned to Rosemary. 'You coming?'

'What – to the poxy canteen dance?' asked Rosemary.

'Aw, c'mon. We'll have a laugh. And I'll pinch some of me ma's gin to put in the fruit punch. Bring your Gracie. Face on her like a smacked arse lately. Maybe she could use a laugh.'

'Maybe we all could,' said Rosemary.

———

'It's not like we go out every night,' Gracie told her ma.

'And you?' Lil Ellis raised an eyebrow, looked over suspiciously at Rose. 'You going to this bun fight, too?'

Rosemary flinched. Her ma could be more intimidating with a single eyebrow than others could with their whole body. She'd had a lot of practice.

'It's the works do. So, *yes* – I'm off to the dance as well,' said Rosemary, defiantly.

'Not like you,' said Lil. 'When was the last time you went anywhere like that? Music, dancing, blokes trying it on.'

'Maybe it's time I had a bit of fun like everybody else, then,' said Rosemary. But her voice was bitter, not like somebody getting ready to go out on the town for some laughs.

'What if there's a raid?' asked Lil. 'What then?'

'Factory's got a shelter, Ma. Stinks a bit, but they all do. And if you're so put out, why don't you come with us? I know Norman's just waiting to see you again.' Rosemary crossed her fingers tightly behind her back. Not that she didn't want Ma there, but there was stuff she needed to talk to Gracie about. Stuff that would put a permanent kink in Lil's straight, lifeless hair easier than her Friday-night Amami wave set.

'Norman, you say. And wouldn't that be a reason for not going? The man's got wandering hands – tried to paw me last time. No, I'll just go down the tube if anything kicks off, and don't you pair worry a single hair on your pretty little heads about me.'

Playing the martyr again. It had been a good idea of hers to use Norman as a weapon. Norman who wouldn't even be there. But Rosemary didn't feel bad. It would give her a chance to escape the cloying atmosphere of the house with Gracie mooning around. Gracie enjoyed dancing and the bob-hops they used to go to before the war. Gracie's dancing had been... Rosemary searched for a word... *exuberant* – that was a good one. One night at the Palais, Gracie had been so carried away that she'd fallen into the back of the stage. Landed in the middle of some poor bloke's drum-kit.

'Do what you like then,' said Lil. 'You will anyway. And don't you think you're having the bath water first, this time. It's my turn.' Her shoulders slumped in a pantomime act of defeat, and she went off to get the tin bath from the yard. One bath a week per household, all five luxurious inches of it. No wonder they all fought about who should be first in line.

'That's sorted then,' said Gracie. 'I'll pass on the bath. I ain't getting in after *her*.'

A few hours later, the pair of them walked to the factory together. Through the blackout. Arm in arm.

Strange as it might seem, Rosemary actually enjoyed the works 'do'. Not that she took much part in it, other than watching some folks make a right fool of themselves. She ate a couple of sausage rolls from the buffet that were not actually sausage, but some kind of mashed-up carrot concoction mixed with bread stuffing. It had been years since any of them had seen a 'real' sausage – the ones you got now from the butcher had so much water in them that when you fried them they exploded. People had started calling them 'bangers'. A new name for sausages, and it seemed like it might stick.

Rosemary watched her sister throw herself manically into the dancing, like she was all set to go to jail tomorrow and this was her final night of freedom. Maybe it was. And of course they asked her to sing a bit. *And how would that go?* Not too well at first, for it took two of them to haul her up onto a table. *Seemed like Gracie's stomach muscles had forgotten what they were there for, other than to wrap around this poor wee sprog of hers. Thank God she wasn't showing yet.*

Still, she managed to come up with a fair rendition of 'Down at the Old Bull and Bush', and the whole place erupted into full-blooded song, every one of them throwing their heart and soul into it. Some of them laughing till they cried.

Maybe it wasn't just she and Gracie that had needed to blow off steam.

'I'm off tomorrow,' said Gracie, when she'd managed to get her breath back and plonked herself down practically in Rosemary's lap.

'I guessed. Not telling Ma?'

'Can you do it, Rosie? I ain't good at that sort of thing.' Her eyes looked desperate.

'Sure.'

'You're a peach, you know that, sis?'

'So I've heard.' She watched her sister knock back some of the fruit punch and giggle.

'Hey, let me taste that,' Rosemary said.

They wrestled over the tumbler, but Rosemary won. 'It's got gin in it.' She looked over at her friend Maisy, who just raised her own tumbler and smiled. 'That won't do you-know-who any good now, will it?'

'Only one small glass, Rosie. Won't hurt. Anyway, he's not *you-know-who*. He's little Harry Ellis, my own wee baby boy.'

And that's when her sister broke down in tears. Massive, plump things – collecting in the corner of her eyes and tracing damp black lines down her face.

Rosemary took out her precious hanky and spat on it like their mother did, rubbed hard, trying to get the black off before anybody saw it. Her sister wouldn't like that: people poking fun at her. Wondering about the waterworks. *None of their business, was it?*

'Silly chump, told you not to put that boot polish on.'

Gracie let go one more shuddering sob and then found a smile from somewhere. 'I only put the boot polish on the bottom lash, I ain't stupid. Saved the last of the mascara for the top.'

Rosemary Ellis laughed until she couldn't stand it anymore, until some of the awful sausage roll she'd had made its way back up into her throat and almost choked her. What a world, eh? Where women found themselves wearing boot polish instead of mascara and beetroot juice instead of lipstick, and poor blokes marched off to fight a war they'd never asked for.

9

What's the first thing you do after being trapped underground for months? Danny rode on the top of a London bus. It was glorious, the freedom. And yet his fellow passengers grumbled about the war, the shortages, the rationing, the lack of clothing coupons and the lack of what they called decent grub.

Danny couldn't believe it. He was in heaven. The food here was a banquet compared to what his friends in Rotterdam had to exist on every day. And to see the sky, that was the best bit.

He was almost delirious with happiness: any minute, he expected to see Rosie. At last, he could marry her. A little later than they'd planned, but then there was a war on. He imagined she would understand. Was that too arrogant of him – to think that Rosie still kept the flame of their love alive? He'd have been posted as 'missing', he presumed, but what if she thought him dead? Would she have moved on with her life – a life without him? A life with someone else! He pushed the thought from his mind.

He was on his way to her house right now. She might still be at work in the factory, sewing those parachutes of hers, but her mother could be home. He'd got on well with Lil, a bit of a character, but they'd hit it off; he'd found her honest, not affected or grandiose like his own mother – or as false.

Maybe it was even better this way. A surprise for Rosie. *Or maybe a shock*, he thought suddenly. He didn't want to frighten her. But what was he thinking? His Rosie didn't give way to fear. She was courageous and plucky and bold. At times she could be feisty and determined. Rosie was straightforward as well, spoke her mind and didn't put on airs. It was what he loved about her, that, and her belief in herself. In who she was and where she came from. An East Ender, and she was proud of it. And he was proud of her. He couldn't wait to tell her that again.

Danny left the bus at Bethnal Green tube station. Her house wasn't too far away and, as he hurried along, he pictured her face in his mind again, couldn't help but smile. People passed him and stared. Some gave him strange and even hostile looks. He was a young man and yet wore no uniform. He was an enigma they were trying to work out. His bearing was military, yet his clothes were rough and unlike any of the civilian clothes around him.

He turned a corner and walked into the street where she lived, full of hope and excitement.

Except she didn't live there anymore. No one did. How could they? It wasn't even a street. Not a single recognisable house was left.

Had he got it wrong? No, this was the place. Because there was that strange quirky schoolhouse, the one she'd walked him around. It was right there. Standing on an island of its own, at the end of the road, stranded, surrounded by rubble, weeds colonising the piles of brick and shattered masonry. Both sides of the street were gone. Only rubbish and foul-smelling debris remained. A sad reminder that people had once lived in this place. Right in the middle of the street was a gaping hole in the ground, cordoned off with rope, the remnants of a broken water main jutting through. A rancid haze hung in the air above where the houses had been and flies buzzed, feasting on the rotten waste.

Danny ran from the place, blinking tears from his eyes as a voice in his head taunted him. *Is she still alive?* And if she was, where would he start to look for her? She'd never told him where the parachute factory was. It was something you took for granted, that careless talk could cost lives. It was a maxim ingrained in all good citizens. Still, he couldn't believe that he'd never asked. But then, they'd spent their time together talking about other, more important things: plans for the future, places they would visit when the war was over. Now, would there even *be* a future for them?

He had to believe she was alive. She must be. And that their love would conquer all, even the hate that came from war.

He squared his shoulders and raised his head high, ignored the negative voice in his mind and went in search of Rosie. There must be someone there who could tell him what had happened, could give him a clue, a trail to follow. The thought put new life in his step and, with a steely resolve, he set off to find her.

In the short space of an hour, Danny's emotions swung from high to low. He was elated, at first, when the landlord from a pub around the corner from Rosie's house had recalled the night of the bombing. Many from Wilmot Street had been fine, the man claimed. Only three had died, and it seemed they were all older folk.

So, it looked like Rosie and her family had survived. Danny allowed himself to feel hope and excitement again. He even found the church hall where many had sheltered and been housed for a while. But the bombing had been chaotic and there were no records of the survivors or where they had gone. That's when the trail went cold, and Danny felt the sharp sting of disappointment and frustration.

Still, he refused to let himself slide into a pit of despair. Decided to move on, tackle the problem a different way.

He was a pilot. He'd crashed his plane in Holland five months ago. His squadron couldn't have their Hurricane back, but at least they would have their pilot. The thought made him smile once more. He would make his way to Kingsway, to the Air Ministry. They could get his papers sorted and his uniform, take him off the missing list – and get him back to his squadron. There might even be someone at the Ministry who could help him trace Rosie.

———

It hadn't taken long for the Air Ministry to confirm that Danny was indeed Squadron Leader Daniel Welland (missing, presumed dead). After that, he'd been handed a cup of tea and passed over to a junior commissioned officer, a flight lieutenant, Danny noted – by the insignia on his uniform. One rank below Danny's own.

Danny followed him into a tiny back office. The chap was an administrator of some kind and Danny spent twenty frustrating minutes listening to several phone calls as the young officer tried to cut his way through miles of red tape.

Danny tried to read the young man's face. He seemed shocked by his last call and Danny nodded as the flight lieutenant apologised, and hurriedly left the room. The officer came back some time later with tea for them both.

'*More* tea?' said Danny.

'Bit of bad news, I'm afraid, sir – your squadron…'

'My squadron? What *about* my squadron?'

'They've gone, squadron leader,' said the young officer.

'Gone!' he said shocked. 'Gone *where?*'

'Egypt. Air defence duties. Your squadron will be back home in September and converting to Spitfires.'

'Okay, get me out to Egypt then,' said Danny.

'Not that simple. They won't just fly you out to 238 Squadron like nothing's happened. There'll be the physical for a start – the Medical Board. You were injured and after what you've been through, the medics'll want to check you out – make sure you're fit to fly before they reassign you.'

'But that's a lot of bollocks.'

'And so it might be. But they don't write the manuals for nothing. There're procedures to go through.'

Unbelievable, thought Danny.

'Take it you've got no ID card or ration book, squadron orders?' asked the young officer.

'Sure. I took all that stuff on a mission!' said Danny angrily, frustration getting the better of him. 'It's back at base, in my locker.'

'We'll need to set you up with papers then and a uniform. Now, don't suppose you've got money?'

'Guy who flew the Lizzie home lent us both some cash.'

'Both? Who else was there?'

'Not important.' *Maybe the other guy was having more luck*. He hoped so.

'We'll sort you out with a chitty for back pay and somewhere to stay. Get the ball rolling on the medical and stuff. Shouldn't take long.'

'*Really?*' he said. He knew how easily bureaucracy could screw up, wasn't as optimistic as this lad opposite him drinking his tea like it was just another day at the office. It wasn't. Yesterday Danny had been in a cellar in Rotterdam. Where had this guy been? Tied to a desk. Polishing the arse of his shiny trousers on a comfortable chair.

'I know this is frustrating, sir. Maybe not what you

expected, but these things take time. Believe me, I know what you're going through.'

'I doubt that.' But when he searched the young man's eyes, Danny saw something there he hadn't noticed before. That haunted look. Like the guy Alexander on the plane home. And he noted the slight tremor in the hand that held the mug.

'We might have more in common than you think, Squadron Leader.' The young man left it at that.

'Look, I'm sorry to be rude – what's your name?'

'Frank Usher. Call me Frank. And I understand – truly. You want to get back in the thick of it. I get that.'

Danny offered his hand, and when he shook Frank Usher's, he could feel the tremor move through his own palm. He decided to cut the young officer some slack.

'Fancy a pint?' asked Danny. 'Noticed a pub round the corner.'

'The Pig and Whistle,' said Frank Usher. 'It's not bad. At least they've got beer.'

So, Danny bought them both a beer and they relaxed into each other's company. Talked about how things had been before the war, places they'd seen. Frank Usher seemed in no hurry to get anywhere, and neither was Danny.

They'd given him a chitty for a bed and breakfast place, but he didn't want to go there, didn't want to waste his time sleeping. He knew sleep wouldn't come easily anyway. He'd be thinking about his Resistance friends in Holland and the danger they'd gone through to get him there, the fear that wove its way through their daily lives. *So who could sleep?*

Maybe he should have gone home. Should have made the effort. But his mother would dissolve into her usual hysterics and start smothering him with concern. No. Home would be a last resort.

And he couldn't have stayed with Rosie, even if he had known where she was. They weren't married yet and her mother had made it plain what she thought about 'that sort of thing'. Married first, fun later, Lil had told him, in that outspoken way of hers.

Danny was settled on one thing: that he must push the Air Ministry to get him back in harness, classify him fit-to-fly and get him reassigned. Rosie knew him as a pilot and that's exactly what he'd be the next time they met. He needed to be useful to his country and to pay back in some small way the sacrifices of his Dutch friends. Rosie had been proud of him and he wanted to hold his head up high again. To show her that her pride had not been misplaced.

'Look, it'll be chucking-out time here soon...'

'Yes, I'm sorry,' said Danny. 'I've taken enough of your time already, and I'm grateful.'

'Not what I meant.' The young man smiled. A lopsided affair, as if the right-hand side of his face wasn't up to the job. He'd obviously lost nerves there. But he looked like he was used to it now. 'If you fancy a walk, my place isn't far. We could have a cuppa, if you don't fancy going to that B and B yet.'

'Why not?' *Nothing better to do.*

'Might even be able to rustle up a bit of cheese and a few biscuits. Still got some left from last month's ration. Could scrape the mould off.' The young man winked. 'Never seem to eat much nowadays.'

That'd be right. The chap gave a whole new meaning to the word 'thin'.

It turned out to be a good idea. The walk through the freezing air cleared Danny's head and although the tiny flat that Frank Usher called home was hardly luxurious, it felt friendly and cheerful; better than going back to an awful bed and breakfast place he'd been lumbered with. He passed on the cheese. Accepted the tea. And sank into the dog-eared armchair where

Frank directed him. Its tapestry fabric was faded and worn with age, but it was comfortable all the same. *The best seat in the house,* he suspected. He watched as the young man lowered himself gingerly onto the hard, wooden dining chair opposite, and knew then that he would like this selfless young officer, that the chap might even become a friend.

Danny used the young man as a sounding board. Getting stuff off his chest that he didn't even know was there.

He hadn't meant to talk about Rosie. Didn't think he was ready to share her with anyone else, but his mouth dived straight in without consulting his head, and Danny found himself narrating the whole of their story from beginning to end. *A love story.* He didn't mention her name, like he was hugging that pleasure all to himself. And when he looked at Frank Usher's face, the surprise and disbelief on there, Danny swallowed hard, felt embarrassed.

'Sorry, didn't mean to go off like that,' he said.

'No problem, old boy. I understand. I totally get it. You've got the old white charger primed up and you're ready to ride off into the sunset with the woman. But what I *don't* understand is why you don't know where to find her.'

'We used to meet in the Lyons Corner House, the one on Coventry Street.'

'Yes, but surely you know where she lives? Her address...?'

'Of course I've got her address. Went there today, but she wasn't there – and neither was the house, bombed-out. Family had moved to a temporary shelter somewhere, but nobody could tell me where.'

'So... other than sitting in the Lyons Corner House every day on the off chance she'll come in, what's the plan?' asked Frank.

'I'll look for this factory she works in,' said Danny. 'Maybe you could help me there?'

'Try my best,' said Frank.

'And anything you can do to get me back in the air.'

'Can't promise that. Above my pay grade, I'm afraid. But I'll organise the medical board. Get that moving, at least,' said Frank.

'Got some other stuff I need to do as well,' Danny said. 'Promises I made to friends in Holland. I hate to impose, but maybe you could help me track a chap down.'

'Help if I can,' said Frank. 'As long as it's not classified.'

'The bloke's called Pietersen. Came over when some of the Royal Dutch Navy escaped. Seems he ended up here.'

'You're kidding, right? The chap's name wouldn't be *Adam* Pietersen, by any chance?' asked Frank.

'Well, yes, but...'

Frank Usher's eyes lit up, his body language became animated. 'Man's a legend.'

'Maybe it's not the same man though. This one works at Dutch Navy headquarters here in London.' *At least that's what Anna had told him.* She didn't know much more though.

'That's the one. Bloke's a hero.'

'Really?'

'Classic stuff,' said Usher. 'Whipped a battle cruiser right out from under the noses of the Germans. Well – him and twenty-two others. Cruiser, for God's sake! Normally has a crew of 400 and they sailed it straight across the North Sea. Took it up to Holyhead. You believe that?'

'Surprised they didn't make him an admiral after that.' Danny grinned. Looked like he'd found Anna's Pa for her. 'Think we'd be able to run him to earth?' he asked. 'I've got something for him.'

'Easy enough, I should think. He's in charge of their shore base. Rank of *Kapitein-ter-zee*, though I don't think he actually goes to sea anymore.'

'Hell. You're well informed.'

Frank Usher shifted uncomfortably in his seat. Didn't like

being thrust into the limelight. 'Just that he's a bit of a hero of mine.'

'So, the man led his own small Dunkirk, eh?'

Usher almost choked on his cheese. And Danny noticed that it wasn't only his hand that trembled now, but the whole right arm, while his foot beat out a rapid-fire tattoo on the floor.

'Sorry. Didn't mean to rake up bad memories.'

'We've all got them,' said Usher. 'It's the war.'

10

LONDON

12 MARCH 1943

He was a trained pilot, a man who'd lived through the Battle of Britain, yet there he was parking his arse in a waiting room while blokes out there with no experience and hardly any flying hours were being sent out to get killed.

Madness.

He'd been back in London for a week now. A busy week where they'd organised a uniform for him, and yesterday the quacks had given him a real going-over. Frank Usher had been responsible for rushing all that stuff through. Danny knew the chap had worked miracles in order to cut through some of the suffocating red tape.

But still he was restless, sitting there in a stuffy little office on a chair that could have been used in the Spanish Inquisition. Waiting. Waiting for what exactly, he wasn't sure. A clerk had poked his head round the door an hour ago, thrown an odd look Danny's way and brought him the inevitable cup of tea, like it was the answer to all woes. He'd tried to read his fate in the man's face; to figure out what his medical report said. But either they didn't know there, or Danny wasn't much of a psychic.

He yawned, stretched, tried to remind his legs what they were there for, and left the small waiting room, looking for a clue that someone remembered he was still there.

Frank Usher rushed by, a lopsided smile on his face and a bundle of files the colour of dung clutched in his arms. 'Shouldn't be long now,' he said.

'For what?' Danny asked. 'Is something happening?'

'Hope so. Bit of a flap on right now, but I'm sure they'll get to you soon.'

'That's what you said two hours ago. Sorry, Frank. Patience – not my thing.'

'Sure. I'll get a mug of cocoa to you, and a magazine.'

Danny Welland laughed. Good old Blighty. Drink cocoa and carry on. Though he doubted there were many households that would be able to get that luxury on their ration books. He didn't know. His own country had become a foreign land to him.

A female secretary brought him a mug of steaming liquid, a Rich Tea biscuit and a newspaper. The young woman looked exhausted, but managed a thin smile. 'Sorry about the magazine,' said Miss Ramsey, apologetically. 'Could only drum up an old copy of the *Express*, I'm afraid.'

'No problem.' He suddenly felt awkward. Was he acting like a bloody prima donna, a spoilt kid, when these poor sods were just doing their jobs? Performing daily miracles, going home exhausted every night and getting up to face the same thing all over again?

He opened the newspaper. War stuff, of course. Good and bad. Not that the bad was given too many column inches. Not good for morale. He knew all about propaganda: putting a positive spin on war news that would scare the bejesus out of ordinary folk busy slogging their way through the mire.

He turned the page and there she was. *Jesus!*

His mouth went dry. Rosie. *His* Rosie. Large as life and the most beautiful creature he had seen, despite the hairnet and the dull unattractive bottle-green overall. War colours, war materials, not meant to flatter, but she wore them like a glamorous ball gown. She was shaking hands with the queen, and the smile on Rosie's face leapt off the page.

He rushed urgently from the room, went looking for Frank Usher, but the man had vanished and there was an excitement and nervous expectation permeating the hallways. Something was on. Some kind of big push, maybe. But of course they wouldn't tell him. Still Danny could feel it; knew the signs, had been involved in operations that had generated that same kind of buzz. Things that were meant to change the course of the war, but far as he knew, had never managed it.

'Can I help you, Squadron Leader?' It was the young woman who'd brought him the paper.

'Do you know where I might find this chap?' he asked, and pointed to the name on the article's by-line. 'Mr Robert Batley.' He grabbed her by the arm, his hold strong enough to leave bruises.

She pulled away from him, confused. 'I'm sorry – what?'

Danny saw fear in her eyes. Had *he* caused it? *What did the young woman see when she looked at him? Someone haggard and thin, with scars on their face? An anxious, troubled man, so intense that he frightened her?* That wasn't at all what he wanted. He'd been through a lot, it was true, with the trauma of the crash and his injuries, the fear of being captured. Still, that was no excuse for bad manners.

'Sorry,' he said. 'That was rude. It's just that – well, I *know* her. The woman in the photograph. Her name's Rosie and I need to find her. We were about to be married, you see.' He didn't know why he'd told her that, something that made him vulnerable. Or maybe he just wanted her to know that he was human and not some kind of monster.

'I *see*.'

But, from the puzzled look on her face, it seemed to Danny that the woman didn't see at all.

'The article doesn't say where this factory is, but then you wouldn't expect it to,' said Danny.

'Exactly,' said Miss Ramsey. 'We can't make it *too* easy for German spies,' she added, and finally smiled.

'If I wanted to find this bloke who wrote the article, where would I look?' Danny asked her. His voice was less frantic now, like he hadn't *really* fallen over some mental cliff edge, and he plastered a smile to his face, hoped it didn't look as fake as it felt.

'You could start at the Ministry of Information, I suppose.' Gloria Ramsey took a closer look at the photograph and the article. 'Yes. I'd try there if I were you. Factory visits, morale boosters – that's their kind of thing.'

'Thanks, you're an angel,' he said, and ran from the corridor as if the building was on fire.

Frank Usher caught up with him on the stairs. 'Bit of good news, old chap.'

'I'm joining the squadron?'

'Sorry,' said Frank. 'Nothing from the medics yet. No – that bloke you were looking for. The Dutchman, Adam Pietersen. I've run him to earth and if you're up for it, he'll meet us tonight. He'll pick us up here at seven. That okay for you?'

'Should be. I've got something urgent to do right now. But if I get held up, I'll give you a shout.'

'Something I can help with?'

'I'm looking for the woman of my dreams,' said Danny. And the grin on his face was real this time.

'Yeah? Good luck with that!' said Frank.

'I'm not a bloody kid, you know!' said Lil Ellis.

'Look, Ma, I know that. But what can I do?'

'You can tell me the feckin' truth. How's that for a start? Why would our Gracie want *you* to go and visit her in the country? And why would the stupid girl go tearing off like that in the first place? Women's feckin' Land Army. What's our Gracie know about farming?'

'A whole lot more than she did a month ago, I reckon,' said Rosemary.

'Less of the cheek. And what about your job? Can Mr Hardcastle spare you for a week?'

'There's five hundred of us in the bleedin' factory, Ma. They won't even notice I've gone.'

'And less of the bleedin' swearin', miss. That's not how me and Da brought you up.' Lil sniffed and turned her head away.

It wasn't often her mother cried and she'd be embarrassed by it, so Rosemary didn't make a fuss or offer a hanky. It was the thought of Da that did it, she figured. So many of the men were missing or POWs. One person's loss was not unique.

'So...'

'What?' asked Lil.

'It's okay if I leave for the week?'

'Do what you want. I can manage. I'm not senile.'

'Never said you were, Ma. And I'll be back before you know. Just promise me one thing, eh? I know you hate the tube shelter, but promise you'll go down there, if a raid starts?'

'Not stupid, am I? I was looking after meself when you and that sister of yours were just twinkles in your da's eyes.'

'I know. And we love you, both of us.'

'And your sister Gracie's got a right rare way of showing it, especially now, when she needs a mother.'

Rosemary hugged her mother, felt sour and underhanded at having to lie for Gracie. Okay, maybe not a lie exactly, but wasn't it the same thing when you didn't own up to the truth?

She clung tightly to her mother and Lil Ellis squeezed right back. A mother's reassurance, a mother's love. And when she looked into Lil's sad eyes, wet with tears, she understood. Too right her ma wasn't stupid. *She'd sussed the whole thing.*

Even so, Rosemary felt a small knot of excitement twist in her stomach. When she'd first had Gracie's letter, pleading with her to come, she'd seen it only as another problem to be sorted, but it might be an adventure at that. A chance to shake off the dismal trappings of wartime London for fresh air and green fields. Plus, there was the train trip. She hadn't been on a train for a long time, had dug a rut for herself: work, sleep, eat. Maybe now was the time to be a bit more adventurous, give her lost optimism a fighting chance.

An hour later, standing in Mr Hardcastle's office, looking at the man's brows as they knit fiercely together into one long hairy caterpillar, and the scowl pasted to his face, Rosemary's rekindled optimism took a small dive.

'*Et tu*, Brute?' Mr Hardcastle said, with feeling.

'Pardon?'

'Never mind, Rose.' The supervisor's voice was resigned. Tired. He had a thankless job to do. Sometimes it seemed impossible, but you did it all the same.

'So, does that mean I can't have the week off, Mr Hardcastle?' A small vibration moved through her calf muscles. Not so much a fear. Nothing really frightened her now, for what more could they do to her? A realisation that she might have to let her sister Gracie down, when she'd already promised she would come.

Rosemary watched his face. Heard the heavy, long-suffering sigh. He was a tough man, but sometimes you had to be tough to get the job done. But she thought him a fair man, as well. Some of them here disagreed and she'd once seen a woman rush from

Mr Hardcastle's office in tears. Well, *she* wouldn't cry – whatever he said.

'Sorry. Can't let you go today. We need to finish that big order. More important things than ourselves sometimes, Rose.'

'So...'

'Finish the day out and you can start on your wee jaunt tomorrow. But I can only give you four days. After that, you'd be looking for a new job. Can't play favourites, here. If I did that, they'd all be going off on charabanc rides to Southend.'

'Mr Hardcastle, I'm not going on a—'

'I know, Rose. I know. Just clear off and work, will you?'

Now she *definitely* wasn't looking forward to the trip. Say he gave her job away – what would they do then? How would the family cope? Her mother wasn't well, couldn't go back to her cleaning job. *Bloody Gracie.* A minute's joy with some skanky Yank and a lifetime's regret. That's what she'd brought on them all. Still, family was family and would always be, especially in the East End where values were cherished – war or no bloody war. She went off to her work station muttering the name *Gracie* under her breath.

'Flavour of the month, eh!' The sneer on Albert Green's face said that it wasn't a compliment.

'What?' Rosemary asked.

'Boss's favourite. You spend more time up there than you do on the factory floor, Rosie Ellis.'

'Not that it would be any of your beeswax *what* I do. And why you messing with Norman's machine? He'll have you for that. He's *very* particular is our Norman. You want to get back to your cutting room, Mr Green.'

'Mr Green? Now that's not very friendly, is it?'

'You're not my friend,' she said, and tried to make her sneer as impressive as his.

'And was *Norman* your friend?' he asked.

'A respected colleague.'

'Is that so? Well, *Rosie* Ellis, you'll need to get used to a new colleague for a bit. I'm taking over this machine. The man's flatter than a raspberry jam pancake, right now. His house took a direct hit last night. Bleedin' great parachute mine. *Boom!*'

Albert Green waved his skinny arms in the air to demonstrate the force of devastation wrought by the parachute mine. Then he dragged his long ferret-like face into a massive grin, as if he'd just pulled off a particularly humorous joke.

Rosemary was treated to a close-up of the blackened teeth in his gurning smile and the spaces in his mouth where teeth had retreated, fallen out, or maybe been knocked out – for Albert Green was that kind of bloke, well known as a scrapper.

And she was surprised by the tears that trickled down her cheeks. She hadn't expected them, or the dam to burst that easily. Maybe its walls were thinner than she thought.

11

They say stuff like 'your heart's coming up your throat'. A gruesome idea, Danny thought, and pretty graphic if you let your mind wander over it. Right then his heart was hammering against his ribs and his throat was dry, and if somebody had forced a whisky on him, he wouldn't have complained.

Not that there was much chance of that, sitting in a dreary office at the Ministry of Information with nothing but his imagination for company and a haughty-looking receptionist who'd tried her best to ignore him.

A wizened little man with a dried-out prune face and wisps of hair pulled thinly across his scalp had directed him to a seat, instructed him to *wait*. Mr Robert Batley was expected 'imminently', the man had said.

Danny figured that meant *soon*. But it wasn't until an hour later that the door was flung open, and a young man in an expensive suit and a camera slung around his neck made a dramatic entrance. He flashed a perfect set of teeth at the receptionist, and she replied with a coy expression and a strange eyelash flutter that Danny found disturbing.

The photographer's smile widened and he winked at the

woman. *Quite a ladies' man, then, this Mr Batley*, thought Danny, for the receptionist flirted with him, giggled at a joke he told. Danny coughed, reminding them they had an audience.

Batley gestured towards one of the small offices, and invited Danny in.

'Tea?' The man looked at the name on the scrap of paper. 'Squadron Leader Welland.'

'No, thanks, Mr Batley. I've had enough tea to sink the *Titanic*.'

'Know what you mean. And call me Robert, please.' Batley flashed a plastic smile, gave his perfect teeth another outing. 'Now, what can I do for you?'

'It's a strange one, this. But I've just come across one of your photographs in the *Express*. Taken a while ago, I gather. I'm after information about someone in the picture.'

'Oh?'

'Long story cut very short: I've been out of the country for a while and before I left, the woman in your piece agreed to be my wife.'

'Congratulations. You happen to know the particular edition?'

'Got it right here, Robert.' Danny produced the paper from his jacket pocket, and slid it across the desk.

Robert Batley paled, his breath catching in his throat as he stared at the photograph.

Danny went on, not noticing: 'So... you know where I might find her now?' he asked.

'Take it we're discussing this lovely young lady and not HM Queen Elizabeth?' Batley grinned – a smile that didn't make it to his eyes.

Danny laughed, joined in the joke. 'You'd take it right. This woman here is the love of my life. And I'm about to put a ring on her finger.'

Batley's eyes lingered on the photograph. It was *her*. The jumped-up little tart who had tried to get him fired. He cleared his throat, studied the man across the desk more closely. So, she'd bagged herself a flyboy, had she? A pretty-boy aviator in a fancy uniform. Same old, same old. These guys only had to look in a woman's direction and men like him didn't stand a chance in hell. Heroes!

Batley's jealousy was like a rabid beast, simmering in the depths of him; a prehistoric giant clawing at him, threatening to overwhelm him with its power. He felt sick with it, trickles of sweat running down the back of his neck.

A shudder of disgust ran through him as he thought about her having a life with this man across the desk from him. *He* should be the one who possessed her. And if he couldn't have her, well...

'You okay, Mr Batley – Robert?'

'Huh?'

'Do you need some water?' Danny asked.

'Thank you, no.'

'Only – you look a little upset.'

'I'll be fine,' said Batley. 'Not sure *you* will, though, Squadron Leader.'

'I don't follow.'

'I hate to be the one to tell you. To break such awful news – especially when you have such *obvious* feelings for the young woman, but...'

'But what? Out with it, man. What the hell are you trying to say?'

'Tragic, really tragic,' said Robert Batley. He shrugged his shoulders. 'Wartime, though. Tragedies happen every day.'

'For God's sake, Batley – what?' Danny grabbed the man by

the lapels of his fancy suit jacket and shook him. 'Christ's sake, man – tell me!'

'Right after that photograph was taken, the young woman bought it, I'm afraid. Whole street got taken out. Direct hit. She didn't make it to the shelter.'

'No! Can't possibly be!'

''Fraid so. I wanted to do a follow-up. Do a poster campaign on her. But she's dead. So sad.'

'You're sure? I mean, how can you be so sure? Lots of civilian casualties, things must get confused.'

'Confused?' said Batley.

'Mistaken identity – must happen all the time. Maybe it's a mistake...'

'We don't make those kinds of mistakes, Welland. Not here! I'm sorry for your loss. Now, if there's anything else I can do for you...'

Danny rushed from the office without saying a word. What could *anybody* do for him? There was nothing to be done. She'd gone. Still, he couldn't believe it. Surely he'd feel it if she were gone? They had a connection that was stronger than blood and bone and breath. It was impossible. He refused to believe it.

———

Danny didn't know why he'd gone back there. Just the practical side of his brain taking charge, guiding him through some weird pre-programmed motions, trying to swamp the sadness that threatened to overpower him.

'Ah, there you are. Wondered if you'd make it back in time. *Kapitein* Pietersen's waiting upstairs. Laid on a car for us,' said Frank Usher.

'What?'

'The Dutchman – he's taking us out to Simpsons for dinner. Quite a treat.'

'Ah.'

'Everything okay, old man? You're not ill, are you?' asked Frank.

'Ill? No. Just...'

'Something happen?'

Danny grabbed onto the door frame. 'Maybe I'll just head home.'

'That bed and breakfast place? You're in no state to make it over there. Come and have a bite to eat.'

'Don't think I can, Frank.'

'Look, old boy, I don't know what's up, but it wouldn't hurt to have some decent grub inside you, would it? Come and meet Adam Pietersen. I've still got that package you brought for him. Why not give it to him yourself? Tell him about his family?'

He owed them that much.

So, he went to Simpsons with them.

It seemed odd to be out celebrating when his own news had been devastating; a part of his mind refusing to take it in. *Was he in denial?* Danny didn't think so. No. Something much more powerful than logic told him she couldn't possibly be dead. Something deep and primal, a thread that had joined his heart to Rosie's. Telling himself that, and promising he wouldn't give up until he found her, he threw himself into the celebration with the pair of them.

Danny took in the luxurious dining room, with its impressive oak panelling, embossed golden ceiling and the sparkling white tablecloths. He relaxed back into the comfortable red leather chair, a distant cousin of the hard wooden seats he'd been trapped in for most of the day.

'How in God's name do they still manage to get beef like this?' Danny marvelled at the feast of riches as he dissected another slice of the pink, juicy roast beef.

'Maybe it's horse,' said Adam Pietersen. He laughed: a throaty growl that shook the whole of his massive frame. He reminded Danny of Anna.

Frank dropped his knife. 'Think so?'

'He's teasing you, Frank. This isn't horse,' said Danny. He winked at Adam Pietersen.

'No?' asked Frank.

'No! I've *eaten* horse – among other things.' Danny remembered a stew he'd eaten in a Dutch cellar. The meat had tasted like rabbit. He'd thought it was. But he'd found out later it was cat.

Adam Pietersen nodded at him. 'You and I have things in common, Squadron Leader. Lots of household pets vanished in Rotterdam, ended up on the dinner table.'

Frank Usher almost choked on his beef.

'Least they were useful,' said Danny 'And call me Dan, please.'

Danny's mind went back to the early days of the war, when people in England were flooding to the vets, having their animals put down. A government pamphlet had recommended euthanasia. '*Save your pet the anguish of the bombing, save yourself the problem of feeding it*'. In one week alone there'd been 750,000 animals killed. A bloody tragedy. His mother had taken her dog to the vets. Come home without him. Danny loved that dog, had tried to persuade his mother against it. But she claimed it was her patriotic duty. Jesus wept! He couldn't believe that so many people had let a government pamphlet do their thinking for them.

'Dan?' The expression on Adam Pietersen's craggy face suddenly became serious.

'Yes?'

'Be straight with me. I don't need to have it whitewashed and packaged in a neat little parcel. I know things are bad back there but are my girls *really* okay?'

Danny pictured Adam's wife. The woman was skin and bone, but still a fire blazed in her eyes. A determination to look after her daughter Anna, to live through the fear and the famine and the humiliation the Bosch had brought on her country.

'Your wife Sara has guts and pride. She's amazing. And she looks fine.' He waited for God to strike him down for the lie. Still, the truth didn't always help. Danny wasn't fat himself, but he could have lifted Sara Pietersen with one hand.

'She's always been a handsome-looking woman,' said Adam. 'And Anna? What about my Anna? There's a sadness about her, a restlessness. She needs a good man.'

Danny swallowed hard, his Adam's apple performing an awkward contortion in the middle of his neck.

Adam Pietersen noticed it and grinned. Pietersen was a massive bear of a man, his huge, unruly red beard tinged with grey; a face weathered by the elements and scarred by life's troubles but still able to produce a huge smile revealing dazzling white tombstone teeth. He winked at Danny. 'It's like that, is it, my boy?'

'Eh? No. It's not what you think...'

'Don't worry, I'm not about to get my shotgun. You have my blessing.'

Danny said nothing. What was there to say? That he would reject this man's daughter in favour of someone else? He threw back some of his wine, tried to cover his awkwardness. He turned to Frank Usher. 'Think you can help me with some information, Frank?'

'Try my very best. This have something to do with that article?'

'How d'you know...?'

'Miss Ramsey – she thought it was important.'

'Could be,' he said, embarrassed as he remembered the way he'd frightened the poor woman. 'I need to know where that parachute factory is. Can you help?'

'I'll give it a fair crack – seeing as we're pals.' Frank Usher smiled, at least with the side of his face that could manage it.

And Danny realised that it was true: the man really was a friend. And maybe he could help him find Rosie. Surely between them they could do it.

A waiter arrived with three brandy goblets and Adam Pietersen stood up and raised his glass high above his head. 'A toast, gentlemen. To the end of the war. Swiftly may it come.'

Danny Welland and Frank Usher both nodded their heads in agreement.

12

The journey had been a nightmare. The train had been stuck in a siding for two hours and no one seemed to know why. So what might have taken a few hours in peacetime had so far taken ten and she still hadn't reached the tiny 'halt' that Gracie had mentioned in her letter, near Brenzett.

You'll love the place, Gracie had said. *Kent's a paradise.*

Love it? Maybe. If she ever got there. When the train wasn't crawling along like a lethargic snail, it was being held up at every junction, it seemed, to let other, more important, trains go by. Goods trains carrying military hardware took priority over passengers, the conductor had explained. 'Not *my* fault,' he'd said. 'Read the posters' – and then he'd wisely disappeared.

A poster above her head showed an engine pulling wagons loaded with coal along with the words: *Food, shells and fuel MUST come first*. And an accusing finger pointing outwards asking: *If your train is late or crowded,* DO YOU MIND?

Well, yes. Right then she *did* mind. But that didn't mean she wasn't a good citizen: just hot, tired and hungry.

She'd been squashed into a compartment meant to seat ten. There were twelve of them in there, mostly people in uniform –

off on leave – or going back. The narrow corridor outside was jammed with bodies as well. Some people sitting on their luggage. Hoping for seats when the 'lucky' ones decanted onto station platforms with strange-sounding names, places Rosemary had never heard of.

She fell asleep, her head coming to rest on the shoulder of her neighbour, a tall, thin army captain with a scar above his right eye.

'Oh, dear.' Rosemary woke with a jolt, and her face flushed crimson.

'What?' asked the captain.

'I'm sorry,' she mumbled. Her arm had gone dead where it was pressed into the man's side. 'That was selfish of me.'

'Really?'

'Using you as a pillow.'

'Not at all.' He doffed an imaginary hat. 'Happy to oblige.'

'Oh God. I wasn't snoring, was I?'

'Very melodic. Unlike any snores I've encountered before,' he said.

'No!'

'Forgive me,' he said. 'I was just teasing. Maybe I can make recompense.'

'Recompense?'

'Repay you in some way for my boorish teasing.'

Had the man swallowed a dictionary? His language, his confidence and that casual air of authority – it reminded her of someone. That, and the slightly dog-eared look to him, like the war had worn him down to bone and sinew.

The breath was punched from her body for an instant. *Danny. My God.* He was another version of her Dan. Older. Different uniform, but the same eyes, and that look behind them. Like they'd already seen too much.

The soldier took a barley sugar from his pocket and offered it to her.

Rosemary looked at the sweet in its crinkly wrapper as though it was an alien object transported from some distant planet. Barley sugar? *Incredible*. She hadn't tasted that for years. She took the sweet shyly, reluctantly, as if accepting it would take her over some line that shouldn't be crossed. In truth, she wanted to fall on the sugary treat, glistening away, tempting her with its amber sweetness, demolish it with indecent haste. *Unladylike*.

'It's okay. It's just a sweet. I've got others.' The man smiled at her.

'Thanks.'

An elderly woman opposite raised an eyebrow at Rosemary and a small tut formed on her lips. *Bloody hell, it wasn't like she'd gone to bed with the chap.* She'd only taken a barley sugar. Some people were quick to judge. You'd think the war would have taught them something – to be kind. There was so much pain around, why add to it? But maybe that was just her. Rosemary Ellis: naive, trusting, unlucky in love – *wholesome*. That's what Danny had called her. She went searching for his face in her mind. Couldn't find it. No! That couldn't be allowed, he had to be there.

'You all right?' asked the captain.

'I'm fine.' But it was a lie.

She closed her eyes. Pretended to sleep, for she didn't want to talk to this man. He reminded her too much of Dan.

The train slowed, and she heard him take his luggage from the overhead rack. He left the carriage, along with several others whose places on the hard seats were immediately filled.

'He left you a note,' said the elderly woman opposite, when Rose finally opened her eyes.

'Pardon?'

'That bloke. He slipped a note in your bag, and some sweets.'

Rosemary reached down to the shopping bag at her feet.

She took out the barley sugar, giving one to the woman across the way, but she didn't read the note. She'd do that when no one was watching.

———

A man driving a horse and cart offered Rose a ride to the hostel. 'They call me Old Arthur,' he told her, when they shook hands. He'd come to the small halt to meet someone else, but they hadn't arrived. The old man shrugged in that fatalistic way that explained everything. *Wartime.* Things got messed up: train timetables, people.

He'd agreed to take Rosemary to Ivychurch Airstrip at Brenzett and the huts where the forty Women's Land Army 'lasses' were billeted. Lasses – that's what he'd called them. And Rosemary tried to think of Gracie as one of these lasses. It didn't work, for Gracie was an East End girl, Bethnal Green through and through: peel her down to the core and that's what you'd find. Like a stick of rock, the place was a part of her that could never be stripped away. Gracie was at home in the big city. She wasn't a country girl, wouldn't fit in there. Rosemary could see that now. No wonder her sister had written such a miserable letter home, and a good job Rose had managed to intercept it before their ma got her hands on it.

She was glad of the lift, thanked the man. Without him, she'd have ended up trudging through endless lanes in the dark, getting hopelessly lost. And the rain sheeting down.

'Come to join the WLA then, have ye?' the old man asked. He puffed away on a pipe that wasn't lit and didn't seem to have any tobacco in it.

'The W—? Oh, the Land Army. No, my sister's been billeted here, said I could join her in the dormitory for a week.'

'A holiday, like?'

'Sort of,' she said. Though if Rose had her choice she'd

rather have gone to Cornwall – looked at the cliffs and the ocean, instead of flat fields that seemed to go on for ever.

'All right for some. Can't remember the last time I had a holiday.'

The man's long face reminded her of Norman when he was having a moan, and brought back the sadness she'd been trying to put behind her. *Bloody war, bloody Gracie, bloody weather, bloody Norman getting himself killed.*

'Thanks for this,' she said. 'For the lift.'

'Only Christian, helping out yer fella man. This sister of yourn, what's her name?'

'Gracie – Gracie Ellis. She's from London, Bethnal Green.'

'And she's never let us forget it,' he said.

'You *know* Gracie?'

'Small place. Folks all know each other round here. But Gracie now – well, she's quite a lass.'

'That's for sure,' said Rosemary.

'Wee slip of a thing, but she can dig drainage ditches with the best of them.'

'What? Our Gracie?' She couldn't imagine Grace digging *any*thing.

'Some of them start out all weak, like. Before you know it, they ain't slips of girls no more. Muscles start appearing. It's wearing them corduroy breeches what does it. They start acting like blokes. Gracie's a tough little nut, works on the same farm as me on the marsh. Give 'er 'er due – she puts in as good a day's work as any bloke. But you'll not be finding her at the hostel, if that's what yer thinkin'– not this time of night.'

'No?'

'They'll all be out at the Fleur De Lys.'

'The what?'

'The old Fleur. Village pub,' he explained, when Rosemary still looked puzzled.

'Our Gracie wouldn't be there,' she said. 'She doesn't drink.'
Shouldn't drink, more like.

'No?' Arthur gave her a cynical look. 'Let's see, shall we? I could do with a pint meself and it wouldn't do you no harm, neither. Something to warm ye. Yer like a drowned rat there. And that's another thing yer wee sister's good at.'

'What's that?'

'She's the farm rat-catcher. Took to vermin control like a duck to water, she did. And there's not many of they Land Girls can get on with it. Too squeamish, like. But Gracie now – it's like she were born to it.' Arthur chuckled when he saw the confusion on Rosemary's face.

Rose pulled her coat tighter around her, wished she'd brought the mackintosh Ma had offered to lend her, and thought about Gracie, and how this man must have mixed her up with somebody else.

Gracie? A rat-catcher? Impossible. Her sister went into hysterics when she saw a mouse, never mind a bloody great rat. And *Rosemary* had always been called on to dispatch any spiders unfortunate enough to cross Gracie's path. Mice, spiders, or any other small beasts, Gracie was terrified of them all. Her squeals could be heard all along the street.

No, this man Arthur had got that wrong. He was thinking of someone else. And Gracie definitely wouldn't be found in any pub, even one with such a fancy French name. Not with her in the family way. But still, Rose didn't object. Something warm to keep the winter chills at bay would be an idea. She was soaked through, and still small icy rivulets found their way down the back of her neck. The Fleur De Lys probably had a big roaring fire blazing away in a cheery hearth. Fuel was in short supply, but these village folk were canny, would have found a way to keep a bit of extra firewood and a few buckets of coal handy.

'Okay,' she said. 'The pub it is.'

. . .

The old Fleur, as Arthur had called it, was a landmark in the village of Brenzett. You could hear the noise from a long way off. Drinkers with voices raised, somebody playing an instrument in there – it sounded like an accordion to Rosemary – and there were others joining in. Less than tuneful, but you couldn't fault them for their raucous enthusiasm. Place must be packed, she reckoned, considering the number of bicycles lined up outside the pub.

'They ride them and God guides them,' said Arthur.

'Eh?'

'After a few jars in there, ain't many of them up to being in charge of a bike. But they always makes it back to billets. God guides them, see.'

'Ah.'

'And your sister's in there.'

'How can you tell?'

Arthur pointed to a rusty old bike, parked haphazardly against the wall, like it had just been abandoned. 'That's hers. And if you listen carefully...' Arthur put his hand to his ear, cupped it for dramatic effect. 'Yep, that's she. That's Gracie all right.'

The voice floated on the night air, high above the others around it: loud, confident, full of life. 'We'll Meet Again'. One of Gracie's all-time war favourites.

'If she's in there with a glass in her hand,' said Rose, 'it'd better be lemonade.'

'Leave the lass alone. She's old enough to drink, ain't she?' asked Arthur.

'Think so?' said Rosemary. 'But is she wise enough?' Rosemary thought again about Gracie's unborn baby – Harry or Harriet.

'Trouble with some of them,' said Arthur, 'is they gets away from the cosy little family nest, bit of freedom for the first time, and it goes to their head, like. But that ain't your sister. She seems like a nice kid and she's got a sensible head on 'er shoulders. Not carried away, takes the job seriously. She's already been promoted. Got a new bar on that armband of hers.'

Rosemary jumped down from the cart. She had to see this woman, the one that Arthur was describing, because no way could her sister have turned into this picture of perfection, this paragon of virtue. *Pure fiction.* It was all in the man's head.

13

BRENZETT, ROMNEY MARSH, KENT

MARCH 1943

Turned out it wasn't lemonade, but a large port-and-lemon that Gracie was clutching in her hand. Rosemary was surprised. She'd imagined her sister serious about keeping the child, concerned for its welfare, yet here she was downing alcohol as if there might be a drought. And she didn't even seem embarrassed that Rose had caught her in the act.

Rosemary frowned. Gracie looked different. It was true, what this bloke Arthur had said. Her sister was nothing like the young woman who had left London. She was self-assured, held herself straight and proud. No longer the youngster who put on a cocky front, but wasn't brave enough to tell her own mother she was leaving, and that some Yank had put her in the pudding club.

Rosemary couldn't help herself: her eyes sought out her sister's waistline and her stomach. Gracie must be three months pregnant now. Surely there should be some outward sign of the small life concealed in there? But there was nothing to see.

'Get *you*,' said Rosemary, after they'd hugged.

'What?'

'The uniform. It suits you. And Arthur over there says you've been promoted.'

'Arthur? Where's Arthur?'

'He was right there. Gave me a lift in that horse and buggy thing of his. Primitive. But sort of nice,' said Rose. 'Apart from the rain pouring into all your nooks and crannies.'

'You came, sis! But you didn't have to.'

'I didn't *what?*'

'I'm okay.'

'You're okay? But the letter! What about the letter? I couldn't sleep nights, thinking how unhappy you were. And trying to hide your letter from Ma. Think that was easy? And I got time off work, specially.'

'Yeah, I'm sorry, sis. But the stupid letter – listen, I wrote that weeks ago, when I was desperate, and before I...'

'Before what, Grace?'

'Before...' Gracie pulled her sister in closer. Whispered the secret in her ear. 'Don't be sad for me, Rosie – *I'm* not, and it's the best way, really. Little blighter wouldn't have had much of a life.'

'The baby? You've lost the baby?'

'Or maybe it lost me, Rose. You know – maybe I just wasn't ready.'

'When?'

'Few weeks back. Just after I wrote you. And I was homesick too. But not now. Now I'm doing stuff I ain't never done before. Stuff I never thought I could do. And you know what, Rose?'

'What?'

'I ain't never been so happy. And they trust me here, rely on me. Think I can do a job just as good as any chap. I never thought that before.'

'Course you're good as any chap, Gracie Ellis. I always told you so, didn't I? Don't let *nobody* put you down, that's what I said – and it's true.'

Gracie hugged her sister again. And Rosemary could feel it, the change in her; the hard skin on her hands, the new muscle. Ditch digging, for God's sake. Her sister dug drainage ditches and caught rats. No longer was she the self-absorbed teenager waiting for confirmation that the world revolved around her, and that it was her world and everybody else was just living in it.

Rosemary laughed. 'So, I've come all this way for nothing. I could have stayed home, you know, and been soaked by East End rain, instead of this awful Romney Marsh wet stuff.'

'Ah, but the rain here is nice and soft, Rose. Admit it. And it was time you had yourself a wee holiday, anyway.'

'Oh, yeah? And what will I do, while you're off digging ditches and catching these rats of yours?'

'Go and look at the sea for a bit. Do some sightseeing. Come back at nights and we can sink a couple in the old Fleur.'

'And what would Ma say if she knew her God-fearing daughters were sinking a few in the pub every night?'

'Maybe she'd be happy for us, Rose.'

Old Arthur appeared at Rosemary's elbow. 'Want a lift to the billet? Unless you fancy sitting on the handlebars while your wee sister here steers you both into a ditch?' Arthur smiled, and the wrinkles on his face made him look a lot less fierce and crusty. Rosemary followed him to the horse and cart, helped Gracie put her bike in the back. Arthur winked at her and looked like somebody's favourite granddad, and much friendlier than when she'd first spotted him.

The rain beat down on them, but right then she didn't mind, because as her little sister had said – the rain here was nice and soft. She wondered how their ma was getting on. Lil was like a creaking door: had lots of ailments, things that might have sent a lesser mortal to their grave. But she was a tough old bird. And as she'd often told her girls – if Mr Adolf bleedin' Hitler was thinking of taking her out, he'd need to drop a bleedin' bomb right on top of her head. And he'd need to make sure it was a bloody great big one.

That thing about Mr Hitler's bomb was false bravado. Lil Ellis had lost an eardrum in the early days of the Blitz, and her nerves had taken a pounding when she'd come back from the shelter one morning to find a gaping hole where the house used to be. After that, Lil wasn't keen on making her way through the blackout on her own. Preferred it when her Rose and Grace were here. Her natural, fierce independence made it hard for her to rely on others, but with family – well, that was different. She'd brought them into the world. And she was right proud of them in her own stubborn, curmudgeonly way.

The siren had sounded while Lil was in the middle of washing her hair. She grabbed a towel, twisted it around her wet, soapy head like one of those exotic Arabian princes. The gas had to be shut down, and the water turned off at the stopcock. But she was used to sorting it all now, and checking the blackout curtains. Didn't take long.

She legged it to the front door. If she was quick, she could join the rest of the strange band of pilgrims that made its way from Royston Street to the tube station shelter. She didn't relish it. Sitting there in the damp musty underground with its cold tiled walls and the smell of its disgusting toilets, but she'd promised Rose that she wouldn't stay in the house when there was a raid on. Because you never knew, and despite all her bravado, Mr Hitler might get lucky one of these days and plant one of his bombs right down her chimney.

'Hang out your washing on the Siegfried Line.' She heard

the singing as soon as she opened her front door. *Good old East End. Whatever happened, they'd all still come out singing.*

'Hey, Lil, pity your Gracie ain't here. She was always good for a tune.' Lil's neighbour, Ivy Brown, was trotting down her front path as fast as her slippers would allow her.

'She's got a voice and no mistake,' said Lil. 'Out in the country now, making sure we all get our spuds and cabbages. Our Rosie's gone to see her.'

'What – your Gracie's one of them Land Girls now?'

'Sure she is. 'Spect she's out there on her tractor as we speak.'

'And maybe you've gone weak in the head, Lil. They don't do no ploughing and stuff in the dark, do they? Anyway, it ain't the time of year for ploughing and all that.'

'Well, whatever she's doing, it'll be important stuff if our Gracie's got anything to do with it. She ain't the kind to sit still and do nothing. Not when there's a war on.'

Lil took her neighbour's arm and helped steer her around the rubble. Along with Ivy's young daughter, Ella, they made their way to the shelter. Friends and neighbours together, helping each other out. It was the natural and kindly thing to do.

The alert siren was still sounding. The red warning – a loud frantic wail whose pitch rose and fell alternately. Folks were used to it now, but even so, it had a black ominous feel, and you tried to get to the safety of a shelter as soon as you could, for it meant that an attack was on the way or already started somewhere. You prayed for the all-clear, still an ear-blasting sound, a long continuous noise, but even so, it was far more comforting than the alert siren. Because it meant one thing.

If you could hear the all-clear, you had survived another raid.

———

Adam Pietersen had enjoyed his evening. Early supper at Simpsons with their superb roast beef and a chance to unwind with good company. He'd been pleased to meet this young pilot, Danny Welland, and to hear news of his family back home in Holland. The guilt of escaping to England, leaving them behind so he could help his country's war effort, often ate at him. But it seemed they were well. And the evidence of his own eyes told him that his daughter had found someone she cared about, a man who could take care of her, should circumstances make that possible. And maybe, in his own small sphere of influence, Adam might be able to give those *circumstances* a nudge in the right direction.

He sucked on his empty pipe. He would light it once the car dropped them off. They were on their way to the East End, Pietersen and Frank Usher. Frank had suggested they all head to Victoria Park, in Bethnal Green, where a new rocket-powered anti-aircraft system was being tested. All a bit hush-hush, Frank had told them. Not many knew about this first test firing of the new Z-battery.

Pietersen had been excited by the prospect. *Rocket-powered weapons that would reach higher than any normal flak?* That could only be good. Bring down more German planes. Maybe even shorten the war, get him back to his family. He'd tried to persuade Danny Welland to come with them, but the man seemed preoccupied, had become gloomy as the evening progressed, and had stayed behind at the restaurant doing some serious drinking.

Their car was only a mile from Victoria Park when a huge searchlight lit the blackened sky and a terrifying volley of sound ripped the air around them. The car shuddered and their driver struggled to keep it on the road. The man was a good driver, used to wartime roads that would have tested other, less skilled, men. He slewed the car to a messy halt and turned around in the road, back the way he had come.

'We should be going the other way,' Pietersen shouted, and pointed in the direction of the park.

'There's a raid on, sir. And I won't be responsible for getting you gents killed.'

'They're testing the guns, that's all,' said Pietersen. 'This isn't a raid.'

'No? And what d'you call that?' the driver asked. The siren screamed its red alert – *attack imminent*. 'I'm getting you to a shelter. Tube station's not far away.'

———

The driver checked his passengers in the rear-view mirror. Some of these VIPs were a right royal pain in the arse. Didn't have the sense they were born with. This bloke with all the fancy gold bands on his sleeve might be able to shout the odds in his own little kingdom, but here, in this car, *he* was the man in charge. *What could they do to him? Sack him?*

The driver rammed his foot down hard to the floorboard and yelled back to them, competing against the siren's frantic wail: 'Hold onto your hats, gents. This could be a bumpy ride.'

14

Lil Ellis didn't think of herself as a coward. But it put the wind up you, right enough, walking through the blackout and the sound of the siren. She clung tightly to Ivy's arm as they made their way to Bethnal Green tube station. It was a dark, dismal night, no moon; and a steady stream of rain slaking the footpaths. Like skating through ice, it was. And miserable. Lil's puny body shook beneath the thin layer of her raincoat.

They were still some distance away from the stairway down to the underground station when a screaming, terrifying sound was added to the siren's wail. It was a sound none of them had heard before. A new kind of bomb, one of the onlookers said. 'Get inside, quick!' the man yelled, as more of the terrifying sounds reached them. 'Close, they're really close,' he said. 'They'll be falling on top of us.'

It was like a scene from hell. Hundreds of people were converging on the entrance to the underground station. The Empire – a dilapidated cinema on Green Street, affectionately known as the Bug Hole because of the massive cockroaches that made it their home – had just let out its customers, which added to the melee of people trying to get into the shelter's stairway.

'What's the bleedin' hold-up?' shouted a woman behind Lil.

The mass of humanity streamed inexorably towards the entrance. Lil and her neighbour Ivy Brown could hear screams coming up from the stairwell, but they'd no idea what was happening there. Both women got caught up in a surge of moving bodies and Ivy's hand was tugged from her daughter Ella's. Ivy yelled a warning as her daughter disappeared ahead of them, pulled through the entrance, tumbling down the stairs below.

Nothing made sense to Lil. A madness seemed to grip people. She was swept up in the crowd as people behind her pushed her towards the stairwell. She could find no foothold as she sank to her knees into a mass of writhing bodies. A woman in front of her had tripped and fallen, and the rest had gone down like human dominoes behind her. People were screaming, warning the others to get back, to retreat from the slippery stairwell. Wet with rain, and steep. So steep you couldn't get a purchase in the dark. And no handrail! And the only bleedin' entrance to the shelter.

'Gawd Almighty, Jesus!' screamed Lil. *Why had no one bothered to put a feckin' handrail there, or a safety barrier?* It wasn't like the locals hadn't asked for one. An accident waiting to happen, that's what they'd all thought.

She heard Ivy calling to her daughter. And then nothing. Not another sound reached her ears as Lil Ellis struggled to breathe. She fell on her face and hands, slid headfirst down a human slide of soft warm bodies beneath her. More heavy bodies piled on top of her and she choked as the remaining breath was punched viciously from her chest.

Some people screamed with their remaining breath. Some people cried. Others prayed. Lil Ellis said her daughters' names, and then blacked out.

. . .

Lil had no idea how long she'd been trapped. When she finally opened her eyes, there was only blackness in the claustrophobic funnel of the stairwell but somehow she managed to move her head to one side, away from the press of bodies above her. Beneath her, nobody moved or cried out anymore. Or prayed.

She dragged in a lungful of stale air and felt pain burn its way from her chest to her throat.

Urgent voices drifted down from above, a surreal mixture of high-pitched sound and low moaning. She saw a faint glimmer of light. It got closer and then a huge head hovered over her. A man with a large, bushy red beard was holding a torch, aiming the beam into her face. He told her to blink. She blinked.

'My God, you're alive,' he said. He bent down, his massive hands plucking at her, trying to get a purchase on her shoulders.

Lil stared in confusion at the man. He had on some kind of uniform and as he bent to lift her, Lil saw the strange cross around his neck. A weird affair, not gold or silver, but some kind of cloth held on with string. She fought hard to make sense of it. Was he an angel? Could this be the Angel Gabriel?

'This one's alive,' she heard him shout. And that's the last thing Lil remembered as the pain of being hauled from the mass of bodies around her made Lil Ellis faint again.

Adam Pietersen pulled many more people from the charnel house of the stairwell that night. Only four were alive. God knows how many were dead. He'd stopped counting. They put them on carts. *Piled them in like animals*, he thought. Like something from medieval times, or the Black Death.

The bodies – men, women, children, babies – were all taken to the mortuary at Whitechapel Hospital and when that became full, the rest were stacked in St John's Church across the road from the tube station. Hardly any of them had fatal injuries, but they all shared one thing in common: they were black and blue from being trampled, and they had died from asphyxiation.

Pietersen had seen many things in the war – things that saddened and disgusted him, but the sight of a small baby crushed in its mother's arms as she'd tried to save and shelter it was something that he knew would stay with him and haunt his dreams for years to come.

He went over to the roadside and threw up his wonderful roast beef dinner.

A woman came over to him. Patted him on the back, kept thanking him, over and over again. She was shaking with cold and shock, and her eyes were wild globes in her head, her clothes filthy and ripped. Her hair was soaking wet and stuck out from her head in a bizarre fashion, bits of soap still clinging to it.

They faced each other on the street outside the church with its sad cargo of casualties, both alive and dead. One massive bear of a man from Holland, and one tiny woman from the East End of London. Tonight, they were one, a single human being, joined in tragedy.

Lil Ellis broke down and cried, and Adam Pietersen picked her up in his bear-like grip and hugged her until her shaking body could find no more tears.

'I can't find my friend,' said Lil.

'We'll find him,' said Pietersen.

'*Her*,' Lil told him. 'Ivy. She's my neighbour. We came together, along with her daughter. I can't find either of them.'

'I'll help you look,' he said.

They found Ivy in a corner of the hall, clinging onto her daughter's lifeless body, refusing to let anyone take the girl from her grasp. Refusing to believe that her beautiful daughter Ella was no longer alive. She didn't have a mark on her, Ivy told them, so how could she possibly be dead? She was sleeping, that's what. It had been a long hard night and the child was weary.

'Why don't I put her to bed over there, then?' Adam Pietersen asked her gently. 'She'll be more comfortable, don't you think?'

Ivy allowed him to take her daughter carefully from her arms and put her on one of the hastily erected camp beds in the hall. *Shock. It took people in different ways.* When something was that painful, you just refused to believe it. Spun yourself a different story. A more acceptable reality. Until the real one kicked in.

'Maybe I should take Ivy home,' Lil said.

'You think so?' asked Pietersen. 'It's warm in here. Get her a cup of hot tea and put her to bed. There's lots of blankets. Take one yourself and have a rest. Better than going back home in the blackout.'

There was a muffled shout behind him. When Adam Pietersen turned around, he barely recognised the man heading towards him, dishevelled, soaked to the skin. A man Pietersen had laughed with only hours before. They had drunk wine in a fine dining room and joked about eating horse. Now there was no laughter. No jokes.

'Christ, man. You're here,' said Frank Usher. 'I thought you'd bought it, old chap.'

Pietersen was shocked. *Did he look as bad as Frank?* The man seemed exhausted but also relieved.

'Been right here,' said Pietersen, 'doing what I could. Little enough, though.'

'Same here. Been ferrying kids to Whitechapel Hospital. Not many survived,' he said, the shock written in the white of his face and the despair in his eyes. 'Took the rest to the mortuary. Been offloading bodies most of the time.'

'I'll get us some tea,' said Lil, taking charge.

'Good idea,' said Pietersen, 'and perhaps you could even rustle up a cigarette, for my friend here.' He looked at Frank.

When she'd left, Adam Pietersen patted Frank Usher on the shoulder. A gesture of support, of understanding. They'd both seen and done things that night that would not easily be forgotten. Nor should they be. 'Bad night,' he said. '*Rum do*, as you British say.'

'Bad as they get,' said Frank. 'They're saying as many as three hundred people were jammed into that stairway. Won't know how many died. Not for a while. And not a single bomb dropped. It was a bloody test. Those damn anti-aircraft rockets exploding overhead. Propaganda nightmare if the Germans get wind of this.'

Adam was grateful when Lil came back with the tea. A cup for both him and Frank and cigarettes for each of them. He watched her take one to her neighbour as well. The WVS volunteers had already set up the huge tea urn, and women were handing out sandwiches and cigarettes. It was something the British did well, he thought. Coping with emergencies. Pietersen swallowed some of the hot, sweet tea. It was supposed to be good for shock. It might not help. And it wouldn't bring Ivy Brown's daughter back. But it couldn't hurt.

15

LONDON

MARCH 1943

Danny had woken up that morning on a narrow, uncomfortable bunk in a local ARP post in the Strand, with a foul taste in his mouth, and several small men banging away with hammers inside his skull. An air raid warden had found him wandering aimlessly near the fire-blackened, bombed-out site of St Clement Danes church. Danny had no idea how he'd got to the church. Or why. All he could remember was drinking too much.

A man walked over from a paraffin stove in the corner and handed him tea in a chipped enamel mug. It was the colour of bark and scalding hot, but it had some life-giving sugar in it. Danny grinned, put it to his lips gratefully.

The man in the tin hat and blue serge uniform grinned back. 'Hard night, eh?' said the warden. 'We don't get many folk just wandering about in the blackout up west. Not before the all-clear's gone off. Most sensible folk stay home or in the shelters.' The man emphasised the word 'sensible'.

'Can't remember too much about it. Except the roast beef in

Simpsons was something I couldn't pass up. Haven't eaten like that in years,' said Danny. 'Sorry if I gave you any trouble.'

'No trouble, mate. You slept like a baby. So, who's this Rosie, then?'

'Rosie?'

'Yeah. You kept on about her. Must be some special lady.'

'She is – *was*.' A shudder went through Danny as he thought about the prospect of a life without her. A world without his Rosie. 'I've got to try and find her. She can't be gone. I won't believe it.'

'Wartime.' The ARP warden shook his head sadly. 'Things get complicated. People survive. Some don't.'

'You're right! People *survive*. And you know what? She'd be one of them.'

Danny threw back the rest of his tea and put the offered cigarette in his greatcoat pocket, thanked the man for his hospitality, and made his way through the chill of a London morning. Fog invaded the air – but it no longer invaded his mind. Whatever it took, he would find this place where Rosie worked. Where she made her parachutes. He had every right to know. Secrecy be damned. And he would finally put that ring on her finger. Right where it belonged.

He started at *The Daily Express* building on Fleet Street. It was an impressive and futuristic-looking edifice, black art-deco, with acres of walled glass, blast tape criss-crossing it in diamond patterns. The newspaper had commissioned a similar building in Manchester, but Danny hoped he'd find the answers he was looking for in London. Answers that would lead him to Rosie.

She couldn't be gone.

It took hours of waiting; impatient, anxious hours when no one seemed to be doing anything to find out where this factory was. 'It's in your bloody newspaper story!' he'd told a young man. 'How hard can it be? You're intelligent people, I presume, not simpletons.'

Frustration had made him angry. Cancelled out his normal charm and good manners. The remark hadn't made him any new friends, either, or encouraged them to go out of their way to help.

Eventually though, a young woman secretary took pity on him. She'd explained the need for security and why they couldn't just hand out addresses of important war factories without proper consideration. But when Danny had shown her his ID card and his RAF papers, she seemed assured that he wasn't a clandestine German spy. She promised to do her best to find what he needed.

'Shoreditch,' the woman said, when she came back. 'I've written down the address for you.'

Danny was grateful when she explained that she'd worked in the archives for twenty minutes to find the place.

'Thanks. I'm indebted to you,' he said, and gave the young woman a huge smile, then hurried from the office like the devil was on his heels. Time was a tricky thing; you never knew how much of it you had, and he needed to get to Rosie as soon as he could.

He had no plan, other than make his way to this factory over in Shoreditch, the East End. Wartime London, though. It took him over two hours to get there from Fleet Street. Only thirty minutes of that was on a bus, as the rest was waiting for it. Even so, Danny felt the excitement building in him, and a small kernel of happiness growing inside, until he found himself smiling inanely at other passengers on the bus. Maybe they thought he'd lost his mind. But he hadn't, of course. He'd found it.

He had no time to spare now. He'd waited far too long already. So when he was told to wait in the supervisor's office, Danny didn't sit as he was invited to, but paced the floor. The young woman who'd ushered him in had offered tea. But he refused. *Politely, this time.* And despite his manic impatience. It didn't hurt to be civil to people who were only trying to help.

Mr Hardcastle hurried in, looking flustered. His normally calm demeanour had vanished, and in its place was a man fraught with strife, facing problems that seemed, for the time being at least, insurmountable. His face was red, and large sweat stains on his jacket marked out the battle he'd been waging on the factory floor. 'I'm sorry, but I can't spare you more than a minute or two,' said the harassed supervisor. 'Maybe you could come back another day? Bit of a flap on here, I'm afraid.'

'Nothing too critical, I hope,' said Danny.

'Two of my best workers have already gone. One of them copped a direct hit from a huge parachute mine. And now a third goes and sews his hand to a machine.'

'Good grief. Anything I can do?' Danny asked.

'Shouldn't think so,' said Mr Hardcastle, 'unless you can handle an industrial sewing machine.' He moved towards the door, needed to get back to the shop floor.

'I'm looking for someone who works here. I'll be out of your hair, once I can speak to Rosie.'

'Rosie? We've got *several* Rosies.'

An elderly man rushed in through the door. 'We've got the transport sorted now, Mr Hardcastle. And they're about to cart him off. Who should I put on Green's machine?'

The supervisor looked over at Danny. ''Fraid I've got to leave you. Got to sort this.'

'But Rosie. Rosemary Ellis,' stammered Danny. 'Where can I find her?'

'Rosemary? One of my best workers, you know. But she's gone, I'm afraid. Gone. *Gone!*' shouted Mr Hardcastle over his shoulder, as he rushed from the office.

Danny left the factory in Shoreditch in a daze. Just walked.

No destination in mind. His head was floating on his body like a balloon that someone had overinflated. It was about to burst. *Direct hit from a huge parachute mine*, the man had said. *You didn't walk away from a direct hit.* First the bloke from the Ministry of Information, and now this supervisor. They'd both said she was gone. You couldn't argue with that. They couldn't both be wrong.

He dropped his head onto his chest in defeat. What could his life be now? Did he even *want* to live in a world that no longer had Rosie in it? No possibility of ever seeing her again. Theirs was a love that could not be replicated. The kind that came only once in a lifetime.

Danny walked for miles, hour after hour of mindless journeying, looking for an answer. And then it came to him. He had to get back into combat. He had to fly. It was the only thing that could make any sense out of the pain. He would go and pester the Ministry, speed up his return. Pester the medics, get them to give him a clean bill of health and ship him out to his squadron. Somewhere he could be of use in this bloody awful war that tore nations apart and ripped loved ones out of your life.

He found Frank Usher in the Pig and Whistle round the corner from the Air Ministry, looking as if he'd been pickled in brown ale. Danny had no idea what sorrows Frank was trying to drown in drink, but doubted they'd be anything as painful as his own. As losing Rosie.

He practically dragged the young man all the way to his tiny flat, then doused his head with ice-cold water from the kitchen tap. It seemed to do the trick, for Frank started to focus a little, and his general demeanour improved once he'd thrown up several times.

'That wasn't necessary, old chap,' said Frank, shivering.

'Cup of tea would have done the trick.'

'I need you to help me,' said Danny.

'Do I strike you as somebody who could help *anybody* right now?' Usher rushed to the bathroom again and threw up the last remnants of the ale.

'This isn't like you, Frank. Anything I can do?'

'Not unless you can bring one hundred and seventy-three people back from the dead. Women, children, babies.'

The young man dry-heaved. Looked as if he might need another trip to the bathroom.

'Jesus H. Christ. What's that about?' asked Danny.

'Hundreds of people injured too. But you're not likely to read it in the daily rags, are you? They'll keep a lid on it. Not good for morale.'

'Tell me.'

'You remember Adam and I were going to see those new anti-aircraft rockets being tested over in Victoria Park? Place near Bethnal Green. Only problem was – nobody told the locals. They all thought it was a raid, and you want to know the funny thing?' Frank asked.

'Always good to hear something funny,' said Danny, drily.

'Not a bomb was bloody dropped. There *was* no raid, Dan. Just those damn rockets of ours being test-fired overhead. And the sirens weren't even *meant* to go off. Once it started, everybody rushed to the entrance of Bethnal Green tube. Only one entrance there. Steep stairway, small space. And it was wet and slippery, been raining. And dark, of course. And not a single bloody handrail to grab hold of. Some poor woman fell and they all piled in on top. Went down like skittles.'

'So, you and Adam – you got caught up in it?'

'Not stuck in the stairwell, no. But we spent the night collecting dead bodies, ferrying them to mortuaries.'

Danny watched the young officer pour them both a drink.

'Brandy?' he said, in awe. 'A miracle.'

'Yes, old boy. Still a few miracles left, it seems. And we'll need them, don't you think?'

Danny Welland said nothing, just threw the brandy back in one. But as for miracles... *Could there really be any left?*

16

BRENZETT, ROMNEY MARSH, KENT

MARCH 1943

Pitch-black. And freezing cold in the dormitory huts where the Women's Land Army were housed in Brenzett. But Rosemary Ellis had seen worse, and it wasn't the first time she'd had to sleep with her coat on.

She could hear them all moving about now, getting ready for the new day, preparing for physical labour that was often back-breaking and took you out in freezing temperatures from early morning till late at night. But the 'lasses' were a friendly bunch and had accepted Rosemary even though she wasn't one of them and was freeloading on one of their bunks.

'Black as the devil's armpit outside,' said Gracie. 'But dawn'll be up by the time we've cycled to work.'

'What – you cycle in the *dark*?' asked Rosie.

'No worse than the blackout at home. And less chance of falling into some bomb crater.'

'What about you and the bike ending up in a ditch?'

'We ride them and God guides them – least, according to Arthur,' said Gracie.

They both laughed.

One after another, the girls left for work, leaving Rosie and her sister alone in the hut.

'You not going?'

'Soon,' said Gracie. 'Need to talk to you first, sis.'

'Oh?'

'That letter the bloke wrote you.'

'I should never have let you see that,' said Rosie. She had almost forgotten the note slipped into her bag on the train, with the boiled sweets. When she'd finally read it, its contents had made her curious and she'd shown it to Gracie. 'What about it? And don't say I should do what he says and go and spend the day in Margate with him.'

'Why not?'

'Because – I don't know anything about the man.' Although his invitation to lunch seemed innocent enough, it struck Rosie as a little wild. Adventurous. He'd written that he would wait for her every day for the next three days of his leave, at the window table of the Montrose Hotel, in the hope that she would decide to come.

'Yeah, but you said he looked like a decent bloke. Bit sad, maybe. Battered and bruised by the war. He was a captain in the army, right?'

'So he said. And he had the uniform. Back on leave for a week,' said Rosie. 'Looked like he could use it, an' all.'

'Well, then – what you waiting for?'

'Guy could be a nutcase for all I know.'

'You know what, Rosie Ellis – you're scared of men. Want to be a virgin all your miserable life?'

'Nothing wrong in saving yourself for the right man,' said Rosie.

'Well, that man ain't gonna suddenly, miraculously come back to life with his RAF uniform on, is he, Rose? Forget him. The man's dead. And you're not the Virgin Mary.'

'Christ, Gracie, you can be bloody cruel when you work at it.' Rosemary turned her head away, didn't want her little sister to see how deep the hurtful barbs about her Danny had gone.

'Realistic. I just want you to see things as they are, and not waste your life waiting for something that's impossible. Go and see this bloke like he wants you to. Spend the day with him. Have some bleedin' fun for a change.'

'Oh, yeah? And if he wants more? What then, Grace?'

'You're a big girl now, Rose. You know how to say no, don't you?'

'When did you turn from my little sister into my mother?' Rosie asked.

'Ma? Think Ma would tell you to go out with some geezer you only just met?'

'Ah *ha*!' Rosie pointed an accusing finger at her sister. 'Just what I'm saying – Ma would have a blue fit.'

'Yeah, but Ma ain't here. Now go and get ready and I'll take you to the bus stop,' said Gracie.

'And how exactly will you manage that, Gracie Ellis, digger of ditches and catcher of rats?' asked Rosemary.

'On the handlebars of me bike,' said her sister. 'How else?'

And that's how, two hours later, Rosemary found herself on a bus heading out to Margate.

Margate, Ramsgate – all those towns on the Isle of Thanet – were strictly off-limits to holiday makers now. No leisure activities allowed. Fair enough, since it was the ideal spot for a German invasion. So the odd stranger wandering around, especially one not in uniform, could easily be a fifth-columnist working for the Bosch.

But her sister Gracie had taken care of that; had kitted her out in a spare uniform and miraculously turned her into a Land

Girl. Green jumper, felt hat, green tie, brown corduroy breeches.

Rosemary stared out of the bus window, watched the fingers of red and gold stretch across the sky, until full dawn finally arrived. The air was clear and fresh, no early-morning mist clung to the earth even though the land was flat. You could see for miles, and it gave her a feeling of freedom, of being able to breathe. She could understand why her sister liked the place.

Gracie would be at her work now. Gracie, the Land Girl. A farm labourer, that's what it came down to. You had to smile. Still, it seemed that she was happy there. Maybe it was just the freedom of being her own woman, the independence, and being away from the confines of family. Rosie could see that as well. That it might be exciting – once you got over the homesickness.

She took out the letter again from Captain Alistair Greenway. *Fine name.* And he looked like a pleasant chap. A man who had promised to wait for her every day of his leave, hoping she would come

It was like something from one of those romantic American films. Not that she'd seen many films lately, but her sister had dragged her along to the Bug Hole to see *Casablanca*. They'd both cried when Humphrey Bogart and Ingrid Bergman hadn't walked into the sunset together. That would have been a happy ending. Still, you couldn't always have happy endings.

Did he really mean it, this Captain Greenway; that he would go to the same seat every day and just wait for her? They'd only spoken for a few minutes on a train and knew nothing about each other. Then again, it was wartime and people took shortcuts when time was such a precious thing. You never knew how much of it you had left.

One thing she guessed about this man, though. Despite his happy-go-lucky exterior, Alistair Greenway was sad inside.

She'd had enough sadness in her life. Did she really want any more?

. . .

'You came,' he said. He had a wide, silly grin on his face – a small boy handed an unexpected ice cream.

'So I did.'

He took her coat and pulled out a chair for her.

A gentleman, she thought. *Or a rogue with acting skills.* Rosemary still didn't fully understand why she'd come. The romantic bit about waiting for her, maybe. Not giving up.

'And I'm glad,' said Alistair Greenway, still grinning.

'But I need you to understand something,' she said.

'Oh?'

'That I don't usually do things like this.'

'Things like what?'

'Meeting strangers in hotels,' said Rosie.

'I don't think that for a minute. If I did, I wouldn't have invited you,' he said.

'Okay then, just as long as you understand. And we need to get one thing straight. The invitation was for lunch, that's all.'

'Yes, ma'am,' he said, and gave her a mock salute. 'Fully understood.'

Was he making fun of her?

'That's all right then,' said Rosemary.

'After lunch, I usually take a constitutional along the promenade. Helps the digestion, I've found,' said Alistair. 'Would that be allowed, Miss Ellis?'

He was teasing her again. But she didn't mind.

'A walk, Captain Greenway? I think I could stretch to that. And call me Rosemary.'

'Excellent. The air's quite bracing along the front. Now, let's see what these fine people can rustle up in the kitchen. I'm game for anything except powdered eggs or spam,' he said. 'And the name's Alistair.' He laughed.

It was a pleasant sound and one that Rose thought she could

get used to. She relaxed and allowed herself to enjoy the company and the food and looked forward to a walk along the prom. And as for anything else? The world was full of infinite possibilities. But one thing definitely wasn't on the menu, and that was breakfast the next morning.

After they'd eaten, they walked for an hour, talked about London and the places they'd been. About their interests, their hopes for the future. The day was fine, the air bracing as Alistair had promised.

But Rose thought it a sad, empty place, for no people walked on the sand, no children laughed and made sandcastles, or hunted in tide pools with their nets. Margate's sandy beach, stretching for miles at low tide, might once have made a perfect picture postcard, but not now. Now it had nothing to recommend it, unless you enjoyed gazing at acres of barbed wire. Images of Cornwall came into her head, of the blue-green ocean that plunged into the rock pools of Havenporth. Crystal clear water. Inviting.

The sea here was brown.

Alistair Greenway asked nothing of her, other than companionship. Lunch, walk, a few laughs, and a gin in the hotel before her bus back. She'd slipped an arm through his as they'd walked to the bus stop. *Her idea.* And it had felt good. Comforting. Like somebody cared.

He told her he would wait in the same window seat tomorrow. Hoped she could make it. But he didn't pressure her. Her decision, he'd said. And so it was, because Rosemary Ellis was a grown woman, her *own* woman. It was a time of liberation, when a woman could do the same job as a man: her in the factory, her sister Gracie on the farm.

As she made her way back to Brenzett, Rose thought about Gracie's words. They weren't true. She wasn't afraid of men.

But Grace was right about one thing. Rose *was* holding on to her virginity, like some kind of precious gift not to be squandered or handed out without thought. *But was that right?* Being chaste seemed like an old-fashioned thing to many, in a world where no one could be sure they'd still be alive tomorrow.

A small ripple of anticipation moved up Rosemary's spine. She'd given Alistair her address. He'd given her his: a place she'd never heard of, in Devon. The family home. He lived there with his sister but hadn't gone back for his leave; wanted a change, he'd told her.

And now it was up to her. She could go back and see him tomorrow if that's what she wanted – and that *was* exactly what she wanted. She'd gone too long without companionship, the kind that a man could give. And who knew, when she went back tomorrow, she might even let him kiss her.

Then thoughts of Danny flooded her mind. Of the love she had felt for him – still did. Theirs was an intense, all-embracing love and having him ripped so viciously from her had left a raw empty hole in her life. A wound that might never heal. Suddenly, she felt guilty. Disloyal to him, to his memory. Guilty for allowing herself to feel happy that day. No one could ever replace him, and should she even try to?

17

Danny had spent the whole impossible day being shunted from one office to another. He could see it in their faces now, the way no one wanted to look him in the eye, that his presence was an embarrassment. What he was asking for was somehow – and he couldn't think how – a boon that no one there at the Air Ministry was prepared to grant him.

What was wrong with people? Couldn't they see he was a valuable asset? An experienced pilot prepared to give his expertise, his passion, and even his life to the noble cause of his country's victory?

Now there was no Rosie to live for, giving his life seemed easier than ever.

His friend Frank Usher caught up with him. 'Bit of a red tape nightmare, old chap,' said Frank.

'I knew it! What now?' asked Danny.

'Remember I mentioned that place over on Oxford Street?'

'What – the "personnel" johnnies, you mean?'

'Right. They're the chaps.'

'The glorified desk jockeys,' said Danny. 'What do they want with me?'

'I've been on to them again. Gave them a bit of a nudge.'

'Thanks for that, Frank. You're a good pal. Everybody else is giving me a wide berth. It's like I've got something infectious they're scared of catching. Know why that might be?'

Now even Frank couldn't look him in the eye. *What the hell was that?* And Danny Welland realised for the first time that there was something they all knew, but no one was brave enough to tell him. No one except Frank, perhaps.

'They've sent this over for you,' said Frank. He handed over an envelope. 'Sorry you've had to wait so long.'

Danny opened the letter with shaking hands, a premonition of doom seeking him out before he'd read a single line. And there it was, laid out on the page, every word a blow. As far as the RAF was concerned, the verdict was cut and dried. He'd been grounded. Admin. A lousy desk job, in a training flight maybe. Watching others take off when he couldn't. It was there in the letter. *Classified unfit for combat duty. Sight deficiencies.*

He wouldn't be allowed to fly. He wanted to strangle the bureaucrats with their own red tape. Because, instead of telling him right away when they'd had the results from the Medical Board, the blasted letter had been sitting in somebody's in-tray over in Personnel. He wanted to knock their heads together.

'I'm sorry,' said Frank. 'I know how it feels. Got grounded myself.'

'You were operational?' asked Danny, surprised.

'Once,' Frank replied. 'You know how it is. It was another time – don't talk about it much, not now.'

'Any time you want to...' offered Danny.

'Good of you. But right now, I need to run something by you.'

'Don't know if this is the time. Rather be alone to think this thing through, if you don't mind,' said Danny.

'Up to you,' said Frank. 'But it's just something that our new friend Pietersen said. Think he might be able to help,' he added.

'He's dropped a few hints and he's invited us both to dinner again.'

'Not feeling very sociable, I'm afraid,' said Danny. 'I need to get this sorted out. Get my future mapped. They can't just chuck me on the scrapheap. I need to be useful; don't you see? There's a war out there and I've got to do my bit.'

'Exactly!' said Frank. 'So why not listen to what Pietersen's got to say? He told me he's got a job for you, if you want it, that is.'

'What – flying?' asked Danny, excited now.

'Not flying. No. But he reckons it's just as important. Stuff that could change the course of the war.'

'As if I haven't heard that before,' said Danny. *Bitter now. But who wouldn't be?* They'd taken his wings away.

'All I'm saying is give the man a chance. Let's meet him, listen to what he's got to say.'

Danny didn't answer. He felt as if the life he'd known had slowly drained away. No more Rosie – the woman who had kept his soul alive. And now, no more flying. No words of his could change that. And nothing Adam Pietersen had to say could possibly make a difference.

'Maybe it's not the end of all things, dear boy,' said Adam Pietersen. 'There are other ways to give Herr Hitler a bloody nose.'

'Oh yes? Flying a desk. Up to your armpits in paperclips.'

'No, not that.'

'What then?' Danny said.

They were all gathered for another of Pietersen's famous dinners. Not Simpsons this time. The restaurant was finding it hard to get beef. Still managing to get salmon, but even so, they'd all agreed that the Army and Navy Club in Pall Mall –

where Pietersen had been greeted with respect – was a good enough bet.

'Let's discuss it after dinner, shall we?' said Pietersen. 'They still manage a fine port here, and can drum up the odd cigar.'

Danny looked around at the grandeur of the room, almost intact despite the austerity of wartime. The fine crystal chandeliers had been removed because of the bombing, but the oak panels and luxurious red drapes still gave it an air of elegance. And the famous paintings in the library – scenes of glorious battles – were a reminder of Britain's military past. *But modern warfare?* Would chaps who sat in this room in years to come describe *that* as glorious? Still, it was necessary, of course. Had to be done, thought Danny. You couldn't just sit back and do nothing while the rest of Europe suffered under Hitler's boot.

Adam Pietersen noticed Danny's glance around the room, but misunderstood it.

'Impressive, eh? An old-fashioned splendour. Bombs dropping all around us and still this place manages to look timeless. Serves a pretty good mutton stew, too,' said Pietersen. His expression suddenly changed, became thoughtful and sad.

'What's on your mind?' asked Danny.

'Oh, just wondering how many of my countrymen will be sitting down to a decent meal tonight. Makes the guilt keener, thoughts like that. And my family, they'll be living on scraps.'

'They're tough,' said Danny. 'I'm sure they're fine. And they've got some good men looking out for them.' He remembered the bluff kindness of Edwin Jansen, hoped the Dutchman was still alive.

'And that's what I need to talk to you about, Dan. Those good men. And how they could use our help, especially after the sad news from Rotterdam.'

'What news?' asked Danny.

'American Army Air Force raid on the docks. They accidentally wiped out hundreds of civilians in a residential area in the process.'

'Jesus!'

The waiter arrived with their drinks. All three men sat in silence. And Danny Welland couldn't help but notice the single tear that rolled down the grizzled face of the Dutchman beside him.

After dinner, Danny was surprised when his friend Frank left the table and said his goodbyes. Danny accepted another drink and then watched Adam Pietersen closely, tried to imagine what was coming next. What the Dutchman had on his mind. Whatever it was, it seemed that Frank would not be involved.

'Ever heard of the SOE, Dan?' asked Pietersen.

'Heard of it, yes.' *And it was true. He'd had a lift home on one of their exfiltration flights.* 'Couldn't tell you what they do, though. Something to do with intelligence, I suppose. Spying and that sort of thing,' said Danny. The question threw him. Not something he'd been expecting.

'Not spying, particularly,' said Adam. 'But you're in the right area with the intelligence thing. It's a specialised unit, certainly. Stands for "Special Operations Executive" and it's a British secret service division, set up to help with sabotage in occupied countries.'

'I see,' said Danny. Though to be fair, he wasn't exactly keeping up. Couldn't see what it would have to do with him.

'I hope that you will,' said Pietersen. 'I have friends in the unit, and they believe you could be very useful.'

'Me?' Danny said, shocked. 'But I don't know anything about that sort of thing. How can I...?'

'Your knowledge of Dutch for a start. Your past experience in Holland. They're setting up a new underground route hoping to get stranded fliers out and back to Britain. My friends feel you'd be perfect for the job.'

'With all due respect, that's insane. I'm not a spy,' said Danny. The very idea was ludicrous, he thought. Dreamed up in someone's fantasy, or nightmare.

'Insane? No, I don't think so,' said Pietersen and he smiled at last 'You'd be perfect, don't you see? A total fit. You'd understand these fliers. And you'd only have to be a "liaison" for the escape line. No one is asking you to spy. You'd be on loan to SOE, on a temporary basis. And you'd still hold the rank of squadron leader in the RAF.'

'A squadron leader *with no squadron*,' said Danny, cynically.

'Nothing's perfect, Dan. Did you really think they'd let you fly – with your bad eye?'

'No. I guess I'm not surprised. And when it comes down to it, I wouldn't want to be a burden to the rest of the Wing. Wouldn't want to put any of them in harm's way.'

'Well, then. What do you say?' asked Adam.

'I haven't spoken Dutch for a while. Don't know if I'd remember how.'

'They'd send you on a refresher course. And you'd get other specialised training from the intelligence wallahs up in Baker Street. You'd be quite an asset.'

Danny reset his thoughts. He was a flier, would miss the life, but the air force didn't want him, had made it plain they'd have no use for him. And he needed to be useful. To have a job that would contribute to the fight.

'Okay, Adam,' he said. 'Maybe it wouldn't be so bad, at that.'

And so it was decided. A new beginning. A start to Danny Welland's whole new life.

18

BRENZETT, ROMNEY MARSH, KENT

MARCH 1943

This time, Rose walked to the village pub. It took longer than it had in Old Arthur's horse and cart, and she didn't even know if Gracie would be at the Fleur when she got there, because Rosemary had no idea of the time. Except that it was dark. And it was raining. It seemed to do that a lot here. But still, it didn't dampen her spirits, and she jogged along the lane to the centre of the village with a light heart. Optimistic about the future. Her sister Gracie was right – this holiday was something she'd needed to recharge her batteries, help her face the challenges that living through a war delivered daily to your doorstep.

Her sister's bike was right there against the wall, just as it had been the night before. She was glad, because she wanted to share the excitement of her day with her little sister. Gracie would be pleased. After all, it was she who had encouraged Rose to go and meet the man.

She went into the Fleur, shaking the rain from her coat. Logs crackled cheerily in the fireplace and she headed straight for it, warmed her frozen hands. But tonight seemed different. There was no excited buzz of conversation. No raucous laughter. Tonight, there was no cheerful sing-along. No bloke playing his accordion.

Rose looked around in confusion. Nothing she could see explained the atmosphere of gloom that hung over the room. Except that overnight the place had changed from a cheery country pub into a funeral home. Some heads turned towards her, a couple nodded, but none smiled and they all went back to their beer.

'Somebody die?' Rosemary asked her sister. 'It's like a wake in here.' She laughed, tried to lighten the atmosphere.

Gracie was sitting at a table near the fireplace, her face a study in gloom, like the rest of them. 'Matter of fact they did, Rose.'

'What? Who? Sorry. It was a joke, didn't mean to...'

'I know,' said Gracie. 'It's war. People die, right?'

'Somebody from here?' she asked, and looked around at the scattering of customers.

'Not exactly. But he came here once, filmed some scenes. Seemed like a good man. This lot's been beating their gums about it.'

'Really?' said Rosemary. 'They seem pretty quiet to me.'

'All talked out, I guess.'

'Well – who...?'

'Leslie Howard. He was flying from Lisbon to Bristol,' Gracie said. 'Civilian flight, brought down *deliberately*, they're saying. Eight Junkers just waiting for it. Shot down over the Bay of Biscay.'

'Why would the Germans do that? Attack an actor?'

'Ask Hitler. Ask Mr Churchill. How the feck would I know, Rose?'

'*Leslie Howard*. God, I used to dream about him,' she said. 'And I cried for days when I saw *Gone with the Wind*. He was this handsome blond creature, Ashley Wilkes, always seemed sad though.'

'He was playing a part,' said Gracie. 'Don't suppose the man was anything like that.'

Old Arthur came over with a brown ale in his hand. Sat down at their table. 'Not you two as well?' he said. 'Like a bleedin' mausoleum in here.'

'Yeah, well. The man was special,' said Gracie.

'Hear what they're saying?' asked Arthur. 'There's talk one of the passengers looked just like Churchill, smoked a cigar an' all. Mistaken identity, that's what I reckon,' he said, and shook his head sagely.

'You don't want to go spreading rumours, Arthur,' said Rose. 'Not good for morale.'

'It's what the bloke on the radio said. Mistaken identity. Reckoned them poor blighters got killed because the Bosch made a feckin' mistake. All seventeen of the poor sods.'

Shot down in mid-air, thought Rosemary. Did those poor people have any idea what was about to happen? Did they have time to feel fear? It made her think of her Danny. Had it been like that with him? He would have put up a fight, she knew that much about him. But was he given the chance?

'You're miles away, Rose.' Gracie stood up. 'Want a drink? I'll get them.'

'What? Oh – thanks,' said Rosemary. 'If you're sure. Half a mild, then. But you should be saving your pennies.'

'Just as well to have no money than not enough,' her sister said, over her shoulder.

'Gracie tell you her news?' asked Arthur. ''Bout the telegram, like. Not often we gets a telegram, here.'

'What news?' Rosemary looked across at her sister, chatting to the barmaid.

Arthur shook his head, his face glum. 'Not my place to say. But the missus in charge of the Land Girls got it sent to her, and she sent me off to give it to your Gracie. Can't say that I know what's in it. Though Gracie didn't look best pleased when she read it, mind.'

'Well?' said Rose, when her sister had come back with the beer. It was weak. She could have done with something stronger, but gin wasn't easy to get.

'Well, what?'

'The telegram? Arthur says you got a telegram.' Rosemary glared at her little sister. 'You were going to tell me, I suppose?'

'Keep your hair on, Rose. It was right next on the list.'

Arthur, looking helpless, picked up his ale and fled. The two sisters glared at each other.

'It's about Da, isn't it?' Rosemary swallowed hard, tried to ignore the sickness in her stomach, and the way her heart slammed into her ribs, beating out its manic tattoo.

People didn't send telegrams, not unless it was something important. Something sad. She braced herself for another blow. *And just when life had cheered up a bit.* She thought back to the day she'd just spent with Alistair, the way they'd laughed. Seemed like you always had to pay for stuff, that life claimed some sort of payback. It wasn't fair.

'No,' Grace said, quietly. 'It ain't Da. It's Ma.'

'What? Ma sent a telegram? I knew I shouldn't have come. She hates it on her own.'

'It ain't that. Somebody in the ARP sent it, official like. She's been involved in some kind of accident in the blackout. Not hurt bad,' Gracie said, quickly, 'just knocked about a bit, few scrapes and bruises. But looks like she's real shook up, Rose. They said she shouldn't be left on 'er own. One of us needs to go.'

'That would be me, I suppose,' said Rose with a sigh.

'*I* could always go,' said Gracie.

'Yeah? And open a whole can of worms? That wouldn't do

you or Ma any good, would it? And if she's shook up like they say...'

'Thanks, Rose, you're a peach, you know that?'

'Sure,' said Rosemary. 'A peach, that's me. Think that's what Alistair will say when I stand him up tomorrow?'

'You could write to him and explain.'

She'd do it when she got back home. There'd be time then to write something special. *And maybe it was even better this way.* If the bloke was really interested in her, wouldn't absence make the heart grow fonder? That's what they wrote in books. Then again, people also said, 'Out of sight, out of mind.'

Words, language. You could make it do whatever you wanted to. Didn't mean it was true.

Rose was sad to leave her sister. They'd got on better together than they ever had before; maybe that said something about this new Gracie, the more grown-up one. The courageous woman prepared to bring a baby into the world. And face the sadness of losing it. Leaving home had performed some sort of miraculous transformation in her little sister, and whatever it was, however it had happened, Rosemary was glad of it. Hoped it stuck. And at least she could put their ma's mind at ease now. Gracie was well. Had settled in. Was happy. Surely Lil Ellis would like that, would be pleased for her daughter?

The train journey back home was just as tedious as the outward one. And this time she didn't have anything to look forward to. Rosemary hadn't even managed to bag a seat; they'd all been taken by the time she joined the train. She'd had to make do with the corridor, seated, balancing on her small suitcase until her legs lost all feeling in them. That's when she gave in and resorted to sitting on the floor. People getting in and out of the train had to clamber over her feet, but she didn't apologise. Rosemary Ellis figured she'd apologised too many times already in her life. It didn't get you anywhere, just made you a mat for them to walk on. She was just as good as any of this lot. *And* she'd met the queen. How many of these people who threw her angry looks could say that?

Exhausted. Fed up with the whole bloody world. Its wars. Its anger. Its stupidity. That's how she was at ten o'clock that night, walking through the streets of London, heading towards their tiny two-bedroom terraced house in Royston Street. Her shoes pinched and her feet were tired and sore from the long walk home, but at least she could sleep in her own bed soon. A bed she'd had all to herself since her sister moved out. There was something to be said for that.

An air raid warden cycled past her on his bike, whistling, 'Nice One Cyril'.

'Put that bleedin' light out,' he shouted fiercely up at a first-floor window. A hand tugged the blackout curtain back into place and the warden carried on his way, seamlessly picking up the tune where he'd left off and whistling cheerfully all the way down the road.

She brightened. *Home*. War or not, the East End was a special place, and although it had been pounded night and day in the Blitz, Mister Hitler had discovered to his cost that some folk were just too stubborn to give up. You'd look hard to find the word 'defeat' in *their* dictionary. And Rosemary was suddenly glad.

She would travel the world one day; an ambition she was positive would come true. And if anyone asked her *how* she knew it – especially when the whole world was in such turmoil – Rosemary wouldn't be able to explain. But one thing was certain. She could travel the earth and still there'd be nowhere she'd feel more at home than the East End of London.

19

'So, you like this bloke Alistair, then?' said Lil.

'He made me laugh. Not easy to find one who does that.'

'Yeah, well. Marriage needs more than just laughs. Serious business – *give and take*. It's the blokes what do most of the taking, mind – and *us* the giving. Always has been. Women do the slaving and have the kids.' Her mother sighed.

'Have you not been happy then – with Da? He's a good man.'

'Men's *men*, Rose. They wants what they wants, and *they* says *when* they wants it.'

God, but it was depressing sometimes talking to her ma. And now, since that terrible night down the shelter, Lil was letting the misery of the war get to her. She wasn't even cantankerous anymore, just accepted things with this new bleak fatalism of hers, like nothing good could ever come from each new day. Rosemary hated to leave her alone, and yet it was good to get away from the dark cloud that hung over the house in Royston Street and seemed to follow her ma around.

As for marriage – Rosemary hadn't even mentioned marriage. She liked this man, Alistair, but didn't know if she would want to spend the rest of her life with him. Or with *any* man. Not if her ma was anything to go by.

Rose had written him a letter when she'd first come home – a few weeks ago, now. But she'd heard nothing back. He'd have returned to his regiment. He could be anywhere, and she refused to think about the danger he would be in. Best to blank it from your mind and let fate do what it did best. *There!* She was becoming just like her mother.

Still, Rose wasn't against giving fate a small nudge now and then. She'd taken on more responsibility in the factory, been promoted to a section head, and the new position had given her an appetite for broader horizons.

When this war finished, she wanted to be one of the women who changed things. A *career* woman. So she'd started educating herself, had joined Boots' Book-lovers' Library, a lending library in Boots the chemist. The few pence investment had been worth it, for she'd taken out a book about modern business practice.

Administration was a complicated affair, it seemed, and it hadn't been simple – how the book described it, but Rose had painstakingly worked her way through it. Her mother had been scornful. When the men came home from war, women would be back in the kitchen again. As far as Lil Ellis was concerned, she could see no other alternative.

'Fancy the flicks?' asked Rosemary, looking for a distraction. 'Supposed to be a good one on at the Bug Hole.'

Lil Ellis said nothing. Just pouted like a kid.

'C'mon, Ma, give ourselves a treat, eh?'

'And won't you be working? You never seem to have time for your old ma now – either working, or got your nose in one of them fancy books of yours. Trying to better yerself! Waste of bleedin' time, for we all know how that works out. They'll hear a Cockney accent and won't want to know no more.'

'Look, you want to go to the flicks or not? I'll come back

early. There's a new Errol Flynn one on. Him and Ann Sheridan. *The Edge of Darkness*, supposed to be good.'

'War film?'

'Think so,' said Rose.

'We got enough war of our own without going out to watch it, Rose.'

'Yeah, but this one's different. It's about Norway. All that lovely scenery, and they ski and do all sorts, I expect.'

'And why would I want to see that?'

'Good to see other places, Ma. And travel. I always wanted to travel.'

'Your da's travelled, now. Seen other places. Don't 'spect it's done him no good.'

You couldn't win. Rosemary slammed the front door behind her, left her ma to her own brand of misery. *Course* it was good to see other places, travel the world. Look at different people, see how they got on with life. And that's what she'd do. She had her mind set on it. Meanwhile, there was a war to get on with.

The cold wind blew through her flimsy jacket, and Rosemary promised herself that whenever she had the chance to start these travels of hers, she would begin with somewhere warm. A place with blue sky, for a change. And an ocean. And golden sands that stretched for miles.

Rose came home early, as promised. Her ma was hovering by the front door, waiting, jumpy, an expectant look on her face. Rose took the envelope her ma impatiently thrust at her – and tried not to smile.

Lil reminded her of a cat getting ready to pounce on an unfortunate mouse that had got in her way.

Rosemary turned the envelope over in her hands, inspected it.

'It won't open itself, will it?' said Lil.

The postmark said Tiverton, Devon. So it must be from Alistair. But she was puzzled. How could it possibly be sent from there? He wasn't *there*, and his leave had been over weeks ago now.

She gave it a closer inspection. Nothing written on the back, and her address in Royston Street on the front. A reply to the letter she sent him? She'd posted it to his home address, although he'd said he wasn't travelling there for the rest of his leave. He wanted a change, he'd said. That was why he'd gone to Margate. But Rosemary knew he lived with his sister in this place in Devon, had hoped the sister would be kind enough to forward her letter to Captain Alistair Greenway.

'Some kind of fancy perfume on there,' said Lil.

Rosemary sniffed the envelope. Her mother was right; there was definitely the faint trace of perfume, and not the cheap scent that Lil used to douse herself with. That was called Night in Paris, used to come from Woolworths, but you couldn't even get that now.

She tore open the letter, took a long time to read it. It was from Alistair's sister. Not him.

She reread it. And when she looked up, there was a fine film of tears in Rosemary's eyes.

'That's that, then,' said Rose.

'What? This one's been kilt as *well*?' Lil Ellis ripped the letter from her daughter's hand.

'No,' Rosemary said, quietly. 'He's not dead, Ma. Might as well be, though. He's getting married.'

'Swine!' said Lil.

'Not that I even thought about marrying the bloke,' said Rose. 'But he seemed nice.'

'You and men, Rose. You ain't got no luck.'

Her ma seemed to struggle with the letter, the same as Rose. The language was stilted and formal, not a friendly letter.

'Well, the jumped-up little bitch...'

'Ma! Language.'

'I'll give you language,' said her mother. 'We're not good enough, eh?'

'That's not what the woman said, Ma.'

'Yes, it is. Only in more poxy, affected bloody words. Not an...? What's that word there, Rose?'

'Appropriate. Means not suitable – not proper.'

'Of course you're proper. That's how we brought you up, our Rose.'

'The match, she means – between me and him.'

'Stuck-up snob. And "East End slum", what the feck she mean by that? Our house might be small, with an outside lav, but it's clean and neat. I've always kept it neat; you know that, Rose. Rugs beaten. Front step shinin'. Sheets changed every week. It ain't no bleedin' slum.'

'I know, Ma.' Rose went over and hugged her mother. Lil's thin shoulders were shaking with rage. 'Ignore it. Some people just ain't kind,' she said.

'Any rate, this was written by his sister,' said Lil. 'It ain't come from the bloke hisself. *He* didn't say he's getting married. Reckon this woman just wants to split you two up, Rose – being as this so-called fiancée's a friend of hers. We only got her word her brother's even promised. And another thing...'

'Enough, Ma.'

'Why'd she open your letter, Rose? Wasn't addressed to her. Somethin' ain't right here. And the bloke weren't even stayin' there for his leave. Don't reckon he gets on with this sister of his. I ain't even met the woman and she's got on my tits.'

'Ma?'

'What?'

'Leave it.'

They left it.

. . .

But although Rosemary refused to discuss it with her ma, she read the disturbing letter many more times until she knew its hurtful words by heart. The thought of Alistair getting married had shaken her, not because she felt any claim to him – she hadn't known him for long – but they'd had some laughs and a little fun. Enough to forget the war for a while. He'd seemed like a decent man. Not someone who could forget he was already engaged. *But maybe he tricked me*, thought Rose. *If he had, then it was a shabby trick. A surprise.*

Still, her mother was right. *You ain't got no luck*, she'd said. Right to the heart of the matter, that was Lil. You could always rely on her for straight talking. Her ma didn't believe in sugar-coating the truth. But it made Rose feel melancholy and brought back the heartache of losing Danny. As if she'd lost him all over again.

Days went by when she allowed herself to sink into a mist of despair. Watching others around her live their lives, like an outsider looking on. The idea finally touched a nerve, reminded her of the plans they'd made together, Danny and her. He wouldn't want her to be sad. Or waste her life moping like this. He'd always encouraged her to reach high, told her she was intelligent and could do anything she decided to do. So, she kept his voice in her head. And made her plans. She would keep on reading, gathering knowledge, because her ma was wrong. Bettering yourself was *never* a waste of time. And she would find out more about a job with the Red Cross, one she heard they were recruiting candidates for. It was something she thought she'd be good at: tracing people lost in the war. It would be the beginning of a new life. Something she'd be proud to do, and she believed that her Danny would've been proud of her too.

PART TWO

20

LONDON

10 JUNE 1944

A year had passed since that last convivial dinner at the Army and Navy Club. And Frank Usher and Adam Pietersen would see a very different person now. Might even pass Danny Welland on the street and not recognise him. He had grown a full beard and put on weight, most of it muscle from hard training.

He'd been sent to Guilford for his induction, and then up to the wilds of Scotland, where he'd had commando training and special courses in survival. Had even done some parachute jumps.

As his training progressed, and Danny passed out successfully from the commando course, he began to feel more positive, less angry about not being allowed to fly. His confidence came back and he was happy with this new, powerful body of his.

And the best bit was that no one in the SOE had doubted his performance, his ability to carry out these new duties. *One eye or not*, they'd believed in him. And he knew that his Rosie would have as well. The ache was still there – the pain of losing her would never truly go away. But that's what came from finding such a great love – a once-in-a-lifetime love. It also brought great sadness when it was ripped from you. He imagined Rosie would have felt the same way if *he* had died.

He'd come to headquarters for a final briefing before he left England. It was strange coming back to the capital; so much of it had changed, with bombed-out buildings everywhere. And Londoners he passed on the street looked weary, their faces grey. The optimism of the early war years seemed to have vanished to be replaced by a jaded acceptance, and a lack of joy. He understood. He'd tasted the bitter ashes of pessimism and defeat too, when they wouldn't let him fly. But now Danny Welland had been renewed. He had a purpose. He was going somewhere he was needed, back to South Holland.

Déjà vu. He was sitting in the Pig and Whistle, nursing a whisky and waiting for Frank. The pub was even more rundown than the last time he'd been there. The ceiling was stained yellow with years of cigarette smoke and a pall of smoke hung in the air, trapped, the residue from countless Woodbines about to join their predecessors.

The propaganda posters still clung resolutely to the walls. They were worn now, but no one had taken them down (that would amount to treason). A caricature of Hitler glared down at drinkers. Hitler with his massive cartoon ear, listening for every scrap of information dropped carelessly in drunken conversation. And Danny smiled at the RAF recruiting poster: the large, busty blonde balanced on the wing of a bomber, enticing young healthy lads with a love of their country to volunteer, to sign up for the air force and 'give them hell'. Go bomb the bejesus out of the enemy. The posters must have been hanging there for years, Danny reckoned. Now, nobody volunteered. You went where they put you.

He took a healthy slug of the whisky and watched his friend Frank limp his way to the table.

Danny tried not to show his shock at the change in the young man. Frank had always been thin but now he was gaunt, and his face had the unhealthy pallor of too many days and nights inside, trapped in an office. And stress – you could see it ingrained in the deep lines around his eyes.

'Good to see you, old boy.'

'And you,' said Danny. 'What's with the limp?' he asked.

'Lucky, really. Could've been worse. Got caught in a raid and a shop front blew out – beggars didn't have blast tape on their windows. Glass and shrapnel caught the old leg. Still, not as bad as some. Lots of civilians bought it that night. Heard on the grapevine you were off.'

'Oh?'

'Adam gave me the nod. Left some stuff for you. Got it at my place if you fancy the walk.'

'The man's got ears everywhere,' laughed Danny.

'Wanted to see you off himself, but he's on a ship somewhere. Hush-hush stuff, I guess. He didn't say where.'

'He's a good chap,' Danny said. 'Tries to help where he can. Thanks to him, I'm now one of the "Baker Street Irregulars".' He grinned. He was glad to be part of something important at last. Doing a real job.

'Won't ask where you're going, old bean. Walls have ears.' Frank Usher looked around at the rest of the customers. 'Mum's the word, eh!'

'No idea anyway.' Danny winked.

'Shall we?' Frank pointed to the door. 'I could rustle up some coffee, the real stuff. And still got a bit of cheese and some biscuits left.'

They both laughed now. Remembered the first time Frank Usher had said that.

'Real coffee, eh?' said Danny.

'Yep. Things are easing up a bit. Looks like we got the Bosch on the back foot at last.'

'We'll see,' said Danny.

He hoped his friend was right. The allied invasion of France had begun, it was true. D-Day. And some of the war news sounded hopeful. But his friends in Holland were still living under an occupying army, being ruled by the brutal S.S. And how many of them were even still alive? People were starving over there. You heard stories of them eating their precious tulip bulbs. Danny sent up a silent prayer for the lot of them.

―――

A year had gone by since Rosemary had left her old job at the parachute factory. *A year can feel like a lifetime. Or the blink of an eye. Depends on what you filled it with.*

Rosemary smiled to herself. *Self-improvement.* It was a guiding thought and the reason she still kept up her library subscription at Boots and read so eagerly. Her ma didn't approve of course, thought it a waste of money and time. But Danny would have understood. Her thoughts and approach to life were becoming more questioning and analytical. She'd also joined a philosophy group: people who examined the basic ideas behind life, human thought and how society worked. She'd been shy at first – just listened and watched, hesitant to come forward with her own ideas in case they would laugh at her. But she'd been taken seriously by the others, her thoughts respected. And none of them expected her to be stupid just because she had a Cockney accent.

She was going there tonight.

'Fancy the flicks, Rose?' asked her ma.

'Got my group meeting tonight,' said Rosemary.

'What's the point of that la-di-da meeting?' asked Lil.

'We discuss things. Analyse them.'

'What feckin' things?' Her mother's mouth pulled itself into a thin line.

'Everything, Ma. How people live. How they think. What makes the world work. Why it goes wrong and folks kill each other.'

'Good luck with that. Folk been killing each other forever. Nothing your fancy group comes up with likely to stop that!' Lil Ellis flounced off in a huff.

'I'm off to work,' Rosemary shouted at the back of the door. Her ma was barricading herself in the kitchen again, got her dander up easily nowadays. Only to be expected though, what with all the shocks she'd had. Rose had tried to be understanding, but life was hard on all of them. Didn't do to just give in.

She took her coat and headscarf off the hook by the front door and picked up her black leather handbag. A luxury. She still felt guilty about using it every day, when few other women could afford such incredible things. But he'd insisted. *You told me how you wanted to visit France one day, so please take this small gift and promise you'll use it and not just look at it.*

When the magical parcel had first arrived, her heart had done a back flip. *Danny. In France. Still alive.* But it wasn't, of course.

It had come from Captain Alistair Greenway. He'd 'liberated' the beautiful leather bag from a shop not far from Paris. He was part of the British force moving through France. He wasn't allowed to say where exactly, for loose lips cost lives.

Alistair mentioned nothing in his letter about his sister, or his engagement. Which could mean that it wasn't true after all. And that he still had feelings for her; otherwise, why go to all that trouble in the middle of a war to get a parcel to her? They must be powerful feelings. That's what Rosemary's newly discovered analytical skills had told her.

And although the thought was pleasant enough, it didn't

give her the thrill that it might once have done. Rosemary Ellis had changed her outlook on life. Her thoughts about her own unique value in it. She had a worth as a person, as a woman, and she wasn't about to throw that away by becoming second fiddle to any man. Equals, yes.

She had no idea how someone like Captain Alistair Greenway would feel about that. But she knew *exactly* what one very special man had thought. Her Danny. It was then that Rosemary realised something important.

No one could ever take his place. Her fault, perhaps – because she'd set him up there on a pedestal, too high for anyone else to reach.

Rosemary sighed. Deep thoughts, introspection, they were all very well, but they didn't get you to work on time, did they? She shouted goodbye to her mother again and closed the front door quietly behind her.

Strange to think that in a time when bombs were dropping and soldiers were getting killed in foreign places, you could still catch a bus to work. At least that's what Rosemary thought. Buses had their own blackout camouflage, roofs painted black and their headlights shaded, blast mesh over their windows. Some were even converted to run on coal gas, saving precious petrol, pulling strange trailers in their wake to make the gas. But they were still the proud red buses that Londoners knew and loved.

And in its way, it was a small miracle that she was able to get all the way from her home in Bethnal Green to the upper-crust world of St James's Palace enclave – the Red Cross had been given a house there on temporary loan to use as an office. Rosemary had some very classy near-by neighbours, including HM Queen Elizabeth. Her ma had joked that Rosie should pop in for tea with the royal lady – seeing as they were old pals.

On a good day, it took three-quarters of an hour to get to work. But today wasn't a good day and she'd already been stuck on the bus for an hour. There'd been a raid the night before and blokes from the Heavy Rescue Service were still trying to clear the rubble. Sometimes it was like that, after a bad night.

Rosemary drummed her fingers impatiently on the back of the seat in front of her. She'd been anxious to get to work today. Her new job with the Red Cross was a far cry from her old one at the factory. They were poles apart, using different skills. Sewing parachutes took nimble fingers, a practical ability and the work had to be meticulous. All skills that Rosemary had been praised for. But she had rarely been called on to use reasoning or analysis, something that this new job needed, and that Rose had discovered she was good at.

Her work with the Red Cross often brought frustration and even sadness, but there were also times when it gave her overwhelming happiness and satisfaction. Those were the days when her research and patience brought results, when she managed to trace missing people and bring families together again.

She hoped that today would be one of those special days. She'd been busy collecting paperwork for weeks, piecing together POW records, telegrams and letters from a family in the Midlands. They were relying on her – or someone like her. *A tracer.* That's what the Red Cross called her. And it was an important job. Sometimes successful. Most often not. For there were thousands of missing soldiers, airmen, sailors – forty thousand alone left behind when Dunkirk was evacuated. Her father had been one of those, and that's why Rosemary had been particularly anxious to get this very special job.

It was often stressful. There were days when she went home to cry, when she found out that fathers, brothers, sisters, daughters had been killed, rather than just gone missing.

She was expecting a call from Geneva, from the headquarters of the International Committee of the Red Cross. Her ICRS liaison in Switzerland had hinted that the news would be good. It was mostly Geneva who did the main overseas searches, while people like Rose gathered information and did the foot slogging and research – going through records and interviewing relatives. She'd done more travelling in Britain in the last year than she had in the rest of her life.

Rosemary loved her job, the satisfaction she got from reuniting people, of locating prisoners of war. And she worked tirelessly, putting in long hours, as she had at the parachute factory. She hoped that one day she might find her own father. He'd been reported as a POW in Poland, but it wasn't true, for she could find no trace of him. She hadn't told her ma though. Lil didn't need to hear that kind of news.

As she passed through the historic archway and opened the massive mahogany front door with its polished brass, once again Rosemary marvelled at the simple beauty of her surroundings. She would never get jaded by it or take it for granted. It was hard to think of such a grand space as an *office*, and it was the very opposite of the place she had worked before, the sooty brick of the factory. It was bizarre.

'You're here! I was beginning to worry,' her colleague Alice greeted her.

'Been stuck on the bus for ages,' said Rosemary. 'Civil Defence out clearing rubble.'

'Could've walked in,' teased her friend. 'I did last week.'

'Yeah, well, we don't *all* live in a women's hostel practically around the corner from work,' said Rosemary.'

'Could do.'

'You know I can't leave my ma on her own. I'd never do that. She needs me.'

'I'll put on a fresh pot of tea,' said Alice.

Rose smiled. 'Thanks,' she said. 'You're a pal.'

'Am I?' asked Alice. 'You mean it? Are we *proper* pals?'

'Absolutely. We help each other out, don't we?' said Rosemary. 'That's what friends do – and families.'

'Not mine,' said Alice.

Rosemary knew all about Alice's family, or lack of it. There were no brothers. No sisters. An abusive father who was off somewhere fighting in the desert and a mother who had thrown Alice out of the house when she was only sixteen.

That's why Rose had been kind to the girl, had acted like an older sister. Had even covered up for her with the boss who ran the office. She knew that Alice found filing hard, sometimes misplacing records because letters got scrambled up in her head. Letter Ps became Bs and almost magically the letter S turned into the number 5. It was a weird thing that Rose couldn't explain and didn't understand, because her friend Alice was far from stupid. But the girl had been too embarrassed and ashamed to admit it to anyone else, only Rose.

Alice Thompson followed Rose around like an eager puppy, making her tea and doing small errands for her. Sometimes it was embarrassing, but Rose didn't say so. That would be unkind, and Alice had already had enough rejections in her life.

'Thanks,' said Rosemary, when the girl brought in the tea tray. There was even a custard cream biscuit. But then Alice was enterprising, a forager who could always manage to find a supply of biscuits despite the ration.

'You're pure gold, Alice. Twenty-four carats,' said Rose, as she bit into the deliciously sweet treat.

'I'll accept that,' said Alice. 'Closest I'll get to the real thing, I expect.'

'Don't do that,' Rose said.

'What?'

'Lower your expectations,' said Rosemary. 'You have a worth. A value. Put a high one on yourself, even if other people don't.'

'Really? Is that what you do, Rose? Is that how come you're

so confident around that lot in there?' Alice nodded at the door in the corner. The inner sanctum. Where the powers-that-be resided.

'Never gave it much thought,' said Rosemary. 'Except that I know I'm equal to them. Work just as hard.'

Alice smiled. 'So, today's the day,' she said.

'What?'

'The phone call from Switzerland. Aren't you excited?' asked Alice.

'If it works out and we've got the right man, I will be.'

'And then you can celebrate. How will you celebrate, Rose?'

'Ma wanted to go to the flicks. 'Spect I'll take her.'

'Really?'

'Sure. Should be a good one. At least Ma's looking forward to it. A musical, I think.'

'Sounds lovely.'

'Yeah? Think so? Why don't you come with us then?'

'Go on!'

'Why not? You could stay over at my place. Nothing fancy. But we could have a bite to eat, and travel into work tomorrow together. What d'you say?'

'That'd be great.'

'I wouldn't get your hopes up. The Bug Hole isn't exactly luxurious, and we live in a tiny two-up-two-down. But we could have a few laughs, at least. Be like having my baby sister back home again. She's in the Women's Land Army, on a farm in Kent. She loves it.'

Alice Thompson grinned. 'Your sister sounds nice,' she said. 'And whatever your house is like, it'll be wonderful. A hundred times better than going back to that pokey hostel room with no heating and a bunch of stuck-up women who think I'm stupid.'

21

The noise in the Lysander was ear-shattering. You could feel the vibration thrum through your body, hammering like a manic drummer. Thermals were plucking at the small plane, too: one minute the Lizzie was rising, the next plunging as if the sky itself was alive and hostile and might pull the wings off her as easily as if she were a frail butterfly.

But Danny wasn't worried. The pilot wrestled with the controls, fought the elements that were set to destroy the small fragile aircraft. The pilot was good. He won.

'Hope you didn't puke back there,' the man shouted into the headset. 'Had a bloke last week threw up in his mask. Messy business.' The pilot laughed.

'Nope. Had worse on a fairground ride,' said Danny. It wasn't true, of course. The small plane was taking a battering, bucking about all over the sky, but Danny was happy to be back in the air. And relieved. *Parachuted into occupied territory.* That's what they'd told him – these people who were carrying out their secret war. But for some reason, which no one at the Baker Street SOE was prepared to share with him, that had dramatically changed at the last minute to this trip in the Lysander.

A result. At least as far as he was concerned. He hadn't been that keen on a parachute drop. Floating through pitch-black skies that any minute might flood with search lights and pin your white silk canopy in their beam? It wasn't his first choice. He hadn't enjoyed any of his parachute training, but you went where they pointed you. Did what they told you to do. If it helped with the war effort.

Danny sat with the precious briefcase balanced on his knees, his arms cradling it like it was gold dust. And so it was. Nine pounds of hardware in a small attaché case. The 'Paraset' radio transmitter could send and receive messages up to 500 miles away. But he was only the delivery man. He'd had no radio training.

It was a hard, dangerous job being a wireless operator. Their estimated life span behind enemy lines was measured in months rather than years. Then there was the loneliness. Wireless operators were usually lone wolves who worked apart from the rest of the underground cell. Safer that way, so their capture wouldn't bring down the rest of the cell with them. And they had to move around a lot to escape detection from the Germans with their specialised equipment. The Bosch could have a transmission pinpointed in as little as twenty minutes.

Danny had no idea who this new toy would end up with, but he was in awe of that person. Man. Woman. Dutch. French. British. Someone with courage.

'Not long now,' shouted the pilot over the headphones. His voice was deep and slightly accented, sounded Norwegian to Danny's ears. But he didn't ask. The bloke was an experienced flyer, had done a good job in terrible conditions and wore an RAF uniform. That was enough. They were brothers.

Hard to believe he was being infiltrated back into Holland. A strange old world. He wasn't a spy; they'd assured him of that.

But what was in a name? And Danny wasn't naive. He wasn't in uniform, was wearing civilian clothes. So, no matter what any of the Baker Street Irregulars tried to say, the Germans might not feel the same way. They shot spies.

'You about set?' asked the pilot.

'We're there?'

'Couple of minutes. Need to get in and out fast. Natives are getting jumpy, I hear. Can't hang around.'

'Appreciate it. Thanks for the ride.'

'Sure. Hold onto your hat, Squadron Leader. It'll be a bumpy landing.'

It reminded Danny of all the times he had brought his own crate down. And now he was scratched from the active flying list. It had rankled at first when he thought about it, the unfairness of it all. Still – water under the bridge. A chap couldn't afford to be bitter.

Danny and his kit and the precious attaché case were out of the rear cockpit of the Lizzie and down the ladder in record time.

He stumbled, managed to save the radio before it hit the ground.

He saw the hooded torch blink on for a second only, and then it was gone. He didn't need an engraved invitation, got the idea and headed in the direction of the light. He ran fast. The training up in Scotland had made a kind of athlete out of him. He wouldn't win the mile, but he was fitter than he'd ever been – and tougher. Ready for whatever they threw at him.

'What's the time by Big Ben?' a voice whispered in the darkness.

He couldn't be sure, but the voice sounded familiar.

'Zero hour,' he answered. *Damn foolish passwords if you asked him. But then nobody had.*

'*Spreekt u Engels?*' asked Danny.

'*Ja,*' the voice replied. 'I speak little English.'

'Good,' said Danny. His Dutch had deserted him for the moment.

'Okay, we go. Quickly,' said the man.

They both ran in a low crouch, jumped over a wall and landed in a lane on the other side.

A few minutes later they were in the back of a small van, a clapped-out boneshaker with bad suspension and tyres that had too many miles on them. It was only then that Danny relaxed, his hands unclenching from the tense fists he'd forced them into. He thought about the miracle the pilot of the Lysander had performed to get them down without leaving bits of the Lizzie all chewed up in the rutted field.

That's when the man beside him shone the torch into his eyes, and produced a loud belly laugh. 'Okay, British. So, you forget every word of Dutch we teach you, *ja?*'

It was De Groot sprawled on the floor beside him, his huge feet up on the wheel arch. Except it was hard for Danny to tell at first. Only the voice and the massive beard gave it away. Nothing else about the man was the same as before: the skin on his face had sagged into deep lines and pockets where the fat beneath it had retreated, and the clothes he wore hung on him as if they'd been made for someone else. Someone much larger.

'So – the British don't want you. They throw you back to us.' De Groot let loose another huge laugh.

The driver banged on the partition. '*Hou je stil!*'

'She wants us to be quiet,' chuckled De Groot. 'Dry up, she says.'

'She?' Danny asked.

'Ah. *Nee.* It's not Anna. You like it to be Anna – *ja?*'

He couldn't answer. Of course he wanted Anna to be alive. But he felt awkward about seeing her again.

'Anna is an angel compared to *this* one!' De Groot grinned.

'This Beatrix is a she-devil. But useful – *and* brave,' he added grudgingly.

'Anna and Sara – are they...?'

'Both safe. Anna's cycled to Amsterdam, but she'll be back. And Sara? Well – Sara is Sara. She gets older and thinner,' said De Groot. 'But then we all do.'

'I can't believe it's you, William. You're still here.'

'*Ja*. Thanks be the Lord. But we've moved from Jansen's cellar. Allies bombed the whole place. Funny, yes?'

'What is?'

'German Blitzkrieg in '40 got most of Rotterdam, but missed us. Then three years later the *Allies* get us. You British must have a name for that.'

'*Irony*. You got yourselves in the middle of a fight.'

'*Ja*.' De Groot produced a theatrical sigh. 'It's the war. Such things happen.'

Danny took his lead from the tall Dutchman and stretched out his long legs, put his canvas kit bag under his head in a makeshift pillow and tried to get comfortable. It was like resting your head on a railway line, for there were lots of hard lumps in there. Tins of ham and corned beef that Pietersen had left for him. A gift for the Dutchman's family and friends.

It wasn't long before De Groot's snores filled the back of the van. Danny had no idea where they were going, which part of Holland even. He was in their hands. But if William was prepared to sleep, then it could be a long trip. He only knew that he was headed for this new safe-house, wherever that was. No one had told him. The less you knew, the safer it was for all. It was a mantra practised by the Resistance.

He pulled his rough woollen coat tightly around him and checked the attaché case beside him once more. The hard cold ribs of the floor beneath him dug uncomfortably into his back, but if William could sleep in the back of this ancient bone-shaker, then Danny could as well. Tomorrow, he hoped, would see him at his destination and he could deliver his important cargo. Then the real work would begin.

'Middelland,' said Danny. 'I've not been here before. Still Rotterdam, though. A city you know well.'

'Sure. And we're lucky to have a home,' said Anna. 'Not as beautiful as the old one. No garden. No harbour. But so far, it's been safe from the bombing. And Edwin has built some interesting additions to the basement.' Anna laughed. 'We'll go down there soon and you can see for yourself. It's where you'll be spending your time.'

'I have some things for you and Sara. From your father.' Danny recalled the last time he had seen Adam. The huge man had tears in his eyes that he didn't try to hide. His craggy face full of sadness. It was something Adam Pietersen had to battle with, the conflict between doing a useful job for his country and the guilt he felt for having abandoned the family he loved.

Anna's eyes were glazed with unshed tears, he noticed. And she bit her bottom lip to stop it trembling. 'That's kind. How is he? Is he well?'

'He's well. Busy. And he misses you both. Speaks of you often. I'm to give you a kiss from him. You and your mother.'

He gave Anna a discreet peck on the cheek. The sort that he felt a father might give. He wanted no romantic complications, but it seems he failed. He watched her face redden, saw a fleeting look of pleasure pass across it. And Danny felt a strange, nervous excitement as Anna took his hands in her own. Hers were almost as large as his and they were rough and chapped. Working hands. Her face had the look of someone who spent most of her time outdoors and not in a cellar like some of the other Resistance workers. She was still as tall as he remembered. As tall as him, unlike any other woman Danny had known. But she had suffered in the same way De Groot had. Had lost a lot of weight. Like the rest of them, he assumed. *Little food. Not much sleep. And too much stress.*

'Mother's gone to try and buy food. Sometimes there's a little available on the black market. There will always be some who profit from the misery of war. Do you not think so?' And that's when Anna Pietersen broke down and cried.

Her shoulders heaved, and a shockwave moved through her tall, bony frame. Danny circled his arms around her, held her tightly to him. Couldn't bear to see this brave young woman break down in front of him. When he'd known her before, when she'd nursed him, she had always held herself with such pride.

'I'm sorry,' said Anna. 'It's just that Mama's had to sell her wedding ring.'

Danny pushed the jet-black hair away from her eyes, wiped her tears with his hand, and then Anna Pietersen did something that shocked and surprised him. She pressed her mouth to his and kissed him with a passion that made his head reel and left him confused.

And Danny Welland, despite his better judgement, kissed her right back.

22

LONDON

JUNE 1944

'Your mother's nice,' said Alice.

'Really? Not a word either me or my sister Gracie would have picked. Growing up with Ma was...'

'What?'

Rosemary tried to think of a kinder word than the one that came automatically to her lips. Her mother was a hard, exacting woman. Believed in doling out punishment to her kids when she thought they deserved it. But Rose figured there was love there as well. You could sometimes see it when her eyes softened.

'A challenge. *Tough love.* Ma believed in it. Me and Gracie picked up a few smacks round the ear. And Ma can unleash a hard, spiteful tongue when she wants to.'

'Couldn't be easy bringing up kids, though.'

'She was right impressed with you, Alice,' said Rosemary.

'She was?'

'Sure. Said you were a sweet kid who knew her manners.

You definitely made a hit there and bringing her the flowers – that was genius.'

'She gave me dinner and we had a laugh at the flicks,' said Alice. 'It was one of the best nights I've *ever* had.'

Rose looked across the desk at her companion. She suspected that Alice was exaggerating, laying it on thick. It's what people did. But she saw no guile in the young girl's face, just excitement. It was a clue to the kind of life Alice had endured before, and maybe even now. Rosemary hadn't given any thought to what happened once the office was locked up for the night and they went their separate ways. Maybe the girl was lonely.

'We'll do it again sometime. Wait till you taste Ma's stew.'

'I haven't had stew in ages.'

'God knows what she puts in there, but it tastes like actual food. Think she's got something going with old Mr Thomas at the butcher's. He usually finds some scrag end of mutton for her. Under the counter.'

'Well – if you've got time to chat, Alice, you've obviously not got enough work to do.'

Neither of them had heard the door open. But now Alice blushed red and scurried off to try and look busy. The girl was an office junior, but some of them treated her like a slave. Showed her little respect. But then if you didn't have respect for yourself, thought Rose, some people saw it as weakness. Thought you were a doormat to wipe their dirty boots on.

Mr Phillips fired a disdainful look at Alice's retreating back and walked to the coat stand. He was a finicky little man, slow and meticulous. The act of putting on an overcoat and hat might take the normal person a few minutes at most, but Mr Phillips was a perfectionist. Five minutes later, he was still fussily smoothing out the fingers of his black leather gloves and had made no attempt towards the street door.

Rose picked up the yellow document folder from her out

tray, thrust it into the man's hands, and opened the front door for him. 'Don't forget to get them to sign it, Mr Phillips.'

'You don't need to remind me of my job, Miss Ellis.'

'Good.'

When he'd gone, Alice came rushing back from the small kitchen balancing a tea tray. 'Made you some tea, Rose. That was very brave.'

'What was?'

'Telling him what to do like that.'

'He's not my boss. And he's not yours, either. You shouldn't let him talk to you like that.'

'Yes – but I'm just a junior.'

'And he's just a messenger. Besides, nobody's *just* anything. We're all equal human beings, and even if he were your boss, he should treat you with respect.'

'Is that what your ma taught you?'

'Nope, I figured that out all by myself, Alice.' Rosemary laughed. 'Something I wanted to ask you.'

'Really?' said Alice.

'Somebody in my library group told me about this course the WEA is running. Sounds exciting.'

'What's the WEA?'

'The Workers' Education Association. Anyway, I've decided to do it. It's only once a week. Maybe you'd like to come along. We could go together after work. Fancy it?'

It would be good to have a companion, someone to share her studies with, but even if Alice wasn't keen, Rosemary was still excited about the new class. It was as if she had suddenly come out of the dark into the sunlight; the world of learning had revealed such thrilling possibilities for her, opened up her eyes.

'I've never been much good at book learning. Takes me a while to read all the words. Not that I'm stupid...'

'No. You're not stupid,' said Rosemary. 'And don't you let

anybody tell you that. C'mon – it'd be fun. And I'd help you figure it out.'

'Maybe. I'm not sure. It's not mathematics, is it? 'Cause I'm not too fond of sums.'

Rosemary laughed. 'No. It's learning all about other countries. European Studies, it's called, and they also teach you some beginner's French. I've always wanted to learn French. Say you'll come. We could go back to my house after. I'm sure Ma would love to see you again and make a fuss of you.'

'Sure she wouldn't mind?' asked Alice.

'She's missing my little sister. Maybe she's looking for somebody else to mother.' *Or to boss around*, thought Rosemary. But she didn't say that. She figured Alice Thompson already had enough on her mind.

———

Guilt and confusion sat heavily on Danny's shoulders. He couldn't shrug the feelings off, for Anna's absence had bought him a reprieve. *And what kind of man did that make him?* But it had been hard to look her in the eye since that kiss – and not just one kiss, either. That was the most confusing. There had been several. And now Anna had the idea that he was in love with her. He'd seen it in her face.

It didn't matter that he hadn't *meant* to lead her on, for Anna was young, naive, had no experience with men, and he was six years older. He should have known better.

Guilt prodded him, a reminder that the girl was off doing something dangerous, something he should have taken on. But she'd insisted on delivering the new radio transmitter, said it was safer that way, until his Dutch was up to scratch.

There'd been some *incidents* lately. She and Edwin had glossed over them, but it was why Danny's parachute jump had been cancelled and they'd ended up landing. Some agents had been parachuted in and been riddled with bullets before they'd even touched the ground, the Germans waiting for them. Even so, he'd wanted to deliver the radio, but Anna insisted it was her job. And he already knew that once she'd set her mind on something, there was no holding her back. In that respect, Anna Pietersen was exactly like her father.

Meanwhile, Danny was a conflicted man. On the one hand, he wanted no harm to come to Anna. If the Bosch discovered her with the illicit radio, she would be transported to a concentration camp, or perhaps even executed. He *wanted* her safe return, but then he would have to deal with a strong young woman with love in her eyes, and maybe even marriage on her mind.

The others threw winks at him. Like they knew of his dilemma. Edwin definitely did, for the big man went into great detail about what happens when a fish is first caught on a hook. How he may twist and turn and wriggle and fight for his freedom, but eventually the fish becomes exhausted with the battle and gives in – gratefully.

Edwin grinned every time he saw Danny. And now he thumped him on the back, like a conspirator who shared a secret.

'Not easy being a courier,' said Edwin. 'Need to be fearless. She's a brave woman. *And* strong. Comes from good Dutch stock.'

'Who, Beatrix? She'd eat you alive, man.' De Groot looked up, his hands black from trying to fix the ailing duplicating machine.

'Both fine women. But you'd need to sleep with one eye open with that Beatrix,' chuckled Edwin. 'No – it's Anna who's fond of our young friend here,' he continued. 'Though what she sees in that ugly face, God Himself could only tell us.'

Danny let them have their fun. For despite his problem with Anna, Danny Welland was happy to be back there among good friends, brushing up his Dutch, throwing himself into the planning of this new escape line. It gave him a purpose.

He was to be a liaison for the new underground line. Much of the planning had already been put in motion by the Dutch Resistance network, the hard work done by Edwin.

Edwin had also made some special innovations to the cellar in this new safe-house. At first glance it appeared as what you might expect, although someone with a surveyor's eye and knowledge might well have noticed a discrepancy in the width and area of the underground space.

Behind the shelves in the cellar was a large hidden compartment where, in an emergency – like the Germans deciding to run one of their periodic raids – up to twenty people could successfully, but not luxuriously, be hidden for a few desperate days. There was bedding and water and candles in there.

Luckily no one had needed to put these emergency evacuation measures to the test. On first inspection, although Danny could appreciate the workmanship and the idea behind this hidden Aladdin's cave, it gave him a choking feeling of claustrophobia. *Better to be in there than captured by the Bosch, of course. But only just,* he reckoned.

Danny's job in this new escape line was to be a friendly face, a go-between and translator, once the British and American airmen and soldiers, who'd been trapped all over Holland, finally made their way here. To get them ready for the journey onward to Belgium.

It sounded easy. But nothing in this war was ever as easy as it sounded. And now that the Germans were on the back foot they were becoming even more vicious.

The sting of a dying scorpion.

23

'What in God's name got into her, Ma?' *Unbelievable.* Rosemary picked up her sister's letter from where she'd dropped it on the kitchen table.

'Mind your language. We don't take God's name in vain in *this* house. You know that!' But Lil was just as upset as her daughter. It had been a shock. Right out of the blue like that. No warning.

'Maybe she really loves the man,' said Rose. She wanted to believe that. 'But he's forty and she's eighteen. How will that work? She's looking for a father, not a husband and a mate.'

'My Gawd, Rose, I just realised...'

So, it was okay for Ma to take God's name in vain then. Just not her!

'What?'

'When our Gracie's forty, this bloke – he'll be sixty-odd.'

'Sixty-two,' said Rosemary. 'But don't let's get ahead of ourselves.'

'Meaning what?' asked Lil. 'She's already feckin' done it. Gone and married the man. And not so much as an invite for her poor old mother.'

'Wartime,' said Rosemary. 'Quickie wedding in a register office. People do it all the time now. Soldiers before they go off.'

'Well, it ain't right. Not to my mind. And a *farmer!*'

'Nothing wrong with being a farmer,' said Rose. 'Country needs them.'

Lil Ellis went and made them a pot of tea. Her hand shook as she poured the dark brown liquid into the teacups. Best teacups. From the sideboard. Seemed right. Being as it was a sort of celebration. Her youngest daughter married.

'So, you going there? Like she asked you?' said Lil.

'Can't do it. Got something really important on at work.'

'That ain't like before, then. When you worked at the factory you was happy enough to drop everything and go and visit your sister.'

'That was different.' And so it was. It had been an important job, certainly, making parachutes that might one day save an airman, but it wasn't something she'd intended doing for the rest of her life. *But this one...* Rosemary Ellis had at last found her rightful place in the world. A job that stretched her, made her fulfilled. And there was a secret that she'd been holding on to. Too precious to share with anyone, in case giving voice to it might make the possibility disappear.

Her boss, Miss Simons, knew that Rose had been trying to learn French. Had encouraged her in her ambition. French, she'd said, would be a useful language to have in their line of work. And who knew, after the war ended (*and please God it would end soon*) there would be places in the organisation for someone like Rose. Someone with skills. A woman with ambition and insight.

Rosemary hadn't realised that she possessed 'insight', but Miss Simons was a clever woman who could see potential. A career woman. Someone who Rosemary looked up to for her single-minded dedication to her work. The woman had no husband. No family. Seemed to have happily swapped those for her job. *But surely a woman could have both?*

Rosemary smiled. The man would have to be special, progressive in his ideas. A thoughtful, analytical man. She felt herself redden, because there was such a man in her philosophy group. He'd taken a close interest in her, had invited her out several times, but she'd always shied away. Geoffrey was an older man. Thirty-one. Nine years older than she was. But maybe that wasn't so bad after all. Not twenty-two years difference in their age, like her sister Gracie's new husband.

Maybe she'd take Geoffrey up on his invitation next week when they met. To watch a film with him. And to let him help with her French studies. What was there to lose? Her sister Gracie would say that there was one VERY important thing to lose. Rosemary felt the blush from her neck move upwards until her cheeks burnt with it. She was only twenty-two. There was still time. And the words of her sister rung in her ears once again: *Do you want to be a virgin all your life?* No. She didn't. Then again, she didn't want to throw away something precious on a man who didn't deserve it.

'Penny for them?' Her mother had that cunning look back in her eye. *It's like Ma can read your hidden thoughts.*

'They're not worth a penny,' said Rosemary.

'I know you. I've looked in your eyes many times, Rose. I can see when you're hiding stuff.'

'Stuff? What stuff, Ma?'

'You've been real chirpy lately. Like some kind of happiness has landed on you and stuck there. Out with it.'

'Out with what? There's nothing to tell.'

'You've got a bloke, haven't you? Some bloke in work, or that fancy French class you go to over in Edmonton.'

'There's no bloke, Ma. Forget that. It's all in your mind.'

Spooky. A mind reader, that's what the woman was. They could use her as a secret weapon against Hitler.

'Do you good,' said her ma. 'Every woman should have a bloke to take care of her.' Lil Ellis let go a small, regretful sigh. It had been a long time since she'd had a cuddle from her own man. Not that Harry was a romantic sort of chap, but he did the necessary. And every married woman had needs.

'I don't need a bloke to take care of me. I want a chap who'll treat me as an equal. Marriage should be a contract between two partners of equal value.'

'Who told you that, Rose?' Lil laughed. 'Somebody in that fancy group of yours?'

'You'll see. There are men out there. Men who value a woman.'

'Yeah. For their ability to lie on their back. And wipe the snotty noses of their kids. And make suet pud on a Sunday.'

'Not just that. For their intelligence – their *minds*.'

Lil Ellis looked at her daughter's intense expression and chuckled. 'Sure they value them. But only if these women of yours keep their *minds* in their knickers. I think you'll find that's where most blokes are looking.'

'You're wrong, Ma. Things are changing. This war's made people start thinking.'

'Grow up,' said Lil. 'This is *real* life. Nothing's changing.'

———

It was almost like she was on the rebound. Rosemary wanted to prove her ma wrong. She set off for the library and the discussion group, her mother's pessimistic words echoing in her ears. Of course things were changing. And not all men were the same: out for themselves; out for sex with no consequences – like the American who got her sister pregnant and then cleared off.

She didn't exactly throw herself at Geoffrey Turner, but when he sat down next to her, she didn't discourage him this time. This seemed to embolden him, at least enough to ask her out to the pub for a drink afterwards. She accepted. It was Friday night. No work tomorrow. Why not?

In the busy pub, Geoffrey apologised for the way he had to incline his head towards her. A burst eardrum made it hard for him to hear. It's what had kept him out of the forces.

He was a man with lots of facts at his fingertips. And they tumbled rapidly from his lips, as if they'd been trapped in his head for a long time just waiting for someone to show an interest in them. He made her head spin. Or maybe that was the gin. She'd had two already.

Geoffrey Turner spoke about places he'd travelled to, strange things he'd seen. But somehow his voice, all in the same humdrum timbre, did nothing to bring those places to life. When he offered, Rosemary accepted another drink – and after it, felt just a little tiddly. She should be getting home soon.

She got up from the chair. A mite wobbly, if she was honest. But he put his hand gently on hers. 'Must you leave so soon? I thought you were enjoying yourself.'

'It's been very nice, Mr Turner.'

'Oh, *Geoffrey*, surely – now that we've put the world to rights between us.' He laughed.

He had a nice laugh. She had to give him that. And Geoffrey wasn't a bad name. Had a sensitive ring to it. And maybe he was sensitive too. Or was that just the gin talking? Maybe what he really was, was boring. She giggled as well.

'Another drink,' he said.

'If I didn't know better, *Geoffrey* – I'd think you were trying to get me drunk.'

'Good grief, no. Just a pleasant night out with a like-minded spirit. Forgive the pun,' he said and smiled.

A nice smile too. Everything about the man was *nice*. Not

earth-shattering. Not the sand-blasting of her soul that had happened when Danny had entered and exited her life. But maybe that was good. Just running Danny Welland's name through her mind still had the ability to rock her to the core.

Rosemary tossed back the rest of her drink. Looked at the other one he had put on the table in front of her.

This was the time she would have told her sister to run.

Run before you did something stupid you might regret.

But she didn't run.

She couldn't give Danny the gift she wanted to – the gift of her virginity. And if Danny couldn't have it, then it had no value, no worth. Why was she saving it? Somebody might as well have it. *And her sister would no longer be able to call her the Virgin Mary.*

24

'So,' said Lil, 'we got that straight then? You'll ask young Alice over for the weekend?'

'I said so, didn't I?'

'What's eating you? You been snappy since you went to that meeting of yours last week. They been putting more daft ideas in your head, girl? Want me to go over there and sort them?'

'Leave it, Ma. You can't always fix stuff. I'm a big girl now. I need to sort my own life out.' Rosemary hung her head in misery. That was right. She needed to get this mess fixed. A mess of her own creation.

'Ah *ha*, that's it! I *knew* it. There's some bloke behind this.'

'Behind what? There's nothing, I told you,' said Rosemary.

'Mooning around like a lovesick bleedin' fool. It ain't like you, Rose.'

'It's not love.'

'Sex, then. It's sex, ain't it? Finally got yerself sorted.' Lil Ellis grinned. 'And it's got you all confused. 'Cause maybe it weren't this lovey-dovey candy floss and fireworks silliness that you thought it was. That you read about in those magazines of yours.'

'I didn't say that.'

'You didn't have to. A mother knows. Got that look in your eye. Well, I just hope you been careful. Don't want no grief about unwanted little sprogs running around.'

'Ma! Stop that. I'm not stupid, am I?'

'Heat of the moment, don't matter how clever you think you are. Passion takes a hold.'

If she didn't feel so miserable, Rosemary would have laughed. *Passion?* There'd been no passion involved. She thought back to the embarrassed fumbling of them both that night. It hadn't been what she'd expected. Her mother was right. But maybe that had something to do with her being drunk, and him being the wrong man. And in the end, *not* a nice man. And definitely a man with *no* passion.

That wasn't the worst bit. He'd asked her out again. She'd rolled out a pathetic excuse, but he'd been persistent. And yesterday, on the bus to work, he'd miraculously appeared, taken the seat next to her. And in front of the whole damn bus, he'd got down on one knee and produced a ring from his pocket; one he said had been his grandmother's. He'd refused to get up off the floor till she said yes.

People on the bus had clapped and cheered. *A bloody circus.* And they'd made her feel like a criminal when she'd refused the bloke. Rosemary had tried her best to let him down gently. *It wasn't him,* she'd insisted. It was *her*. She couldn't marry anyone. She would *never* marry anyone. She just wasn't the marrying kind. She wanted a career. To better herself. To learn things. And to travel the world. There wasn't room for a man in her plans.

Geoffrey Turner had left the bus an angry man. And he had fired one last hurtful salvo at her. She would never better herself. She was just a little tart from the East End and no amount of education could ever wipe that out, or her accent.

She'd thought he was a sensitive man. A cultured man.

Someone who believed that all people whatever their rank or station should be treated with equality, with dignity. Those were the theories he'd expounded at the discussion group. But Rosemary had been wrong about him. She'd been naive. And he'd been a liar. He only believed in those principles when they didn't affect him. When they hadn't been put to the test. He was a hypocrite. Geoffrey Turner was just the same as the rest of them who believed in the class system. He was a middle-class man who didn't want his happy little bubble tainted by somebody from the working class. Someone he thought was inferior. Someone born in the East End of London. Somebody with a Cockney accent. Lose the accent, pretend you're someone else and that would be fine by him. She'd be *allowed* to move one rung up the ladder and join him.

Well, Rosemary Ellis had one thing to say to people like Geoffrey. She was proud of who she was. She would make her way in the world, not despite where she came from, but because of it. And she would never, ever forget where she came from. *Or lose her accent.*

Alice looked so miserable that Rosemary forgot her own problems.

'He giving you grief again?' Her eyes went towards the small cubicle where the office messenger, Mr Phillips, reigned over his fussy little kingdom.

A huge shudder overtook Alice and the gullies in her eyes filled with plump tears, ready to roll down her sad, pale face. 'No. It's not him.' *Another shudder.* 'It's nobody here.'

'Who then, Alice?' Rosemary put her arm around the girl. The young woman's body was thin, almost skeletal. She was younger than Rose but much taller, and her gangling height often made her awkward and clumsy, adding to her lack of self-esteem. Liquid from her nose joined the tears and Rosemary pulled a handkerchief from her pocket, one that her ma had made her for Christmas. Her sister Gracie had one the same. And they were only to be used for *emergencies*; Lil had been keen to stress that.

This *was* an emergency.

She wiped the tears from her young friend's eyes, handed Alice the handkerchief, and steered them both towards the ladies' bathroom.

'What's this about?' she asked.

'You'll think I'm silly,' said Alice. 'You'll think I'm weak – but I'm not, Rose. I try my best to ignore them. To put up with them. *Dignity* – that's what you said was important. Respecting yourself. And I've tried to do that, honestly – I've tried my very best. But they still won't leave me alone. Keep making fun of me. Get me to read posters and stuff, and I panic, get it all wrong. They think it's a great joke.'

'That lot at the hostel?'

'They keep saying I'm weird.'

'If you're weird, then we should all be so lucky.'

'Think so?'

'I think you're brave. That's what I think. Now, blow your nose and go back to work. We'll pick your stuff up from that digs of yours when we close up – and you're coming to stay at our place.'

The day moved on slowly, seemed to last forever. How was it that good times went by so quickly, but the bad ones filled an eternity? Of course it only seemed that way to Rosemary, that the day dragged its feet, because she didn't relish the thought of going home unannounced with a 'boarder'.

Her ma would most likely be okay with a visit from Alice Thompson. After all, she'd invited her for the weekend. Lil had a soft spot for the young woman. Hard to find softness in her mother at times, but somehow Alice had tapped into it. That was fine and dandy. But how would she explain that the arrangement might have to go on for some time?

Alice had nowhere to live, needed a safe bolthole away from the women who had made her life miserable. People could be unkind. Some of them saw difference as a reason to make themselves feel better about who they were. *Don't get her started.* Between those idiots at the hostel and having to go back to the philosophy group and face Geoffrey bleedin' Turner, life wasn't always a bundle of laughs – but you had to get on with it. And so she would. Rosemary was determined. She wouldn't let him stop her going. She hadn't done anything wrong, and she could marry who she damn well pleased. Or not. Answered to no one but herself. Let them all put that in their philosophical-bloody-pipe and bleedin' smoke it.

———

How easy that had been! Lil Ellis had been thrilled when Rosemary brought her friend Alice back home again. She enjoyed the young woman's company.

'It's a bit tricky,' explained Rosemary.

'What is?' her ma asked.

'The situation with Alice,' she'd said. She'd waited until the young woman had left the room to put her few belongings up in Rose's bedroom.

'I ain't exactly blind. I can see she's been crying.'

'She needs somewhere to stay, Ma. Least for a time, till we can find her some new digs.'

'And she'd be paying for these new digs, would she?' asked Lil.

'Well, yes. But places that take young women – hostels and the like – they're not that easy to find quickly.'

'I see.' Lil went over to put the kettle on. When in doubt, tea was always a good idea.

'Do you?'

'I understand, Rose. We need to take this wee girl under our wing. Protect her. She ain't got nobody else. Or am I wrong? Somebody else there for her?'

'No. Alice's got nobody. And those idiots at the hostel been giving her grief.'

'So...'

'What? What's on your mind, Ma?'

'I could always get a spare mattress. Ivy's got one she's been lookin' to get rid of.'

'And?'

'We could put it on your bedroom floor. And this money she'd be paying for her hostel – no reason she couldn't pay it to us, right? And she likes it here, she's said so. She could throw her ration book in with ours and we could give her bed and lodgings. That okay with you, Rose? And it's not like your sister's coming back, her being a married woman an' all, and living on a farm.'

Rosemary was dumbstruck. It was a solution she'd never thought of. One that would work out for all of them. Her ma would be happy, for she'd have company when Rose went out to her classes. And Alice would be happy because she'd have somewhere to live and more decent grub than she'd been getting. And she'd have a real family at last, warts and all. And Rosemary wouldn't mind sharing her floor. She liked Alice. Alice who treated her like an older sister.

Someone other than her mother to talk to. Someone to ride the bus to work with. Her mother was a sly old fox. There was more than one sort of intelligence. Common sense was a special kind, and Lil Ellis had it by the bucketload. A result all round.

25

ROTTERDAM

JUNE 1944

They heard Sara Pietersen long before the first screams began. Heard her clattering noisily upstairs above them. Warning them. For a small woman, she made a lot of noise. *For a thin woman with next to no weight.* And then the buzzer sounded in the basement.

They'd tried the buzzer out before, just a dry run, to make sure the wiring was connected properly and the emergency signal worked. No one would have hit the thing again, not even by accident. They had all been very clear on that. *No ambiguity.* If it sounded again, it meant the real thing: the Gestapo was on their doorstep.

There was no panic. They were adults. Experienced adults who'd been fighting this secret war for many years now. In the basement, they each went to their allotted tasks quietly, smoothly, opening the hidden compartment behind the stained shelving, and making sure there was nothing left out that would betray their presence behind the barricade that Edwin had fashioned. Good enough. Best they could do in the circumstances.

Danny had been surprised by his immediate thoughts. They had not been for himself or for Edwin and De Groot down here with him; his first thought had been for Anna. Relief that she had gone to the capital, would not be caught here like a rat in a trap. And his second thought had been for Sara. She was a brave, stalwart woman. She'd suffered her share of heartache and deprivation already. Danny wished he could spare her any more. But it didn't work like that. They all knew it. No matter how much they all loved Sara Pietersen, no one could help her now. *Fate*. That would be her saviour – or her nemesis.

It was hard to listen to. The sound of the jackboots above. The angry orders meant to intimidate. Sara was alone. She was a proud woman, and courageous, but it was hard to be brave when you were alone, when vicious men were threatening you, laying into you with their fists.

Like the rest of them, Danny heard her screams, wanted to go out there and help her. Save her from the boots that would be landing their brutal, callous kicks into her stomach. Fists punching her in the face. Blood choking her, filling her mouth, her nose. Her eyes closed. All these pictures were sharp in Danny's mind as he imagined them.

He remembered Adam Pietersen, and how kind the man had been to him. How the Dutchman had been conflicted, tugged between his love for his family, his guilt at leaving them and his love for his country.

If there was a chance, even a small one, they had to try and save his wife, Sara.

The thought made Danny move towards the concealed door. But Edwin saw him, pinned him strongly by the arms, and De Groot put his large hands over Danny's mouth before he could give away their presence here.

Sara was a lost cause. But with any luck, the rest of them could carry on the fight.

Under cover of darkness, the three silent figures moved through the city. They all carried rucksacks with the more incriminating things from the safe-house hidden inside. De Groot took the heaviest one. He'd insisted on it. Big man, big weight. It was digging painfully into his shoulders, but he didn't complain. None of them did. Their burdens were nothing compared to the one Sara had to bear. They didn't know if she was alive or dead, where she had been taken, if she was being interrogated. It was likely she would tell them nothing. But you never knew. A body could only stand so much pain before you went insane with it, and told everything you knew.

Danny had thrown up several times thinking about her, imagining the kind of torture they might subject her to. Hoping she was already dead. And Anna. *What about Anna?*

'She knows. Once she sees the signal, she'll follow us to the other safe-house.'

'What?' said Danny.

'Anna. You asked about Anna. She'll know what to do. She's not a child, and she's done this before. We all have,' said Edwin.

He hadn't realised he'd spoken her name aloud. Thought the question had simply been in his head. *Fear and trauma.* The twin evils that emasculate you; make your brain seize up. He wouldn't let that happen. He'd been in danger before. Had found his courage and survived.

Hours later they arrived at another safe-house. Danny had no idea which part of the city they were in. Still Rotterdam. But it didn't matter. All he could think about were the gruesome images his mind had conjured up of Sara Pietersen's haunted face with blood gushing from it, matting her hair, running into her eyes. And the brutes that had taken her – callous bullies, all of them. A tiny woman at their mercy, with no means to fight back. He threw up again. In the garden of a rundown tenement block. All over his own shoes.

The others laughed at him. There hadn't been much to laugh about lately, and it broke the tension.

'So,' said Edwin, 'a bad night.'

'*Ja*,' agreed De Groot.

'And now?' asked Danny. 'What do we do now?'

'We wait,' said Edwin. 'For Anna. And for any news of Sara. Good or bad. We'll soon hear.'

'The bad quicker than the good, I think,' said De Groot. 'People are happier spreading bad news.' He shrugged his shoulders. 'It's the way of the world.'

'Bastards!' said Danny.

'Yes. Sadness follows us, I'm afraid,' Edwin said.

'But, Sara... we have to do something,' said Danny.

'Like what? Knock on the front door of Gestapo headquarters and ask for our friend back? And make no mistake, Dan – we *all* love Sara Pietersen. We knew her better than you did. A good woman. A loyal friend to all here. But that would be the same as destroying the whole cell. You see that, don't you?'

'So, what – we just leave her there?' asked Danny.

'We wait,' Edwin said, and shrugged. 'You'll get used to it. We've all had to. Meanwhile, let's unpack and settle into our new *luxurious* quarters. Which, I should like to point out, even has a kitchen,' he added.

Danny tried to think of a word that meant the opposite of luxurious. He'd already taken a tour of their new base and the inevitable cellar where they'd all spend most of their time. It was cold and smelled foul and the Spartans would have felt at home there. But, as Edwin had pointed out, at least it had a kitchen.

So, Danny made himself useful, brewing up coffee, *real coffee*, from the store of goodies that Adam Pietersen had sent.

They had been frugal with it so far, but Danny believed that now was the time when spirits needed a boost. And he was right. The black, glutinous coffee worked a treat. It warmed them up and prepared them for the Herculean task ahead of trying to make their surroundings less derelict and more like a home.

An hour later, they had more coffee and opened up the precious corned beef. It was a muted celebration. Not a lot to celebrate, except that Anna had arrived and she was safe. When she found out about her mother, the young woman was distraught. She turned to Danny for comfort and spent the rest of the night sitting on the dusty, cold basement floor, nestled in his arms. She finally fell asleep and he went upstairs to the others, hoping for news. None yet. Which in its own way was good, because if De Groot was right in his prediction, the bad news would come quickly.

'And what about the escape line?' asked Dan. 'I suppose that's buggered now.'

'You give up too easily, British. We get a message through and the radio operator will pass it on. Just a setback. We're all still here.'

'And who'll take the message?' said Danny. 'Anna? Don't say Anna. She's in no state to do that now. She'll give herself away.'

'Not Anna, no,' said Edwin. 'Beatrix can do that. And we'll need to get started on a new crawl space down in the basement.'

'Good idea,' said De Groot. 'The last one was a lifesaver.'

'Not for Sara,' said Danny.

'No, not for Sara,' Edwin agreed. 'But let's at least try and keep Anna safe.'

'I'll go back down,' said Danny. 'Don't want her to wake up on her own. Got any bedding I can take her?'

He went back to the damp, mouldy basement, slipped a pillow under Anna's head and covered her with a thick twill blanket. She deserved better. Despite her height, she looked so young and vulnerable there, her face relaxed in sleep. Like a child. But she wasn't, of course. She was a grown woman, had been forced to grow up quickly, living through a war in occupied territory, doing dangerous things that no young woman should ever be asked to do. But she'd done them willingly. No father to spoil her. And now no mother. An orphan. Little orphan Anna. He smiled, thinly. She wouldn't want anyone feeling sorry for her, was strong like her mother, pig-headed and determined like her father.

Anna had a strange quality in her face that drew you in. That drew *him* in. Gently, he moved the hair away from her face. She'd let her hair grow now – much more feminine than the last style she'd had when he'd been here before. It made her look like a child from a fairy tale.

He planted a kiss on her forehead and one on each cheek. And before he knew it, Danny was kissing her mouth. Not a simple peck, but the hungry, full-mouthed kind that woke Anna Pietersen from her troubled sleep, and encouraged her to kiss him back with the same ferocity. And before either of them could help themselves they gave in to their basic human needs. It didn't feel like sex, just a gentle osmosis, when two bodies turn into one.

26

BETHNAL GREEN, LONDON

21 AUGUST 1944

'He don't look too bad. What d'you think, Alice?'
'He has a nice face, Mrs Ellis.'
'Told you to call me Ma,' said Lil.
Alice Thompson blushed. And Lil stared once again at the photograph, trying to look behind the flat façade of the portrait.
'They look happy. Don't you think so, Rose?'
'Yes,' said Rosemary. And they did. If you put those two in a room with a hundred people, they would find their way to each other. Would light up the room with their happiness.
'Think he looks old?' asked Lil. 'This Joe.' She threw the question out to whoever was up for it. Rosemary caught it. She knew her ma. Knew she needed reassurance that Gracie had done the right thing.
'Not a day over ten,' Rosemary said.
'C'mon, Rose, this is important.'
'No, he doesn't look old, Ma. The man could easily pass for thirty. And what's it matter what he looks like, anyway? He

obviously dotes on her. Look at the face on him. Grinning like a lovesick fool.'

'Few months with our Gracie, he'll soon get over that.' Lil laughed. But she was pleased. Pleased with the photograph that would end up right next to Rose's award in its fancy golden frame.

They'd been surprised and excited by the post. There'd been a very long letter from Grace, as well as this picture taken outside the register office, with the newly married couple both beaming like kids who'd met Father Christmas.

Her sister looked well in a grey tweed suit and tiny pill-box hat with a veil on it. Rose had never seen the hat before. *Something old, something new, something borrowed, something blue.* The suit was 'utility' – a simple, practical style of clothes that were inexpensive, didn't use extra material for fancy frills. An idea brought in by the government to save wartime resources. Plain, unadorned, yet Gracie wore it like a Paris model. Rose wasn't surprised her sister could pull that off. Glamorous, even in tweed. The bloke had a suit on. Like it was a special occasion. A suit borrowed from a mate, maybe, for it didn't fit him. But he wore it with the kind of pride that came from knowing this was the day in his life he would remember, when everything else had faded. It gave a special quality to the man, and the suit.

As well as the letter, there'd been a postcard delivered to Royston Street. A postcard with a photograph of the Eiffel Tower on it. Not much information – just signed by Alistair Greenway (Captain) along with the words: 'We've done it!'

Rosemary filled in the blanks by herself. Paris had finally been liberated. All three of them had sat in the parlour a few nights ago listening to the exciting news on the radio. It was a scene played out in countless homes around the country, people waiting to hear the deep voice of Alvar Lidell as he read the news in that calm, reassuring way that had become his trademark. A man you felt could be trusted. A man you could believe. Someone with gravitas whose words held not only weight and authority, but also comfort. A friend you invited into your parlour.

They'd all cheered when he delivered those words. *Paris was free!*

But while of course that was great news, it didn't mean that Hitler had given up. For the last few months those terrible V1 rockets had been landing in London. Flying bombs – horrible frightening things that people were calling 'doodlebugs' and 'buzz bombs'. Their targets were random and they just fell to earth when their engines cut out. They made a sinister buzzing noise, but when that sound stopped, that's when you'd need to worry – and pray that these strange bombs with wings would pass you by, fall to earth somewhere else.

'He still fancies you, then,' said her ma.

'Who?'

'*Who*, she says!' Lil rolled her eyes to the ceiling. 'The fancy army captain what sent you the French handbag. That's *who*.'

'We're just friends,' said Rose. *Ships that pass in the night*, she thought. They had little in common, just companions who had enjoyed each other's company for a while. She suspected that Alistair knew it too and when the time was right, she would write to him, let him down gently, humanely. She didn't want to be unkind.

'Yeah, well. You could do worse,' said Lil, warming to her theme.

'Ma! Stop marrying me off, will you? I'm not interested.'

'You'll be sorry,' said Lil. 'Just saying.'

'Well, don't!'

'When you're stuck with a copper boiler that don't work. And a plug that needs fixing.'

'I'll do what I do *here* when stuff goes wrong,' said Rose. 'I'll fix it myself.'

'Or call a plumber,' said Alice. 'They fix boilers – and sink plugs too.' A beam spread over her face and then she laughed.

Both women looked at her in surprise.

Was this really Alice? Had she just told a joke? Okay, a feeble one. But all the same, it was the first time. The young, timid woman was starting to relax. To feel at home.

'Right,' said Lil. 'Your turn to make the tea, Alice. Rose – you can read out that letter of your sister's for me. The old peepers aren't what they used to be.' Lil didn't like to admit that she couldn't read too well.

Rose read the letter slowly, so they could both savour it. She tried to picture the places Gracie talked about, and the people. Old Arthur wanted to be remembered to her. Said how he'd raise a glass to her at the Fleur. Told her he couldn't get any baccy for his pipe, and maybe if she was of a mind to, Rose might find some in that fancy capital city she lived in, and pass it on. He'd reimburse her.

She pictured the old man's face in her head – rough with deep lines dug into it, like a scouring pad, but with a twinkle in his eyes, sucking away on an empty pipe like a kid's dummy. She'd try and find some baccy for him.

And the exciting things her sister was getting up to. Gracie had started a small group for the village children, evacuees returning home from all over the country – the east coast and the marshes especially had been thought a dangerous place for kids in the early days of war, Gracie told them. Ripe for an invasion. Flat country. On the coast. Hitler's first port of call, many reckoned. And now she'd marshalled the kids into a 'friendly rabble' (her new husband's words). She took them on hikes, taught them how to cook. 'Our Gracie, cook?' said Lil when she heard. Miracles really happened then.

'And she's made them into a choir,' said Rose. 'A dramatic group as well – that'll be for the adults, don't you think? Says here they're rehearsing for *Oklahoma!* They'll put it on in the village hall at Christmas.'

Rosemary took the teacup from Alice, swallowed a small sip, and then spluttered it straight out as she continued reading.

'Well, *that's* ladylike,' said Lil.

'God Almighty, Ma!'

'What now?' asked Lil. 'Haven't we had enough? What with your da, and the upset down the shelter and Ivy lost her mind. I don't want no more bad news.'

'Not bad news.' Rose grinned at her mother. 'Gracie left the best news till last. How d' you fancy being a grandma?'

'That's really good news, isn't it?' said Alice. Unsure whether it was or not. Looking from one to the other.

'If we had some sherry, we'd celebrate,' said Lil. 'And that's the truth.'

'Two lots of good news in one day,' said Alice. 'What with Rose's promotion in work and all.'

'You been promoted? You never said! S'pose I'm the last to hear.' Lil Ellis put on one of her famous pouts.

Couldn't win, could you? 'Not exactly a promotion,' said Rosemary. 'Least not yet. But when Miss Simons tests me on my French, next week, and I'm okay, she'll move me up a grade. We get letters and postcards from France – people looking for their lost families.' She thought about the good news she'd had from Geneva some months before. A case she'd become close to. The phone call from Switzerland had confirmed the young soldier she had searched for was still alive and in a POW camp. *The man's mother had cried when Rose told her*.

'And there was that German you tracked down and the thank-you note from his wife. You'll keep that, won't you, Rose?' said Alice.

'German!' spluttered Lil. 'You been doing favours for bleedin' *Germans* when they got my poor Harry locked up in one of them camps of theirs?'

Her ma's face screwed up with anger and her thin body shook. Lil raised a bony fist in Rosemary's face, but didn't unleash it. That was why Rosemary didn't bring her work home with her, never discussed the finer points of it with her mother. Lil would refuse to understand. Her mother was a good woman, in her own way, but she could be narrow-minded. People were human beings. And the Red Cross made no distinction between countries or creeds, apportioned no blame. It was a humanitarian organisation, not a political one, giving help where it was needed. To whoever needed it. Whatever side they were on.

'He's a POW, Ma. In one of our camps *here*. You think we don't do exactly the same things as those *bleedin' Germans* you're on about?'

'That's different,' said Lil.

'And why's that?' asked Rosemary.

'Because they started the bleedin' war. And if you can't see that, then you're no daughter of mine.' Lil Ellis stormed from the room.

'Sorry, Rose. Didn't mean to make trouble. I thought she'd be pleased.' Alice's lip trembled as she tried to hold back the waterworks.

'Not your fault. And it's not Ma's, either. She's had a rough time these last years – too much work, too much worry. We got bombed out and then there's my da. She'll never forgive the Germans for that. She's put on years these last months. She's still a young woman, but you'd never guess.'

'Should I go and talk to her, Rose?'

'Up to you, but I'd leave it. She'll barricade herself in her bedroom for a bit. Make us suffer.' Rosemary smiled. 'She doesn't mean it, though. She's a good-hearted woman, my ma. But anger's the only weapon she's got against these sad, crazy times. We can't take that away from her.'

Sobs shook Alice's thin frame and Rosemary went over and hugged the young woman, ruffled her hair, like she sometimes did with her own little sister Gracie. Gracie, the married woman. Soon to be Gracie, the mother. Times were changing and they were changing with them. And *hope* was still a word in Rose's mind. Hope for a swift end to this punishing war. Where people suffered in camps. Where innocents died. And families were separated. Hope that she'd see her da again.

'Let's make a pact, shall we? That we'll be special friends. Friends for life, Alice.'

'I'd like that,' said Alice. She offered her pinkie finger and they both entwined them, a sort of promise, not a blood oath – but binding all the same.

'So, you still think I can stay?' asked Alice, blowing her nose on the hankie she'd pulled from the sleeve of her thin cardigan. 'Maybe your ma wouldn't like it now that...'

'You want to leave? You don't like it here?'

'I never been so happy *anywhere*, Rose. It's just that – maybe your ma blames me for you two fighting.'

'Fight? You call that a fight?' said a voice behind them. 'She ain't seen it when we really fight, has she, our Rose?'

'No, Ma.' Rosemary Ellis smiled at the woman who'd brought her into the world, had guided her path, sometimes with a hug, sometimes with a clip, when she figured it was needed.

'And as for you – you ain't thinking of leaving us?'

'I love it here, Ma.'

'Right,' said Lil. ''Swat I thought. And we get on right well with you, Alice Thompson. Put the kettle on, there's a good girl, freshen that tea up a bit.' She patted the young girl on her hand as she went past. 'And why don't you rustle us up some bread and dripping for supper? There's a skim of dripping still left in the larder. Careful now, don't cut that bread too thick.' She turned to her daughter. 'Now you...'

'Yes, Ma?' asked Rose.

'Tell me about this promotion of yours.'

Rose smiled. 'Like I said, if I can pass the test next week, Miss Simons promised to move me up a grade, and I get to translate some of the letters sent from France. She normally does all that, but she's off to Geneva soon.'

'You're a clever girl. You'll do it. And Rose...'

'What?'

'I'm right proud of you.'

Rosemary Ellis dropped her head, so her ma wouldn't see the tears that had begun to build behind her eyes. Tears were a sign of weakness. Her ma had always told them so. But these were tears of happiness, for praise wasn't a thing that came lightly from her mother's lips. And when it did, it was something you cherished. Felt you must have earned.

'Thanks,' said Rose.

'This new grade of yours...' her mother said, thoughtfully.

'Yeah?'

'That come with any more money?'

And there you had it. War, peace, whatever – there was one thing you could rely on. Something as natural as night following day. Lily Ellis would always appreciate the buying power of a pound note.

27

LONDON

OCTOBER 1944

In the days that followed, Rosemary Ellis learned one important thing about herself. She was *strong*. Not physically perhaps. But mentally. She might be small. Danny had once called her petite, which she took as a compliment, an accolade she wore with pride. And her tiny frame sometimes gave people the wrong impression when they first met her: that she was weak, a pushover. It was often useful when she went to meetings. It threw some people off the scent, meant they were unprepared for the tenacious way she fought for her agenda, for change.

She was a champion for POWs. For displaced people. For refugees. And there were lots of them now. There would be even more refugees, she knew, before the war dragged itself to a weary end. And for Rose Ellis, it didn't matter which country they came from.

She was liaising more now with ICRS in Geneva, and her old boss Miss Simons was out there most of the time. They were being swamped with requests to find people, and by the rising tide of refugees. And as some prisoner of war camps were being liberated it was putting a strain on resources. *Good news and bad news.* Men were going home, but not her da.

Her job had become more exacting. Long hours, but then she was used to that. She sometimes stayed overnight at the office, tried to squeeze in a few hours' sleep there. Alice would make her a flask of tea and a cheese sandwich, or a meat paste one when the ration ran out. Alice had turned into a mother hen, fussing over her, complaining that Rose pushed herself too hard. Then the young girl would wave goodbye, and make her own way home to Royston Street. But what was the end of Alice's day was often just the beginning of a long night for Rose. Still, it was good to know that someone was there for her ma, to keep her company and take her to the odd musical at the flicks.

There was little time for anything outside work. Leisure time was a thing of the past and Rose's French class and the philosophy group had taken a back seat for the last month. She was getting more proficient at French now anyway, as it became part of her everyday working life.

As for the philosophy group, Rose had been determined not to let Geoffrey Turner put her off going back there. So she had gone back. She'd had the guts to face him – but the strange thing was that he hadn't. He had not been back since their confrontation on the bus. Her final evening with the group before she left to make time for her work had ended with a happy and unexpected celebration. People brought her small leaving gifts: a diary, a fancy blue notebook as well, with her name printed on the front, *to write down her random thoughts.* Many of them agreed that Rose did, at times, have random, unusual thoughts, but that she must keep on having them. And someone had used their precious ration to make her a leaving cake.

Rosemary had cried. Sometimes you didn't know what good friends you had until you said goodbye.

. . .

It had been a sad, trying day in work that day. She'd finally discovered the fate of two British soldiers she'd been trying to locate for some time. They'd been friends, taken prisoners on D-Day and she'd traced them to a POW camp. But today she'd found out that they'd both been killed in an unsuccessful escape attempt. It had happened months ago. But sometimes, it was like that, the information slow to come through – and you held on to false hope.

Still, Rose would try to put the sadness behind her and go home early for a change. It was Ma's birthday and Alice had been bugging her all day about making a special effort and coming home for a celebration. It was very important. *She had to be there*, Alice nagged. Something special was arranged and *God would put a black mark against her name if she missed it.*

Alice wasn't frightened to use God as a deterrent or an encouragement when it suited. (Although never in front of Lil, it had to be noted.) Alice Thompson may have grown in confidence since she'd first come to live with them, but Ma's unwritten law that you didn't take the Lord's name in vain in *her* house was one you ignored at your peril.

Rosemary smiled when she thought about her friend. Alice had proved herself a steadfast and loyal companion. Alice, with those massive eyes. Blue, too. The kind that made men look at her with lust on their faces, though Alice seemed unaware of the effect she had on them.

Rose had seen the young girl change over the last months, become more settled and sure of herself. Not so eager to please everyone – to make them like her. She didn't have to *buy* their approval, Rose had told her. She only had to be true to herself. And if that meant you weren't always popular, did that really matter?

They'd had lots of discussions about it, late into the night. Alice on her mattress on the floor. And Rose in her bed. The bed she used to share with Gracie. And now Alice was becoming special, like another sister.

'Quick, get a move on,' said Alice. 'We need to be there before she arrives.'

'We're taking Ma to the *pub* for her birthday? She'll never go for that. You know how she feels about it.' *The public house was a place of sin and depravity where folk forgot their inhibitions when 'the drink' was on them.* Although her ma had been known to knock back the odd sherry at home if it happened to cross her path.

'This is different, Rose. Ivy's going to collect her. She won't refuse Ivy, will she?'

'And poor old Ivy Brown's in on the surprise, is she?' asked Rosemary. 'Will she even remember to get Ma? You know how confused she's been since she lost her daughter, Ella, last year.'

'Ivy's been getting better. She'll be okay. Now will you hurry up and get moving? We need to put the bunting up before she gets there,' said Alice.

'My God, you're worse than Ma. *Bully!*'

'Yeah?' Alice smiled.

'Yeah.'

They went off arm in arm to the pub several streets away – on Green Street, just down the road from the Bug Hole. It wasn't as hard as it used to be, walking through these streets at night, for the blackout had been changed to a 'dim-out', except when there was a raid on. The dim-out was equivalent to moonlight. Things were looking up. It made people a bit more cheerful, Rosemary thought. You could see it their faces. The blackout had been necessary, but it hadn't been good for morale. Lots of folks got lost in the dark, especially if there was fog as well. And there'd been loads of accidents. Some poor bloke had taken a wrong turn and ridden his bike into the Regent's Canal. Dead before they could get to him.

Rosemary squeezed her friend's arm. 'This bunting you're on about. I don't see it.'

'Already at the pub,' said Alice.

'Smooth. You haven't managed to lay on food as well—? 'Cause I'm starving,' said Rose.

'Taken care of. Nothing exotic – a few bloater paste sandwiches and some pickles.'

'God, Alice. You're a bleedin' magician.'

'Yeah? Tell that to my new boss, will you?'

'Alice?'

'Uh huh?'

'I *am* your new boss,' said Rose.

'I know.'

They both laughed and Rosemary thought about the sandwiches waiting at the pub. *Life wasn't too bad at all, was it now?*

'Rose?'

'Yep?'

'What age is Ma?'

'You don't know? Not that she ever talks about it. She never talks about herself – you notice that?' said Rosemary.

'I figured fifty-something.'

'Really?'

'She's not?'

'Ma's had a tough life. Been worn down by it. Had us when she was young. Lost her own ma and da early on. Then Da going off to war like that and getting captured at Dunkirk... She looks older than she is. Today's her fortieth birthday.'

'Jesus!'

'What?'

'Just that – well, she acts old.'

'She is what she is,' said Rose.

'Sure, but... don't you think it's odd...?'

'Odd? How's that?' asked Rose.

'She's the same age as this new son-in-law of hers.'

'Hadn't thought about it. But maybe that's why she kept going on about the bloke's age,' said Rose.

'Think your Grace loves this bloke?'

'Seems like it. Seems they're both smitten. Least, they look happy in the photo.'

'Reckon your ma's in love with your da?'

'What's this? Twenty questions? I got no idea if Ma's really in love, or Da for that matter. They rub along together and they're company for each other. But love? Shouldn't think so. Not the kind that smacks you between the eyes.'

'You in love with this Captain Greenway, Rose?'

'No.'

'You sure? I mean, how're you supposed to know?'

'Oh, you'd know.'

'You ever had that kind of love, Rose – the one that hits you between the eyes?' asked Alice.

'Kicks you in the stomach, makes you feel sick, slams you in the heart, stops your breath, makes your head reel? That kind of love?'

'Hell's bells!' said Alice. 'And did you have it?'

'Sure, Alice. I had it. Seemed too perfect to be real, like it couldn't last.'

'And did it?' said Alice.

'It did. But *he* didn't.' Rosemary's voice trembled with the remembered sadness. 'His plane went down two years ago.'

'God, I'm sorry Rose. I shouldn't have asked.'

'It's fine. Time helps. Whoever said time heals was right. The wounds get less painful, but they never disappear. And I don't think I'd want them to. I don't want to forget him.'

'Maybe somebody else...'

'It's okay. I like my life, Alice. But does this mean what I think it means? You've met someone?'

'Yes. But how can I tell if he's the *one*? He's kind, and considerate, I reckon. He said he likes me. And I guess I like him too. But, don't you need more than that?'

'I'm not the one to ask. You need to ask yourself. Nobody else can tell you. And for God's sake, whatever you do, don't ask Ma. Her idea of a woman's place in marriage will make you stay single.'

'I didn't say I wanted to *marry* him. I want to be an independent woman – just like you. A man would need to understand that.'

'Good grief,' said Rose. 'What have I done?' She chuckled. 'I've created a sister for Frankenstein's monster.'

28

LONDON

OCTOBER 1944

'Best night of my life, Rose.' A smile tugged at her ma's face. A face older than its calendar years, marked with toil, disappointment, but sometimes pride. And now happiness filled in the gullies her battle with life had put there. Softened the harsh features. And Lil had waved her hair – something special for her birthday.

'I'm glad, Ma.'

'I mean it, Rose. Thanks for all this.' Lil Ellis looked around at the table, at her friends and her wonderful family, including Gracie with her husband Joe who'd made a special trip.

Rosemary was thrilled that the party had been such a success. And it had been a true surprise for her ma. You could tell that by the look on Lil's face that she hadn't expected any of them to remember. Her ma had so few expectations from life. In a way it was sad, at least Rose thought so.

'Don't thank *me*. It's all *that* woman's doing.' Rosemary threw a mock salute at Alice. She was on the other side of the long trestle table, listening to Ivy trying to sing a tuneless 'We'll Meet Again'.

'Thank you, daughter number three,' said Lil. But the drink had got to Lily Ellis a while ago and it came out as 'thraughter number dee'.

'The blether's near your eye, Ma.' Gracie shouted up at her mother and laughed.

Rose smiled at her sister, happy to see her again, glad for a chance to celebrate. Gracie was right, their ma was definitely under the weather, the drink taking its toll. Rose had never seen her ma this worse for drink before. Somehow it made her more human.

'Hey, our Gracie. Why don't you give us a tune?' said Lil. 'Show Ivy how it's done.'

Gracie didn't argue, for once. Just got up on the floor – not the table this time, for she was a married woman now, and a bit of decorum was called for. Besides, she was carrying a huge bump in front of her.

Her enthusiastic and tuneful rendition of 'We'll Meet Again' proved that Gracie had lost none of her natural musical ability. And the man sitting at the head of the table smiled and nodded in approval.

'Vera Lynn's got nothing on your Grace,' said Ivy Brown. 'Credit where it's due.' Ivy's voice was loud and her large, round face had red spots blooming on both cheeks, for she had downed more than a few glasses of porter as well.

Some of the guests could hold a tune, but others wouldn't have been able to find the melody even without the considerable amount of beer and sherry that had made its way along the table in front of them.

Rosemary studied all the eager, happy faces. Laughter. Fun. Joy. Not a single argument. *A miracle*. What a night. Like her ma, Rose would not forget it. And to have them all together like this. She still didn't know how Alice had managed it, to get

Grace and her husband Joe there – and all without Ma sussing a thing. It showed great admin skills. Alice would go far.

As the last strains of the song petered out, Rosemary noted her sister take up her fighting stance. *Lord, no, it wasn't about to go belly up, was it? Not now, when the evening had been such a success and so* – she tried to think of a word – *cordial.*

'Listen, everyone,' said Grace. 'Want you all to know something. Glad this celebration came up, and thanks for organising it, Alice...' She beamed over at Alice.

Maybe not belly up then. Could even be something good, what with Gracie smiling an' all.

'We would like to announce' – Gracie gestured rather grandly towards her husband – 'that is, *Joe* and I would like to announce that our joint production here' – and now Grace placed both hands dramatically on her prominent belly – 'has two heartbeats.'

'Two heartbeats?' said Lil, confused.

'Twins, Ma,' announced Gracie, proudly. 'We're having twins.'

'My *Gawd*,' said Lil, breaking her own rule about taking the name of the Lord in vain. 'Two for the price of one!' And that's when Lily Ellis passed out, her head coming gently to rest between a platter of bloater paste sandwiches and a half-glass of excellent porter.

Her mother's piercing scream woke Rose from a wonderful dream. She'd been walking the cliffs of Havenporth with Danny and they were about to kiss when the frightened howl from her ma's lips jolted Rose awake. Danny's face had retreated, replaced by Lil's ghostly white one, creased up in pain with tears streaming down it. A thing Rose had rarely seen.

Her ma was shaking with fear and Rosemary took hold of her, the thinness of her mother's body a shock.

'Shush, Ma. It'll all be fine. Just a nightmare.'

'Gawd, Rose. He was right there. Hovering over me. Great big man with that cross of his. Like something from the beyond, he was.'

'Who was, Ma?'

'Bloke in my dreams. Don't you listen to nothin', Rose? He came to get me.'

'Nobody's come to get you, Ma. Only in a dream. And they can't hurt you.'

'And how's that, Rose? 'Cause the bloke was right here. Grabbing me. Wanted to kill me. Tried to pull me down them steps in the tube. Said I should have been kilt that night.'

Rose watched her ma shake her head. Like a dog shaking off water. 'Just a panic attack,' she said. 'You'll be fine, you'll see. I'll make us both a drop of cocoa. How would that be?'

'You're a good girl, Rose. And don't tell no one else, mind. Don't tell your sister. She's got enough on her plate. And Alice would only fret. She ain't like you. You're strong.'

Rosemary put the phone down, stunned. She couldn't bring herself to smile, although every cell, every molecule of her being wanted to do just that. Smile until her face hurt with it.

Her boss had called from Geneva, had made travel arrangements for Rose to join her there.

It was dangerous, flying to Geneva – Miss Simons had been clear about that. If she would rather not make the trip, she didn't have to. Her choice. A civilian aircraft flying from Lisbon to Bristol, the trip she would do in reverse, had been taken out of the sky by German planes. Leslie Howard had been on board. She remembered it.

There was to be a stopover in Lisbon. An ICRS delegate and her on the same flight. And the following day, they would both pick up the weekly flight from Lisbon to Switzerland – an even more hazardous trip.

Her whole body screamed with excitement, but she couldn't let any of it escape – because that would be unseemly in the circumstances. Her great news was bought with other people's suffering. It wasn't a cause for celebration.

Rosemary pictured life as a set of balance scales. Right now, her side of the scale was soaring high, which meant that others – the refugees fleeing persecution, the POWs trapped in camps far from home – were at the lowest point in their existence.

Alice hovered over her, looking worried.

'You're not *going*, are you?' asked Alice.

'She's given me twenty-four hours to think about it,' said Rosemary.

'But you can't! It's not safe.'

'Miss Simons got there okay. And the other people on the plane, they're expecting to get there in one piece.'

'And what does she want you to do there that you can't do right here? It's mad. You shouldn't even be thinking about it, Rose.'

'The boss has moved over to deal with Relief now. Wants me to take her place in the Central POW Agency over there.'

'And what about your ma?' asked Alice. 'She'll go off her head with worry.'

'Ma's tougher than you think. And she'll soon have two grandkids to take her mind off stuff. She's got Gracie and...'

'And?'

'And she's got you as well. Look – I know it's a lot to ask. And it puts you right there in the trenches with Ma. I'll understand if you want to move on with your life instead of babysitting her... I tried to sort out a place for her,' said Rose.

'She told me,' said Alice.

'Down in Brighton. Away from the raids, and she'd have her own small bungalow in a complex. Lots of other people her age, and activities and a warden to look after them. And she could have a cleaner in.'

'You know Ma. She'd never have a cleaner,' said Alice. 'Reckons they'd only snoop. Says nobody could clean as good as she does.'

'Anyway – she wouldn't go,' said Rose.

'So – you still leaving?'

'I am.'

Rosemary waited. Silence. She watched as her friend Alice left the room, heading for the small office kitchen. There was the noisy clatter of cups and saucers and the sound of running water. *Tea!* Karl Marx claimed that religion was the opium of the people. He was wrong. *It was tea.*

The tea was ferried in on a silver tray with a crisp white cloth on it. Weak-looking liquid in china cups, no milk, no sugar, no biscuits.

'There's a war on,' said Alice, and grinned.

'We still friends, then?' asked Rose.

'Best friends forever.' They linked pinkie fingers.

'So...?'

'Doesn't mean we always have to agree, though, does it?' said Alice. 'I'll look after your ma. She's been good to me. But I still think you're wrong.'

'I know. But it won't be for long. It's only a temporary posting. I'll be back soon.'

'We'll see,' said Alice, and she shook her head. 'We'll see.'

Rose was relieved. But it wouldn't be that easy with her mother. Lily Ellis was a woman who didn't believe in change, and yet there'd been so much of it lately. Some of it good, of course: Gracie getting married, about to have kids, two of them. Her ma had been knitting bonnets and pull-ups. In strange unbabylike colours, you had to admit, but then it had mostly been wool from old unravelled cardigans – her own, and others donated by neighbours. Sacrificed for the greater good. *Make do and mend.* Like the pamphlet said.

On the bus back home, both women were quiet: Rosemary thinking about how she would break the news to her ma, and Alice thinking about how Ma would take the news.

In the end, it was simple. Rose just came straight out with it as soon as they'd walked in the kitchen.

Rissoles again. Praise the Lord. And pass the lentils.

You could hear the scream all the way along Royston Street. It reminded Rose of the time Gracie had found the mouse in the pantry. And the woman had gone on to kill rats! There was no accounting for life and the strange paths it took you along.

Lil Ellis flounced off in a huff, slamming the front door with a power that almost took the thing off its hinges. But then hinges weren't what they used to be. *How could somebody that small, that thin, pack such a punch?* Motivation, Rose figured. When her ma fixed her mind on something, the heavens shook. It's what made her who she was. And Rose and her sister had inherited it. You had to laugh.

———

Surprising how much you can pack into a week. Rosemary had tied up loose ends at work, sorted through her clothes; borrowed a suitcase from Ivy next door: a proper suitcase that you could take on a plane. Her own pressed cardboard one would have done the trick – she wasn't too fussy about how stuff looked – but Ivy had insisted. And her ma had agreed. Rose was representing the street. And a brown leather suitcase (battered though it may be) was better than letting them all down with a blue pressed cardboard one. Meant you could hold your head up high.

'Not bad for an *East End slum!*' Lily Ellis had proudly announced.

Rosemary had been surprised at how the insult from Alistair Greenway's sister had wormed its way into her mother's psyche.

There'd been a truce between her and Ma. Instigated by Lil. *Joy of joys.* Rose wrote the date down in her fancy blue notebook, a day that should be remembered in history, for she couldn't recall any other time her ma had been the one to give in.

Friday night. One last sleep in her own bed. Tomorrow night, with luck, she'd be sleeping on a plane. The thump of her heart speeded up at the thought of it. The start of an adventure.

She'd told them all she wasn't frightened, but that wasn't true; when she allowed herself to dwell on it, the whole thing was terrifying. Two and a half hours in a plane, clinging to the sky, the roof of the world. How did the things defy gravity like that? It would either be brilliant or the most fearful night of her life.

Not that she'd be alone. There would be others on the flight, and this Swiss chap travelling to Lisbon with her and then on to Geneva. The ICRC delegate. He was due to pick her up from the station at Bristol; take her to the airport with him. A chance to practise her French.

Alice had been strange all day in work. Detached. Had misplaced a file, something she hadn't done for months now. And when they'd arrived home earlier, she had been secretive, whispering in corners with her ma. There was something on. You could feel it in the air. *Not a going-away party, please. She couldn't stand it.* It was hard enough to leave them all behind, to ignore the guilt that it should be her looking after her mother and not her best friend Alice drafted in to do the job.

Only one thing for it. Rosemary would get in first, a pre-emptive strike. She picked up the things she'd been hoarding under her bed; a strange collection, each of the items wrapped carefully in brown paper, tied with the used string that she'd diligently saved. She'd always known she'd be leaving, that this day would come, just maybe not this soon. But sometime. It was written in the heavens and in the blue notebook, and even as far back as the cliffs in Havenporth if she'd known it.

She needn't have worried. There was no huge embarrassing going-away party with the whole street invited to share in the triumph – her ma showing off about her girls. That might have been better. She might not have cried then, like she did now.

Ma was in the front room, cradling the certificate of Rose's achievement. Handed out by the queen herself. And the best glasses were out on the sideboard, and a bottle of something coloured dark red that Rose had never seen before.

'It's made with berries,' said Alice. 'It'll blow your head off, Rose. Best we could get, though.'

'What you mean, "best you could get"? I made that meself!' said Ivy Brown. 'You didn't think we'd let you go without a wee celebration, did you?'

'An' there's real sausage rolls. Got three proper sausages from the butcher,' said Lil proudly, puffed up with the achievement. 'No bread or carrot in there.'

'Ma – you shouldn't have used up your coupons.' But Rosemary smiled all the same. A treat. 'I've got a few things for you, as well,' she said. 'But you're not to open them till after I've gone.' It didn't seem right, just then – Rose stealing the limelight, when they'd all gone to such trouble to give her a send-off.

She'd wrapped a small tin brooch for her ma. The shape of a heart with a pair of hands wrapped around it. Rose had found it in a pawn shop. Her mother would scoff at it, she knew. Call it sentimental. And then shed a few tears when nobody was looking.

And for Alice? She'd left her the black leather handbag that Alistair had given her.

Gracie's parcel had a thin silver bangle in there, the one her da had given Rosemary before he left. Gracie had always wanted it, preferred it to the brush and comb set he'd given *her*. Her ma promised to post that off along with the gifts for the twins – a pair of bootees each for them.

'One for you too, Ivy. Think of me when you wear it. It's your favourite colour.'

Rosemary had bought a new headscarf for her. The old one was falling to bits. Purple and white. Some might call it garish, but she knew Ivy would like it.

'Right, before you lot start bawling your eyes out,' said Lil, 'let's make a start on this sherry.'

'Blackberry wine,' corrected Ivy.

They opened the wine. Enough to blow your head off, Alice had said. And it didn't let them down. That's why Rose only had one glass. Tomorrow was a big day and she wanted to remember every bit of it.

'And how will we know you've got there safe, Rose?' Ivy came out with the question her ma had been reluctant to ask. *All that flak in the sky. It wouldn't know she was working for the Red Cross, now would it?*

And of course that was true. Rosemary had thought about that many times. Planes were shot down every day. Passenger planes and war planes. Bombers and fighters. Aircraft like Danny's. Yes, it was a possibility. It was wartime, she was flying through a warzone, might even be shot down, just like him. How peculiar that would be if she should share the same fate. After all, fate had brought them together that day at the Corner House on Coventry Street when Danny had taken a seat at her table. Would the same fate that had united two soul mates bring them together again in some afterlife?

Her ma's sharp tone invaded her thoughts, brought Rosemary back down to earth. 'Ivy's talking to you!' said Lil.

'Sorry, Ivy. I was somewhere else.'

'Hope it was nice,' said Ivy. 'So – how *will* we know you've arrived?' she asked again.

'Easy. That's all sorted. When I get to the office over there, I'll phone Alice. She'll be waiting in work for a call.'

'But it won't be for a while,' Alice jumped in. 'Could be days,' she warned, 'all that travelling. And getting sorted out in her new job.'

'We've agreed a week,' said Rosemary. 'If Alice doesn't hear in a week, then she'll use the office phone to get through to Switzerland.'

'And you can do that?' asked her ma. 'Speak to another country like that?'

'We do it all the time, Ma.'

Lil Ellis looked amazed.

'But don't worry. There's no way it should take a week. I'll be sending you lot a postcard before you've even had time to miss me.'

But Rosemary Ellis was wrong. They wouldn't be hearing from her for a long time.

29

ROTTERDAM

NOVEMBER 1944

It was almost Christmas. Not much to celebrate, though. Not for Danny Welland and Anna Pietersen and the others trying to stay alive in war-torn Holland. It was nearly the end of 1944, and the sad, battered city of Rotterdam was *still* in enemy hands: although parts of the Netherlands had been liberated, the Germans had not been defeated there. So in Rotterdam, their job went on.

That meant that Danny and Anna had already made several hazardous trips through the evening blackout. They were still there. Still escorting escaping men and women through the rubble, dodging patrols, bringing them to this stinking cellar, to the transit station the cell had set up, moving their 'cargo' on whenever they could. So far, they'd all been lucky. But Dan figured their luck couldn't last.

Beatrix had been taken, hauled off her bike on her way to pass information to Amsterdam. Information that she carried in her head, because no one could risk notebooks or documents –

nothing written down. That would be handing a gift to the Bosch.

They'd found the poor woman tied to a post in a miserable brick courtyard, its walls pockmarked with bullet holes and bloodstains. Executed without trial. No trip to Gestapo headquarters. The Germans were taking shortcuts. Time was running out. They were on the retreat. Just not quickly enough.

Everyone in the cell had felt relief – and guilt. *Relief* that Beatrix, a fine young woman, if at times overbearing, had had a quick end, suffered no torture. And hadn't given them up to the enemy. And *guilt* that it was a twenty-year-old in the prime of her life who had paid the price for them all chasing freedom. A sadness to add to other sadness.

But the good news was that the same fate had not yet been doled out to Sara Pietersen. As far as they knew.

The thought that her mother was still alive had made Anna even more reckless in her fight for her homeland. Danny had tried to keep her out of danger, but the young woman was feisty, insisting she didn't need a nursemaid.

Dan had kept one opinion to himself, as it wouldn't help to voice it. The fact that Sara had not been shot didn't mean she wasn't suffering. Even now she could be in a cellar at Gestapo headquarters or maybe even forced to work in one of their brothels. They'd heard the enlisted men's brothels were even worse than the officers'.

Edwin came down to the basement with a large, bulging hessian sack thrown over his shoulder.

'What've you got there?' asked De Groot.

'A miracle,' Edwin said. 'A gift from the intrepid Christiaan. Payment from our *captors*.' He spat out the word.

'Christiaan?' said Danny. 'Who's Christiaan?'

'The doctor who checked you out? You don't remember?' asked Edwin.

'Never knew his name. So, what's the payment for?' Danny asked.

'One of the officers caught the clap.' Edwin smirked. 'Christiaan's been treating him. Worth a sack of spuds and a few carrots.'

'Stew,' said Anna. 'God be praised, we can have *stew*. Got any onions in there as well?'

'Might be,' said Edwin. 'But you can't have all the spuds, just a few.'

'Why not?'

'Saving them – for something special. You'll see. And you'll fall at my feet, giving thanks.' Edwin gave a hearty laugh.

Dan looked up in amazement. Edwin had shrunk to half the chap he used to be and as for laughter... well, there hadn't been any.

'We'll have some stew tonight,' said Anna. And she laughed as well. Winked at Danny. 'You see? I said things would get better and you didn't believe me. Pity we haven't got any meat, though. Now that *would* be a miracle. Or even the odd bone. Give it a bit of flavour. Still, I'll do my best,' she said.

De Groot left suddenly. Just like that. No explanation. Mysterious.

'Maybe he doesn't fancy stew,' said Anna.

'What, *him*? He'll eat anything that's standing still,' said Edwin.

They all laughed again. *Laughter, the best medicine.*

'We should invite Christiaan. After all, it's his booty,' said Edwin.

'I'll go,' Anna said.

'No, I'll go,' said Danny. 'You cook.'

And for once she did as she was told. And even smiled.

―――

They ate their stew late that night, and it had the most wonderful smell, and taste, and didn't seem like just vegetables boiled in water.

'It's brilliant, Anna,' said Danny. 'How did you do it?'

'Ask *him*.' She pointed at De Groot, who'd slunk back into the house two hours after he'd mysteriously vanished.

'Bones,' he said, and his shoulders shook with laughter. 'She said she needed them. For the stew.' De Groot rubbed his belly in satisfaction.

'Bones? What kind of damn bones?' asked Danny.

'The stew was good, *ja?*' said De Groot.

'A masterpiece of culinary perfection,' said Danny.

'Then you don't need to know *what* kind of damn bones, do you?'

For the next few weeks, they feasted on boiled potatoes and onions. Better than most of their countrymen were eating. Meanwhile, Edwin was doing something mysterious with the rest of the potatoes that he'd squirreled away. None of them could guess what.

Then on 5 December the miracle happened. Danny discovered that Christmas celebrations in the Netherlands centred around *Sinterklaas* – St Nicholas – bringing presents for the children on the fifth day of December, the day before St Nicholas's Day. And today, they had their own delivery from *Sinterklaas*.

The first slug of the vicious moonshine, made from potatoes, made their eyes bulge and grabbed at their throats with an iron fist, burning its way through to their stomachs. After that, it was easier as Danny's system got used to it.

'Is this stuff safe?' he asked, after a coughing fit.

The rest of them laughed.

'Pussy. You'll get used to it. You might have a few pimples

on your face when you wake up tomorrow and a head like a lead balloon – if you wake up,' laughed Edwin.

'If?'

'Okay – *maybe*,' teased Edwin. 'Happy Christmas, British.'

It was the best day they'd had for months. Years. But it was only a day. One day of light among so many days of pain.

―――

The news was delivered by a ten-year-old boy named Willem. A boy who had already seen far too much for his tender years, almost half of which had been spent living in a war zone. But the young lad was proud of his 'job' as a courier for the Resistance.

Sara Pietersen had been shot in a grimy backyard near Gestapo headquarters. Her executioners had shaved the head on her shrunken, beaten body. Strung a sign around her neck. It translated as *Traitorous Dutch Whore*. Some German with a twisted sense of humour had painted her swollen lips scarlet. They stood out on her pale dead face like a cartoon caricature. The German propaganda machine swung into action and for days afterwards, posters of her face had been plastered on shop hoardings and public buildings. A terrifying warning, should anyone else decide to disobey German rule.

At first Anna was hysterical, producing banshee-like screams that were sure to give them away. Edwin was forced to knock her out. A sedative would have been better, but they had no such thing, and he tried not to break her jaw.

Later, Danny watched her disappear into a dream-like state, staring off into the distance for days on end. And then came the uncontrollable shakes. That's when he lay down beside her on the ancient mattress, and pulled her body into his.

. . .

Then, one day, Anna woke up and seemed normal.

Although almost a month had passed since the trauma of her mother's horrific death, Anna seemed to have no sense of time. The world had closed down around her, but now it was beginning to open up again as her brain finally accepted the awful truth.

Danny was behind the partition in the cellar, where he'd been making I.D. cards for two of the British fliers they were hiding.

Anna Pietersen wrapped her arms around him. 'I've got no mama,' she said.

'I know.'

'She's left me.'

'Yes.'

'And my *papa*,' she said. 'He's left me as well.'

'Yes, but...'

'Promise *you'll* never leave me. Promise me we'll be together... forever.'

Did he make an excuse? Or say yes, and later break that promise? Danny's thoughts went into overdrive. *Together – forever?* That was a promise he'd made to Rosie, and with her, it would have been an easy one to keep. His one great love. But fate and the war had been cruel, taken her from him. Anna was a fine woman, but it wasn't the same. Could never be. She could never replace his Rosie.

That's when they heard Christiaan's voice and the sounds of feet on the floor above. Several people, not just Christiaan's. And raised voices. They swung the shelving quickly into place, closed the partition door and joined the three men in their hiding space. Two British fliers and one American.

Danny remembered another time. Another hiding place. And every fibre of his being throbbed with fear. The fear that this time, they might not be so lucky.

30

LISBON, PORTUGAL

NOVEMBER 1944

Rose's sense of adventure had overcome any residue of fear. Fear of flying. Fear of the unknown. And things had gone well so far. Her colleague had picked her up at Bristol station and taken her to the airport, where they'd both boarded a plane for Lisbon.

Two outcomes, she'd said. Her first flight would either be brilliant or the most fearful night of her life.

She was right on both counts. It was totally, mind-blowingly brilliant to rise into the air as if your body had grown wings. But it was also the most fearful night of her life, and all because the authorities in Lisbon had mistaken her travelling companion for someone else.

Anders Müller, a small, quiet, innocuous man, pleased to be finally going back home to Switzerland, had been mistaken for one *Andreas* Müller: a man with a history of smuggling gold.

At first it had just been inconvenient, a hold-up in their travelling plans, and even slightly humorous. Because, as Rosemary saw it, no one as dull as Mr Müller could possibly have criminal tendencies.

Portugal was a neutral country, a country that appeared to play off both sides in the war against each other. A country you wouldn't expect to imprison people working for the Red Cross and heading for Geneva as part of a humanitarian mission. Spies from all sides happily frequented the bars of the city unmolested, and refugees used Lisbon as an escape route out of war-torn Europe, so such a mistake was bound to be corrected. *Wasn't it?*

At first, the pair of them had been put under house arrest – not particularly unpleasant, but worrying all the same. It meant they were stuck in a hotel for two weeks unable to leave, even to take a walk. Then suddenly, a police escort arrived and took Mr Müller away. Rose had no idea where and that was the last she saw of him. Later in the day, the same two men came for her and suddenly the relative comfort, and safety, of the hotel was exchanged for a dank and cheerless cell in a police station. She was questioned about her involvement in a smuggling operation. *A ludicrous idea*, thought Rose – but somehow the mistaken identity of poor Mr Müller had expanded to include her. An incredible fantasy, but the authorities seemed to think that both of them were using the cover of the Red Cross for some kind of illicit trade.

She imagined her boss in Geneva urgently trying to sort it out. Miss Simons was a resourceful woman; it shouldn't take her long to put things right. But days went by, and she heard nothing.

Christmas turned into a sad affair and Rosemary felt increasingly homesick, imagining her family back in Royston Street. Gracie would be getting bigger now, but she would have made the effort to go home for Christmas and bring Joe. He seemed a good, decent man. Rose had only met him that one time, at Ma's birthday do, but she'd been impressed with the love that he showed for her sister. A quiet man, generous and gentlemanly. The kind who doffed his hat to women. She imagined her ma and Alice, in their paper hats, listening to the wireless and eating Christmas fare. Not that there would be much of that, but her ma always managed to work small miracles with the rations.

Her own meal was a lump of cheese with mould on it and a sausage with a skin so tough that Rosemary's teeth couldn't break through it. She was allowed no knife, no fork. Nothing of any kind that might constitute a weapon. In desperation, Rose had sawn the sausage backwards and forwards over a crack in the concrete wall. It took a long time. How long, she couldn't say, because she didn't own a watch anymore. They'd taken it from her. And it hadn't been worth the effort, for the meat inside the skin had been mostly gristle.

But instead of crying in frustration, she finally smiled and remembered the exploding sausages that her ma had first cooked in the frying pan. So plumped up with water that they hissed and fought and wriggled out of their skins. The image made her laugh.

No one had beaten her, or physically attacked her. But there are other kinds of torture, and when Rose heard the noise from outside: the celebration, the fireworks on New Year's Eve, it had been the lowest point of her captivity.

Just when she thought she could take no more, two men had come for her one day, and taken her back to the hotel. They gave her back the brown leather suitcase, instructed her to take a bath and change her clothes. She shook with terror. But surely if they were going to execute her, they wouldn't have let her take a bath – but who knew?

Rose was put on board a bus with her two police guards and escorted to the airport. They walked her out to a waiting plane and handed back her passport before she shakily mounted the steps. She knew she would always remember the feeling in the small of her back; the fingers of ice that crept their way along her spine. Waiting for the bullet that would end her life.

But when Rose's trembling legs finally took her to the door of the plane, she looked around at her captors. They were both smiling, and one even touched his cap in a salute.

A New Year's Amnesty, they told her, when she arrived in Geneva three hours later. And Miss Simons, white and shaken, picked her up in a Red Cross ambulance. She never saw poor Mr Müller again. Nobody did.

Rosemary stayed on in Geneva, working hard, trying to shake off the memories. Trying to escape the recurring nightmare of being trapped in a cold, dank cell. She was having it a lot, night after night, waking up with her heart thudding in her chest, her sheets drenched.

By then they were finding out all kinds of things about the trauma that came with war: psychological scars that others couldn't see in you, but were there just the same. Rose had thought herself immune, but it wasn't true. Nobody was.

It always surprised her that the nightmare was not about the haunting sights she was seeing in squalid refugee camps; things that had happened to others, the sad wreckage of people's lives. It was her own trauma that played itself out in her dreams.

Then in May 1945, suddenly, as if someone had simply turned off a tap, the war in Europe came to an end. *What had it all been for, this madness?* A senseless, cruel waste of life, Rose thought. A generation of young men from countries all over the world, gone, never to live their lives. Would it make a difference now to how the world worked in the future? She hoped so – because *sometimes* hope was all you had.

Rosemary went back home to finally join her family. They would need her now, especially her ma. For Rose had at last traced her father. She had made it her mission to find out what had happened to her da, had used all of Geneva's extensive resources. She discovered that after his capture at Dunkirk, he hadn't been taken to a proper prisoner of war camp, one where some humanity still operated along with the Geneva Convention and Red Cross parcels.

Instead, Harry Ellis had ended up in a slave-labour camp in Trzebinia-Siersza, Poland, where British soldiers had been used to dig iron ore alongside the Polish slave workforce.

Rose had wept on and off for days when she'd found out that he had died in the camp. The cruel life he must have suffered.

He had been a casualty of war. Another of *the fallen*, just a name and service number on a list. A very long list. But he was far more than that. He was her da. It had been a miserable, melancholy day when she discovered the truth and now there would be the inevitable telegram. She knew that it would come, and she would be there when it did, to help Ma face it.

They had a street party to celebrate VE Day.

Ivy brought out some of that awful homemade wine of hers, closer to cleaning fluid than a decent Beaujolais.

The next day, the telegram arrived. Harry Ellis was dead. Rose saw tears glisten in her mother's eyes and understood. Felt her ma's raw grief. It was the same as her own. They'd both lost good men to this hateful war, an indiscriminate slaughter of brave men and women.

The details in the telegram were vague, and Rose was relieved.

She hadn't told her ma what she'd found out about the grim Polish camp. But she'd told Gracie and Alice, and they'd both agreed with Rose – that it was something Ma didn't need to know. He was dead. *Dead was dead.* Too late to do anything about it now.

But Rose did find out one more thing. According to the War Department, Lance Corporal Harry Ellis was due to be reburied in a military cemetery in Poznań, Poland.

Ma didn't want to go, so Rosemary went alone. Gracie didn't see any point, she said, for Da had left their lives a long time ago.

There was no sunshine that bleak day as she stood in front of his grave. The rain had pounded her, bouncing off the dull grey headstone. Brittle. Relentless. It had been a day shrouded with sadness, but something she'd needed to do.

The thought sent an ice-cold chill through her. Hands reaching out from the grave. But then, there were many of those, including Danny's.

Rosemary could never bring them back, Danny or her da. But she made them both a promise standing there. She would cherish their memories, think about them both in her quiet times. She would remember Danny's smile, his strength and courage when he flew out daily to face the terror in the skies. Now she must have courage too. Courage to draw a line under the savagery and move on.

There would be so much to do in the aftermath of war. So many families torn apart. Refugees with nowhere to go. There would be a lot of rebuilding to do – of homes, of cities, of people's lives. If Rose could help in some small way, then that's what she would try to do.

The war in Europe was finally over! It was an amazing, incredible thought that after all these years of struggle was hard for Rose to take in. *Could you really just call it THE END and that was that?* she wondered. It was more like the beginning. The start of a new time, a new era.

Rosemary Ellis held her head high. Determined to face the future. Whatever it would bring.

PART THREE

31

LONDON

JULY 1982

'C'mon, you lot, you're lagging behind.' Rosemary opened up another bottle of champagne, the cork leaving the bottle like a bullet, almost embedding itself in the ceiling.

She poured the wine into Grace and Alice's glasses, some of it making its way sloppily onto the coffee table in front of them. Rose was right; Grace and Alice had some catching up to do before they were as tiddly as she was. Not that Rosemary often drank like this. But it was a special occasion.

A double celebration – Rose was about to retire, and Alice had become engaged to a wonderful man. None of them had met him yet, but if he had persuaded Alice to finally marry then Rosemary thought he must be a remarkable man. They would all meet him tomorrow at the inauguration of the Bethnal Green tube monument.

At last, there was to be a special memorial to all those people who had lost their lives in that awful disaster in 1943. Rosemary was thrilled, especially for her ma, who still had nightmares about that terrible night. Perhaps now Lil would be able to put the memories behind her. Rosemary hoped that tomorrow's ceremony would finally bring her ma some peace.

'Won't you miss it, Rose?' asked Gracie. 'The job? All that rushing around all over the place. Putting the world to rights.'

'Don't know that I put much of it right,' said Rosemary.

'Yes, you did!' said Alice, coming to her defence.

Rosemary smiled at her friend. Alice could always be relied on to make her feel good about what she'd done in her job, both in the war with POWs, and later with refugees. But really, it had been a drop in the ocean. She'd left the Red Cross many years ago, had been attached to the office of the United Nations High Commissioner for Refugees since then. It had been born out of the war, created in 1950 to help the millions of Europeans displaced from their homes. It was meant to be a temporary measure, yet there it was over thirty years later, still going strong.

Rose sighed. She had liked her job, but at times it was harrowing, and stressful. New conflicts. New refugees. *You never ran out of refugees*. It was time to slow down. Have something else besides work in her life. Now, perhaps, she could finally get to live in her tiny flat in Bonner Street for more than a few weeks at a time.

Bethnal Green. She'd always known she would come back to it. Although it had changed a lot – mostly young professionals had moved in where there once were families in cheek-by-jowl terrace houses – it still felt like home. Bethnal Green station on her doorstep and Victoria Park. Memories. Good and bad.

And Ma and Ivy weren't far away. Over in Shoreditch now. She used to work in a parachute factory there in the good old bad days.

She raised her glass. 'A toast,' said Rose, and she turned to her sister, Gracie. 'To you, Grace. Want you to know how proud

I am of you,' Rose said. 'You've worked hard on the farm and bringing those girls up on your own. I'm guessing *that* wasn't easy.'

'I'm not a victim, you know,' said Grace. 'I chose my life.'

'I know,' said Rose. 'We all make choices, right?' Her voice was wistful. No kids in *her* life. No man either. Two brilliant nieces, though.

'I've had a good life,' said Gracie. *Defensive now.* 'Don't need nobody feeling sorry for me, sis. I had a lovely man. Ten wonderful years with him. Lots don't get that much.'

'Joe was a good man,' said Rose. *She'd cried at his funeral, same as Gracie.* 'They don't make many like him.'

'Anyway,' said Grace, quickly changing the subject, 'this a celebration or a wake? What about Alice? She's the one we should be toasting.'

Rose raised her glass in the air. 'Of course.' She inclined her head towards her friend. 'Another toast. Here's to you, Alice, and your mystery man.' Although it wasn't strictly true, because Alice had spoken of him often, but only to Rose.

'Not very mysterious, I'm afraid,' Alice said. 'He's a modest man. Some might think him a little dull. But not me,' she added, quickly. 'He's been very good to me. And he's worked so hard to get the memorial set up.'

Rosemary thought about how the pair had met. Both Alice and her fiancé, Frank Usher, had worked tirelessly together to get the memorial garden organised. Alice had been a driving force for the project and when she'd advertised for people to help, Frank had answered the call. He had been there on that terrible night and had helped in the rescue. Now, he had gone to Holland to pick up his friend, a man called Adam Pietersen, who had also been at the underground station after disaster struck. This Pietersen was a much older man, though, and a little frail. Rosemary was worried for him. About the strain it might have on the man, both mental and physical, for he would be in a wheelchair.

They all toasted Rose's new life. And Alice's man. Then they finished the rest of the wine.

The day of the memorial service dawned. It had taken many hands to bring about. People from all walks of life, but they had one thing in common: they wanted to right a wrong, and give victims of the disaster the recognition they should have had so many decades ago.

Several of the survivors had come, as well as a few of the rescuers, and perhaps for them it would bring closure. The Mayor of London had announced he would be there. Something that hadn't gone unnoticed by Lil Ellis. She'd bought herself a new hat.

Now people were smiling, discovering friends and neighbours that time and distance had separated. And although there was a feeling of reverence for the victims who had lost their lives in the disaster, there was also a rekindling of the old wartime spirit.

They were all packed into a corner of Bethnal Green Garden outside the tube station, clustered around the impressive memorial. 'The Stairway to Heaven' was a full-sized replica of the original stairway where the disaster had happened.

It was a thing of beauty; Rose had thought that the minute she'd first seen it. An inverted stairway made of teak, over a simple but impressive concrete plinth. The teak had been reclaimed from a ship sunk during World War One. A poignant reminder, Rose thought, of the ability of humans to repeat their own mistakes and warlike idiocy over and over again.

The names of the dead were carved on the outside, and the

top covering had 173 small holes for the light to shine through. *The number of the dead.* Twenty-seven men, eighty-four women and sixty-two children.

Bronze plaques, stark against the sparkling white of the memorial's base, held the words of survivors, rescuers and relatives of the dead.

Rose thought it a fitting monument. The architect had been inspired, for it was exactly right. Simple. Dignified. Not pretentious or elaborate. Truthful. A sculpture that truly represented the spirit of the East Enders, both victims and survivors.

The short remembrance service was almost over now. The mayor had said his bit, had handed out certificates of thanks to the rescuers, and commemorative certificates to the survivors. She watched Ivy read hers. Watched the poor woman's shoulders heave in grief as she remembered her lost child. Saw her ma pat Ivy's lined hand. A gesture of sympathy, of solidarity. They had both suffered that night. The two women had a special friendship, a bond that had lasted a lifetime now. And Rose was glad of that.

A bugler played 'The Last Post' and Rose noticed Adam Pietersen give a shaky salute. He'd worn his naval uniform, an impressive-looking outfit. He must have cut a fine figure in his youth, but now the uniform hung from his shrunken shoulders and Rose wanted to weep for him. Still, he held himself proud and erect in his wheelchair, but there was a look of sadness on his grizzled face.

They all gathered around the buffet and an elderly lady in a WVS uniform served them tea from a massive urn. *Like old times.* And then Gracie jumped up onto the platform and started a spontaneous singsong. 'We'll Meet Again'. The voices may not have been as strong and boisterous as they once were, but the emotion poured out and smiles spread throughout the audience. Gracie was in her Women's Land Army uniform too.

How on earth had she managed to hold onto that, Rose wondered.

'See what they gave me? Aren't they gorgeous?' Alice thrust the massive bouquet under Rose's nose.

'Lovely. No more than you deserve, though. Hadn't been for you, Alice, this whole thing might never have happened,' said Rose.

'Me and a whole lot of others, especially Frank,' said Alice.

'*Especially Frank*,' agreed Rose. Although she hadn't long met him, Rosemary could see that he was special and that the love the man felt for Alice was real and honest. He would be a rock, she thought. Like Danny would have been for *her*, had he lived. A love that was unshakeable, steadfast and above all had its foundation in the respect they felt for each other. Equal partners, that's what this pair would be, Rose was convinced of that.

She swallowed hard, the remembered sadness almost choking her. The day and the uniforms and the overpowering emotion of people reliving the past – it had brought it all back. Had tripped her up, brought back the sadness of loss. But you had to let it go.

She nodded to Frank Usher when he smiled at her. Rose didn't know why, but they seemed to have formed an instant bond, as if they shared a history. Though, of course, that wasn't so. They had never met before, although Alice had spoken of him to her.

Rose watched him push his old friend Adam over to the tea urn. Eighty years old, Frank had told her, but Adam Pietersen was still determined to look life in the eye, give it a good run for its money. *Always had been*, Frank had said.

'Never understood the British obsession with tea,' laughed Adam Pietersen. 'Don't suppose you've got a nip of brandy somewhere? Keep out this damn English weather.'

'Pub,' said Gracie. 'Just around the corner, near where the old Bug Hole used to be. Remember it?'

'Ma and I practically lived there,' said Rose.

'Speak for yourself, Rose.' Lil Ellis moved her mouth into a small, tight pout. 'I ain't *never* lived in no pub. It ain't Christian.'

'The *Bug Hole*, Ma. Not the pub,' said Rose.

'So – shall we?' asked Adam. 'Warm the inner man with a small nip.' He smiled at Lil. 'And did I mention that you haven't aged a mite since I last saw you, Mrs Ellis? And still as charming.' He took her hand and pressed it to his lips in a very gallant, and distinctly continental, gesture.

And Lil giggled like a schoolgirl. 'Call me Lil,' she said.

———

They all gathered in Rosemary's flat the next day and talked about the ceremony.

'Your friend seemed like a very sweet man,' said Rose.

'Good-hearted and kind,' said Frank. 'But Adam's had a lot of sadness in his life. It's taken its toll. He's not a well man.'

'A gentleman,' said Lil.

'So, he got back home okay?' asked Rose.

'Arrived safely,' said Frank. 'A friend picked him up from the airport.'

'Not his wife?' asked Lil.

'No,' said Frank. 'Not his wife.'

'He's not married, then?' said Lil.

'Ma!'

'What, Rose? Just askin'. Ain't nothin' wrong in that.'

'It's sad. When we were talking about that awful night down the shelter, he started to cry. It was weird. I've never seen the chap cry before,' said Frank. 'Great big man like that. Hero – you know?'

'Probably brought it all back. The ceremony yesterday. Couldn't have been easy for anybody,' said Rose.

'You know what he said?' asked Frank. '"God allowed me to

save a few people that night, but I couldn't save my own wife, my own daughter."'

'Jesus! That's tragic. They die in the war, Frank?' asked Rose.

'His wife, yes. She worked for the Resistance. Got captured. The Gestapo killed her.'

'Horrific! said Rose. 'And his daughter?'

'Anna. She was in the Resistance as well, but she didn't die in the war. Still, I wish he'd told me. I wouldn't have asked him to come over if I'd known,' said Frank. 'Not when he'd had such a shock.'

'What?' asked Alice.

'Her death. Anna's passing. Unexpected like that, must have been a hell of a shock for the old chap. It's still fresh, the grief.'

'So, she wasn't sick or anything?' said Rose. 'You said *unexpected*.'

'Only two months ago. They found her sitting in her chair one day. Like she'd just nodded off. It was a heart attack.'

'To die alone – that's sad,' said Rose. 'How old was she? Did Adam say? Not that it makes any difference, she's gone now.'

'Fifty-seven. Not old, really. One year younger than me,' said Frank. 'Makes you think.'

'Certainly does,' said Gracie, and she stared pointedly at her sister, a challenge in her eyes.

'What?' said Rosemary. 'What did *I* say?'

'It's like I'm always telling you, Rose. You want to live a little. You need to bury the past, get on with your life before it's too late,' Gracie said. 'Never know how long you've got.'

'Well, now that we've cheered ourselves up a wee bit…!' started Lil, drily.

'So, the poor man's had his troubles,' said Rose. 'Can't believe he'd still travel over here for the ceremony in the middle of all that.'

'Told me Anna had always wanted him to go,' Frank said. 'Said he did it for her as much as himself.'

'And to think that he rescued me,' said Lil. 'If it weren't for him, I wouldn't be here. It's a funny old world and that's the truth. It'll kill us *all* before we leave it.'

It wasn't often Lil Ellis told a joke. They all laughed.

32

CORNWALL

27 JULY 1982

What a beautiful summer it had been. Who needed to go to the Med when you had everything you needed right there?

Rose was going to Cornwall one last time. On the anniversary again. She'd done her bit. Had been to Havenporth several times now, keeping faith with the promise and the memories. But the time had come to say goodbye to the past, to finally slip the silken knot and allow the future to take whatever course lay in store. Soon she would be sixty. A *young* sixty, she reminded herself yet again. She remembered her sister Gracie's words. That Rose should bury the past and live a little before it was too late. Have some fun for a change. She'd had a busy life, but most of it was work, not much play.

Maybe her sister was right. Maybe it wasn't too late. While you were still breathing. And with any luck, Rosemary Ellis intended to keep on breathing for a long time to come.

Her sister waved her off, was house-sitting Rose's flat for a while.

'Why not stay?' Gracie had asked her. 'We could go to the

flicks. I'll cook you a meal. We'll have a bottle of wine, Rose. Just us two. Forget Cornwall.'

'Tempting,' laughed Rosemary. 'But I need to get off. Twenty-seventh of July. It's our anniversary.'

'Rose!'

'Last time, I promise.'

'You're stuck in a rut, Rose. And you won't find anything there,' said Gracie.

'No. I guess not,' said Rosemary.

———

Her drive to Cornwall had been an odd, dream-like affair. Once she'd arrived, she had tried to recall the moors: had the usual early-morning mist been clinging to them? Sometimes it was like driving your way through porridge. But, strangely, the whole thing had been surreal. And maybe even dangerous, driving on autopilot like that. She had been surprised when she arrived in Havenporth. Remembered little of the journey after that last goodbye to her sister.

Maybe that was it – the unsettling thoughts about the future. *Stuck in a rut*, that was her sister's parting shot. And was she? Clinging on to a love story that belonged to the past? A love that had never been tested in the furnace of life. Even now, the passage of time gave it a feeling of fantasy, as if the whole thing had been in her mind only. Had Danny Welland even existed, or had she made him up?

A dashing pilot. A wish. A dream.

Time was a strange thing. She supposed she should feel ancient by now, but she didn't. Rosemary felt like the same person who had once stood on the cliffs of Havenporth with so much expectation of a future with Danny. And she was lucky, she knew that, for although she was no longer the stunning young girl of her youth, time had not been too unkind to Rosemary.

She only needed glasses for distance and her green eyes were still clear, could become animated – especially when she laughed. *She should do that more often.* Not try to take the world on her shoulders. Her skin was good too, the odd wrinkle here and there, and her hair still that rich brown that admittedly nowadays had to be given a helping hand. It had been cut into a sculpted bob, for she'd given up her long tresses in her fifties. *Not a good look for an older face.* But heads still turned on the odd occasion.

The role of spinster was one she'd grown into gradually. And it suited her, even though there were times she felt lonely. Not that she'd lived the life of a nun. There had been men. Some proposals of marriage along the way. But although she'd been flattered, Rose had never found anyone special enough to share her life with. That was the legacy Danny had left her. Up there on his pedestal. But she couldn't blame him, of course. *Could she?* Dead men can't speak in their own defence.

'Good to have you back, Miss Ellis. Jack will show you your room,' said the young woman at the front desk of her hotel.

'Not my old room?' Rose was looking at the room key's fob, at the unfamiliar number there. 'I wanted my usual room,' she said.

'Sorry, but we're fully booked right now. You're in the new extension. If you'd booked earlier...'

'That's okay.' She didn't want to make a fuss. Wasn't this young girl's fault. Still, everything changes. Nothing stays the same forever.

She unpacked. Changed into her casuals, and took a stroll up East Cliff to work up an appetite. Most of the holiday-makers were already trekking back from the beach for lunch. Back to hotels and boarding houses and those awful, boxy holiday flats that had sprung up all over the bay. Lots of changes were taking place; a subtle kind of vandalism was turning her precious Havenporth into a haven for slot-machine addicts. So different from the place she'd fallen in love with forty years ago. Their magical Brigadoon.

This would be her final pilgrimage, she'd told Gracie. And in a way she was relieved, the heavy sigh that left her lips resigned. There was nothing there for her now. Only sadness for a time that no longer existed.

Halfway up the cliff she stopped to catch her breath, sitting down on a bench that, after so many visits, she considered hers. She looked out to sea and smiled. That was one thing they couldn't change. Still as awesome as the first time she'd seen it.

She jumped, startled as a large black Labrador bounded over to her, covering Rose in muddy paw prints.

'Oh! I'm sorry about that. Winston gets carried away at times.'

Rosemary's eyes were instantly tugged to the source of the voice. She swallowed painfully as the sight of the man's face dried her mouth, and her heart tried to punch its way through her chest.

'You okay?' asked the man.

'What?'

'I hope my dog didn't upset you. He gets over-excited when he's chasing sticks.'

She felt sick. Her skin turned white and clammy. Her breath, caught in the tight funnel of her throat, came out in shallow gasps and the young man looked concerned.

'Look – should I get a doctor or something…?'

Rose smiled weakly. The poor young man looked scared to death. How stupid of her. Of *course* it wasn't him. How could it possibly be? He was dead. And if he'd lived, he'd be two years older than *her* by now.

The man returned her smile, relieved, and joined her on the bench. They talked. He was easy to talk to and Rose decided that she should talk to more young people.

'So, is this your first visit here?' she asked.

'Probably sounds foolish, but it was something I promised my dad we'd do,' the young man said.

'Oh?'

'He *loved* this place!'

'Really? Maybe I've seen him,' said Rose. 'I've been here a few times myself. Did he visit often?'

'He's only been once, but he always wanted to come back. When Mum died, he was all set to, then he got sick. A stroke. It was very sudden.'

'I'm sorry.' She searched for another word but couldn't find one. *Sorry*. It seemed an inadequate reply to the news of a death. It sometimes sounded trite. But she truly meant it.

She couldn't explain why, but Rosemary felt a strong affinity with this personable young man who'd lost both his mother and father.

'It's okay. He's had a good life. Must have been quite a character in his youth. He was a war pilot.'

33

Rosemary felt her face empty itself of colour.

'You okay?'

'Impossible.' She whispered the word.

'Sorry, I don't understand.'

Rose's hand fastened urgently onto the young man's arm.

'Your father...'

'Ye—es?'

'What did he fly?'

'Hurricanes, I believe. Quite romantic, really. He was shot down and my mother hid him. She was in the Dutch Resistance.'

'No!' It came out as a wail. And Rosemary felt the earth gape into a massive chasm beneath her, sucking her life into the centre of it.

'Something wrong?' *The woman was obviously one loaf short of a bakery. And his arm – what was that about? She was hanging onto it with a ferocity that belied her small frame.*

'His name, what was his name?' The urgency of her words gave them a brittle edge and the man looked embarrassed.

'I don't follow.'

'Your father's name – what was it?'

'Well, most people called him Dutch, but his name's Daniel.'

'Welland?'

'Yes...! But, how did you know?'

'Danny!' The name exploded from her lips. *He'd been alive – for all those years.* 'Why did he send you here?'

The man gave her a puzzled look. Rosemary tightened the grip on his arm. 'Look – it's important to me.'

'Did you know my dad, then? Are *you* the reason I came here?'

'I don't know.' Her voice was flat, forcing out the small puffs of speech as if the effort was too much for her. A plump tear hung at the corner of her eye.

Rose hadn't cried in a long time.

'He told me there was someone special. Someone he loved very much. Was that you?'

Rose shook her head. 'Hardly, if he married your mother,' she said.

'Yes – she was a good woman. A good mother. And he was grateful to Mum, but I don't think theirs was a love story.'

'He made a life with her.'

'She looked after him when he was shot down. He lost his memory for a while, couldn't remember who he was. Didn't even know there was a war on, that he was a pilot.'

Rosemary pulled a small lace handkerchief from her pocket and dabbed at her eyes. The man shifted uncomfortably on the bench.

'Do you have any brothers or sisters?' she asked.

'A younger sister.' He grinned. 'Rosie's a beaut! Always been the apple of Dad's eye. You know how it is between fathers and their daughters.'

So, he'd named his daughter after her. *Consolation prize.* No, that was stupid; he'd obviously still loved her. But it seemed that by the time he even remembered her name he was married to another woman. And he hadn't left her, because Danny was a man of principle. It was one of the reasons she'd loved him; so, hardly a reason to hate him now. No point in being bitter, it was such a self-defeating emotion. Besides, it wasn't in her nature.

Rose sighed. Life was such a strange concoction of twists and turns, some happy, some sad. No point in crying over what might have been. Not when life had been so very good to her.

'I'm sorry if I made you unhappy, talking about my family,' he said.

She smiled. 'No harm done. And I'm glad we've met.'

'You *are* her, aren't you?' he said.

'Who?'

'The love of his life.'

'Maybe. I'd like to think so,' said Rose.

'I'm sure of it. Don't you see, that's why he made me promise to come here – to this spot on the cliffs? He was *very* specific. Kept going over it to make sure I'd got it right. And the date...'

'What about the date?' she asked, urgently.

'Said I should go on the anniversary, whatever that meant.'

'What?' Rose's breath choked in her throat.

'July twenty-seventh. He said it was important.'

Rosemary Ellis felt pure joy. It was right. He *did* love her – he'd remembered. He'd gone all the way through his life and still remembered the date. The day he'd proposed to her. The day he'd wanted to keep special.

'I'm sorry he didn't make it back here.'

'So am I.' Her words were wistful, but not sad.

'But I'm glad *I* did. Maybe we can be friends.' The young man's Labrador came bounding back and jumped up on Rosemary, licking her hand. 'There you are, Winston agrees.'

She laughed. It was infectious, a laugh that had the life-force in it and all the joy that came from remembering life still had good things to offer.

'I should get back,' said Rose. *Just being polite*, for she didn't really want to leave. To break the spell. She wanted to stay and talk. Talk about Danny and the life he'd made for himself. Talk to Danny's son. But the young man probably had better things to do with his time than sit there and listen to her reminisce.

'I'm here for a while. If it wouldn't make you feel uncomfortable, perhaps we could have dinner together. What about tonight? I hear there's an excellent restaurant down in the valley.' He winked. 'Dad told me he used to take someone special there.'

Rose blushed. She hadn't done that in years. 'They knocked *that* old place down years ago. But there's a bistro on the beach that I'm sure he'd have liked. And dinner would be lovely.'

'It's a date, then. Well, not a *date*, obviously... you know what I mean.' It was the young man's turn to blush.

She patted his hand in a motherly fashion and it felt like the most natural thing to do, as if an instinctive bond already existed between them. Danny's son got ready to leave, but instead of shaking hands, he grabbed her in a spontaneous hug, said he hoped she would find time to come and meet his wife, Angie, and their two little girls. If she *wanted* to, that was.

It was only then that he told her his name, and she knew then why she'd been drawn to this lovely young man. He had his father's sensitivity, hadn't wanted to hurt her by revealing that they were both called Daniel. Except friends called *him* Dan.

She smiled at his thoughtfulness, and at the irony of the circle of life. It sometimes took you right back to where you started and if you were lucky, you learnt from it.

'He was gutted he couldn't make it back here himself,' said Dan Welland.

'Yes... well. Life can be unkind.'

'But he's hoping that when he gets his strength back, he'll be up to the trip.'

'What! Wait. Danny's alive? I thought you said he was dead.'

'Dead? No! Look, I'm sorry if I gave you that idea. He's had a stroke, but he's a real fighter. Getting better by the day. Can't wait to start rehab.'

'Alive. My God, he's *alive*.'

Dan Welland laughed. 'Alive and kicking and giving us all hell. Wouldn't use a wheelchair. Wanted to walk out of the hospital by himself.'

'Is he allowed visitors? Would it be okay if I...?' She couldn't say it. Didn't dare allow herself to hope. To see him again. To look into those eyes. Older now, but all the same, still Danny's eyes.

'You mean you'd go over to Holland?'

'I'd go to the moon if I could see him again.'

'Hey – my old man was right. You are one sparky lady. And I'm sure he'd be thrilled to see you.'

Winston jumped up on them both in turn.

'Time to get him back, before he disgraces himself. Until tonight then. Do you mind if I bring my wife? I'm sure she'd love to meet you, and she's a Londoner like you. You'd have a lot to talk about; she's always been really close to Dad.'

'That would be wonderful... *Dan*.'

A grin took hold of her face the whole way back to the hotel, and refused to let go. And who cared what people might think? That one of her ducks was missing? Well, you know what? She didn't care. Maybe it wasn't *natural* to go around smiling to yourself like that, but it should be. And despite her dodgy knee, Rose Ellis quickened her step and felt like a twenty-year-old again.

34

It wasn't a date, but a fly on Rose's bedroom wall might have been excused for thinking it was. She'd tried on everything in the small wardrobe, and still couldn't decide what to wear to their meal in the bistro that night. Most of the clothes she'd packed were holiday casuals, things you could wear on the beach. She hadn't expected to be invited out to dinner.

Only two things were front runners: her long kaftan, and a white lace dress that came to just below the knee. Rose had always liked the dress and with her summer tan it was striking, she felt. But maybe just a bit too formal. Still, it was a special occasion, after all: dinner with Danny's son and daughter-in-law.

Make-up immaculate. Hair perfect, conditioned to within an inch of its life. The graduated bob complemented the shape of her face. Her hairdresser was a genius, and it was so easy to deal with. She looked in the mirror – and almost changed her mind. The overall effect was maybe a little showy, like she was trying too hard. But Rose picked up her handbag and closed the door behind her, before she could change her mind again.

She walked slowly to the bistro on the beach. It had been

built on the footprint of the old restaurant that both she and Danny had loved. The thought sent a tiny shiver through her and she pulled her short jacket more tightly around her. He was *alive*. She was still struggling to believe it, but it had to be true, because this young man was obviously Danny's son, the image of his father. And why on earth would he lie to her?

They were both waiting for her at the door, Dan and Angela Welland, smiles of welcome easing her into a meeting that could easily have been strained and choked with emotion. But it was as if Rose had known them forever.

'Dad said you were a stunner, and he was right,' said Angie. 'That dress is gorgeous too.'

'Thank you, Angela. I wasn't sure. Thought it might be over the top.'

'Beautiful – and call me Angie, please. And are you Rosemary or Rose?' she asked.

'I answer to both,' said Rose. 'Except Danny used to call me *Rosie*.'

'He told me.' The young woman smiled.

'He *did*?'

Angie took Rose's arm and guided her to their table, ahead of her husband. 'We'll talk later, if that's okay,' she whispered. 'Things I need to tell you.'

It was a promise that intrigued Rose and set a whole butterfly farm loose in her stomach. She hardly touched her salmon en croute, but managed to down a couple of large glasses of wine with indecent haste. She pulled herself back from the brink. Didn't want these good people to think she was just one step away from the Betty Ford Clinic.

When Dan left to pay the bill, his wife suggested that she and Rose should meet the next morning for coffee, just the two of them.

'Unless you're going back home?' she said.

'No, that's fine. I'd love to get together. The Engine House café over on West Cliff has some lovely pastries.'

'Sounds great,' said Angie. 'Never say no to a pastry. Just us girls, then. Dan's been dying to take the kids surfing. And we've got things to talk about. Stuff Dad couldn't tell his son, or his wife Anna.'

'But he told you?'

'I suppose he felt he could trust me. And I lost my own father when I was young. Danny and I became close, closer than a normal father-in-law, I guess. He told me to call him Dad, and maybe I reminded him of you, being British. He shared some secrets. You need to know all the facts before you go rushing off to see him.'

———

How could she sleep? She didn't even try. Excitement made her feel like a kid again and she thought about phoning Gracie, but that was stupid. She could hardly wake her sister in the middle of the night. Maybe Alice, then. But that was equally as daft: Alice and Frank would be in India now, enjoying their honeymoon and sitting on a bench in front of the romantic Taj Mahal, making lovesick doe eyes at each other.

Rose woke up freezing cold on top of the bed. Six in the morning, and the book she'd been trying to read last night still there on her pillow. Stiff, sore, shivering. Every joint in her body hurt like she was suffering from the flu, and the feeling of euphoria from the previous night had all but drained away. *Reality check. Hangover! Drank far too much last night. Can't drink wine anymore*, she reminded herself. Allergy or something. She should read up on it.

She couldn't even remember getting back last night. Dear God, they didn't have to drag her home in an alcoholic stupor, did they? And then it came to her – Dan had dropped her at the front door of her small hotel, and she'd made it through with hardly a wobble.

A hot shower. And coffee. Lots of it. That should do the trick – and a couple of aspirins. Rose believed strongly in the restorative power of aspirins and coffee. *Note to self – no more booze!*

The shower was disappointing: whatever they'd done to the plumbing in the new extension hadn't worked. The water didn't pound down on her in the flood she hoped for but was a sad, desperate trickle. Still, at least it was hot and Rose manoeuvred under its miserly stream like an acrobat, managing to get her whole body wet and washing off the shampoo suds.

She had a flashback to another time. Her hair being washed in a bowl in their kitchen sink in Royston Street, her mother rinsing off with cold water thrown over you from a chipped tin jug. And no more shampoo left. Shampoo had been one of the first luxuries to go in the war, at least in their household. Red Lifebuoy soap with its strange chemical smell. That's what they'd washed their hair with, and no fancy conditioners to make it soft. A dash of vinegar in the washing bowl did the same thing.

Still, happy days, though, as well as bad. But then maybe she was remembering things through the far-off sentimental prism of distant years. Rose-coloured glasses. That was funny, right? At least if your name was Rose.

She towelled off her hair and gave it a quick blow dry. Slapped on some eye make-up, decided on the black and white striped trousers with the white tee and her sandals. Might as well give the sandals an outing: she'd had her toenails painted in their summer regalia. Shame to waste it.

Coffee next. By the time Rose arrived in the small breakfast lounge, it was beginning to fill up with hotel guests. Holiday-makers believed in getting a head start on the day. Getting their money's worth out of the beach. And Havenporth had a beach worth shouting about: golden sand for the kids to build sandcastles with moats, and rock pools teeming with life at low tide. Tiny creatures waiting to be discovered along the shoreline. Crabs, prawns so transparent you could see their internal organs through their fragile skin. Pipefish, thin and long, and those strange snakelocks anemones, vivid green with purple on their tips. Elegant-looking things, but with stings in their tails, tentacles built to stun passing fish. And cushion starfish, hidden among the weeds, tiny five-legged miracles no bigger than a fifty-pence piece.

Back in her room, she called her sister Gracie.

'You're right,' said Rose. 'Life doesn't last forever...'

'You sound happy,' said Gracie. 'I'm glad. I was worried for you, Rose.'

'I've had some incredible, colossal, life-changing news.'

———

Angie Welland was waiting for her inside the café.

Rose took a deep, calming yoga breath, like her teacher recommended. She headed for the table in the corner with its pretty lace cloth and one of those cute afternoon-tea stands in the middle of it. The cake stand had three separate layers, each with more stunning goodies on it: tiny cocktail sandwiches on the bottom layer, a Cornish cream tea on the next, and the most exquisite and tempting iced buns and cakes on the top.

'Hope you don't mind, but I took the liberty of ordering their special afternoon tea.' Angie laughed. 'Though obviously it's still morning, but I thought we'd indulge ourselves. Bit of luxury never hurt and this is quite an occasion for me. Finally meeting you like this, Rose. Never imagined I would.'

'Looks fabulous,' said Rose. She'd only had coffee for breakfast, and that carrot cake looked inviting with its lush butter icing. *Maybe just a little.*

'Tea okay?' asked Angie. 'Or would you rather have coffee?'

'Tea's fine,' said Rose. 'As "builders" as it comes. Can't be fiddling around with all that fruit stuff.' She had once had an unsuccessful battle with green tea and shuddered at the memory of its medicinal taste.

When they'd got over the housekeeping stuff – poured the tea, filled their plates with the tiny sandwiches – there was silence. As if something extraordinary and memorable was about to happen.

'Where to start?' said the young woman. 'I suppose the most important thing is that we shouldn't do anything that could make Danny's situation any worse.'

'Oh?' Rose prickled slightly. Of course she wouldn't do anything that would hurt Danny. And how could Angie Welland think that she would?

'It's just that it might be quite a surprise for him, maybe even a shock, when he's had so many lately.'

'You don't think I should go? That I'd give him a heart attack or something? Is that what you're saying? Of *course* I'd be sensitive,' said Rose. She felt hurt. And misunderstood. She had always put Danny first, in front of her own feelings. Couldn't this woman see that she loved him? Wanted only the best for him?

Angie reached over and patted Rose's hand. 'I'm sorry. That isn't what I meant. Of course you must go, but you need to think carefully about how you prepare the ground, that's all I meant. Just to appear out of the ether like that, when Dad thinks you've been dead for the last forty years. It could shake him up a bit. Just wanted to warn you before you go rushing over to the nursing home in Rotterdam.'

Rose's hand stopped halfway to her mouth, her salmon and cucumber sandwich hovering in mid-air. 'He thinks I'm *dead*? How in the name of God could the man ever imagine I was dead?'

'We need to talk about that, I guess. It's very important. Because it changed his whole life. He would *never* have married Anna Pietersen if he'd thought there was one chance in a million you were still alive. But he had confirmation from two different sources that you'd died. And that's the *only* reason he went back to Holland. He made a life with Anna, but he never loved her. And I guess her father Adam was a bit of a matchmaker there as well. Nudged him firmly in Anna's direction when the war ended. Your Danny respected Adam Pietersen and the man had been kind to him, helped him get a job in the SOE – Special Operations.'

'Adam Pietersen?' *It couldn't be the same man surely? Not the bloke they'd had drinks at the pub with? The one who'd come over for the inauguration even though he'd been in such distress himself.*

'Anna's father,' said Angie.

'Is this the *same* Anna who just died?'

'A few months ago. We all went to her funeral. It was hard enough for my Dan to lose his mother. For Danny to lose his wife. But Adam was inconsolable, wasn't expecting her to go before him. You know how it is with your kids. You expect them to outlive you, and Anna was his only child.'

'Anna Pietersen. My Danny married Anna Pietersen?' whispered Rose.

'Yes,' said Angie. The look on her face was confusion. Like there was a complicated plot and no one had warned her about the twist. Had left a bit out. She just wasn't following. 'Is something wrong? I don't understand.'

'It just seems such an odd coincidence,' said Rosemary. 'I suppose it's the *same* Anna Pietersen. And her father's definitely called Adam?'

'Adam Pietersen, yes,' said Angie.

'And did he just travel over to London?' asked Rose.

'He went there for a memorial service at Bethnal Green,' said Angie.

'It *must* be the same man,' said Rose. 'We met him there. Took him for a drink in the pub.'

'We didn't want him to go by himself,' said Angie, 'but Adam insisted. He can be stubborn at times. And he said that his friend Frank would look after him.'

'It *is* him. The same man. Incredible!' said Rose.

'What is?' asked Angie.

'You know that thing about it being a small world. Sounds trite, but it's mind-blowing.'

'Why's that?' asked Angie Welland.

'Danny's father-in-law. This Adam Pietersen. He's the man who rescued my mother in the Bethnal Green tube disaster.'

'That *is* incredible,' said Angie, 'a strange twist of fate – that they should both be there on the same night.'

'Yes, strange. But then life can be strange at times,' said Rose.

'Adam used to have nightmares about it. The things he saw that night,' said Angie.

'My mother too,' said Rosemary. 'It sounded horrific. And they tried to sweep it under the carpet, so the real tragedy didn't even come out at the time. Wouldn't have been good for morale. And Hitler would have made a propaganda nightmare of it.'

'That's war for you,' said Angie. 'A terrible thing. And you're right. It's an odd coincidence. The two families being intertwined like that, especially after what you and Danny felt for each other. Seems like it was meant to be.'

35

They both agreed that Angie should be the one to break the news to Danny Welland. And that it shouldn't be done over the phone. Face to face, so that Angie could prepare the ground, would be there to help with the fall-out. So many wasted years when he could have been with his Rosie.

Even Angie, who knew him well, had no idea how her father-in-law would react when he found out Rose was alive. Had been all this time.

And the worst bit was that Rose could do nothing. It was all in someone else's hands. Not something she was used to or could deal with well. She was the one who sorted things. Always had been. Both in her family and in her life. Now all she could do was wait.

Angie and Dan and their two girls were still on holiday, and there was no reason to cut it short and rush back home to Rotterdam like there was some kind of emergency. Danny was on the mend, had friends around him, was being looked after. Rose could understand all that, but it didn't help. She wanted to be with him right then, that second. Waste no more time.

Rosemary drove home, images of him filling her head, the

sound of his voice in her ears. He'd have changed, like her, the years putting lines on his face perhaps and his hair – that beautiful hair of his – would it still be there? She forced herself to ignore any more thoughts like that. It would be how it would be.

Meanwhile there was something she could do. Something positive to fill the wait.

She should share this new, exciting news with Gracie and Ma. Make them understand how things might change, tell them about these happy, miraculous things that Rose hoped would guide her into a future where Danny would play a part. How much of a part was something that fate would decree, as it had done many times in her life before. Hopefully fate would be on her side now. Help Danny to recover. But would he still want her in his world? Now, after all this time?

Still, she had to be optimistic. How perfect life would be if this man whose memory she had cherished for so long could finally be a part of her world again. Here, beside her, not only in her dreams. Perfection!

Rose had told Ma and Gracie to dress up a bit. It was a celebration, after all. Drinks and a meal out, she said.

Her ma arrived in a taxi. Rose paid the driver.

'Didn't bring my purse,' Lil said.

Rose gave her ma a knowing smile. It wasn't anything new for Lil to 'forget' her purse. Being frugal during the war was a habit that had stuck with Ma. But Rosemary didn't mind, believed Lil deserved to be looked after now. She'd struggled for her family, brought them safely through to adulthood. Tough love. Lil's sort of love wouldn't be written about in poetry. But it was real, Rose knew that.

They walked arm in arm to Bethnal Green Road and they

all struck up a song. A happy, wartime song, with Gracie taking the lead.

'You're perky,' said Lil. 'You got something to celebrate, Rose?'

'Tell you when we've got a drink in our hands.'

'I guess there's a bloke in there somewhere. Am I right?' said Grace. 'Did you finally listen to your wise little sister, who's got more common sense in her small toe than you've got in that whole body of yours?'

She took them to Pellicci's. The best of both worlds. It was a café where Lil would be able to get her steak and kidney pie and she and Gracie could have something Italian. A result all round, especially when the waiter brought the wine.

'So...?' said Gracie. 'You waiting for a drum roll? Out with it, Rose. And don't say *"what?"*, 'cause you know you're bursting to tell us.'

'It's kind of monumental, I guess. Hard to know where to begin, without giving everybody a bloody heart attack.'

'Jesus, Rose. You want an Oscar? Just tell us, unless you think Ma and I are stupid and won't get it.'

'It's not that. It's just...'

'What?' asked Gracie.

She'd tried to think it through. The least dramatic way, that wouldn't give them both the kind of shock she'd had. Her ma was old. Wouldn't be easy. She decided to work up to it – slowly.

'You know I went to Havenporth...'

'God's sake. 'Course we know. *You* know she went to Havenporth, Ma?' Gracie grinned.

'Not an imbecile, Gracie. Though there's some treats me like I was.' Lil looked over at her daughter Rose, an eyebrow arched. No one could arch an eyebrow as critically as Lil Ellis.

Okay, straight in. Deep end. No lifebelt. 'Well, I met somebody there. On the cliffs. Right where Danny and I used to walk.'

'Knew it!' said Lil. 'You got yerself a fancy-man at last. 'Bout time, girl.'

Could you still be a girl at nearly sixty? Maybe she'd always be a girl to her ma. Sort of comforting.

'He's already married to a lovely woman. And he's half my age.'

'So, why we even discussing him?' asked Gracie.

'Because,' said Rose, 'he's Danny's son.'

There was a long pause. 'Not yer man that was ready to marry you, our Rose?'

'The same,' she said. And now Rosemary couldn't hold back the grin any longer.

'Don't get it,' said Gracie. 'And call me thick, though I don't think I am – but how the hell can you produce a son from beyond the grave?'

'You can't. You'd need to be very much alive for that and living in Rotterdam,' said Rose, still grinning. She studied their confused faces. *But then who wouldn't be?*

'Nope. Still don't get it,' said Gracie.

Her ma didn't say anything. Just sat there hanging on to her glass of wine like it was the only thing in the world that made sense.

'Exactly what I thought, at first,' said Rose. 'He's the image of his da. Gave me a bit of a turn. And he explained that he was there on our special anniversary, because Danny had asked him to go.'

'He know who you were, Rose?' asked her ma.

'Not at first. And the strange thing was that Danny hadn't told him everything. But he'd told his daughter-in-law all about me. Lovely lady. We get on well.'

'No,' said Gracie. 'Still not totally with you. Why would he tell this woman everything and not his own son?'

'I guess it would be hard for a son to hear that his father had loved someone else before his mother, and always would do. Besides, there're some things you can say to a woman, that a man might not understand. She's British as well, like Danny, her father-in-law, and they're very close. He told her all about coming back home to look for me, after he'd been shot down. But some people told him I'd been killed. That our house had a direct hit.'

'So it did.'

'Yeah, the old one. But we weren't in it, were we?'

'So, the bastard took hisself off and got married, Rose. Left you at the bleedin' altar,' said Lil.

'He didn't know, did he? Angie said that if he'd known I was still alive, he'd never had gone and married this Dutch woman. Had two kids with her. Made his life with her.'

'And where's she now?' asked Grace. 'This wife?'

'She died last year. And then Danny had a stroke. The shock, I suppose. Being with somebody all your life like that. Bound to take a toll, their passing.'

And that's when Rose broke down. She'd been holding back the tears, but some things were just too overpowering to ignore.

Lil moved closer. Put a scrawny arm around her daughter's shoulder and squeezed. 'It's okay, Rose. You still got us. And what you never had, you can't miss. Stands to sense. He's gone, and that's that.'

'That's what I thought. Forget the man, he's gone now, and I reckoned even though he'd married this Anna... well, he wouldn't have done if he'd known I was still alive.'

'There you are then,' said Lil.

'And it was kind of comforting to think he hadn't forgotten me. All those years and he still remembered our anniversary, the day he proposed. Told his son to go there on the same day.'

'That's nice,' said Gracie.

'It's better than that,' said Rose. 'True, Danny's had a stroke, but he's still *alive*. And I'm off to see him. Soon as Angie phones to tell me it's okay.'

'Angie?' asked Lil.

'Keep up, Ma. That's his daughter-in-law – right?' said Grace.

'Right. She thinks it's better if she breaks the news gently to him, before I go racing over there to Holland. Tells him I've been alive all these years. The man's been ill. Don't want to kill him off. Not now, when I've just found him.'

'Proper pair of numpties, then.'

'What, Ma?'

'You pair. Not safe to be let out on your own. *You* thought *he* was dead. *He* thought *you* was dead. Probably best you never had kids.' Her ma laughed and tossed back the rest of her wine. 'And I'll have another one of these,' she said. ''Cause if I'm not mistaken, there's more to come.'

And that was her ma. Cunning as a fox. And still in charge of all her marbles, even if they weren't as shiny as they used to be.

36

Danny Welland looked longingly out of the window of his room. It was on the ground floor. *Should be easy just to step outside.* Make his escape from this place where they treated him like a decrepit idiot with no brains, a child who couldn't think for himself.

He'd only had a stroke, for pity's sake – wasn't stupid. He could fend for himself if they'd let him. But here he was in this damn nursing home being told what to do, what to eat, when to nap.

He'd been forced to eat rice pudding, suck down jelly. Baby food. When what he really wanted was to tuck into a huge fried breakfast, oozing with grease. Food that put a lining on your stomach like concrete, gave you blowback for at least a couple of hours later. Or a large helping of fish and chips. But he hadn't had proper fish 'n' chips for years: the English kind, cooked in beef dripping. Not that these busybodies would let him have that now.

He'd only agreed to go there to get out of the Dijkzigt-ziekenhuis, the Dijkzigt hospital, where he'd spent the first few weeks recovering from his stroke. The hospital was fine, the care good, the food okay, the staff friendly, and some of the nurses were easy on the eye. But the whole place was full of sick people. Didn't help you get better, looking at that lot everywhere.

Here, in the nursing home, they made him use a walker like an old man. And he wasn't! He was only sixty-two – plenty of good mileage left in him. He'd been doing the exercises and the strength was coming back to his legs, and soon he'd ditch the Zimmer frame.

Danny was feeling more upbeat than he had for ages. His good friend De Groot had been to visit that morning, bringing his lady friend with him. A fine-looking woman with large breasts that shook when she laughed, huge teeth, and a smile that put dimples in her cheeks.

They'd laughed a lot, talked about old times, and Anna and Beatrix and Edwin and Sara. All gone now, but somehow the wounds weren't as raw as they'd once been. Except Anna, of course – the pain of Anna's passing was still like an open sore that hadn't healed. But with time it would. And probably long before it had any right to. And that was a guilty barb that sometimes ate into him.

She'd made him a good wife, had been a good mother, but if he had his time over again, Danny Welland knew he wouldn't have married her. After the first few years there'd been no love between them, just an understanding that they needed to be together for their children. And there was Adam, of course. A divorce would have finished the man. And he was a good man. A man who had already lost a wife. Danny couldn't take anything else away from his father-in-law.

He'd wanted to go with Adam. Over to London, for this inauguration thing at Bethnal Green. Bethnal Green had always held a special meaning for him. It was where Rosie came from; the place she had loved. And even though Danny hadn't been there at the tube shelter that night with his two friends, hadn't witnessed the sadness and devastation of the disaster, he'd always felt with them in spirit. And it would have been great to see Frank again, renew old friendships. Sometimes life just got away from you, and friends fell through the cracks. Easy to lose touch. *Must be forty-odd years since they'd last sunk a pint together in the Pig and Whistle. Probably pulled the old place down now. Stuck up a high rise in its place.*

When he'd asked his hospital doctor to let him travel to London, the man had blustered. *Impossible.* And who would look after him? Adam was going as well, he'd explained. *And would an eighty-year-old man with terminal cancer be up to looking after someone who'd just had a stroke?*

Danny had thought about roping in his daughter, Rosie, or his son, or that wonderful daughter-in-law of his. But the idea was selfish. They all had their own busy lives, and he wouldn't put that guilt on them. And soon now Adam would be coming to visit, when he felt well enough, on one of his good days, and would fill in all the blanks.

His phone rang.

'*Met Danny Welland*,' he answered.

'Papa, it's me,' said Angie.

'You're home,' said Danny, happiness and relief in his voice.

'Can I come and see you, Papa? We need to talk about something,' she said.

'Sounds serious. Something wrong? Not you and Dan or the girls, is it?'

Angie Welland laughed. 'No, nothing like that. Nothing wrong at all. In fact, something very, *very* right. Exciting.'

'Well then, *tell* me, girl. Don't want you trailing all the way out here, not if you're busy.'

'Never too busy to see you; and the girls are off swimming with friends.'

When he'd put the phone down, Danny went to the small cupboard in his room. The treats cupboard. He wasn't supposed to have it. *Contraband.* But they couldn't stop you having some fun in life and he knew how much Angie liked her pastries, had a sweet tooth, just like him.

She was very good to him, a kind of surrogate daughter. Different from his own daughter, for Rosie was far more feisty; still, he loved Rosie as only a father could love his daughter – not that he saw much of her nowadays.

Rosie was a live wire, sparky, intelligent, but she was often spiky, hard to be around at times, especially now she was in her late twenties. She thought she knew everything about the world, and that her father had forgotten everything. It was how children were, he supposed, before they matured. And if he was honest with himself, he'd probably spoilt Rosie a bit.

But Angie was different. She had a serenity about her that calmed down everyone around her. He'd missed her. And now she was back with some kind of exciting news. *Ah!* He'd just thought about it. Of course. And how brilliant was that? He was about to become a granddad again. And, strangely, the thought didn't make him feel old, but young and vital. New life. It was something to cherish. Something to rejuvenate you. He put the kettle on, and began to whistle to himself. A tune he hadn't whistled for a long time. Something from the First World War. 'Pack up your troubles in your old kit bag and SMILE, SMILE, SMILE.'

'You look good,' said Angie.

'You too,' Danny said. 'Might even say glowing.' He smiled. Waited for her to break the news.

'Really? Must be all that sea air in Cornwall.'

'You liked it then?'

'I see why you adored the place,' said Angie.

Danny pushed the plate towards her, the top of the cake

shimmering like satin; passion-fruit, mascarpone, luscious white chocolate.

He'd taken his walking frame, slipped out past the battleaxe of a nurse patrolling the hallways, looking for escapees, and gone to his favourite patisserie, for the contents of his sweet cupboard didn't seem up to such an important task. Not the sort of celebration you needed when you were about to welcome another small life into the family.

'De Groot came,' he said. 'We had a few laughs.'

'He bring his famous homemade gin with him? You know you're supposed to lay off that with your medication.'

'One small glass,' he said, and chuckled. 'Can't hurt. And not nearly as lethal as that stuff Edwin made with his potato skins. Made us all ill for a week.'

'William bring his lady friend?'

'Sure. Nice woman!' Danny grinned.

'Oh yeah?'

'Keeps him young, I guess. You know William, he's always had an eye for the ladies, especially when they come in large containers.'

'You too?' she asked.

'A man can look, can't he? I might be getting older,' he said, 'but I'm not dead.'

Angie mopped up the remaining precious crumbs with her fingers.

'Well?' asked Danny.

'What?'

'This exciting news of yours,' he prompted.

'Need to ask you an important question first,' said Angie, her face suddenly serious.

'Fire away.'

'If you could change anything about your life, what would it be?'

'That's a hell of a question.' The look on Danny's face turned from excitement and anticipation to concern.

'You and Anna – would you still marry? If you had to do it again, I mean?'

'Dan and you, you're not having problems, are you? Splitting up?' he said.

'Good God, Papa. Nothing like that. He's the love of my life, and my girls.'

'Well then, what?'

'I did that all wrong,' she said, and smiled. 'Not exactly what I meant. It's just – well, if you could have one wish in your life that might change it, what would that wish be?'

He was confused now. This wasn't about her being pregnant, then. And one wish? In the whole of his life? So easy. But how could he say that, for it would be disrespectful to Anna's memory.

'I don't know what you're asking for.' He leaned forward, rested his elbows on the table, head in hands.

'I just need you to say it. I think I know what's in your heart, and I can see it in your eyes sometimes, the regret. One wish – if I had the power to grant it, what would it be?'

'I can't...'

'Okay,' said Angie. 'I'll give you two choices then, and you just pick one. That should be easier.'

'Sure there's nothing wrong with you and Dan?'

'Positive. Okay, ready for your choices?'

'If we must.'

'Choice one: they'd rescind the "unfit to fly" order and let you back into your squadron to fly Hurricanes or Spitfires or whatever you fancied. Or choice two...'

'This is daft. That was never about to happen...'

'Choice two: Rosie and you would get married and go riding off into the sunset.'

'I don't understand. I mean, both of those things are impossible. And if this is some strange metaphor or a mid-life crisis with you and Dan—'

'Nothing to do with me and Dan, I told you. It's about you. And I need you to choose – right now – before I give you my news.'

'Hurricanes or Rosie?' said Danny. 'No contest. I loved flying, but I lived for my Rosie. Rosie any day. Now, will you stop hounding me? You're worse than Nurse Ratched upstairs.'

Angie Welland laughed. *He'd be okay. Maybe he'd get a bit worked up. Wouldn't believe her.*

'What if I were to tell you there'd been a mistake years ago, and that Rosie was... well, she was still alive?'

His face froze into a startled mask. 'I'd think that was a cruel thing to say, Angie. And you never struck me as being cruel.'

She left the table. Lifted her handbag from the sofa. Took out the photograph. Placed it in front of him. 'Taken a week ago. In Havenporth,' she said. 'On your anniversary.'

The gasp was loud in the small room. And the silence that followed stretched out, took on a life of its own. Was finally broken by a sob.

Angie plugged in the kettle. Tea. For shock. And he'd definitely had a shock, but at least he hadn't keeled over like she was frightened he might. It would take time to process.

'If it's true... if this miracle is really true...' Danny wiped his shirt sleeve across his eyes. 'Then I have to go to her.'

'You don't need to,' said Angie. 'She's coming here.'

37

LONDON

AUGUST 1982

Lil Ellis could be persuasive at times. And getting Frank to come over to Rose's flat when the poor man must be wiped out after his long flight seemed a sadistic thing to do. But Lil had been single-minded. *His honeymoon was over, the man had been lucky to get one. Wasn't like they'd all been that lucky. Day out in Brighton, that's what she'd had with her Harry. Hardly call that a honeymoon, could you?*

'Don't see why we need Frank here,' said Rose. 'How will that change anything?' she asked her ma. 'The past is the past. Gone. Can't be re-invented. Anyway, it's the future I'm interested in.'

'We got stuff to clear up, Rose. And Frank was pals with Adam, that nice Dutch bloke what came to the ceremony,' said Lil. 'Maybe he knew this Anna too – and yer man, Danny.'

'Can't see that it makes any difference,' said Rose.

'Don't you want to know if the bloke's on the level, Rose? He left you at the altar. Rushed off and married this Anna woman...'

'Adam Pietersen's daughter. He met her in Rotterdam,' said Rose.

'Don't care if he met her in Tesco's. Something don't seem right.'

'Ma! It's Rose's business, not ours,' said Grace. 'Her life.'

'Just making sure she don't screw it up,' said Lil.

'Same thing. Her life. Her screw-up. Not our job to interfere, Ma.'

'Family first and last. That's what I taught you pair. And now when Rose needs our help, she'll get it, whether she damn well wants it or not. Your job don't stop when your kids are born, you should know that, our Gracie. And what you call "interfering", I call doing my job.' Lil Ellis slammed the door on her way out.

Rose nodded gratefully at her sister for the backup. She didn't have the energy for a full-blown argument. The last week had been a blockbuster, an emotional roller-coaster, and she didn't fancy getting back on the ride again. Wanted some time to regroup and think about what lay ahead. What she'd say to Danny when the time came. How she'd react.

'Think Frank'll come?' asked Gracie.

'He's had the royal command. Don't see him refusing. And now that Alice is back at work, it'll give him something to do. Can't see the man as a house-husband, can you?' said Rose.

'You excited?' asked Gracie.

'I am. And scared,' said Rose.

'You? You never been scared of anything in your life, sis. What about when I used to make you look under our bed for monsters, and in that horrible old wormy wardrobe of Ma's that smelled of mothballs?'

'This is different, Gracie. I always knew the monsters weren't real.'

'You *did*?' Gracie laughed. 'And yet you told me you were braver than me. Made me give you my fizzy chews in payment.'

'I remember those,' said Rose. 'Used to gum your mouth up.'

'So – you're not really scared, are you, Rose?'

'Nervous,' said Rosemary.

'Why on earth...?'

'Long time ago – we were young. Different people maybe. Say Danny's disappointed in me?'

'Well, then – he doesn't deserve you. And that cuts both ways. Maybe you'll be disappointed in him. Maybe because you couldn't have each other, you've both made up these wonderful, beautiful, perfect people. Fantasy people. For there ain't no such thing as perfect. You *know* that.'

'I know, sis. That's what scares me. Say the reality is nothing like the dream?'

'It won't be, will it?' said Gracie. 'Big deal. Just join the club like the rest of us poor slobs. Time to put up or shut up, sis.'

'I know.'

'You can do this, Rose. Go and see the man, and don't judge him. Perfect memories are one thing, but we're all just human, warts and all. Cut your expectations by half. It'll be fine.'

'Think so?'

'You got my personal guarantee,' said Gracie.

'Yeah? And what about Ma's?' Rose laughed.

'Don't be daft, she won't be speaking to either of us,' said Gracie.

'Enjoy it while it lasts, shall we?'

―――

They took Frank out to the pub around the corner. Seemed only fair, Rose said, after dragging the poor man away from home, stamping all over his honeymoon ardour and snatching him from Alice's passionate arms.

She tried to imagine Frank as a lover, the amorous sexual being that Alice claimed him to be. It didn't work. *Best not try.*

The man always struck her as shy and reserved. A gentleman, and good in a crisis, not the sort of bloke with loads of notches carved into his headboard. An image of Frank Usher in a pinstripe suit, rolled brolly held high, leading the charge into their bedroom in Dulwich, launching himself onto their fancy new king-size bed, lodged in her mind. *No. Stop.* She'd never be able to look the poor man in the eye again if this kept up.

'Now – you said you had some questions, Lil?' said Frank.

'It ain't just me, son. Important to Rose as well.'

Only Ma could get away with calling Frank *son*. Rose suddenly pictured the poor man as a ten-year-old, skinny legs protruding from short trousers, an old-fashioned school cap on his head and a blazer with the school motto embroidered on the pocket. She imagined it was the kind of uniform Frank Usher would have worn, felt at home in. Would he have worn his cap at a jaunty angle? Probably not. Danny would have. She was sure of that.

'Really?' He looked around the circle of women, couldn't imagine why he'd been invited. But Alice's family were his family. He'd insisted on that. And even though at times it could be confusing, sometimes overwhelming, it was flattering that they treated him as one of their own.

Frank's family had been an odd, disparate collection of strangers, and now they were all gone. Not that they'd been much of a comfort when they'd been alive. His father and brother had both been fierce advocates of the stiff upper lip, and his mother had ignored everyone else, drinking her way through a bottle of sherry every few days.

Frank looked over at Rose, a question in his eyes. Rose didn't answer it. Said nothing. Her ma was in charge. *Best to follow the script, see what happens.* Made no difference anyway. She would go and see Danny, build a bridge to the past, and attempt to build a new one to the future. No one else could help them with that.

'So, let's get down to business,' said Lil.

Frank Usher looked confused. Took another long draught of his beer. A temporiser. He was mystified, had no idea what 'business' was. Why he was there.

'This Dutch friend of yours – Adam. The one that hauled me out the stairway that night. He had a daughter, you said?'

'Anna. She died.' Frank had seen the old man cry. This once-strong man who'd stolen a battle-cruiser from under the noses of the Germans, and from sheer willpower led its meagre crew of twenty-two desperate seamen, and sailed it across the North Sea to safety at Holyhead. A powerful, charismatic man, crying like a baby, brought to his knees by grief. Mourning his lost child.

'Hard to lose a child,' said Lil. 'My friend Ivy… she lost her girl that night.' A small shudder shook Lil's thin frame. 'Not something you forget.'

'No,' said Frank.

'Still, at least *his* daughter got to grow up. Have kids of her own. Not like Ivy's girl.'

'Anna? Yes, she was an adult,' said Frank. 'Got married. Had children. Gave Adam grandchildren.'

'And her husband? He still alive?' asked Lil.

Her ma would have made an excellent interrogator. The woman was going at it like a dog with a bone. Rose felt sorry for Frank Usher. Noticed he'd finished his beer already.

'Far as I know.' Adam hadn't said anything about Danny. Been preoccupied with the death of his daughter.

'And you happen to know who this husband was?' Lil asked. 'Where he came from? How come he married Adam's daughter?'

Confused, Frank looked from one face to another, around the group of women. He had a dazed expression on his face.

'Ma! Stop badgering Frank with all these questions,' said Rose. 'And how could he possibly know that stuff?'

Rose caught the eye of the waiter. Circled her hand in the air – a mime for another round. They all needed another drink. Nobody argued.

'Not all of it, no. But some,' said Frank. And all eyes turned back to his face.

'Oh?' said Lil. 'Which bits?'

'Long time ago, Lil. Wartime. It's a long story.'

'We got time,' said Lil.

'I know nothing about Anna's wedding. Except it was after the war had ended. Rotterdam had been liberated and Adam finally went back home. I guess that's when it happened, but I never even met Adam's daughter.'

'But you know *some*thing...' said Lil.

'Well – yes. Adam was a friend, and so was Anna's husband, Danny.'

'What! You *knew* Danny?' said Rose, astounded. 'You never said. I can't believe it. You knew Dan and yet you never once told me! What the hell is that, Frank?' Rose grabbed the wine from the waiter's tray, didn't say thanks, downed half of it.

'Knew it!' said Lil. 'Knew there was more to this. You need to think clearly now, Rose. Before you go tearing over there and throw yerself at this bloke's feet.' Lil Ellis crossed her arms. Confirmation she'd been proved right.

'What? Bit at sea here, I'm afraid,' said Frank. He couldn't understand what he'd done. And why was Rosemary, who was normally so friendly, suddenly angry with him? He fought for a word. *Bizarre*. Not too strong a word.

'*Danny Welland*,' said Gracie. She tried to throw some oil on troubled waters, but even Gracie had to admit that it was all just a bit surreal. 'Think what Rose is trying to say is that considering how important Danny was in her life, that you never once discussed him with her. She was all set to marry the man when his plane went down.'

A tiny glimmer of light flickered its way into the darkness.

And Frank Usher grabbed the anorexic flame with both hands. 'Wait... you were *her*?'

'What's that mean?' asked Rose. The wine hadn't helped. Just made stuff even more fuzzy.

'I never knew her name. He never *told* me her name. But when Dan escaped from Holland, got back home, he came to the Air Ministry. That's where we first met, and I tried to help him. Bloke was in a bad way. Lost an eye when his plane went down. They wouldn't let him fly and he...'

'What – Danny's blind?' said Rose.

'Only in one eye. Stopped him flying in combat, didn't stop him searching for this girl, though. Told me he was off to find *the woman of his dreams*. That's exactly what he called her. But I swear, Rose – I never knew it was you.'

'I thought he was dead. I plagued the Red Cross, his squadron, the Air Ministry. Nobody knew anything. Listed as missing, presumed dead, that's what they told me.'

'It was the war. Things fell through the cracks,' he said. 'I remember the day he was told you'd died. Almost lost his mind. Started drinking. We left him in the restaurant, Adam and me. We went off to Victoria Park. The night we first saw you and Ivy, Lil.'

'God's sake. You mean yer man would've been there with you pair? If he hadn't carried on drinking, like?' said Lil. 'We'd have found out he weren't dead. Rose could've married the man.'

'Who knows?' said Gracie. 'Fate's a funny old thing. Still, at least it means Danny didn't rush off to marry this Dutch woman and leave you at the altar, Rose. You happy now, Ma?'

'Never said I wasn't. Didn't seem right, that's all I said.'

'Need to make a quick call,' said Rose.

'You're leaving?' asked Grace.

'Back in a jiff. Get the next round in.'

She smiled as her ma pulled her bag even closer to her body.

No surprise there. The massive handbag was as secure as Fort Knox. Just as hard to prise the cost of a round out of it.

Rose left the table but the buzz of their conversation followed her across the floor. She could hear Ma's excited, high-pitched voice above the rest. The barman was kind: he gave her change for the phone and directed her to the spot through the doors where she could make her call.

Rose put her coins in the slot, lots of them. Then she carefully dialled Angie Welland's number. A loud set of clicks filled the receiver jammed to her ear, followed by a high-pitched whine, and then an insistent ringtone. She pressed button A and listened as the coins dropped noisily into their collection box.

'*Met Angela Welland.*'

'Hi, Angie. That you? It's Rose here.'

'Rose – what a nice surprise. I was just thinking about you. You okay?'

'Fine. I was wondering... you know...'

'So – you ready to travel?'

'You mean, you've done it? He wants to *meet* me?' said Rose.

'Bit of a shock, but he survived.' Angie laughed. 'Was all set to go there to you. He's excited, Rose. Like a kid. But he's nervous as hell.'

'Nervous?'

'Thinks you might be disappointed in him. He's older.'

'Daft beggar. So am I,' said Rose.

'Yeah, but he doesn't look the way he used to.'

'Neither do I.'

'He says you do. I showed him the photograph. Says you haven't changed. Just as gorgeous.'

'Then he's a liar, or he needs glasses.'

'His face – he was injured when his plane was shot down.'

'I don't *care* what he looks like.'

'That's what I told him, Rose. You still want to come?'

''Course I want to come.'

'Brilliant. Call me with your flight details. I'll pick you up from the airport. And if you'd like to, we'd love to have you stay here with us – unless you'd rather a hotel.'

'I'd love to stay. If you're sure it's no problem.'

'Great. And Rose...'

'What?'

'Thanks. And welcome to the family.'

38

AMSTERDAM

AUGUST 1982

The sun was high in the sky, bathing the concrete and tarmac with a soft glow, smoothing out its harsh edges, giving the stark industrial complex of the airport a patina of romance. Or maybe that was just her. *Rose with her rose-coloured glasses.* Nothing wrong with a bit of romance. She smiled. Tapped into that part of her nature that had once marked her out as a romantic, refused to let the sensible, analytical side swamp it, especially today.

The summer sky above Schiphol airport was smiling down on her. A good omen. And things only got better when she met up again with Angie Welland, who hugged her tightly and grinned. She took Rose's hand and led her to the parked car.

'A sister,' said Angie. 'That's what you feel like, and I've never had a sister.'

'A much *older* sister, you mean,' said Rose. But all the same she laughed. Was flattered. She liked this woman, had been drawn to her from the first time they met.

'Glad you came in at Amsterdam,' said Angie. 'Should only

take us thirty minutes to get to Danny's place. Gives us a chance to get re-acquainted and you can enjoy the scenery. Some of the views are stunning.'

But she noticed none of the scenery outside the car window. It went by in a blur. And her head was doing strange things, confusing things. Writing its own scripts. What would she say to him? How would they fill a chasm of forty years? Would it be awkward, embarrassing? A meeting of strangers, each trying hard to be polite?

'You're not sitting there fretting, are you, Rose?'

'Huh?'

'You worried?' asked Angie Welland. 'Because if you are...'

'What will I say to him? How stupid is this – a grown woman trying to relive the past. It's feeble. I shouldn't have come. And poor Danny, I've railroaded him into this.'

'You think so?'

'Don't you?' asked Rose.

'Here's what I think – there's nobody on the planet could force Danny Welland to do anything he didn't want to. I practically had to handcuff him to a chair to stop him racing over to London to see you.'

'Really?'

'Yes, *really*. And he's just as nervous as you are. So why don't you stop worrying and enjoy the view?'

So Rosemary looked out the car window and tried to ignore the butterflies fighting a full-frontal assault in her stomach, and the hot sour acid that pushed its way up into her throat. She dug in her handbag for some Rennies and smiled over at Angie. The young woman was right. The view *was* stunning.

'Ma had no right to drag you into her arguments,' said Alice.

'Wasn't really a fight.' Although Frank had to admit that at times he'd felt a little overwhelmed by the woman. In full battle mode Lil could be as intimidating as a Panzer tank regiment on the move. Fascinating to watch. And Frank Usher was definitely a people-watcher, found their strange machinations intriguing. If his life had gone another way, he'd probably have been a psychologist, instead of ending up an accountant. But after the fraught war years he'd been looking for something steady and secure. A job that was ordered and calm. There wasn't much excitement in balancing the books or preparing a bank reconciliation statement, but Frank wasn't searching for that. Order. Serenity. That's what he'd longed for. *And then the whirlwind that was Alice had come into his life. And the blandness of his days had been transformed. And he'd been amazed at how much happiness she'd brought with her.*

'So what exactly was it?' asked Alice.

'Huh?'

'Why did Ma make you go over there when you were totally knackered?'

'Looking out for Rose. That's what she said. Did it to make sure Danny Welland hadn't just dumped her to marry Anna.'

'Good job your friend Danny's got you in his corner, then,' said Alice. 'Especially when the whole Ellis clan is lined up in the opposite one. Enough to make you throw the towel in.' Alice laughed.

Her husband grabbed her in a provocative clinch. 'Not the *whole* clan,' he said.

'True. But sometimes it's hard. They're the only real family I've ever had. And although Ma's a challenge at times, she's always been good to me.'

'She's a pocket-sized warrior,' said Frank. 'Won't give up till she sees it through. Lot to be said for that.'

'It's the generation, I guess,' said Alice. 'And the war.'

Alice felt her husband shudder. It was still raw in him, all these years later, and something he rarely spoke about, even to her. Maybe one day. She changed the subject.

'Hard to believe this friend Danny of yours was the man who turned our Rose into Miss Havisham.'

'Who? Don't believe I know the lady.'

'Yes, you do.' She poked him playfully in the ribs. 'The sad, slightly loopy spinster in *Great Expectations*.'

'The one who lived in a room full of cobwebs and rotting wedding cake and wore her old tattered wedding gown?'

'See. You *do* know her.'

'Yes, but Rose wasn't jilted at the altar, and she didn't put her life on hold, did she? She had a powerful job, fought her way through to it on her own merits, a woman's voice in a man's world. Impressive!'

'Sure. She was single-minded, gets that from Ma. And she's my hero, always has been...'

'Heroine,' said Frank.

'Okay, heroine. Anybody tell you you're a nit-picker?'

'Only you. *Precision*. It's important for an accountant.' He laughed. Stroked her hair, tucked an escaped strand behind her ear. Kissed her earlobe.

'And don't change the subject. *Rose*...' said Alice.

'What?'

'Rose definitely put her life on hold, and this Danny of yours made her do that.'

'Danny? No! He was besotted with her,' said Frank.

'Maybe so. And maybe it wasn't his fault, but Rose stuck him up there on a pedestal, a perfect bloke. Impossible for anybody else to match up. When Danny Welland got ripped from Rose's life, so did every shred of romance she'd ever had.'

'Well,' said Frank, 'here's hoping this trip to Holland will put it back.'

'Talking about romance,' said Alice. 'I've had a hard day.'

'Soon fix that. Back massage?'

'I'll run the bath,' said Alice. 'You coming?'

'Always good to save on bath water.' He grinned.

'Let's get the candles out.'

Frank didn't understand this fixation of hers with candles and romantic lighting, but he went along with it. A female thing, he reckoned.

'And I'll put the bubbly in to chill,' he said. Looked like this could be one of those *special* nights.

Danny wanted it to be perfect. Had put a huge arrangement of chrysanthemums on top of his special linen tablecloth. Yellow, white, orange, gold, it lit the whole place up. He tried to look at his room with an outsider's eye and discovered that it was bland and colourless: white walls, grey architrave and cornices moulded in stark polyurethane. Not a bit of warmth in the place. It was modern with clean lines, that was true, but where was the heart, the personality? But at least the flowers threw in a splash of colour. He was glad he'd done that. And he thought Rosie would like it. She'd always loved flowers. Pity the tulip season was over. He could have taken her to the bulb fields. But then maybe he was getting ahead of himself, maybe she wouldn't want to go anywhere with him.

He'd ordered a special tea from the kitchen, hoped she would enjoy it: delicate cucumber sandwiches, scones with homemade jam, and a cake with sugar icing with her name written on it. The cook had been just as excited as he was as he'd gabbled away like a silly schoolboy explaining about the reunion and how he wanted to pull out all the stops, make it memorable.

Angie had warned him against getting over-excited, or stressed. It wasn't good for him, not after the beating his body had taken. And of course they'd all been worried about him.

Which was comforting, to have the warmth of family around you. But he wasn't a child, was he? And he'd been recovering well; his balance was coming back, his legs getting stronger with the exercises, and despite how they all fussed over him about taking the medication, he was on top of it.

Life was a gift. And it was finite; had a sell-by date on it. Problem was nobody told you the date. You never knew when the man upstairs would pull the plug on it. That's why Danny Welland was determined to get the most out of whatever time he'd got ahead of him.

He'd been given a reprieve, and he'd been given it for a reason. And now that Rosie had suddenly appeared like a miraculous intervention, he knew why he'd been handed this new lease on life.

He would treasure every second of it.

The thought changed his state of mind. The nervous agitation vanished, to be overtaken by a weird kind of euphoria. A happiness that put a cheesy grin on his face.

The doorbell rang. He opened up. The grin stayed right where it was.

39

Of course he'd changed. They both had. But forty years' worth of living had extracted an unfair toll from Danny Welland, and then there was the crash which had left him with a small scar on one side of his face and an eye that didn't work anymore. And the slight droop to his mouth, a result of the stroke, she guessed. But his face was alive with pure joy, which made it the most beautiful face Rose had ever seen. She wanted to cry with happiness, but held herself back. He might misunderstand. Might think it was sadness and that she felt sorry for him.

'Rosie, Rosie, Rosie.'

His words were charged with emotion. And robust. Far stronger than she had expected coming from his lean, angular form. He was still tall, didn't stoop, carried himself with the assurance she remembered. And the hair. She'd imagined his hair had retreated, had tried to picture him bald. But he'd been lucky and the wavy hair was still there. Thinned a little, maybe. And not black, but white. *Regal*. A silver fox. Still attractive despite the scars.

Ridiculous. All those fears she'd had, about what she would say. She said nothing. Just reached out and held him. Both of them standing in the open doorway, clinging on for dear life, refusing to let go. A single thought joining them. If they let go now, they might lose each other again.

Angie coughed discretely behind them. A gentle reminder she was there. But still they both clung to each other in their own magical bubble, neither daring to breathe, in case the bubble might suddenly burst.

Rose stretched out her hand, touched his cheek, gently explored his scar with her fingers. A loving touch. A caress. A small moan left Danny Welland's lips. She smiled up at him and the years fell away from her. She could smell the salt in the air, hear the crash of waves as the ocean beat against the rocks at Havenporth, could hear the cry of gulls overhead. And then he was holding her hands in his, kissing her fingertips.

A tiny ripple of excitement woke up the butterflies in Rose's stomach and a delicious shiver of expectation walked its way along her spine.

'Okay then,' said Angie. 'Shall we go inside?' She cleared her throat and waited. 'Papa...?'

'Yes?'

'Maybe we should go in?'

'You worried about my reputation?'

'Papa!'

'Just teasing. You see my beautiful, loving, thoughtful daughter here?' he asked Rose. 'I'm truly blessed.'

'I see that,' said Rose.

'Okay, let's go in,' he said. 'I'll make some tea and the kitchen has laid on treats for us. Or shall we wait?'

'Treats would be nice,' said Rose.

'I'll get them,' said Angie. 'Just make sure he uses the walker,' she told Rose.

'Did I mention she's also a bully?' said Danny. Laughing. Grinning at them both. He wanted to keep on grinning. Didn't see how he could ever stop.

'And if I didn't bully you, where would you be?'

'Well, I've always fancied trying a skateboard for size, like those kids in the park.'

'Idiot! Just make the tea,' said Angie and she closed the door quietly behind her.

'I need to know *everything*,' said Rose.

'What, right now? I remember that about you, Rosie.'

'What?'

'One of the things I loved about you. Honest, straightforward, to the point. And impatient. But maybe we can just sit and enjoy our tea first...'

'Sure, but before Angie comes back...'

'If I know my lovely daughter-in-law, she'll give us time.' All the while he spoke, Danny didn't shift his eyes from Rosie's face. Not for an instant. He didn't want to miss a second of drinking her in. Her eyes, her hair, her smile. And her smile was huge right now.

They sat in silence. Broken only by the rattle of his teacup as he put it down on its saucer. He preferred mugs, but Angie had brought him this delicate set of crockery, had been trying to civilise him.

'So...'

'What?' said Rose.

'Personal questions allowed?' asked Danny.

'We need to be honest with each other, don't you think? So, I guess there are only personal questions,' said Rose.

'You married, Rosie?'

'No. And I've got no one in my life, if that's what you want to know. Never have had, not really. Only ever you.'

'You never married?'

'No. But I've not been locked up in a nunnery.' She

laughed. 'Just no one I'd want to spend my life with. And my job...'

'Angie told me about your job. Incredible. You did all those things you said you would. I'm so proud of you, my wonderful Rosie, even though I didn't get to see any of it.'

'I never really gave up hope, you know,' she said. 'A tiny bit of my heart said you were alive, even though I had no reason to believe it.'

'I looked for you,' he said.

'You did?'

'Went to your house when they flew me back home. But the house wasn't there.'

'We got bombed out.' A small frisson of fear moved through her. The fire in the street that night. The bodies they'd had to step over. She remembered the gaping, toothless hole where their house had once been. Ma and her sitting down in the road and Lil shaking with hysterical laughter, looking at the only evidence they'd ever lived there. The kitchen sink. And then they'd cried. Holding hands together.

Danny moved closer to her on the sofa, pulled her shaking body into his. They'd all got memories. Things that brought back the fear and the sadness. Things that woke you up in the middle of the night.

He smoothed her hair. Still that glorious colour. 'You changed your hair,' he said.

'Old faces – long hair looks strange on them. Mutton done up as lamb.'

Danny laughed. 'Trying to picture you as mutton. No. Can't see it. You'd be just as gorgeous whatever you did to your hair. I'd love you even if you were bald, Rosie Ellis.'

'Same here,' she said, suddenly serious. 'I need you to know that. I love what you looked like before, but it doesn't matter to me, even if you think you've changed. It's the man underneath that I loved, and I can see he's still there.'

'I remember everything about you,' said Danny. 'Your strength of mind. Your independence. Your gutsy determination to follow your heart and achieve the things a woman wasn't supposed to. All of that. I had a picture of you in my mind. It's what kept me going through the bad times. Going over it all in my head. Sometimes I thought I'd go insane with it. Especially when I heard you were dead.'

'Shouldn't believe all you hear. And I can't imagine who told you that.'

'I wanted so much to believe it wasn't true, but when two different people told me you'd gone, well...'

'It was the war,' she said. 'Wires got crossed. Doesn't matter how, I guess. You're here. I'm here.'

'I saw your photograph in the paper. You were smiling. A massive grin. And the queen was right beside you.'

'Ma's still got the certificate they gave me that day. Pleased as punch, she was.'

'And so was *I*,' said Danny. 'Took the article to the Ministry of Information. Found this guy who shot the picture. Figured he'd know where to find you.'

'Say that again,' said Rose.

'The guy at the ministry, he was the one who told me you were gone. Bomb took out the whole street, that's what he said.'

'Whoever he was, he was wrong,' she said. 'You remember his name?'

'Can't be sure. Began with a D or a B. Something like that. But I remember the bloke, bit of a creep. Figured himself for a ladies' man, smarming all over the young woman receptionist.'

'Batley!' *She'd never forget his name.* 'Robert Batley,' she said.

'Believe you're right,' said Danny. 'Bit oily, all teeth and false charm. But maybe I'm doing the guy a disservice.'

'Shouldn't think so,' said Rose. 'The bastard lied to you.' She spat the words out.

All these years... Who'd have thought that manipulative swine Batley was the reason she'd lost Dan?

'Rosie? You okay?'

She was shaking, but it wasn't fear, it was pure, white-hot rage.

'He did it on purpose,' she said. 'But why? What did you tell him?'

'Told him we were getting married, but I don't understand. You mean this guy deliberately lied to keep me away from you? But why would anyone do that?'

'He fancied me, but I told him no. He got upset, assaulted me.'

'The bastard! If I'd known that, I'd have broken his jaw,' said Danny. 'I'm so sorry, Rosie.'

'Not your fault. And I broke his camera on him.'

'Good for you. That's my girl.'

'*And* his nose,' she said.

When Angie came in with the tea trolley, she was greeted by loud raucous laughter, more suited to a barrack room than a genteel nursing home where they served delicate cucumber sandwiches and scones for high tea. A place where, she reminded them both, there were *sick* people. *Frail* elders who took naps in the afternoon.

Her reprimand only made them both laugh louder.

40

It was hard for Rose to sleep. The excitement of it all, and how they'd both gabbled away at a hundred miles an hour, trying to fit so many missing years into a few magical hours.

Rose had told Danny about her job, the pain and the triumphs of it. And she'd even recounted that terrible Christmas she'd spent in a police cell, the cold shock of fear that had gripped her mind and pure terror when she mounted the plane steps, waiting to be shot in the back. Maybe she shouldn't have painted such a graphic picture, but the stuff came pouring out, a cathartic river gushing from her, cleansing her.

Maybe now the nightmare would release its hold on her.

She'd heard the pain come from his lips, seen the tears glisten on his cheeks, roll down onto his beard. The beard had been a surprise. She'd held his hand, apologised for giving him any more sadness, but she'd wanted him to know everything about her. No secrets.

And he'd done the same. No secrets, he'd agreed. And now Rose knew all about his wife, Anna. How they'd first met. How well she'd looked after him, patiently nursed him back to health.

How brave the woman had been. She'd saved his life, not once, but twice. The second time, when they'd all been hiding in a crawl space, a false compartment in a cellar.

The war had been drawing to an end, but there had been pockets of Germans still hanging on fanatically, and two of them had forced their way into a safe-house owned by the Resistance. As soon as they'd heard the heavy boots overhead, Anna had rushed up the cellar steps to join Dr De Jong, and flirted with the men. De Jong had killed one of them, strangled him with a bootlace. And Anna had stabbed the other soldier in the throat with a small penknife. It was something Anna had always carried with her, but she'd felt no remorse in using it, or sending a man to his grave. It was justice, she had claimed, payback for her mother. But Christiaan De Jong had never been able to wipe the guilt from his mind, had taken it with him to his grave many years later. It was the first and last man Christiaan had ever killed. It was war, but even so, he was a doctor, tasked with saving life not taking it. *Do no harm. The Hippocratic Oath.*

The reunion had taken a toll on both her and Danny. They'd stayed late into the night talking, holding hands, drinking tea and the one brandy that Angie Welland had agreed to. It had been a glorious, wonderful but exhausting few hours. Angie had asked the nurse to look in on her father-in-law, a precaution, but Danny was well, buzzing with excitement, and the pair of them practically had to be prised apart when it was time to leave.

Angie had left them alone to say their goodbyes. And the kiss that followed was not a simple peck on the cheek, or a polite interaction between friends, but the passionate, full-blooded promise of lovers.

'Just a down payment,' Rose had told him.

'Glad to hear there's more to come,' he'd replied.

And now, replaying it in her head, like a reel from some panoramic film of their lives, Rose let go the tsunami of emotion building up in her. Relief, sadness at the wasted years, happiness for such a simple thing as holding hands, hearing each other's voices once again. And joy at that kiss, and the possibility of something more. Maybe even a life together. *It's never too late*, her sister had said. And her sister was right. Her sister Gracie was an Oracle.

Finally, Rose was able to sleep, exhaustion overtaking the excitement of the night and the film spooling in her head. And in her dreams she saw that it was not the film's final reel, but that there was more to come. It meant she slept with a smile on her face.

She was woken a few hours later by a noise in her room and her face no longer smiling, but wet. A dog's rough and abrasive tongue was slobbering across it, leaving a wet slimy trail. There was some shouting by her open bedroom door, a light went on, glaring in its sudden intensity, and a deep booming male voice. Shouting. Then apologising.

'Winston, come away from there! Bad dog. Leave Rosemary alone.'

'I'm sorry,' said Rose. 'I must've slept in.'

'No, *I'm* sorry, Rosemary,' said Dan. 'Winston's got some more dog-training classes in his future. Bad dog!' he said again. 'But the phone woke him up. I've just put the coffee on. Angie's out in the kitchen – she's making breakfast if you'd like some.' He headed off down the hallway.

'That'd be great,' she called after him. *Might as well get up. Get a handle on the day.* She hugged the dog round the neck. 'No hard feelings, Winston.' Winston padded out after his master. Maybe he'd heard that breakfast was on the go.

'Shower room's on your right,' Dan shouted over his shoulder. 'Boiler's a bit cranky at times – let the water run for a while before you commit. Could be a shock to the system.' He laughed.

Such a lovely, easy-going family. Rosemary felt like she'd known them her whole life. And she decided to go with the shower. Angie had left out a towelling bathrobe for her, obviously one of her own, because when Rose put it on it reached the floor. Angie Welland was tall. Rose was small.

She joined Angie in the kitchen. The shower had been a good idea, waking her up, especially when the final few moments suddenly turned the pleasantly warm water into a raging ice-cold torrent.

Angie poured her a coffee. 'Cream and sugar?'

'Just sugar, thanks.' Rose looked around the kitchen. Small. Compact. Everything to hand. You wouldn't have to move around much to get from your cupboards to the cooker. Or maybe they called it a stove here. It was massive in the small space. One of those range affairs you found in places where folks took their cooking seriously. Maybe Angie was one of those cooks. Rose's eyes were drawn to two ceramic wall tiles, hanging side by side. One was a caricature of two cute Dutch characters, a boy and a girl. In national dress, she guessed, their lips meeting. The wording underneath in English said *Kiss the cook, she's Dutch*. The other tile said *I married a Dutchman, feel sorry for me*.

Angie put the coffee in front of her. 'A present from my father-in-law.'

'What?' asked Rose.

'Saw you looking at my cheesy wall plaques. Danny's idea of a joke. He believes a bit of cheap tat is good in a room, stops you taking yourself too seriously. I leave them up there to please him.' Angie winked.

'He'd love my place in London, then. Made up of *tat*. But I wouldn't exchange any of it for a Picasso. Mostly stuff my nieces have made me over the years.'

'Family heirlooms,' said Angie. 'Precious.' She pointed at the childish drawings on the cork board. 'Don't think I'll ever take those down. But the girls get embarrassed now. Figure they're far too old to have their pre-school artwork on display.'

'They grow up too quickly,' said Rose, wistfully. 'Same with my sister's girls – twins.'

'Twin girls, wow. All those raging teenage hormones kicking in at the same time.'

'Gracie's done a great job with her girls and now Beth's made her a grandma. Kind of surreal – the way the years rush by.'

'Can't imagine that,' said Angie. 'Must be wonderful. Your first grandkids. Right, let's get on with breakfast. I'll make us a proper Dutch one. You ever had *Boterham met hagelslag*?'

'Shouldn't think so. I'd know if I had, wouldn't I?' laughed Rose.

'Oh, you'd *know* all right,' said Angie. 'And every day should start with it. But then I've got a proper sweet tooth. It's toast loaded with lots of chocolate sprinkles on top. Like the stuff you put on cakes,' she said, when Rose looked confused. 'Or you can have coloured sprinkles. Gives it a crunch. You'll think you've landed in heaven.'

Rose liked the odd bit of chocolate. And sometimes Gracie laughed at her, for the Easter eggs and the Christmas chocolate goodies lasted months in Rose's flat. *Can't be normal*, Gracie had said. Normal or not, Rose's stomach was even now starting to rebel at the thought of that chocolate overload on her breakfast plate.

Bacon and eggs, that's what her stomach craved.

The phone on the kitchen wall rang out noisily, its tinny, piercing bell splitting the silence, making both women jump.

'Second time this morning,' said Angie, as she picked up the receiver. 'Can't think who's trying to get through this early.'

She didn't speak. Just listened. And her expression became

graver as the seconds ticked by. The colour left her cheeks, leaving in its place the dull grey of day-old ashes. Then words came gushing out, like a cork stopper suddenly pulled from a reluctant bottle.

She put her hand over the mouthpiece and shouted the words, 'Dan, get the car. We need to go.' Then into the phone: 'We'll be there. *Which* hospital? Right, okay. Meet you there. Shouldn't take long, not much traffic this early. Oh, and William – thanks.'

A lot of things happened at once. Dan arrived in the kitchen, his wet hair sticking up comically, a comb still grasped in his hand. Angie collapsed into the chair next to Rose's, her breathing shallow, as if the conversation had stripped her of energy.

Rose felt her face turn into an older version of Angie's, the colour leaching from it, deep furrows digging their way into her brow. And her brain refused to find words. Instead, frightening images filled her head. Danny lying on the floor. Danny fighting the agony of another stroke or a heart attack. Danny alone and in pain. But that couldn't be right, for this man William was there. He wasn't alone.

'That was Van den Berg,' whispered Angie. 'He'll meet us at Erasmus. We need to go *now*. He said this could be it!'

'Danny!' The word came out in a primal wail. 'No. It's not *fair!*'

'What?' said Angie.

'I've only just found him! How can the world be so unfair?' She wanted to cry. But her eyes were bone dry.

'Danny? No. Not Danny.' Angie rubbed a tired hand over her eyes. Massaged the bridge of her nose. 'I'm sorry if I scared you. I'm sure Danny's fine.' She turned to her husband, took his hand in hers. 'It's Granddad. He was staying with his friend, William Van den Berg...'

'Not Danny?' said Rose. 'That's wonderful.'

'It's Adam Pietersen, Dan's granddad. He's very sick. Terminal cancer,' said Angie.

'That sounded awful,' said Rose. 'I'm really sorry. And I didn't mean it was wonderful that Adam...'

'I know,' said Dan. 'Don't worry, I get it. Of course you're happy that it's not my dad. But we need to go right now.' He turned to his wife. 'Think we should take the girls?' he asked. He seemed conflicted.

'I don't know,' Angie's shoulders heaved with silent tears. 'I really don't know.' She looked across at Rose. 'What you think, Rose? Ten and twelve, maybe it's too young to see him like that. Then again, if we don't take them...' She squeezed her husband's hand. 'God, Dan. They might never forgive us. One last time. A chance to say goodbye. You know how fond they are of Adam.'

'Why don't you explain, then?' said Rose. 'Just ask them.'

Half an hour later, Rose waved the car off as they drove into the city. Dan, Angie and their youngest daughter, Lotte. She was only ten years old, but with serious eyes, much older than her years. And she understood, she said. That Great Grampy might not be able to talk to her. Might even look a bit frightening, but that he was still the same man, just a bit poorly. So she wouldn't be frightened, she told them all.

Rose stayed with their other daughter, Emma, a twelve-year-old who loved drawing and disco and having her nails painted. Rose got her to draw a picture. The young girl painstakingly drew a horse galloping across a field. It seemed a sophisticated attempt, at least to Rose. But then she didn't have much experience of twelve-year-old girls. Emma's small pink tongue darted out from between her lips, her face a study in concentration. And occasionally a smile flitted across it.

And Rosemary Ellis had a momentary twinge of regret, a

small sharp pain of sadness that she'd had no children in her life. She hoped Emma would have no regrets. Later in life, would she wonder why she hadn't been brave enough to face the sadness of seeing her great granddad one last time? Of never saying goodbye?

41

'I've taken your advice,' said Gracie.

'What particular gem of sisterly wisdom might that be?' asked Rose.

'About Larry. I've invited him to the farm.'

'Ah *ha*! And? What did the romantic physiotherapist say?'

'That's why I phoned, Rose. He said *yes*.' Gracie's excitement came galloping down the phone line.

'That's great. See. Told you he likes you.'

'And I like *him*, Rose. But we've only known each other a month. Don't want him to think I'm easy. Maybe it's a little fast.'

'So? Maybe fast is good. Wasn't it you who told me to get on with life? Just one thing, though,' said Rose.

'What's that?' asked Grace.

'Don't tell Ma. You know what she'll say.'

'*Separate bedrooms!*' They said it together and laughed. Their ma was hot on that sort of thing.

'And what about you? How are things? Didn't phone before. Figured you'd have other stuff on your mind. You and Danny...?'

'Think of perfection and double it.'

'That's great. I'm happy for you, Rose.'

'Yeah, but every silver lining has a cloud behind it.'

'What's that mean?'

'Adam Pietersen...'

'The bloke Ma took a shine to. What about him?' asked Gracie.

'Ma fancied him?'

'Sure. He kissed her hand, remember? She went all girly.'

'The poor man's sick, Gracie. Really sick. Just a matter of time. Whole family's up there with him today. Danny too.'

'What's wrong with him?'

'Not sure,' said Rose. 'Some kind of cancer, I think. But it seems bad.'

'So... you'll be staying over there for a while?'

'Danny's improving all the time and we're taking it as it comes. No long-term plans, but...'

'You're hoping.'

'No harm in hoping,' said Rose. 'Positive vibes...'

'...promote positive results,' parroted Gracie. 'I know. So you're always telling me.' She laughed.

Rosemary laughed too. And she was still laughing when she put the phone down. Laughter was good for you, for your health; there was science out there that said so. It made you feel better. A good hearty laugh got rid of stress and tension, relaxed you. Boosted your immune system. And it released those happy endorphins in your brain. *Laughter should be on prescription.* She tried to imagine some of those sour people she'd come across in her job, suddenly breaking out in maniacal laughter. *Maybe not, then. Some people it wouldn't suit.*

She made herself tea in Angie's small, cosy kitchen. She'd need to have a quiet word with Angie soon. The whole family had been kind and welcoming to her, but Rose didn't want to outstay her welcome. The future would take care of itself, whatever direction it took. All the same, she might end up staying here in Rotterdam for a while. So she'd need to find herself a hotel. One close to Danny's place. No point imposing on her future relatives. No! Did she really just think that? That Danny's son could be *her* son? Okay, a stepson, but all the same. It seemed an incredible dream. But not an impossible one, perhaps. For she thought back to what she'd told Gracie (several times, it seemed) – positive thoughts promote positive outcomes. It made her smile.

Rose was still smiling a few minutes later when the car returned and the family came back. And her smile widened when she saw that Danny was with them. And then, she didn't smile anymore.

———

He took her to a small park near his son's house. He didn't use his walker, but seemed happy enough to accept her help. To allow her to steer him to the pretty coloured wooden bench. Yellow. Something cheerful about the colour yellow, she'd always thought. But not now. Right then their mood was sombre, and an eerie sadness had wrapped itself around the whole Welland household. Angie had gone upstairs with the girls, tried to reassure them, calm the sobs of her daughter Lotte.

'I'm sorry,' said Rose, and held his hand in both of hers. She wanted to say more, to do more. But there was nothing to be said. Grief took its own path.

Tears wet his eyes. He wasn't ashamed of them. Adam had been a fine man, a strong man who'd looked out for his family; put them first ahead of himself. The definition of love.

'I'll miss him,' Danny said. 'He was more than just a father-in-law, he was a friend. We understood each other. He had a lot of grief in his life, but he bore it with dignity.'

'I didn't know him,' said Rose. 'Only met him once, but he still had a twinkle in his eye.'

'You met him?'

'Only for a day – when he came over for the ceremony before Christmas. He charmed Ma. And there's not many could do that.' She smiled.

'Of course, the disaster memorial. You were there for that?'

'My sister, Alice – she organised the whole thing.'

'Alice? You've got another sister?' he asked.

'Not technically a sister, but the family's kind of adopted her. She's special. I think you'll like her.'

'So – you okay letting me loose on your family?' he said, and smiled at last.

'Well, you already met Ma. A long time ago, I know. But she's just the same,' said Rose.

'I liked her, the way she spoke her mind – and she made that fancy cake for me,' Danny said.

'I remember,' she said.

'Think your mother will remember me?'

'She'll remember – and she'll be giving you marks out of ten. But you're halfway there, being Adam's son-in-law. She'll never forget what he did for her. Or how kind he was to Ivy that night.'

'That night?'

'The rescue at the tube station. He saved Ma's life. Pulled her out from under those bodies. Tried to save her friend Ivy's daughter.'

'What – you mean your mother was one of the people Adam rescued?'

'She was. Thanks to him she's been able to see her granddaughters, her great grandson. A gift, Adam gave her a great gift.'

'That's amazing. And bizarre.'

'Bizarre?'

'That it should be your mother. And he's my father-in-law. It's...'

'Spooky,' said Rose. 'Some kind of karmic thing going on there.'

'I'd no idea. He's never said much about it. Adam's a humble man – *was*. He just got on with stuff, no fuss.'

'Him and Frank,' said Rose. 'Both the same, then. Frank rescued kids that night as well, but it's the ones he didn't manage to save that give him grief. You could see it in his eyes at the memorial.'

'Frank Usher?' asked Danny. 'You know *Frank*?'

'Sure. He helped Alice get the memorial fund up and running.'

'*Frank Usher*. My God, I haven't seen Frank in years. Good man. Steady. Trust him with my life.'

'Me too,' said Rose. 'Anybody who can navigate the weird waters of our peculiar family needs a medal. 'Spect Alice has already given him one.' She winked.

'Why Alice?' he asked.

'Alice and Frank. They're married.'

'So, Frank – he's your *brother-in-law*?' His face creased up, like he was working his way through a puzzle. 'You're saying somebody who was a good friend of mine, somebody I haven't met in years, has come into the life of the woman I love, a woman I haven't seen in years – as a brother-in-law?'

'Got it in one.'

'You're right. Spooky.'

'*Destiny*,' said Rose. 'Fate. A weird and wonderful thing. It twists and turns and comes right back on itself.'

'A complicated Gordian knot,' he said.

'You couldn't make it up.' She laughed.

They both laughed. And Danny put his arms around her. Held her close.

The gloom he'd felt suddenly lifted, and Danny Welland

was sure of one thing: Rosie would always be able to strip away the veil of sadness and bring him joy.

Frank's arrival had been a surprise, though now, when she thought about it, making the trip to Holland for the funeral was the sort of thing you'd expect from Frank Usher. He was a quiet man. Never wasted words, spoke only when he had something important to say. But above all else, Frank was a kind man, loyal to friends. And Adam Pietersen had been a wartime friend, someone he seemed to have things in common with.

Rose learned other things, mostly about the Dutch, the new generation, and about funerals. She'd been to several at home. Been invited to more funerals than weddings lately, but then that came with age. She was philosophical about it. Didn't dwell too long or hard on death, or old age. She and Alice had decided they'd never get old, or talk about their dodgy hips and knees.

Adam's funeral wasn't a sad affair; there was some laughter and lightness. It didn't take place in a chapel, but in a large airy hall called an *aula*. Its walls and furnishings were bright, not dark wood pressing in on you, and a huge wall of glass at one end where the mourners could look out onto a stunning meadow of wildflowers. The meadow was a sublime carpet of colours; the intense blue of cornflowers, spectacular red poppies in abundance, and a vibrant yellow flower that Rose couldn't put a name to.

And inside, the *aula* was covered with flowers as well, and drawings and artwork and all kinds of craftwork, including wood carvings. It was inspiring and touching, how people who knew Adam, family and friends from the past, had made something to celebrate his life. It wasn't like any funeral Rose had ever been to. More uplifting than sad.

Angie's daughters had both painted pictures, and Angie had

sewn a new tobacco pouch, which she put beside his beloved pipe. But the most beautiful piece was sitting on top of his coffin, and almost as long as it: a stunning, hand-carved wooden replica of the ship that Adam Pietersen had taken across the North Sea.

And although the idea struck Rosemary as the kind of thing ancient Egyptians had done in their tombs, these artefacts weren't meant for Adam's journey to an afterlife, but as a tribute to him. To show how much he was loved. And for his family to keep.

The thing that took pride of place? It was a large cross made from leather, creased now and worn with age, but with a new piece of string that Danny had threaded through. She watched him place it on the table and saw the tears make their way down his cheeks.

He'd told her the story behind it: how he'd seen Anna sitting on a crate in a damp cellar, sewing the strange thing. A gift for her father. A talisman.

Was he crying for his wife? Or the loss of his friend Adam? Or a deeper sadness that she knew nothing about? Rosemary had one hope. That whatever lay in store for him, for the pair of them, she would be able to restore some happiness to Danny's life. There would always be sadness of course, but facing it together would make it less.

42

LONDON

OCTOBER 1982

'The blushing bride,' said Rose. 'How's it feel?' She hugged her sister and neither of them wanted to let go.

'Great. Exciting. Unreal. Like it's all happening to somebody else,' said Gracie.

'Well, it's not. It's *your* big day on Saturday, and you enjoy it, kiddo. You've earned it. You've had some tough times, sis, but I always knew that you'd get through.'

'Ma's finally agreed to give me away.'

'So – all that stuff about it being a man's job...'

'I guess we all change, Rose. Even Ma.'

'I wish Danny could have made it. I miss him already,' said Rose.

''Course you do, but maybe it's for the best.'

'How'd you figure that?'

'Man's still recovering. A full-blown Ellis family knees-up might not be the ideal place to take him for a test drive.' Gracie laughed.

'Maybe you're right.'

'You hear about Frank and Alice?'

'Heard nothing about anything, Grace. Give us a chance. Only just got back yesterday.'

'They're moving to Brighton. Bought a small hotel there. Alice's retiring and they'll run it together.'

'Good God. Can't see Frank behind the bar doing the *mein host* bit,' said Rose.

'Me, neither. He'll do the books and stuff, don't you think?'

'Suppose this means a new hat for Ma.' Rosemary grinned. 'And a mother-of-the-bride outfit.'

'Already done. She dragged me through Camden Market for hours looking for a bargain. Don't know where the woman gets her bloody energy; she's like a wind-up toy.'

'And thank God for it,' said Rose.

'Amen to that.'

———

The ceremony was simple. The kind of thing Rose would have chosen for her own wedding. Her sister Gracie glowed with happiness, the smile on her face giving her an air of other worldliness. Her voice was strong, never wavered as she took her vows. The groom looked uncomfortable in his suit and kept tugging at his tie, for Larry Wilson was a tracksuit kind of guy, but even so, he seemed happy. Kept staring into Gracie's eyes like they held the key to paradise. And maybe they did. The vows he gave, written by himself, and sweated over for a week – according to Grace – were corny, straight from the cob, but came from his heart. What more could you ask? Gracie's daughter Ray sang 'Ave Maria', her voice clear as crystal, for she'd inherited her mother's talent. People cried, including Rose.

She was happy for her sister. And for Ma, who looked like a small china doll in her massive hat – that blocked out everyone's view – and the smart coral suit, a tin brooch pinned proudly to it: a heart with hands wrapped around it. Rose wanted to cry, but then weddings did that to her. And Alice, tall and elegant in a matching dress and coat, holding onto Frank's hand, and grinning widely at him. Her smile so massive you'd think the government was about to put a tax on smiling. Maybe she was remembering her own wedding.

Looking around at her family, at the happiness of the day, Rose felt Danny's absence even more keenly. He was improving, had bequeathed the dreaded Zimmer frame to an elderly lady in the nursing home who seemed convinced the act was the overture to romance. Danny had spent his final week of convalescence dodging the poor woman. And now he was staying with his son and daughter-in-law. Being spoilt by Angie and drawing pictures of Hurricanes and Spitfires for his granddaughters.

Once he felt stronger, he would travel. Come over to London and spend time with her and the family. He was looking forward to a pint with Frank, he'd said. Christmas, he'd promised. *Let's make it a big family Christmas*, he'd told Rose. And as they parted at the airport he'd asked Rose for a promise in return. That they would make one last trip to Havenporth, the pair of them together, like they'd pledged to all those years ago.

She hadn't wanted to leave him. She'd lost him once before, couldn't bear to lose him again. But he insisted she go to Gracie's wedding. He'd be fine being fussed over by his family. And the only sadness on his face was when he spoke of his daughter Rosie. Rosie who'd gone to live in Amsterdam and hadn't bothered to come home for Adam's funeral. Rosie who seemed to have swerved off the path well-travelled to find a more exciting, lesser-travelled one of her own. Nothing wrong with that, of course. Rose was all for youth carving its own way, especially young women. It was their rite of passage. A journey of discovery. Of aspiration. Of hope. Of equality. Something she believed in. But even so, a chilling feeling of foreboding crept over her when she thought about Danny's daughter. Her namesake.

43

LONDON

CHRISTMAS, 1982

Christmas came. But Danny didn't. She phoned Angie and Dan's number several times, imagined the tinny bell reverberating around the small, homely kitchen, but nobody answered. She phoned the overseas operator, asked the woman to check on the number. Was it working? Maybe the number had changed. No, the number was operating *perfectly*, the woman had replied (she had been a little prickly, if Rose was asked for an opinion). Perhaps whoever she was calling had gone on holiday, the operator suggested. *And not told her? That didn't make sense.* The operator wished her luck and Rosemary changed her mind about the woman.

She took no part in any of the Christmas party games, just sat sourly in a corner of Alice and Frank's front room in Dulwich, while others tried to guess the names of songs and titles of films. Her ma was on top form and Ivy got drunk and had to be put to bed in the spare room.

Gracie looked radiantly happy and announced that she and Larry had bought a smallholding in Devon. Chickens, turkeys, a cow, a pig and two goats, that was the plan. And they'd grow as much of their own food as they could. Gracie's idea of bliss. There was a barn on the side of the house, too, which Larry was going to turn into a physiotherapy clinic. Small to begin with, just enough to keep him busy – sports injuries maybe. He admitted he wasn't much of a landsman, had an allergy to goats, had never been up close to a pig. But still he smiled at her sister. *The things we do for love.*

Everyone's obvious happiness made Rose feel worse. She downed another large gin and tonic and phoned the number in Holland again. Nothing. Maybe they'd all gone out for Christmas. She slammed the phone down so viciously that all heads turned towards her.

'You should leave,' said Gracie.

'What! Not you too, Grace. Ma's just told me I'm a miserable cow and a pain in the arse.'

'Ma's drunk, and that's not what I meant. You should go there.'

'No. I'll not go where I'm not wanted,' said Rose.

'Fer Christ's sake, Rose, get over yourself. How could you not be wanted? Maybe something's wrong. You need to go and find out.'

'I'll not beg for love,' said Rose.

'No? Isn't that what you been doing for years, sis?'

Rosemary ran from the room, grabbed her coat and slammed the front door behind her. She walked all the way home – it took her nearly three hours – but it gave her time to bring her fuzzy brain back into some kind of working order.

Maybe Gracie was right. What if Danny was sick again, had had another stroke? They might have been trying to contact her, and the number Angie had was the flat in Bethnal Green. Yes, that made sense.

She opened her front door gratefully, went straight to her tiny kitchen. Coffee, strong, black, enough caffeine to perk up a baby elephant with a hangover. She took it through to the lounge, sat in her leather massage chair and waited by the phone.

It didn't ring.

Days went by. She couldn't remember eating. She lived on coffee and started smoking. Weird, to go all your life without touching a cigarette and start when you have a pension book tucked away in your handbag.

Alice came around, fussing. And when that didn't work, she sent Frank. But he wasn't good with embarrassing silences, and left ten minutes after he'd arrived. They all had a go at trying to make her *see sense*. To eat. To sleep. To shower. To dress. But Rose only dug her heels in.

Then everybody arrived at once, lecturing her, as if she were some sort of idiot child. A *family conference*, Larry Wilson, her new brother-in-law had called it. But it hadn't been a success and he'd looked out of his depth.

'You'll make yourself ill, Rose,' said Gracie.

'Don't care,' she said. A petulant child. What was the point? You tried in life, gave it your best shot, tried to be happy. But bastard life just ganged up on you anyway. Wouldn't give you what everybody else seemed to take for granted. Her sisters, her ma. They all had *some*body. And what did she have?

New Year passed her by. Rose didn't celebrate. Didn't eat. Got thinner. Started to feel ill. The family left her alone. They hadn't given up on her, she knew: it would be their new strategy, leave her to get on with it, she'll soon come around. But she didn't.

Time elapsed. She didn't know how much, because now she lived in a strange land, half real, half dream. And that peculiar blue light flooding through her window. What was that? And look – there was her little sister Gracie, lifting her onto a bed, her lips forming words, and Rose struggling to hear what they were. And some strange men coming into her bedroom, poking at her, putting something sharp into her thin arm. Whispering. *Why was everybody whispering? What was wrong with bloody people? Why couldn't they speak normally, so she could hear? But then this was a dream, right? Things weren't normal in dreams.*

Gracie grabbed one of the paramedics by the sleeve. She hadn't wanted to cry, to waste time and energy with futile tears, but some things you had no control over. This was her sister, the woman she'd looked up to all her life. They'd shared good times and bad times, laughed together, cried together, fought each other.

'Will she make it? Tell me she'll be okay.'

The young man gently removed her hand, took it in his own. Patted it and smiled, gave Grace a look of reassurance. He seemed like a kind man, a man with empathy; good at his job.

But he didn't give her the answer she desperately needed. He didn't say *yes*.

44

Danny Welland was no stranger to pain, mental or physical. And yet this feeling eclipsed anything he'd ever experienced before. And funerals, he was used to them – a fact of life. In the midst of life they were something normal, almost routine, now that the years were piling in on him. But this! This was anything but normal. He felt like the pain would never leave, never diminish, whatever he did. No matter how many years he tried to outlive it, he never would.

Rosie. *God damn, Rosie! Damn her to hell!* How could she do this to him? How could she leave him like this? He'd given her love, what more had she wanted from him? Maybe it wasn't enough. Had he loved her too little? Too much? It must be his fault. Who else was to blame?

He'd never expected to go to her funeral. His knees weakened and the woman by his side held him up. His balance had been better lately. His whole body had somehow been renewed with the reappearance of 'his Rosie' in his life. He was stronger, much stronger, had even started going to the gym.

He nodded gratefully at Angie, her arm linked through his, giving him her strength. And his son on the other arm. Not much longer to go, surely? He had to hold his head up high, make it through. But he felt like screaming into the awful silence. A silence that was meant to allow them all to reflect. But he didn't want to reflect. He wanted to go into a darkened room and cry and never stop. And then he wanted to shout the name *ROSIE* at the top of his lungs.

But he didn't. Instead he allowed Angie to lead him from the room, guide him to a small anteroom, where his son Dan poured him a large brandy. Danny devoured it, as if it was the answer to his pain. But it wasn't. Nothing could blot that out. Or the guilt that he should have been there for Rosie. Should have done more.

'Sit down, Papa,' said Dan. 'I know it's hard, but we need to talk. Something you have to hear.'

Danny said nothing. Just stared into the brandy glass like the cure for all his sadness could be found in there.

He felt the weight of his son's arm on his, felt the warmth of Dan's hand, guiding him as if *he* were the child. He collapsed into the deep leather chair, a tremor taking hold of him like a river of pain surging through him, looking for somewhere to go. He saw the pity on their faces.

'Things have happened,' said Angie. 'Things you need to know about.'

'Things?' asked Danny, his voice thin, reedy, trembling like an old man. 'I don't want to know about "things", Angie. Don't you think I've had enough? A heroin overdose, for Christ's sake. How could she do it?'

'Some things there are no answers to, Papa. No good looking for one,' said Angie, gently. 'Doesn't make any kind of sense. But Rosie always was a headstrong girl. Got that from her mother, *and* you. No point denying it. She loved experimenting with life. Got into the wrong crowd. Experimented with the wrong things. None of us can blame ourselves, *or* her. It's just life, Papa. Sometimes it's cruel.'

'And that's it! That's what I've got for consolation? Well, it's not enough,' spat Danny, some of his old spirit coming back.

'It's all we've got. All of us. And we're all sad,' said Dan.

'Yes, but your kids going before you – imagine how you'd feel?'

'She was my sister, Dad.'

'Yes, but not your *child*. What if it was Lotte – or Emma? What then?'

'I'd be like you. Angry with the world. But Angie's right. There's something else you need to hear. Don't want to heap anymore sadness on you, but you wouldn't thank us for not telling you. Not when it's someone you care for. Waited so long to find.'

'Rosie? Is this about Rosie? Something happened to my Rosie?'

'She's in hospital. Been very ill. She's—'

'Not more. You're not telling me I could lose her as well...' Danny hurled the brandy glass angrily. He'd once played cricket, been a decent pace-bowler, so it flew from his hand with precision and speed. Shattered against the bright yellow wall, leaving a trail of sticky liquid in its wake, showering the expensive beige carpet with jagged shards of glass that caught the light, glittered like a bed of diamonds.

Laughter – she'd always said it – was the best, the *very* best medicine. Better than all your pills. Not that Rose needed pills anymore. After two weeks in her hospital bed, she'd taken a giant leap forward and her health had improved so much that they were thinking of sending her home. And that day she had laughed so hard that she had started to cry. But then Gracie had always been able to make her laugh.

Though it was hard to make Danny laugh. And Rose

hadn't tried. Didn't think it was right somehow, to minimise his suffering, the natural grief he felt at his daughter Rosie's death. But her sister Gracie had no such scruples. She'd sat in the padded visitor's chair and ploughed on with her daft comments and feeble jokes, until at last even Danny had cracked a smile. You had to admire her tenacity. At least that's what *he* said, and Rose had to agree. Gracie was a natural performer, always had been, and she thrived when there was an audience, no matter how small. This one was small. Rose, Danny, and Frank.

Frank had been doing his bit for the cause. It seemed to be his natural role in life: running errands for people, making life a little easier for everyone. So maybe he would be okay behind the bar of the Oak Tree Inn. That's what they were calling their new hotel, although no one was sure why. There didn't seem to be a single oak in the vicinity, but Alice just smiled when asked, like it was a private joke. She was there now, in Brighton, bullying builders into submission. Sorting stuff, shoving actions into spreadsheets.

Organisation, it was something Alice was good at. She'd changed so much over the years. Like all of them, Rose thought, as she remembered the shy, unsure office junior who'd once admitted she got her letters jumbled up. People were giving that a name now. It was called dyslexia. And if you had it, it didn't mean you were stupid; the opposite, for it meant you were often brilliant at lots of other things that sometimes you weren't given credit for.

Danny and Frank were sitting next to each other in the small hospital room. They'd had a lot of catching up to do. They'd once been friends and you could tell from their reunion that they'd be good for each other, had things in common.

'You hear the latest, Rose?' said Gracie. 'About Ma.'

'What about Ma?' she asked, hesitant. It had that effect on you – a query with *Ma* tagged on.

'She's moving,' said Gracie, and the look on her face was nothing if not triumphal. A told-you-so expression.

'Don't believe it,' said Rose.

'It's true. And guess where?' Gracie's expression had graduated into smug now.

'No idea. Peru?' said Rose.

'Idiot! Course not Peru. But you'll laugh when I tell you.'

'Well then, *tell* me,' said Rose. The others looked on. Interested. Not that it was earth-shattering, but it was always good to have a heads-up on anything that involved Ma. For it generally had consequences for the rest of them.

'Somewhere you know, Rose. Somewhere you tried to get her to go years ago.'

'Not that place I found in Brighton?'

'The very same. She reckons it'll be handy. What with Alice and Frank's new place so close.'

They all stared at Frank. Expressions of sympathy on most faces. And Frank himself tried not to look shocked or swallow his Adam's apple by mistake. It was news to him.

'Jesus, Frank – I'm sorry,' said Rosemary.

'Not your fault, Rose. I'm sure it'll work out.'

And that was Frank for you. A pragmatist. Change the things you can in life, and as for the rest – you made the best of it.

'Maybe she can pop in and do a bit of dusting for you and Alice. Get the bedrooms ready for changeover day.' Rose smiled. *No, that wasn't right.* It wasn't fair to taunt Frank, even though he was an easy target. He was a good bloke. All the same, he smiled back. Could be he was finally getting the hang of the weird and wonderful Ellis family.

'But what about Ivy?' asked Frank. 'Won't she miss her?' Frank Usher suddenly looked like a man who'd had a last-minute reprieve, someone who'd been thrown a lifebelt, a glimmer of relief crossing his face.

'Ivy's going too. Likes the idea of "an elegant retirement complex, close to the sea, warden patrolled with lots of activities, and a friendly community".'

'Gracie...'

'What?'

'You're a smartarse. Can't believe you remembered all that,' said Rose. 'Although, as I recall, you wouldn't help me persuade Ma at the time.'

'Rosemary Ellis – you are my big sister. The fount of all knowledge. And I remember and believe *everything* you say – even though I might not always agree with it.'

'Fool!' said Rose.

She looked over at Danny. He was smiling again. It was getting easier for him, she noticed. He mouthed the word 'NOW?' and his eyes had a question in them. Rose nodded.

'Okay, everybody,' said Danny. 'If we could keep the noise down to a dull roar. I'd like to say something.' All heads turned towards him as he rummaged around in a carrier bag behind his chair. Like a genie, he produced two bottles of champagne and some plastic cups.

'Think we're due a small celebration,' he said. 'The doctors are happy with Rosie's progress and she's put on enough weight to be released from hospital.'

'When?' asked Gracie.

'Tomorrow,' said Danny, and he went over to her bedside and brushed his hand across her cheek. 'We're going home to Rosie's together.'

'And who's going to look after you, Rose?' said Grace.

'I am,' said Danny. 'We'll muddle through together. We're both grown-ups, last time I checked.'

'That's great news, Rose,' said Frank.

'Yes, it is,' said Gracie. 'But don't tell Ma yet.'

'Why's that?' asked Rose.

'You know what she'll say,' said Gracie.

'*Separate bedrooms!*' chimed both sisters together.

Danny, who knew there must be a joke in there somewhere, just smiled, shrugged his shoulders and opened the champagne. He'd find out. He'd have time to find out. He was looking forward to discovering lots of things about Rosie.

EPILOGUE

HAVENPORTH, CORNWALL

27 JULY 1983

They held hands walking up East Cliff, not that either of them needed the support. They were both much fitter now and strong, only had to stop once to catch a breath. Danny had been going to the gym, had put on muscle, and the summer tan gave him a healthy glow. And along with her yoga class, Rose had discovered Zumba. She loved the dancing and the music, the incredible Latin rhythms that went with it. She always came away from a Zumba session with a huge smile on her face.

'I've rediscovered my core muscles,' said Danny. 'It was a surprise to find they were still there.' He laughed.

'And here's one old girl who's happy about that.' She grinned. People didn't talk about it, as if sex was something to be shunned once you'd hit some invisible barrier at the age of fifty. But it was a miracle. A happy miracle for them both. She'd waited four decades to find out how it would be with Danny. And the wait had been worth it.

He squeezed her hand. 'Mature,' he said.

'What?'

'You, my Rosie. You're mature, not old.'

'What – like wine and cheese? Remember when you called me *wholesome?*'

'Did I?' he asked. 'I must have been very wise.' He winked.

'Don't know about that.' She poked him in the ribs.

'Wise enough to fall in love with the best girl on the planet.'

The bench was only halfway up, but they stopped and sat down.

'This is new,' he said.

'I've been here many times,' said Rose. 'It's where I met your son – and Winston. The day my life began again.'

'And I've only been here in my head,' he said. 'This is better.'

'Yes,' she whispered. 'This is better. Much better.'

'And now...'

'What?'

'I'd like to do something I should have done years ago.' The boyish grin she remembered was back there on his face.

He'd ditched the beard. It had made him look years older. But he'd been conscious of the scars on his face. He had a wonderful face, she'd told him, and he'd been brave enough to shave off the camouflage. She hadn't asked him to. But was happy that he had.

Danny fumbled in his pocket. He'd had it all planned out. Smooth, it should have been, suave and sophisticated, the way they did it in the movies. But real life wasn't like a film, choreographed to perfection. And anyway, perfection wasn't so hot. Life with all its imperfections was real; something solid you could grab hold of.

'You okay?' asked Rose, worried.

'Never better.' He pulled out the precious box. Held onto the bench as he got down on one knee. True, the core muscles weren't too bad. But the knees... still, you couldn't have everything.

'What's wrong?'

'Nothing.' He laughed. 'Everything's just about right. And now, Rosie Ellis...' He removed the ring, held it out to her. '...a bit late, I know, but still, better late than never. Will you do me the honour of becoming my wife?'

'What!'

'I'm asking you to marry me. I've been practising this. Even so, don't think I can keep it up for long. You'll need to be quick about it, or you'll have to haul me up.'

'*Yes!*' she said. 'You're sure?' she asked. 'You really want to do this?'

'Of course I'm sure,' said Danny. 'Now pull me up before I rupture something important.'

She pulled him up and they both laughed. And Rosemary looked at the stunning ring on her finger. A square emerald at its centre and two sparkling diamonds set either side; all in a white gold band.

'It's fabulous,' said Rose. 'But how did you get the size right?'

'Measured your finger with thread while you were sleeping. It fits okay, then?'

'It's incredible. But I'd have married you if you'd given me a sixpenny ring from Woolworths. Could have saved yourself a fortune.' Rose grinned.

'Now she tells me.'

'And my family. My weird and wonderful family? You okay with all that?'

'I'm not marrying them, Rosie. I'm marrying you. But if Frank can do it, then I guess I can.'

She hadn't meant to cry. And they were tears of joy. Danny Welland pulled her into his body, the two of them like one person. And they stayed that way, touching each other's faces in awe, smiling, kissing, cuddling.

A couple of young lads swaggered by, sniggering. 'Get a bloody room, you pair,' said one of them.

'Gross,' said the other.

'Hope you can still do it when you're my age,' Danny shouted after them. He laughed, didn't care what people thought. They knew nothing about him. About Rosie, the woman he loved. Would carry on loving till the final breath was sucked from him.

'You could teach them a few moves,' said Rose. They laughed together.

Man and wife. They'd be friends, companions, lovers. And there'd be lots of laughter in their future, she knew that. Happiness. *And* sadness. It was life, after all. You had to meet it head on. Couldn't take any of it for granted.

Rosemary Ellis gazed once more at the ocean, tranquil today. She'd looked at the Atlantic so often now from this same spot. It had many moods, but was always there, waiting for her. Constant. Reliable. Timeless. They were old friends now, her and this beautiful ocean.

She watched the waves roll in, embracing the shore; renewing, cauterising the pain, wiping everything clean.

A LETTER FROM ELAINE

Dear reader,

I'm thrilled that you chose to read *Promise You'll Wait* and I want to say a huge thank you. I hope you enjoyed joining Rosie in her world and if you did and would like to keep up to date with all my latest releases, just sign up at the following link. Your email address will never be shared, and you can unsubscribe at any time.

www.bookouture.com/elaine-johns

I hope you loved *Promise You'll Wait* and if you did, I would be very grateful if you could write a review. I'd love to hear what you think, and it makes such a difference helping new readers to discover one of my books for the first time.

A massive thank you to YOU, the reader, for putting your time, energy and enthusiasm into my book. You're a very important part of the whole writing and reading experience, because until you started to read it, the book was just words on a page – it was you who brought it to life! That's why sometimes, when I'm writing, I imagine a reader looking over my shoulder, spurring me on, and wondering what's going to happen next. (There are times when I wonder that myself!)

I hope you enjoyed following the book's characters and their lives. Rosie and Danny became an important part of my life and I hope you welcomed them into yours as well, and cheered them on through their trials and their triumphs. At times I felt quite mean at pulling them apart when they had both discovered such a special loving bond between them, but hopefully, their joy at finally finding each other again made up for it.

In writing about Rosie and her family and Danny, I wanted to think about how ordinary people might deal with the fear and anxiety of war – would it turn them into heroes and heroines? I believe it did and when you think about some of the *real* people who lived and struggled during those trying times of WW2 and managed to keep life going, often with a smile, they became the real heroes. I believe we owe a great deal to such 'ordinary' folks because they were far from ordinary; and I thank them for what they did, for the sacrifices many of them made.

The idea about *elder* love came to me one day when I saw a lovely older couple that I know sitting on a bench in my local park. They were holding hands. They had been married for over fifty years and yet they still looked at each other as if they were very much in love. We don't seem to talk too much about this kind of love – a love that can exist in advancing years; but why should it not be equal to that first rush of youthful love? That's what I wanted to know. That's what I wanted Rosie and Danny to enjoy – especially as I had been so mean to them!

If you would like to get in touch with me, I'm always thrilled to hear from readers, and you can do that via my website or Facebook. Meanwhile – happy reading!

Thanks,

Elaine

elainejohns.com

ACKNOWLEDGEMENTS

Lots of people have been generous with their time in helping with my wartime research and I thank them all. Any errors are mine and not theirs! Peter Hancock's book *Cornwall at War, 1939–1945* has also been a useful source of inspiration (see Bibliography).

Many thanks to the friendly and enthusiastic team at Bookouture for all their work and support in guiding *Promise You'll Wait* safely and seamlessly through the publication process. Special mention to my editor Ellen Gleeson for her endless encouragement and hard work; also, the invaluable contribution of Belinda Jones and Jane Donovan. Thank you all.

BIBLIOGRAPHY

Hancock, P. *Cornwall at War, 1939–1945* (Tiverton, Devon: Halsgrove, 2006)

Images of War: The Real Story of World War II (London: Marshall Cavendish Partworks Ltd., 1988/9)

Printed in Dunstable, United Kingdom